THUNDER BAY

THUNDER BAY

THUNDER BAY

A THRILLER

Douglas Skelton

ARCADE
CrimeWise

An Arcade CrimeWise Book

First North American Edition 2020

First published in Great Britain in 2019 by Polygon, an imprint of Birlinn Ltd.

This is a work of fiction. Names, places, characters, and incidents are either the products of the author's imagination or are used fictitiously.

Arcade Publishing books may be purchased in bulk at special discounts for sales promotion, corporate gifts, fund-raising, or educational purposes. Special editions can also be created to specifications. For details, contact the Special Sales Department, Arcade Publishing, 307 West 36th Street, 11th Floor, New York, NY 10018 or arcade@skyhorsepublishing.com.

Arcade Publishing® and CrimeWise® are registered trademarks of Skyhorse Publishing, Inc.®, a Delaware corporation.

Visit our website at www.arcadepub.com.

10 9 8 7 6 5 4 3 2 1

Library of Congress Cataloging-in-Publication Data

Names: Skelton, Douglas, author.
Title: Thunder Bay : a thriller / Douglas Skelton.
Description: First North American edition. | New York : Arcade CrimeWise, 2020.
Identifiers: LCCN 2019043279 | ISBN 9781950691340 (hardcover) | ISBN 9781950691357 (ebook)
Subjects: GSAFD: Suspense fiction.
Classification: LCC PR6119.K45 T48 2020 | DDC 823/.92—dc23
LC record available at https://lccn.loc.gov/2019043279

Cover design by Chris Hannah, www.chrishannah.co.uk, courtesy of Polygon/Birlinn Ltd.

Printed in the United States of America

'We are tied to the ocean. And when we go back to the sea . . . we are going back from whence we came.'

—*John F. Kennedy*

THUNDER BAY

THUNDER BAY

PROLOGUE

She felt sand beneath her feet and a warm breeze on her face, yet around her she could hear the shriek of a much fiercer wind.

She opened her eyes and saw the water, so blue, calmer than she had ever seen it before. Where it met the rocks, it was more a kiss than a slap. Even the seabirds seemed less predatory. They did not dive for prey but hung against the clear sky like a child's mobile, as if to pierce the smooth surface of the water would be nothing short of a sin.

She closed her eyes again, breathed in the air. It was sweet with no salty snap, no sense of the damp stench of rotting seaweed that could be all-pervading.

She was happy here. She was always happy here. They used to come to the bay when they were children, the five of them, leaving their homes early in the morning to walk across the island. The journey took them hours but they always made it. And no matter how tired they were they raced down the trail from the clifftop, eager to be the first to hit the soft sand, the wind catching their hair and carrying their laughter to join the echo from the rockface. More often than not she won the race because she was always the fastest runner, the boys too busy trying to best each other to notice she was way ahead of them.

Then they would wolf down the lunches their parents had packed, or in Henry's case some housekeeper or other, and they would splash at the water's edge and play on the rocks that fringed the bay, seeking out sea creatures and discarded shells, daring each other to see how close they could swim to the caves, but no one actually attempting it. They were young but they knew it was too dangerous, even for immortals like them.

But they weren't immortal. She knew that now. They all knew that now.

Voices.

She heard voices.

Distant. Incoherent. Swirling around her within the fierce wind she couldn't feel.

They said there were beings that lived in the winds, elemental creatures that breathed and sighed around the land and the beaches and the bays. But she didn't believe that. It was a tale of the old island, along with the witches on the mountain and the creatures in the water and petrified sisters standing watch on the shore.

And yet . . .

Voices on the wind, surrounding her, calling to her.

Mhairi

Her name. She heard her name, muffled and remote but she heard it. She looked around the bay, but she was alone, only her footprints in the sand. She didn't remember walking down the track. She didn't remember driving here. She didn't remember . . .

Mhairi

Louder now, more distinct. A woman's voice. She scanned the clifftop but saw no figure etched against the sky, so blue, so very blue and peaceful. She looked out to sea—perhaps a boat?—but nothing bobbed on the silky surface.

It looked so inviting, the water, and she felt that, for the first time, she would be able to swim out past the jagged rocks, out to sea, far out to sea, where all was calm and she was free of pain. And there *was* pain, she noticed it now, dull certainly, but it was there. She hadn't been aware of it until she heard the voice, but there it was. An ache that spread from her head to her face and throughout her body. And something else now, something warm seeping from her hair and trailing down her forehead. She put her hand up, wiped it away, saw the red on her fingers. She was bleeding. She'd hurt her head and she was bleeding. How did that happen?

2

She tried to ignore the voice and knelt to scoop up a handful of water from where it lapped against the land. It felt so cool, so comforting. She dabbed her face with it, washed the blood from her fingers. The waves crept around her but she didn't mind. They took some of the ache away and she felt at peace here.

But the voice kept calling to her. Stronger now.

And there were other voices, men talking but not to her. Only the woman spoke to her. Saying her name, over and over and over and over . . .

Mhairi

Mhairi

Mhairi, can you hear me?

The waves built around her, the level rising quickly, but she wasn't alarmed. The water was her friend, it soothed her, she would become one with it and it would take away all the pain. It would heal her. She let its coolness take her under, but it was deeper than she thought, for soon it enveloped her and she floated there in the welcoming gloom, looking up at the sunlight playing on the surface before it fractured and stabbed down towards her. She didn't want it to touch her—she was happy here, she was safe, she was free—but she could still hear the voice beckoning to her and she knew if just one of those beams of bright light touched her it would drag her back. She wanted to push away through the rippling water but she couldn't move. All she could do was dangle, yet her body did not feel loose. One arm was bent away from her, it didn't look right; the other was draped across her stomach. She saw her fingers trembling, still covered in blood—*hadn't she washed that off?*—while one leg was trapped beneath her body. She could feel it wedged there. She was underwater, she liked it here, so why didn't she drift? Why couldn't she move?

The light reached down for her and touched her like hands. Not rough, not like before, but gentle. Caring. Comforting.

And she heard the voice saying her name again as her twisted body was drawn slowly back to the surface, back to the light, harsher now, not sunlight, not warm and pleasing and filled with the laughter of summer. She wanted to stay, she wanted peace, but she couldn't fight it. She had to go back, she knew she had to go back, if only for a short time.

The wind shrieked and howled as she broke through the surface, but where she lay wasn't warm and comforting and soft, it was hard and unyielding. Her vision swam. She didn't know where she was at first, but she knew she wasn't in the sea. Everything was blurred, the light so bright it hurt her eyes and she couldn't see anything clearly. And there was pain, real pain, agonising pain, coursing through every part of her. She wanted to scream, to eject the hurt with sound, but she couldn't. She couldn't even move.

Stay with us, Mhairi.

The woman, still distant but she heard her clear enough, reaching out to her through the blinding whiteness. But then her voice muffled again, merged with the others, only certain words rising to the surface, words she didn't understand.

Open-vault fracture

Zygomatic

Frontal sinus

She tried to speak, but no words came. She knew they were talking about her. She knew she was in trouble and she longed to be back in the bay where she was safe, where the pain could be washed away. But she couldn't go, not yet. One thing came into her head, a name, and she had to know. She forced herself to focus on that name, to say that name. It was a fresh sting, sharp and fleeting, that helped her.

'Sonya.'

A face emerged from the light. It was a kind face. A caring face.

'She's fine,' said the face. 'Your baby is fine.'

Relief then, and it seemed to wash away some of the agony.

'I've given you something to ease the pain,' said the voice. 'You need to stay with me, Mhairi.'

'Ask her who did this.' Another voice. A man. Gruff. She knew the voice but couldn't place it. Couldn't see him. Just a shape behind the woman who was helping her, blurred, indistinct despite the unforgiving glare from the overhead light. Too stark. Too severe. She saw irritation flash across the woman's face.

'Not my concern right now, Jim.'

'It's important.'

The woman turned her head. Mhairi saw her brown hair was cropped tight. 'Jim, not my concern right now.'

Mhairi saw now, not clearly, but she recognised his heavy dark uniform. Sergeant Rankin. Everyone on the island knew him. She couldn't see his face, but she knew it would be flushed and the whisky on his breath would nestle beneath a coat of mouthwash. He smoked too much and he drank too much, that's what her mum said. He'd never see sixty, she said.

Neither would Mhairi. She knew that now.

Whatever she had been given was bringing her further into this world. The wind she heard at the bay but could not feel was throwing itself against the cottage. She could see a blue light strobing against the windows, could hear the logs hissing and crackling in the grate, although she could not feel its warmth. The thought made something within her wince. The logs . . .

She remembered.

The policeman was bending over her now. 'Tell me who did this, lass. Who did this to you?'

She tried to turn her head but the pain screamed at her. Even moving her eyes was agonising. Whatever she had been given wasn't enough. But she had to see if he was there, she had to let them know.

And then she saw Roddie.

He was standing just behind Sergeant Rankin, another policeman at his side. She had seen Roddie like that once before, wedged between two officers, when he'd been arrested for shoplifting back when they were children. He hadn't done it, of course; it had been Henry. It was always Henry, getting them into scrapes and getting away with it.

No, she was wrong. He hadn't been quite like this back then. There hadn't been blood back then, covering his clothes, his hands. Her blood, she knew that. Her blood.

She looked straight at him, saw the fear in his eyes as she tried to speak, as she tried to tell them, but the effort was too great. She felt herself slipping away, could hear the splash of the waves and the cry of the seabirds, urging her to return. And she longed to return. There was too much pain in this world, too much heartache, too much disappointment. She wanted the water to lap at her body again, wanted it to caress her and wash everything away. She could tell them later, tell them later . . . Now she needed to simply bask in the sunlight, away from the groaning wind and the numbing pain and the paralysing terror.

But still she heard the policeman's voice, asking her again who did it, and the woman telling him to back off. Mhairi knew that she had to give him something about that night—he had a right to know, it was important that he knew—but she was so comfortable back in the bay. That was where she belonged, where the breeze carried the promise of contentment. Where memories lived and laughed like old friends.

She managed two words before she once again felt the sand between her toes and was welcomed by the water as it washed softly back and forward against the land.

Back and forward

Back and forward

Back . . .

. . . forward.

1

The present day

The woman's face rippled as she battled her emotions. Her chin twitched. Her cheeks developed a tic. Her eyes became reservoirs. But she maintained the ritual of pouring tea. The well-used strainer was carefully placed on the rim of the china cup bearing a blue floral pattern. The matching tea pot was hidden under a knitted cosy with only its curved handle and spout showing. The tea, perfectly tanned, fell steadily into the cup, even though the electric impulses that thrummed around the woman's facial muscles conducted along her arm and made the pot tremble.

To Rebecca Connolly, more used to a teabag thrown into a tannin-stained mug, the process was old-fashioned, almost quaint, but she understood why it all seemed so important to Maeve Gallagher.

'Sugar?' The question was asked without any eye contact. Maeve's focus remained on the tray in front of her, as if the paraphernalia was something that needed to be closely watched at all times.

'No, thanks,' said Rebecca, her voice soft.

'Milk?'

'A dash.'

The forced banality of the conversation, like the heightened emphasis on the process, was necessary. The woman needed time. She had to fix on the little things, the everyday matter of simply making and pouring a cup of tea, because it held her steady and kept the grief at bay.

The sing-song of children's laughter floated in from the street outside. It was a warm autumn day and they were enjoying it. Rebecca saw Maeve glance through the window of her neat, over-furnished front room to watch the group of teenagers walk by directly outside. There was no garden to act as a barrier, just the window facing directly onto the street and, beyond it, the river. There was no irritation in the woman's slight movement but rather something wistful, as if that laughter was not the laughter she wanted to hear.

'Tell me about Edie,' said Rebecca. Her voice was still gentle but she had to get Maeve to talk. That was why she was here.

Maeve said nothing as she handed over the delicate cup and saucer. She remained silent as she offered the tea plate piled with chocolate biscuits, which Rebecca refused with a shake of the head. Maeve carefully laid the plate back down on the tray perched on the wide footstool. Too carefully, as if she was delaying the inevitable. Rebecca gave her time, sipped the tea, waited. After all, Maeve had agreed to speak to her. She had something to say, and now that she had given her a gentle prod Rebecca knew she had to be allowed the time to say it.

Rebecca gave the room a brief scan. There were four large armchairs and a long couch arranged around a rectangular coffee table with a shelf underneath bearing a variety of magazines and a couple of jigsaws. In the corner beside the wide windows a large flat-screen TV sat on a black unit and through its smoked-glass doors she could see a satellite box and a DVD player with a few DVD cases sitting upright beside it. The gas fire in the tiled fireplace was dark, but the room was warm, thanks to the radiator under the window. The gas fire was no doubt only used in winter, which can be harsh in Inverness. On the mantle sat a reproduction carriage clock but its hands were still, as if time had ended at twelve minutes past three. This was not a room that had a lived-in feel, but then no one actually lived in this room, they just sat here on occasion, either on their way to or just back from elsewhere.

Eventually, inevitably, Rebecca's eyes fell on the heavy sideboard taking up much of the wall beside the door. The piece of furniture looked old, second-hand. It was polished, but she could see scratches and gouges in the dark wood of the doors, perhaps made over the years by carelessly handled luggage. The sideboard itself was not what drew Rebecca's attention; it was the photograph sitting on it. Encased in a silver frame, a shot of a teenage girl with long dark hair falling in waves to her shoulders. A pretty girl holding a black and white kitten. She was smiling. Her eyes danced with delight. Edie Gallagher.

Rebecca wondered where the kitten was now. It would be older, but not much. Rebecca guessed the snap was a year old. The cat would be in the rear of the house probably, where the family lived. Not allowed here, in the business part of the building, even though the Belle View Guest House hadn't had a guest for many months.

Rebecca returned her attention to Maeve. She sat erect in the armchair, her cup and saucer clasped in both hands on her lap, her eyes fixed on the window, her head slightly cocked as if listening to the fading voices and laughter of the young people, her eyes still misty as she longed to hear that one laugh she would never hear again. On the other side of the street Rebecca could see the River Ness reflecting the blue sky. Across the water church spires punctuated the heavens, but Rebecca knew Maeve wasn't seeing them. A small sigh, a tiny shiver, and then—finally—a solitary tear erupted.

'She was my lass,' she said, the simple statement and that lone tear almost breaking Rebecca's heart. She blinked, told herself to concentrate on the job in hand. She heard the voice of her own father, still bearing the lilt of the islands, talking about police work but insisting it worked with journalism too.

A good officer doesn't need emotions, but a great one knows how to use them. Without emotion, we cannot empathise. If we can't empathise, we cannot understand. And if we can't understand, then why the hell are we doing the job?

Maeve didn't move as she spoke again. 'She used to come in that front door like a hurricane, always full of energy, always full of . . .'

She stopped and her face quivered again. Rebecca knew what she had been about to say.

Always full of life.

9

Maeve swallowed the word back and spoke again. 'I would tell her to shut the door behind her, but she never did. Always left it wide open, rain or shine, as she dashed up the stairs, desperate to get her school uniform off and into her jeans and T-shirt, or whatever. Every time I hear that door opening now, I think it might be her.' Her eyes glistened as she stared into the sunlit street. 'But it's not, of course. It's never her. Never will be.'

Rebecca laid her cup and saucer on the tray. Her pad was tucked beside her, against the arm of the roomy armchair, and she wanted to scribble Maeve's words down but didn't want to do anything that might draw the woman from her thoughts.

Her editor had sent her to get Maeve to do something no one else had managed. *Get her talking. Get us quotes, something none of the others have.*

He'd sent Rebecca because this was what she was good at, getting people to talk, getting people to trust her. It was a skill she'd inherited from her father. At least that's what her mum said.

He could always get people to open up. It was a gift.

That gift had served Rebecca well during her three years in newspapers. People warmed to her. People spoke to her, told her things. People like Maeve, who had not spoken to a single journalist since her daughter Edie had died.

'I wonder if he thinks about her?' Maeve said, suddenly. 'That man . . .'

Greg Pullman. The London trader who slammed his hired car into Edie while he was high on booze and cocaine. Who left her broken and dying in the street while he roared away in his high-performance dick extender. Who was that day to be sentenced.

'I wonder if he considers the life he took,' said Maeve, her voice low, barely above a whisper. 'I wonder if he cares at all.' Finally, she looked at Rebecca. 'What do you think he'll get?'

'A custodial sentence, I think. He'll do time.'

A tight little nod, satisfied. 'Good. I'd hate to think that he'd get off with it just because he's got money.'

He'd been staying in his cottage on the Black Isle for the week and had met up with some mates for a weekend jolly in Inverness. He'd decided that he was fit to drive. He didn't even remember hitting the teenager, or so he said.

'That won't influence the judge,' said Rebecca. 'He'll go away, Maeve. I'm certain of it.'

Another bob of the head, then Maeve's eyes drifted back to the window and the sunlight and the river flowing across the street, as if seeking out the red brickwork of the castle, where the court sat.

'Ralph's down there now. He said he wanted to see it. Wants to see the man's face when he hears that he's going away.' Her gaze swam back towards Rebecca. 'You're certain he'll be jailed?'

Rebecca nodded.

Maeve's eyes hardened. 'He'll get, what? A few years? His licence taken away? But then after those few years he'll be out again and getting on with his life. He'll be out again to work and play, have a family. To drink again, to take drugs again, probably even drive again, won't he?'

Rebecca didn't answer. She couldn't. She knew that everything Maeve had said was possible but there was no way she was going to say so because she sensed where this was leading and didn't want to break the flow.

'But my Edie can't, can she? She can't get on with her life because he took it away. She won't ever work. She won't ever have a family, won't ever grow old. He took all that away from her. He took all that away from me and Ralph. He took it all.'

Maeve placed her untouched cup of tea on the tray, then stood and walked to the window. It was a sudden movement, as if she simply had to move, compelled by the rage building inside her. She hadn't spoken to anyone about her grief, as far as Rebecca knew. She'd kept it contained, bottled up. Rebecca recalled a snatched shot of her outside the court on the day Pullman was found guilty. The muscles were drawn, the mouth a tight line, her head held so erect Rebecca could see the tendons of her neck standing out like cables. She must have wept, but privately. Now that single tear had breached the dam and it was about to burst. Maeve leaned on the sill, her head slightly bowed, and Rebecca saw her shoulders shudder.

'Maeve . . .' Rebecca began to rise but the woman held up a hand, shook her head. She didn't want Rebecca's sympathy. She needed to get this out. Rebecca sat back again, feeling she should somehow offer comfort but grateful she didn't have to.

Her phone, nestling beside her pad, vibrated against her thigh, but she ignored it. Whoever it was would have to wait. The flow, it was all about the flow.

'I hope he dies in prison,' said Maeve, her voice strong and not watered down by the tears that now fell freely. 'I hope some other prisoner kills him. I hope he feels just a portion of the pain Edie felt as she lay there in that gutter. I hope someone guts him, the way he's gutted me and her father.'

Rebecca sat back. She had her quote. She had the line that would make that week's splash. She had what no other paper had.

The reporter within her was delighted.

The human being was saddened.

* * *

She convinced Maeve to agree to a photograph, which she took with her phone. Newspaper cutbacks. No need for staff photographers; if you were lucky a freelancer would do (though none were available that day). Rebecca was too young to have known how it was in days of yore—those days actually far from yore, being just a few years earlier— but she'd heard from old hands how things had been done. There was a time when a snapper would have been sent out with her, or at least arrangements made for one to visit. But the industry had changed, moved on, become more efficient in the bid to protect profits. She was wise enough to know that 'efficient' didn't mean improved.

The shot she took was typical tabloid: Maeve holding the framed photograph of Edie and looking heartbroken. It was cheesy and it was basic. A professional photographer might've been more creative, but Rebecca was a mere scribbler. She waited another fifteen minutes before she made her excuses. She thought Maeve was ashamed of her low-key outburst, of her display of near-public emotion, and was relieved to see her go.

As Rebecca walked towards her car, the October sun welcome after the interview, she glanced back at the guest house and saw the woman at the window, still clasping the framed photograph of her daughter to her chest. Rebecca gave her a small wave but it wasn't returned. Maeve Gallagher looked so alone, it was doubtful she even saw her. She was lost in the mists of grief and anger and memories of a stolen young life.

Rebecca turned away and dug her phone from her coat pocket. The missed call was from Chaz Wymark. He was a photographer, young certainly but she had no doubt he would have come up with a far better shot of Maeve. She reached her car, settled on the small wall separating the roadway from the riverbank, and thumbed the call back. As it rang she raised her face to the sun. *Make the most of it*, she thought, *winter isn't far.*

'Rebecca.' Chaz sounded pleased to hear from her. He always sounded pleased to hear from her. They'd never met face-to-face but had spoken often on the phone.

'What's up, Chaz?'

'Oh, big doings over here, you better believe it.'

Over here. Chaz was speaking from Stoirm, an island off the west coast where he lived. He provided local snippets and photographs in return for a payment so small it made minimum wage look overly extravagant. Storm Island, they called it. Her father had been born there, but the only thing he ever said about it was that it was aptly named. But *big doings*. On *Stoirm*? She couldn't believe it.

'What's going on, Chaz?'

He told her. While he spoke, she knew she was on to something. This time, though, there was something new, a quickening of the pulse, the flutter in the gut as nerves prepared to take flight.

This time it was about Stoirm.

13

2

This was the longest he had been apart from his wife since before they were married. The hill on which he stood had been Mary's favourite spot on the island. *You can see the world*, she used to say. Her world, anyway. Below him lay Portnaseil, the only sound the grumble of the morning ferry as it prepared to set off across the Sound, which on this fine autumn day was a refreshing deep blue. Portnaseil was the largest settlement on Stoirm, its buildings nestling around the sheltered harbour, while the other villages clung to the eastern coastline. There was nothing to speak of on the western side, for that was where the weather so often lashed at the land and the cliffs. Not today, though. He lifted his eyes towards the dark bulk of the mainland across the water, where white splashes of villages reflected the sunshine. Behind him was the island, the houses and crofts dotted across the grasslands and heather until they gave way in the west to the corrugated hills that shouldered the sky on either side of the island's mountain, Beinn nan sìthichean. *That's where the fairies live,* Mary used to tell their children. *They let you visit in daylight but not after dark. That's their time, and anyone caught on the mountain after nightfall is theirs forever.*

The breeze whispered through the reeds and tall grass around him. *Spirits*, Mary would say, *singing to us from the other side.* He listened carefully but he couldn't hear her voice among them. He longed to hear it again, even if only once. Maybe, someday, he would.

Two days.

That's how long she'd been gone.

14

Just two days.

It felt like a lifetime.

The church stood above Portnaseil, the old graves scattered around it like standing stones, the newer burial ground off to the side more ordered. For all her love of the old stories, Mary had been a believer, never missed services. The wind could be sharp enough to cut her in half, while the rains could attack as if it was personal, but every Sunday she would pull on her coat, grab her Bible and head out. She'd be back in the kirk soon enough, he thought. Only this time she wouldn't come home and start preparing the roast. This time she wouldn't stop for a chat with the ladies. This time she wouldn't come up to this hill if the weather was fine, just to find a moment to herself and listen to the spirits singing in the grass. This time she'd stay in the kirkyard forever.

He closed his eyes and concentrated again on the soft sigh of the breeze. *Just one word*, he prayed. *Just my name. Just one more time.*

'Dad.'

For a moment he thought it was Mary. Just a brief flash of something like hope. She always called him that in front of the children. Never Campbell, never darling, never anything but Dad. But that would mean his prayer had been answered and he'd long ago given up on any help from that quarter.

He turned and saw his daughter Shona heading up the hillside. She'd always favoured her mother—the same smile, the same laugh, the same look when she was irritated with something he had done—but now she was in her late thirties she was Mary's double. Even her own daughter was showing a strong resemblance. Shona had defied modern naming traditions and called her only child Mary. That pleased him, because it meant a little something of his Mary would live on.

He said nothing to Shona. He knew why she had come to find him. He stared across the Sound, his jaw clenched.

She reached his side and stood for a moment, following his gaze.

'She loved it here,' she said.

'Aye,' he said.

There was another silence between them while around them the world played its own symphony. The soft melody of the breeze. The glissando of the waves as they caressed the yellow sand at the bottom of the hill. The bass rumble of the ferry engine as it pulled away. The percussive cry of a gull.

Shona slid her hand into his and squeezed. He squeezed back. He loved her but he didn't want to hear what was coming next. He'd seen it in her eyes as she'd climbed the hill. He'd felt it in the touch of her hand. He already knew.

She said it anyway, her words so subdued that they were almost swept away by the wind and the waves and the cough of the ferry.

'He's coming back,' she said.

3

Barry Lennox had been editor of the *Highland Chronicle* for a year. He was a big man, probably muscled at one time but those had long since turned to fat, and he kept his hair in a mullet. He dressed in jeans and denim jackets and he thought he looked like Mel Gibson in *Lethal Weapon*. He didn't. He'd been in newspapers for more than twenty years—first with the dailies, then a time with a Sunday tabloid—and Rebecca thought he'd come to the *Highland Chronicle* to stay out of the rain, probably in the belief that working in weekly newspapers would be easy. He'd barely deposited his widening backside in the editor's chair when he was landed with overseeing two other weeklies in the north of Scotland, the owners in London deciding that one editor was enough for all titles on the frontier of their empire. Lennox thought he could manage, because he still believed life in the weeklies was a holiday camp compared to the cut and thrust of national journalism.

He now knew that wasn't the case.

He looked tired and harassed and, Rebecca noted, extremely pissed off. That seemed to be his fall-back position these days. To his credit, he didn't take his frustrations out on his staff, or rather what was left of it, for the owners' cutbacks did not stop at editors and photographers. Profit margins had to be defended and that meant staff had to go, even though they produced the product that created the profits. There didn't seem to be any reduction in management, Rebecca had noticed; there was always somebody new appointed to come along and tell them all how to do their jobs.

When the previous editor, a smart, tough and funny woman named Elspeth MacTaggart, had finally decided she'd had enough she fired off a stinging memo to the suits in the south outlining exactly where she thought they were going wrong and how much they were damaging not just the business but journalism as a whole. They ignored it and waved her goodbye. Lennox was her replacement.

He looked up from his computer screen as Rebecca walked into his office. 'How did you do?'

In the car, Rebecca had scribbled the quotes on her pad before she forgot them. She read them back and saw the beginnings of a smile on his broad face.

'Get it written up, three hundred words for page three but we'll splash on the front. I'll send you a box.' He began to punch the keys again. It didn't matter if a story called for more words or less—that was the way the designer had formed the page and that was it. Lennox would read her piece, though, and tweak it—knowing him, make it more sensational. He could also amend the page design if he had to, but that was a complicated business and, truth be told, an art he had not yet fully mastered. Only one person in the office had been adept at manoeuvring the intricacies of the page design system but he had been made redundant two months before. The new system, said management, who had never punched a key in anger, was so wonderful sub-editors were no longer needed. So the suits started to call them 'content managers' and that made them feel a whole lot better. Rebecca could write neat, clean copy but she had news for them—subs were needed, no matter what they called them. Barry had two content managers but one was on holiday and the other spent much of her time on Mondays and Tuesdays dealing with the various sport pages, meaning the bulk of the news fell to Barry. Hence his current mood.

'You get a pic?' asked Lennox.

Rebecca held up her phone. 'Not a great one. A snapper would've done better.'

He shrugged that away, stared at his monitor. 'As long as it's in focus and we can see the woman's face, it'll be fine. Bung it in the system and I'll slap it on the page.'

'Okay,' she said, fighting down a sigh. She'd only been in the job for three years but even she could see standards were slipping. 'There's something else, Barry.'

His eyes flicked a question over the top of his monitor, but he kept banging the keys.

'I spoke to Chaz on the way back,' said Rebecca.

'Chaz who?' He still wasn't looking at her.

'Wymark, the freelance over on the island.'

'What island?'

Rebecca had never visited Stoirm but she called it simply 'the island' like a native. Her father had only ever called it that, even though he rarely mentioned his childhood home.

'Stoirm,' she said.

'Right, okay,' he said, remembering. 'The freelance.'

Which is what she'd said. 'Anyway,' she went on, 'he's come up with a belter of a story.'

Lennox stopped typing, gave her his full attention. 'Okay.'

'A woman called Mary Drummond died a couple of days ago, massive heart attack. Her son was Roddie Drummond and fifteen years ago he was tried for the murder of his girlfriend. Acquitted on a Not Proven. He's not been on the island since, but there's a chance he's coming back for the funeral.'

'Okay, get on the phone, see what you can get. Get that Chaz boy to nose about . . .'

'There's still a lot of bitterness over the case, Chaz says. It's a fairly big island but Portnaseil is a small community, everyone knows each other.' She immediately regretted using the words 'small community' because that translated to tiny sales. She also knew it was unlikely that everyone knew each other, but she thought the idea might strengthen her pitch somehow. 'But I think this is bigger—prodigal returns, locals resent it. And then there's the murder mystery, too.'

Lennox sat back, lifted a dagger-shaped letter opener he kept on his desk, even though there were very few envelopes to slit open these days, and twirled it in both hands. This was his habit whenever he wasn't poking at the keyboard, as if his hands were so restless they simply had to do something. 'So what you saying, Becks?'

She took a breath. 'I think I need to be over there.'

His body language had formed 'No' before she'd completed her short sentence. 'I can't afford to send you over there,' he said. 'I need you here. You can do ten stories in the time it would take to get one.'

A story's not a story unless it can be done on the phone. That was the pronouncement of one of the nimrods sent up from London to tell the staff they were doing everything wrong. It was during her first year on the job but she knew it was bollocks as soon the words came out of his mouth. The thing was, she felt even he didn't believe it. It was merely the company line.

'Barry . . .' she began.

'Becks,' he interrupted, 'you're not Lois Lane and we're not the *Daily Planet*. You're not going to go over there and solve this mystery . . .'

'I don't expect to. I just feel I can get people to talk if I'm meeting them face-to-face. You know I'm good at that.' A slight incline of his head told her he was forced to agree. 'So think about this—where's this Roddie Drummond character been for fifteen years? What's he been doing? How does he feel about going back home after all this time, with a cloud still over his head? What happened back then? And we'll get more than one story out of it. I promise you we'll get a front page splash and a feature piece right off the bat. And who knows what else I'll trip over. But I need to be there to do that. Some things you can't do on the phone.'

He dropped the letter opener on the desk and stared at her. She heard his breath exhale as he considered her speech, which, given it was delivered off the top of her head, was a good one. She was bound to have won him over but she hit him with one final blow.

'And we're in on this at the beginning, Barry. It's an exclusive. The *P&J*, the *West Highland Free Press*, *The Courier*, even the dailies won't have a sniff of this. Not yet. But we need to move on it.'

She had gambled this would appeal to the old-fashioned newspaperman that she hoped still lived inside him. An exclusive. A chance to splash something that no other newspaper had. Journalistic pride. She thrilled at the possibilities. But she had another motive to get to Stoirm. One she wasn't sharing that with her editor. It was personal.

He shook his head. 'Can't swing it, Becks, you know that. See what you can get on the phone. If it's that exclusive then you don't need to be there.'

Damn it, she thought.

He turned his attention to his monitor once again and she knew she was beaten. Disappointed, she turned away, then a new thought struck her. 'Did you hear from Yvonne?' Yvonne Adams, the only other journalist on the *Chronicle* team now. She was at court for Greg Pullman's sentencing.

Lennox didn't look up from the monitor. 'He got ten years, banned from driving and a ten grand fine.'

Rebecca left his office, smiling. That was something, at least.

* * *

Her mobile beeped just as she was putting the finishing touches to the Maeve Gallagher piece. She had gone straight for the heart, as befitted the story. Even so, she didn't fool herself that this was news. In university she'd been taught the adage, attributed to some long dead press baron, that the news was something that someone, somewhere, didn't want printed. Everything else was advertising. It could be argued, she supposed, that Greg Pullman wouldn't want this printed, but he had other things on his mind now. What it boiled down to was voyeurism. As much as she sympathised with the bereaved mother, this was a chance for the reader to enjoy someone else's pain. Rebecca knew she was being hard on readers but that was the way it was. And yet, she provided the suds for this particular soap opera. She did her job because that was what she was paid for, it was what she was good at, but stories like this were not what drew her into journalism.

She scanned her words as she answered her mobile without checking the caller display. Her heart sank when she heard Simon's voice.

'It's me.'

21

She contemplated simply disconnecting, but she didn't. She couldn't be that hard, even though she'd made it clear to Simon that it was over.

'Becks?'

'I'm here.' Her voice sounded strained, even to her.

'I was wondering if you were free for a coffee, or lunch. Or something.'

'Kind of busy, Simon. Working.'

'Right.' He sounded deflated and she thought to herself, *what did he expect?* 'Yeah, sure, but . . . well . . . I was in the area and I just thought . . . well . . .'

Rebecca looked around to ensure no one else was listening. Who would be, though? Yvonne was still out, Barry was hunched over his screen in his office, the reporters on the other titles, two per paper, were busy, the sole content manager was at the table at the far side making herself a coffee while the advertising department was based in another room.

'Simon, look—it's not a good idea, okay? You can't keep calling me.'

'I know, it's just . . .'

'No,' she said, firmer than she meant it, so she deliberately softened her voice. 'This has to stop. You know it has to stop.'

'Becks, you know how I feel. You know I . . .'

Don't say it, she thought.

'Love you.'

And he says it.

'I can't let things just end, Becks.'

'But they have ended, Simon.'

'Maybe for you.'

'Yes, maybe for me, but that's still an ending.'

There was a pause 'It wasn't my fault, Becks. It wasn't anyone's fault.'

She could hear his voice beginning to waver and she couldn't take it. She knew what had happened wasn't his fault. She knew it wasn't hers, either. It had simply happened. She certainly didn't blame him but afterwards she had come to realise there was nothing between them. As the saying went, it wasn't him, it was her. She didn't know what she was looking for but she knew Simon wasn't it. Not now.

She didn't say any of that, though.

'Simon, please, let it go. There's nothing to be said. Sorry, but I'm under the gun here. I've got to get back to work.'

She hung up. She felt bad, but she couldn't get into that discussion again. It had been six months since it had happened. She'd tried not to think about it too much, but his voice always brought it back and she couldn't have that, not here, not in the office. She moved to the window and looked down into the street, scanned the cars parked on either side. Yup, there it was. Simon's blue Audi. Simon was a solicitor based in Dingwall. It was possible he was down in Inverness at court but he had no reason to be out in the industrial units where the *Chronicle* had its office.

She leaned against the wall beside the window and closed her eyes, blocking the memories. She hoped this wasn't going to be a problem. She couldn't let it become one.

4

If Rebecca had a guilty secret, it was that she was a fan of Robbie Williams. It wasn't something she broadcast, he not being cool among the oh-so-cool twenty-somethings who were her peer group. He was on her iPod, swinging both ways, as she sat on the floor of her small flat, bound copies of the *Highland Chronicle* opened and spread out around her. She had liberated them from the file room before she'd left the office, sneaking them into her car without being seen. The digital archive only went back nine years and so there was nothing online about the Stoirm murder, hence the need for the bulky volumes containing every edition from the year of the murder and then the trial a few months after.

They didn't tell her much. The *Chronicle* reports were far from comprehensive—perhaps things weren't much better in the good old days after all, although there was a very good in-depth feature on the case following the trial. To be fair, a murder like that, the first on the island for fifty years, was well covered by the dailies, and by the time the weekly title came out there wouldn't have been much that was fresh. She found further reports on the websites of the dailies, but even their digital records from back then were patchy.

She did uncover a lengthy entry on the case on a site detailing unsolved murders in Scotland but knew better than to accept what was there as gospel. Technically, the case *was* unsolved. Roddie Drummond had faced trial but was acquitted on a Not Proven verdict. It was a controversial issue in Scotland, the infamous third option for juries—'that bastard verdict', it was called, neither guilty nor not guilty. But an acquittal all the same.

She hooked her glass of wine from the floor beside her and leaned against the settee. The A4 notepad on her lap was covered in spidery handwriting which was unreadable by anyone except herself, and sometimes not even then. She liked to scribble notes down, it made her feel closer to the material. She then let her eyes roam towards the open pages of newsprint and finally to the screen of her laptop. A grainy shot of Mhairi Sinclair, obviously scanned in from a newspaper, stared back at her. She was beautiful, with high cheekbones, dark hair pulled back into a ponytail. If it had hung loose it would have fallen to her shoulders, as straight as a waterfall.

She had a child, the reports said. She was living with Roddie, although he was not the father. Rebecca flicked back through her handwritten notes. The father was another local man, Donnie Kerr. On her pad she'd written the words FIND HIM and underlined them. Twice.

She stared at Mhairi's eyes. The photo was in black and white, so she couldn't see what colour they were. They looked dark. Dark and deep.

What happened back then, Mhairi?

Who killed you?

Rebecca pulled the *Chronicle*'s trial report towards her and looked for the section detailing Mhairi's final few minutes. Paramedics from the newly opened community hospital had responded to Roddie's 999 call. Mhairi had been badly beaten. Rebecca had noted phrases like *open-vault fracture*, where the hair and scalp had come into contact with the brain, *zygomatic and frontal sinus fractures*, which meant she had been beaten so badly the bones around her eyes had been smashed, leaving her left eye bulging from the socket, *Cushing's triad*, where arterial pressure had increased, probably due to swelling of the brain, while her respiration was irregular and pulse rate down. There were further deep lacerations and contusions where someone had compressed her throat. All of this was reported in the dry, emotionless manner of expert witnesses until the pathologist was questioned about the nature of the injuries. 'It is my opinion that the individual who did this was suffering from deep and uncontrollable rage,' he said. Naturally, defence counsel didn't like that one bit and objected to the speculation, but the thought was already out there.

The paramedics did what they could but they were fighting a losing battle and Mhairi died in the ambulance. She had regained consciousness once, while they were still in the cottage. Rebecca scanned the report, found the passage she was looking for, read it again:

The Advocate Depute asked the witness: 'And did the deceased say anything before she died?'
The witness replied: 'Yes. She asked after Sonya.'
'Sonya being her one-year-old daughter?'
'Yes.'
'And where was Sonya at the time?'
'She was in her cot in the house. She was asleep.'
'And the daughter was unharmed?'
'She was perfectly fine.'
The Advocate Depute then asked: 'And did the deceased say anything else?'
The witness replied: 'She did.'
'And would you tell the court what that was?'
'She said "Thunder Bay".'
The paramedic was asked what she thought that meant and she explained that Thunder Bay was a well-known location on the west coast of Stoirm.
The witness was then asked: 'And what do you think she meant by that?'
'I don't know,' she said.

* * *

Rebecca had printed THUNDER BAY in her notes and underlined those words too. Three times. Thunder Bay. She'd logged into Google Maps and zeroed in on it. There was only a satellite image, no ground-level view. It looked fairly remote, with what seemed like a dirt trail running

26

from the roadway that ran the length of the island, although it was difficult to tell. It might've been a tarmac single-track road. Underneath her notes, she'd written one word: VISIT.

If she was honest, she'd decided while she was speaking to Chaz that she would go to the island to follow the story. It didn't really matter what Barry said. She had hoped he would see the importance of the story and let her go but it seemed any news instincts he might have once possessed were smothered by the need to satisfy the number crunchers and their spreadsheets. On one level Rebecca understood his position but her own instincts told her there was no way she could do it justice with a few phone calls.

There was so much here. The murder fifteen years before. The enduring mystery. Roddie Drummond.

And then there was Stoirm.

The island on which her father had been born. The island he'd left when he was eighteen. The island to which he'd never returned. The island that had fascinated her since she'd first heard of it, even though she'd never visited.

It had been one of the reasons she had been delighted to land the *Chronicle* job. Though Stoirm was a far-flung area of the paper's circulation she had always hoped to be sent there, but so far the opportunity had never arisen.

But now it had.

Rebecca found her mum's number on her phone and made the call. She only glanced at the clock on the wall as she listened to the dial tone. Ten o'clock. Mum would still be up. The phone continued to ring. She began to doubt herself. Maybe she *had* gone to bed. Or maybe she was out. Maybe . . .

'Becca, what's up?'

Her mother's voice sounded worried. Rebecca visualised Sandra Connolly sitting in her spacious kitchen in Milngavie. The sound of the TV in the sitting room reached her, some comedy show or other.

'Nothing, Mum, why?'

'It's late.'

'It's ten o'clock, Mum.'

'Still very late for a phone call.'

Rebecca smiled to herself. Her mother hated the phone and wouldn't even allow it in the living room. It was always in the hall, then, after some petitioning from her husband, in the kitchen. That was a victory for him. At least he could sit at the table to chat.

'After all,' said her mother, 'I could be entertaining a gentleman caller.'

Rebecca smiled. 'You're beyond the age of having gentlemen callers.'

'I'm only fifty-two and that's no age at all. Anyway, that's very ageist of you. I thought we brought you up better than that. Even mums have needs, you know.'

'Mums don't have needs.'

'Of course we do—how else do you think you got here?'

Rebecca felt herself smile. She knew her mother was winding her up. 'Behave yourself, Mum. You know Dad was the only one for you.'

Her mother laughed. 'Yes, that's what he used to say too. And I hated it when he was right. It's the man's job to be wrong, all the time. So, why *are* you calling so late?'

'Sorry, Mum, but this couldn't wait. I'm heading to the island tomorrow.'

There was a silence. When her mother spoke, Rebecca heard the familiar, guarded tone she always used when the subject came up. 'Why?'

'A story.'

'What kind of story?'

Rebecca told her.

When she'd finished her brief outline, her mother spoke. 'I don't know anything about all that.'

'I didn't think you would. What I wanted to know was this: why did Dad never speak about the place?'

Despite her pleas for stories from the island, her dad had said very little about the place, except in passing. And further enquiries from her

28

were adroitly averted. He had no photographs to show, nothing of his childhood. It was as if it wasn't part of him.

There was another silence at the other end of the line, filled only by the faint laughter from the TV. Rebecca made out Stephen Fry's voice. When her mother still didn't speak, she said, 'Mum?'

'He just didn't,' said her mother.

'Not even to you?'

'Not even to me.'

Rebecca was surprised. She had meant it when she said that her father had been the only one for her mother. They weren't merely married, they were connected. She'd never seen two people who cared for each other so much. She really thought that he would've shared something with her over the years. 'But why?'

A sigh. 'Why do you need to know?'

'Because it's a part of him I don't know about. I know the rest. Going to sea . . .'

Her father's voice: *I went to sea to see the sea and once I'd seen it I came back again.*

'Then joining the police. But I don't remember him ever once mentioning the island, apart from casually. I tried to get him to talk about it . . .'

Daddy, tell me about the island.

Nothing to tell, Becca.

Can we go and see it?

Nothing to see, Becca. Just a lot of grass and heather and some hills and a mountain. Nothing to interest a wee lassie like you.

'. . . He just shut me down. Said it was all ancient history. Then he changed the subject.'

Her mum gave out a slight laugh. 'Yes, that was your dad. He didn't like to talk about the island, you know that, not even with me.'

'But he must've said something about it. You really don't know why?'

'I tried, Becca, many times, but he shut me down too. In the nicest possible way, as only your dad knew how. But it was still case closed, as far as he was concerned.'

29

Rebecca had encountered that side of her father many times. He had a way of letting you know not to push too far without having to turn nasty. He'd laugh, or say something really stupid, then change the subject entirely.

'Do we have relatives over there still?'

A pause, then the words came, as if they were being dragged out. Talking about the island—it felt as if she was betraying her dead husband's confidence somehow. 'I've no idea. Your dad's mother, your grandmother, died when he was young, his father a few years after he left, before you were born.'

'Do you think whatever happened on the island, whatever made him leave, involved the family?'

'Becca, believe me. I haven't a clue. I wish I did, I really do. But he never at any time said anything of note, just that he really didn't want to talk about it—and even that was done obliquely. Whatever it was, it was enough to make him hate the place.'

Pen poised, Rebecca suggested, 'There must be somebody over there I could talk to.'

Another sigh breathed down the line. 'Becca, something always told me that sooner or later you'd go over there. I knew you wouldn't do it while your dad was here but you would go sometime, as soon as you could justify it to yourself. Now you have a reason. But I wouldn't go over there and open up any cans with worms in them. Nothing good will come of it.'

'You *do* know something, don't you?'

Her mother laughed again. 'Don't go all conspiracy theory now. Your father said nothing to me. He didn't want to talk about it and I respected his wishes.' She paused. 'Well, eventually. When we were first going together I would ask him, even after we were married, but then I realised that there was no way I would get anything out of him.'

'But weren't you curious?'

'Of course I was! Still am. But after all this time I don't think there's anything to be found.'

'So why are you advising me not to go and open cans of worms? What are you frightened of?'

30

'I'm frightened you *will* find something.' They both laughed, then her mother said, 'I'm not going to talk you out of this, am I?'

'Mum, what do you think?'

Another sigh. 'You were always the same, Becca. Once your mind was set on something, that was it. So like your father.' She fell silent and Rebecca knew she was struggling with herself. Finally, her mother said, 'There is Fiona.'

Rebecca felt something quicken in her chest. This was a chink in the armour. 'Fiona?'

'His old girlfriend. Fiona McRae. Well, that's her name now. She was the one person from the island your dad kept in touch with. She was at his funeral.'

Two years. He'd been gone two years. Cancer took him too young and Rebecca still missed him. 'Did I meet her?'

'Yes, briefly. She's a minister.'

Her father was never religious and had insisted on a humanist service at the crematorium, but Rebecca recalled a stout woman with short hair and a dog collar among the mourners. Later she approached them with a kind smile, a brief hello, nice to meet you, sorry for your loss, then she was gone. Rebecca had no idea then what her connection had been to her father and put it down to someone he'd met through work.

Her mother's tone had betrayed no sign of jealousy, but Rebecca was still slightly taken aback. There was a note of incredulity when she said, 'She was his old girlfriend?'

'Yes, when they were teenagers. What did you think—I was his only sweetheart? Your dad was a handsome man. He broke many a heart before he settled down with me.'

That was something she'd never considered. As far as Rebecca was concerned, her mum and dad had been together forever and neither had exes in their lives. She wondered if her mum was still in contact with any former boyfriends. Then wondered if she had hooked up with any since her dad's death. She put that thought out of her mind immediately. Despite their jokes about gentlemen callers, the idea of her mother having sex with anyone, even her father, was not one she wished to explore.

'She's the minister for the island, has been for a few years, she told me,' her mother said. 'She moved off the island after she graduated but managed to get back. She missed the place.'

'But Dad never did.'

'No. Dad never did.'

Fiona McRae. The local minister. She'd been wondering where to start. Now she knew.

5

The *Kelpie* rode the slight swell with ease, its bow biting into the waves and sending spray flying upwards. Donnie Kerr heard laughter as the salt water hit the tourists. Standing at the wheel, he glanced over his shoulder, his mouth tightening into a mirthless grin as he watched the half dozen passengers giggling to each other. *If that wind picks up any further they won't be laughing,* he thought as he ducked slightly to study the sky through the spray-speckled glass in the wheel house. It was still clear, with only a few clouds, but they had a darkness at their centre that he knew was a forerunner of worse to come. He'd felt it this morning, the pressure on his temples that signalled a storm would hit over the next two to three days. He'd always been able to predict their arrival, even in his 'wilderness years'. It was a gift, he supposed, but when he was younger he didn't see any point to it, apart from warning his father that he shouldn't go out that day. Now it was useful, if not particularly profitable, although as October neared its end predicting rough weather on Stoirm was like saying rain will be wet. It was simply that inevitable. When it did hit, there'd be few chances to get anyone out on the boat. The ferries would be confined to the terminal and the *Kelpie* would huddle down with what was left of Portnaseil's fishing fleet and any stranded pleasure craft in the harbour. It was nearly the end of the season anyway and it hadn't been a great one for him. His mind turned to the pile of bills sitting on his kitchen table. He wasn't facing the streets just yet, but some decisions would have to be made. He'd think of something.

He slowed the boat down and killed the engine. The current caught the *Kelpie*'s forward momentum and swung the bow around slightly to starboard. Donnie turned to the passengers and waved a hand towards the water.

'Okay, folks, this is the best spot to see anything.' He nodded towards the mainland. 'You can see the ferry coming over now. Sometimes the dolphins leap around the bow, as if they're guiding it towards the island.'

A couple of the passengers were visibly touched by the notion that the dolphins were piloting the ferry home, but Donnie knew the mammals were simply riding the bow wave for fun. Dolphins were smart and they knew how to enjoy themselves. The ferry could suddenly veer off course and the creatures would continue to frolic. The thing was, they didn't do it every trip, so the chances of seeing them really was a lottery. You can't go through life just having fun, even dolphins know that. The thought took his mind back to those bills again. He pushed the worries away.

'We've also seen whales two or three times this year around this part of the Sound, as well as basking sharks.' The passengers exchanged nods and smiles. This is what they came for, so cameras and binoculars were readied. 'We'll just drift here for a wee while, see what happens. Keep your eyes peeled and if I spot anything I'll let you know.'

He left them to talk quietly among themselves, eager eyes scanning the water for their first sight of a creature. He hoped they saw something, he really did. They'd paid for the trip, but when there were successful sightings the tips were generous. Donnie longed for a repeat of the whale pod from the year before. He'd had a full boat that day, luckily, and the cash pressed into his hand as his passengers stepped excitedly onto the jetty doubled his take. And non-taxable too.

He rested his hands lightly on the wheel, stared through the window again. He felt the current pushing at the *Kelpie*'s bow and glanced around, just to make sure there was nothing they could drift into. The Sound was clear. He could remember back when there'd be fishing boats dotted all around, mostly locals heading in and out of Portnaseil, including his father, but there was only a handful of men working the nets now. When his father died and he inherited the *Kelpie*, Donnie had

34

vowed he wouldn't sail the volatile waters of the fishing business. He believed tourism was the way forward, a view he shared with His High and Bloody Mighty Lord Stoirm. Donnie stared across to the island, his eyes picking out the big house. He could see the scaffolding even from here, and further south he saw the white walls of the distillery. The castle was being turned into an upmarket hotel so that Lord Henry Stuart could attract big money from the shooting-and-fishing set. He also wanted to turn it into a wedding venue, a conference centre even. The Stoirm Hotel in Portnaseil wasn't good enough for the kind of visitor he wanted to attract, even though he owned it along with much of the village. He was even going to stock his land with game so his customers would be guaranteed their jollies shedding some blood. He'd reopened the distillery and was refurbishing it. It had created some jobs and when fully operational would generate more, which Donnie couldn't argue with, but he had no time for Lord Henry Stuart of Stoirm. Not any more. His father, the old lord, had been okay, and Lady Stoirm had been likeable, even though they spent most of their time as drunk as, well, lords. But the son was a different matter. He was a businessman first and foremost. His parents saw the island as their home, but to him it was just another asset in his portfolio.

The question was, where was he getting the cash for all these 'improvements'? Donnie knew Henry was wealthy, but he was not the kind to use his own money. He'd brought in specialist trades people from the mainland because the local workforce could supply only so many skills. Much of the raw materials for the work had also, by necessity, been imported. Roddie heard that Henry had tapped into some grant funds, but there was no way that would cover the amount of work being carried out. He was sure it didn't come cheap.

The suggestion that Henry had foreign investors with deep pockets made Donnie uneasy. Henry had linked the island to such businesspeople before and it had not turned out well.

The faint thrum of engines carried across the surface of the water and Donnie turned his attention to the ferry heading towards them from the mainland.

He wondered if Roddie Drummond was on board.

He couldn't believe the bastard was actually heading home, not after what he did. The Roddie Drummond he'd known would never have had the balls. Word of his return had surged round Portnaseil like flood waters. It wasn't a big place and it was difficult to keep secrets. Not impossible, though. Donnie himself knew that.

He had waited fifteen years to meet Roddie again. He had been in no condition after the trial to seek him out and by the time he'd got himself clean Drummond had cleared off to whatever hole he'd been hiding in all this time. Once Donnie had got his head together, he'd tried to find him, but it was as if he'd dropped off the earth. The only person who knew his whereabouts was Shona, but she had refused to give her brother up. Donnie had nothing against Mary Drummond— she was a pleasant woman—but part of him was glad her death might be bringing her son back to the island.

A dolphin broke water on the starboard side in a flash of pale yellow and grey, and Donnie heard the excited cries of his passengers and the chatter of shutters as they attempted to catch the shot that would grace their Facebook pages. Another dolphin arced from the foam on the port side and there was more delight as cameras and phones swung across. They were short-beaked common dolphins, more plentiful than the bottlenose and the Risso's variety, but still good to see this late in the season. Donnie smiled. He was always glad when the tourists got what they wanted.

He gazed once more across the water towards the ferry cutting through the Sound.

Maybe Donnie would finally get to look Drummond in the eye.

Maybe he'd get some answers.

6

Rebecca nursed a bad coffee and a half-eaten bacon roll and wondered if the man two tables away was Roddie Drummond. She'd seen his face often enough in the press coverage she'd studied the night before, but this man looked too old. Certainly fifteen years had passed, but if this guy was Roddie Drummond then those years had not been kind. The man's brown hair was thinner but his face was fatter, the beginnings of jowls dragging at his cheeks. In the photographs, she'd seen a twenty-five-year-old man who was solidly built and who wouldn't be ashamed of taking his shirt off, but the frame she was looking at now was much fleshier: a middle-aged man gone to seed. He was wearing a cheap windbreaker that wouldn't withstand the chilly gusts she expected to find on the island. The trousers weren't threadbare but they were well-worn, the shoes polished, but as he'd walked to the table she had noticed the heels were worn down and the leather was scuffed. He sat alone, both hands wrapped round a coffee cup as if he were praying its taste would improve.

The ferry's café was nearly empty. During the spring and summer months it would be filled with tourists, but the season was coming to a close. In a week's time the frequency of ferries making the ninety-minute crossing would slow as the winter schedule came into force and islanders who needed to get to and from the mainland would have limited opportunities to do so, even less when the storms hit. Island life was not as idyllic as some would believe.

She tried to study the man without appearing to be staring. If he was Roddie Drummond, then this was an ideal opportunity to speak to him, for he was a captive audience, so to speak. But what if he wasn't? People were always ready to complain about press intrusion, and she didn't want to begin her trip by making a huge mistake.

Mind you, it was possible the trip itself was a huge mistake and would cost her her job. She'd phoned in sick that morning, pleading a vomiting bug. She suspected that Drummond would not remain on the island any longer than he had to, so that would give her five days, the limit of self-certification. She felt guilty, not just for landing Yvonne with an additional workload but also for following the story against Barry's orders and what seemed like company policy. If she was right, and she got this story, he'd understand, she really believed that. She knew under that jobsworth exterior the old-fashioned hack yearned to be set free. At least she hoped that was the case. If she was wrong, or if Barry discovered she'd faked illness, then she would soon be finding out how far Jobseeker's Allowance went.

Damn it! She just could not be certain if this was her man. She had to get closer.

She picked up her cup and her bag, left what remained of the breakfast roll behind her and wandered back to the counter for a refill, studying the man as closely as she could without being too obvious in case he took fright and left. He looked settled in, though, and apparently lost in his own thoughts. She had her cup refilled, paid for it, then casually wandered to the table beside him and sat down at the far corner, where she could scrutinise his face while still keeping a respectable distance, as if she was honouring his personal space. If he noticed her he didn't show it. He still gripped his cup like it was the last life preserver on the *Titanic* and stared at the remains of the brown sludge within.

Rebecca stirred her coffee with the little wooden spatula and examined his features again. Now that she was closer she was certain he was Roddie Drummond. There were lines that hadn't been there before, naturally, and his eyes were empty, as if he had seen things that he wished he hadn't.

She sipped her coffee and her nerve was gathering to make an opening conversational salvo when a bald man slid into the chair opposite her target. He was wearing an insulated outdoor jacket with the North Face logo on the left breast. It was unzipped to show off a denim-blue V-neck jumper, with a blue polo shirt showing at the neck. Rebecca would lay money they were from Pringle. His watch was heavy, not ostentatious but a good quality outdoor item. His skin shone with a healthy tan that spoke more of spending many hours in the open air than baking on a beach somewhere. He was in his fifties but he looked after himself. His face was familiar but she couldn't place it.

'Roddie,' he said quietly.

Rebecca could tell from Drummond's body language that the man was no stranger. He stiffened and his eyes darted around the café, as if searching for an exit.

'Relax, son,' said the man, his voice bearing traces of a Highland upbringing. 'Just here to say hello.'

The newcomer's eyes glinted with amusement as he enjoyed the discomfort his arrival had caused. Then they shot towards Rebecca, so she busied herself in her bag, seeking a book she'd brought. She dug it out, opened it and stared at the pages. She didn't see the words, though, as she concentrated on the conversation taking place.

She was aware of the man leaning across the table and Roddie pulling back slightly, still looking for an escape route.

'I heard you were coming home, son,' said the man. 'I heard your mother died. Shame that. She was a lovely woman, heart of gold.'

'Leave me alone,' said Roddie. His voice was reedy but Rebecca couldn't tell if it was stretched by fear or anger. Maybe both.

'Why? I'm just here to pay my respects.'

'I've done nothing wrong.'

The man laughed. 'Now, Roddie, we both know that's not true, don't we?'

Roddie scowled at him. 'Go away. I don't need to talk to the police if I don't want to.'

'I'm not police any more, son. Retired, three years now.'

Rebecca knew who he was now; his photograph had also appeared in the press coverage of the murder. Detective Sergeant William Sawyer had formed part of the investigation and had arrested Roddie Drummond. He had also, according to Roddie's defence counsel, fabricated an admission of guilt.

Sawyer's tone was reasonable, but it did nothing to ease the tension evident in Roddie's posture. 'Can't say I miss the job. My pension's good, I do a wee bit of security work to top it up.'

Rebecca risked a quick glance and saw Roddie's flesh had paled even further. To his credit, though, he was holding Sawyer's gaze and when he spoke his voice had gained some muscle. 'Why are you doing this?'

Sawyer's smile became a tight little line. 'Doing what? Sitting here saying hello to an old . . .' He stopped himself, cocked his head slightly. 'Was going to say old pal there, but we were never that, were we, son? Never pals. Acquaintances, maybe. That more accurate?'

'Leave me alone.'

'Och, that's not very friendly, is it? We've not seen one another for fifteen years and I get the Greta Garbo! Where's your Highland hospitality? You haven't even asked after my health.'

Drummond stared at him for second. 'How's your health?'

'It's fine, thanks for asking. Hale and hearty. I get to do a lot of walking, a wee bit of climbing if I feel like it. Plenty of time in the great outdoors, enjoying the fresh air out there in God's country. I go back to Stoirm often. Love it there.' He waved in the general direction of the window. 'You should try it, son. You look as if you need a bit of exercise. Put on the beef since I saw you last, eh?'

Roddie didn't answer. It didn't seem to worry Sawyer.

'Anyway, all that communing with Mother Nature gives me stacks of time for reflection. D'you know what I reflect on, son? D'you want to take a guess?'

Roddie's lack of response suggested that he was not in the mood to guess.

'Justice, son. And the lack thereof in this sorry world we live in. We're surrounded by injustice, don't you think?' He didn't wait for a reply.

'Politicians fiddling their expenses then taking decisions on welfare. Big corporations dodging their tax. Self-regulation in industry leading to tragedy. It's all meaty stuff. Gets the old grey cells exercised while I'm taking in the beauties of creation. Naturally, during all my walking and climbing and thinking about justice you come into my mind. So when I heard about your old mother, God rest her soul, and a wee birdie told me you were going home, I just felt I needed to come and catch up. Been a while, son.' Sawyer studied Drummond. 'So, where you been all this time? What you been doing?'

'What do you care?'

'Seriously, I'm interested. After the trial it was like you were there one minute, gone the next. So, where were you?'

'None of your business.'

Sawyer ignored him. 'I tried to find you, did you know that?'

'Why?'

'Because I wanted to keep tabs on you. I'm sure you know why. I've got you now, though.'

Drummond looked away, then got up suddenly, as if he'd heard enough. He didn't move away, just stood motionless for a moment, then he said, 'I was cleared. The jury cleared me.'

'The jury found you Not Proven, which is far from a ringing endorsement of your innocence. You walked free, but it told the world the ladies and gentlemen just weren't sure. But I'm sure, son. I'm sure.'

Drummond looked down at him again. 'I didn't do it, Sergeant. I didn't kill Mhairi. I loved her.'

Sawyer's face broke into a smile that was very nearly a sneer. 'You always hurt the ones you love, son.'

Roddie turned and left the café. Sawyer watched him go, the scornful look sliding away to leave his face blank. His eyes turned towards Rebecca and he winked, as if he knew she'd been listening to everything that had been said.

7

Rebecca found Roddie Drummond on the open-air deck, leaning against the railing with his eyes on the island as it loomed across the Sound. The ferry was not yet close enough to distinguish any real details, but the mountain was clear and the rolling hills around it. There was a legend that it was the head and shoulders of a giant, cursed by the Three Witches of Stoirm to forever watch over the island. If that was true, the giant had one hell of a pointed head. Beinn nan sìthichean, they called it, but most people pronounced it *Ben Shee*. Fairy mountain. The story was merely one of many legends on Stoirm, she had learned.

She could just make out the little dots of houses around Portnaseil and the jetty at which they would dock in another thirty minutes. The wind caught at her hair as she moved to Drummond's side and for some reason she wondered if he was cold in his thin jacket. He gave her a glance, then resumed studying his old home once more. Below them, the bow churned up white water and sent waves fleeing across the surface to die. She laid a hand on the rail, partly to steady herself, partly to grip something unwielding for support as she steeled herself to speak. The faint vibration of the engines travelled from the white-painted metal up her arm. She had decided that there was no time like the present to approach him. It had to be done, so why not now?

'Mr Drummond,' she said, her voice raised against the wind and the drone of the engines, 'my name is Rebecca Connolly. I'm a reporter with the *Highland Chronicle.*'

He gave her another look and something like weariness stole into his brown eyes. Then he sighed and turned away again. When he spoke, she almost missed his words as they were caught by the breeze and snatched away to sea. 'Go away.'

'Mr Drummond, I'm here to help you.'

He gave her a mocking laugh, as he turned to face her, resting both elbows against the railings. 'Really? How can you help me?'

'I can tell your side of the story. It's never been made public.'

'What makes you think I want to tell my side of the story?'

She took a half step towards him, aware that if she got any closer they'd have to put the banns up, but she didn't want to have to shout above the rumble of the engine and the snatching wind. 'I heard what Sawyer said to you. He still believes you're guilty.'

Drummond's laugh was rueful this time. 'Aye, him and the rest of the world.'

'That's why you need to talk to me, Mr Drummond. That's why you need to get your side of it out there.'

He looked her up and down. 'And you're doing this for my benefit, I suppose?'

'No,' she said. 'I want the story.'

Something like amusement crinkled his eyes. 'It'll help you in your career, is that it?'

'That's it. But I do also believe it will help you. Sawyer was right back there. Not Proven, Mr Drummond. To a lot of people that means guilty, but there's nothing we can do about it.'

If he was surprised she'd been listening in downstairs he didn't show it. He turned away to fix his eyes on the island again. 'Do you think I'm guilty?'

She'd expected he would ask that at some point. 'I don't know. Only you know that. Are you?'

She studied his profile as he considered her answer, his gaze still centred on his former home. The amusement she'd seen earlier had been replaced by very real sadness. He gave her a slight shake of the head, as if he'd grown tired of denying it, then scanned the surface of the water, his eyes coming to rest on a small blue fishing boat in the distance. Rebecca could see dolphins leaping out of the water on either side.

'Go away, Miss Connolly. I don't want to talk to you.'

Rebecca hadn't expected him to talk right away, but she was still disappointed. 'I'm staying at the Portnaseil Hotel. If you change your mind, you can find me there.' He didn't acknowledge her in any way, his attention focused on the fishing boat, as if he were trying to see who was on board, but it was too far away to make out any particular individual. 'Think about it, Mr Drummond. I think I can help you.'

When it was evident he wasn't going to say anything further she left him to his thoughts, whatever they were. She saw Sawyer watching them from the top of the steps that led back down to the café. He stepped aside to let her pass but didn't say a word.

8

Sonya Kerr let the voice of the teacher drone on about the Corn Laws and allowed her attention to wander towards the large window on her left and across the Sound. It was a beautiful day and the blue water looked so inviting, although she knew it was as cold as a witch's tit. She'd heard Gus McIntyre use that expression and she quite liked it. She'd never say it out loud, though. Gran would have a fit. Gran was an islander through and through: Christian certainly, but with a healthy respect for the netherworld. Using the word *tit* would be bad enough, but to somehow disparage a witch would have her moving around the house muttering some bloody Gaelic incantation or other to ward off evil.

Sonya looked away from the window, gave the teacher a token glance and tuned in briefly—*no, still saying nothing of interest*—then phased out again, as she scanned the classroom until she found Gus sitting in the back corner. He looked as bored as she felt. His eyes were glazed as he slumped in his chair, his left hand resting on his lap, his right casually twirling a pen. He was a good-looking guy and the problem was he knew it. She knew he had his eye on her, and why not? Sonya was well aware she wasn't bad looking. He'd told her he wanted to meet her tonight at the old jetty on Loch an Eich-uisge. She knew what he wanted, of course, but there was no way he was getting it. She was only sixteen, but she was smart enough to know that once she gave in, once he got what he wanted, he'd lose interest. That was the way Gus worked. He was all puppy dog eagerness, professing love and devotion, until the girl let him in. He'd pursued Sylvia Lomond earlier in the year and Sonya knew for a fact she'd let him shag her after the prom dance. Soon after that Gus moved on—to focus on Sonya, as it turned out. Poor Sylvia was left hanging, but luckily not pregnant. There was no way Sonya was going to run the risk of that, not with Gus McIntyre, no matter how gorgeous he was.

She hadn't decided whether to meet him yet. He was fun and she enjoyed kissing and touching, but that's as far as he would get. She knew he'd try to get her to try some blow—he always had access to the best stuff, or at least that's what he boasted—but she wasn't interested. She didn't know where he got it, but it wouldn't be that hard on the island. There wasn't much else to do apart from drink, smoke and shag.

Sonya knew that was how she had been conceived. Her granddad had told her because he believed she should know. Her mum had shagged her high school boyfriend, Donnie, when they were both out of their heads on blow. But Donnie was a waster, her granddad told her; he was no good at all. Her mum was left while he went off and tomcatted around—that's how her granddad put it, tomcatted. He did worse things, too, her granddad said, but didn't expand. She wondered what those worse things were because Donnie—she never thought of him as Dad—seemed okay. He had been attentive to Sonya for years, even though she didn't live with him. When her mum died, her grand-parents had taken her in; she didn't know where Donnie was then. Her granddad just said he was tomcatting around. He was really fond of that expression.

She could see his boat bobbing about on the Sound. She knew it was his boat, didn't need to see the number or the name. His business was doing as well as could be expected—at least he always seemed to have money to spend on their occasional trips to the mainland. There was hope of growth, too, once the big house was running properly and the distillery was fully open. There would be more visitors to the island and Sonya was convinced that could only help Donnie's business, even though whenever she mentioned anything along those lines his eyes grew hard and he dismissed the thought. Donnie didn't like Lord Henry much, he'd made that clear.

She was only a baby when her mum died. She knew what had happened, of course. Those who were island-born all knew what had happened to Mhairi Sinclair. For a time, when she was little, she was aware of people's expressions softening whenever she came into a room. That stopped a few years ago, though, as memories dimmed and incomers took root. But the past couple of days, since old Mrs Drummond died, she'd felt there was something in the wind, and she suspected it was about her mother. She would come into a room and her gran and granddad would suddenly stop talking. They actually looked guilty and she sensed they'd been talking about her. She had done nothing wrong—that they knew about anyway. If they'd got wind of anything, they would've given her a lecture, whether it be about boys, or drugs, or sex, or generally all three. She'd helped out in the shop below their flat a couple of times and she'd seen some of the older folk give her *that* look. The pitying one.

The bell rang and snatched her from her thoughts. She could feel the relief surge around the class that the torture was over. Chairs scraped on floor tiles, books were shoved into bags and young voices that had been grounded for nearly an hour of tedium were able to take flight again. Mrs Calder said something about reading, but Sonya paid her no heed. She hated history and any intention she might have had of spending further time reading about eighteenth-century laws that meant absolutely nothing to her fluttered from her mind as soon as she stepped into the corridor. It wasn't a big school, so the din of pupils being let loose for lunch wasn't that great, but it was loud enough that she didn't hear Gus call her name. He caught her arm and said it again.

'Sonya,' he said, 'hang on a minute.'

'Gimme a break, Gus,' she said. 'I'm starving.'

The entire school population, including the primary school, was around 250 pupils, most of whom were now converging on the cafeteria, so Sonya didn't want to get trapped at the back of the queue.

'Okay,' he said, 'but what about tonight?'

Despite his six-foot frame and his rugby muscles, Gus looked like a wee boy as he stood there with his neat blond hair and expectation burning in his blue eyes. She knew it was an act, but she liked it all the same. She decided suddenly, just as she always did.

'Aye, I'll meet you. Any of the others coming?'

She saw something in those eyes, a hesitation. He hadn't planned on inviting any of their pals. 'Maybe, I'll ask around. Maybe Alisdair will drive us.'

Alisdair McGovern was an older boy, a friend of Gus. He helped out on the estate and had his own pick-up truck.

She smiled and turned away. 'You do that. I'll speak to the girls, too.'

She left him alone then, her grin widening. She had no intention of telling anyone, but she loved tormenting him. Sylvia waited for her at the double doors leading to the cafeteria, her face hard as she glared at Gus. *Get over it, it's not the end of the world*, Sonya thought, then instantly felt guilty. She didn't know how she'd feel if a boy dumped her as soon as she let him in.

As they shouldered their way through the doors, Sylvia asked, 'So you going to meet him, then?'

'Haven't decided,' Sonya lied.

'He's a bastard.'

Sonya didn't say anything. She picked up a tray and took her place at the end of the queue. Gus had held her back too long, it'd be ages before she reached the food. She pursed her lips in irritation and leaned against the wall, watching the other pupils edge along the line. Sylvia did the same.

'So what do you think of the news?' she asked.

'What news?'

Sylvia stepped away from the wall to stare at her friend. 'You mean, you haven't heard?'

Sonya gave her a slight shake of the head. 'Heard what?'

Sylvia looked guilty, her hand darting to her mouth. 'Shit, I thought you'd have heard.'

'Sylvia, if you don't bloody tell me what the hell you're going on about you'll be wearing this bloody tray.'

'That guy . . .' Sylvia began.

'What guy?'

Sylvia stooped a little and lowered her voice. 'That guy. The one who . . . well, the one who was accused of, you know, your mother.'

Sonya felt something cold take hold of her. 'What about him?'

'Jesus, I can't believe they haven't warned you. If I'd known I'd never have said nothing.'

Sonya spoke very slowly. 'Sylvia, what about him?'

'He's coming back. To the island. For his mother's funeral.'

All thoughts of food left Sonya's mind, as a deep chill settled on her body.

49

9

Portnaseil stretched upwards and out from the harbour as if someone had carelessly thrown it at the land. The harbour itself was a stone finger curving into the Sound, as if beckoning the vessels to port. Private leisure vessels, a mixture of power and sail, populated the harbour now, the masts of the latter bobbing at anchor like a floating copse of trees.

The most concentrated part of the town was what the islanders called the Square, bounded by the Stoirm Hotel, the town hall, the old police station (now an arts and crafts centre), the general store and post office, and a bank which had shut its doors two years before—all built of grey granite imported in the late nineteenth century from the mainland. There were more modern buildings, one housing the much smaller police station, a health centre and the library, another a hair salon and a butcher. The road climbed uphill from the Square through the scattered houses, some brick, some stone, some wooden, towards the single main road that ran the length of the island from north to south. There was no pavement, and very little street lighting, apart from around the Square and at the harbour.

Rebecca waited for the ferry staff to give her the all-clear to walk down the gangway. She felt a thrill of anticipation at finally setting foot on the island. There was something else, too, a voice breathing over her in the faint breeze. She liked to think it was saying *Welcome home, Rebecca* but it could just as easily have been saying *Go home*.

She leaned on the guardrail, her suitcase at her feet, and scanned the scene before her. Portnaseil itself, the mountain that towered above the western coast, the hills that undulated towards it. She looked south, where the land flattened out into a patchwork of fields and bristles of woodland. The coastline was peppered with a succession of cliffs punctuated by tiny sandy coves, bays and inlets.

Stoirm wasn't one of the largest of the islands on Scotland's west coast, but it certainly wasn't the smallest. It covered an area of just over 400 square miles, narrowing in the middle like a waist before widening out again. As such, it was slightly larger than Islay to the south but not anywhere near as vast as Skye to the north. At the last census it had a population of around 3,000 people, but that was five per cent down on the previous findings. In the summer, visitor numbers helped swell the figures but not as much as the communal coffers would like. Rebecca knew there were plans to rectify that—the distillery producing the peaty whisky for which Stoirm was once famed, the sporting estate, the conversion of the big house into a hotel. These were the facts she had gleaned from her swift research the night before, but there was so much hidden, so much she didn't know. She heard the voice on the breeze again, still could not tell if it was a welcome or a warning.

Time would tell.

Roddie Drummond was ahead of her as she headed down the ramp and onto dry land, his shoulders slumped, a battered old sports bag held in one hand. He travelled light, she noted, an art she had never mastered. The inability to take only what was needed was something else she had inherited from her father. She could hear her mother now, setting off on family holidays. *It's not a taxi we should be getting to the airport, you two, it's a removal van.*

Rebecca was dragging a case that was large enough to house a family of four, yet still feared she hadn't packed everything she would need. She was glad she could pull it along, although the handle was ready to detach itself at any moment and one of the wheels was on the dangerous side of dodgy. She hoped nothing embarrassing would occur while she was bouncing over the rough surface of the ramp. Or on the harbourside. Or anywhere, for that matter.

She made it off the ferry without incident, her eyes still fixed on

Drummond. She wanted to see if anyone met him and was rewarded with the sight of a woman in her thirties waving to him from the side of a battered old Volvo estate. She was too far away to make out her features clearly, but Rebecca would bet her Robbie Williams collection that it was his sister Shona. They hugged—well, she did, he kept his arms at his side—spoke a few words and then he climbed into the passenger seat. As they drove off, Rebecca wished she could follow them, but that wasn't possible. She was on foot and was soon manhandling the bag-cum-holiday home up the incline towards the Square.

The hotel looked old-fashioned from the outside and it didn't disappoint inside. The reception was panelled in dark wood and carpeted in dark green tartan. She carefully propped her case upright, the handle threatening to detach itself momentarily, then leaned on the rich polish of the reception. A Sikh with a blue turban was sitting behind the desk and gave her a wide smile. The face around that smile was warm and friendly and welcoming. She saw the handles of a wheelchair behind his shoulders.

'Good morning, and welcome to the Stoirm Hotel. How may I help you?' She heard more than a hint of Glasgow in the voice.

'My name is Rebecca Connolly. I've got a reservation?' She didn't know why she made it sound like a question; she knew she had a room reserved, as did he.

'Ah, yes, Miss Connolly. It's all ready for you.' He produced a sheet of paper from below the lip of the desk with a magician's flourish, laid it in front of her and set a pen at its side. 'If you could just sign this, please. Do you have a car?'

Rebecca signed the form without reading it. 'No, I left it on the mainland.'

'Okay-doke.' Another flourish and a key attached to a large wooden fob took the place of the registration sheet and pen, both of which vanished beneath the desk. 'You said when you booked that you didn't know how long you'd be staying?'

'That's right,' she said, taking the key and wondering if the fob would act as a life-preserver if she fell into the water. 'At least two nights, maybe more.' She didn't know exactly how long she would be on the island but felt some kind of answer was required.

'Stay as long as you like.' The smile widened, which was quite something. 'As long as you pay your bill, of course.'

She smiled back, instantly liking this cheerful young man. 'Does that happen a lot?'

'People not paying their bills? Not much, we're on an island and it's not so easy to slink off. My mother would track them down and give them hell.'

'Your mum pretty fearsome, then?'

He laughed. 'She has made grown men cry. But my brother doesn't like to talk about it. You're on the first floor, nice room with a view of the harbour and the sea. You'll be able to see the seals frolicking.'

'They do a lot of that?'

'Well, mostly they lie around on the rocks, but there's an occasional frolic. How else do you think they make the baby seals?'

He turned and wheeled himself out from behind the desk. 'Forgive me for not taking you to your room. My brother is usually around but he is working the kitchen right now along with my sister, preparing lunches. We're short-staffed at the moment.'

'Not a problem.'

He punched a button on the doorway leading to a hall and it eased open with silent efficiency. 'There's a small lift down at the end of the corridor here, but the stairs are just on the left.'

Rebecca thought about the dodgy handle on her case and decided the lift was a safer bet.

'You need anything, just give me a shout,' he said. 'They call me Ash. I'll never live down burning those potato scones.' That smile again. 'I'm kidding, it's my name, short for Ashar. The phone in the room connects right to the desk here, just press zero and I'll pick up.'

She thanked him and, as she grappled with her case, glanced through the glass-panelled doorway to the Square. Outside, she spotted Sawyer talking to a man in camouflage gear and a baseball cap. His face had the florid look of a man who had been skelped too often by the elements and she could tell by the way he was jabbing a finger at Sawyer that something was getting his goat. The former detective's face was set so tight you could bounce pennies off his jaw. He said something that made the man pivot and stride off out of her line of sight. Sawyer watched him, his face still grim, then picked up the bag at his feet and began to push his way through the hotel door. Rebecca took that as her cue to move away.

As she vanished into the gloom of the hallway she heard Ash say, 'Bill, good to see you again, mate. Have a good crossing?'

She didn't hear Sawyer's response, but he had been greeted like an old friend. She didn't know yet if that was a good thing or a bad thing.

10

Campbell Drummond prided himself on the fact that there was nothing mechanical beyond his skills. Cars, trucks, lorries, tractors, motor cycles, quad bikes, fishing boats, even washing machines and lawnmowers—they held no mystery for him. He could repair them all. If it had an engine, he could take it apart and put it back together again. He could listen to their individual voices and hear whatever ailed them. His wife had believed in the whispers of spirits; he believed in the throaty rumble of cogs, gears and motor oil.

He was bent over the open bonnet of a Vauxhall Astra when Shona appeared at his elbow. He didn't need to look around to the open doors of his workshop to know that his son was standing there. So he didn't bother. He continued to check the spark plugs without a word.

He felt Shona's eyes on him, waiting for him to say something.

Finally, she broke the silence. 'Dad, Roddie's here.'

He jerked a plug from its socket, inspected it with an expert eye. It needed to be replaced.

'Dad.'

'Aye, I heard you.'

He laid the plug aside, worked at the next one.

'Dad ...' Shona managed to inject both an appeal and a reprimand into that single word. Mary could do that, too. But Mary was gone. He heard his daughter sigh and he glanced at her, saw she had that familiar determined look on her face that told him she wouldn't stop until he acknowledged Roddie's presence. He wiped his hands on a rag and turned, raising his head slowly as if fighting a strong counter-force, and looked on his son for the first time in fifteen years. He was framed in the sunlight in the doorway, his travelling bag still in his hand.

'Hello, Dad.' Roddie's voice was hoarse.

Campbell nodded and Shona gave him a slight nudge with her arm to prompt him to say something. 'You've put weight on,' he said.

Roddie nervously looked down at his stomach. 'Aye. My diet hasn't been the best the past few years. Too much fast food, too many quick meals.'

Campbell stared at his son for a few moments. He felt he should say more. He wanted to say more. But he didn't know whether the words would be of welcome or rebuke. If Mary had been here she'd have been in floods of tears and would have been embracing her prodigal, then fussing over him. Mary wasn't here, though. If she had been, Roddie wouldn't be here. Campbell knew that. The boy had come back because his mother was no longer with them. He could not face her fifteen years before and he wouldn't be able to face her now. Shame was powerful. Campbell knew that only too well, for he had felt it every day since that night. Every time he looked on his wife he'd felt it, but never discussed it with her. He dealt with it himself, ratcheted it down. That was his way. And so there were no words of welcome from him and no display of affection, only a curt nod and a few words. 'You know where your room is. Your mother kept it as you left it.'

He turned back to the engine. He understood it better than his own feelings. A few moments later he heard his son walk away.

'For God's sake, Dad,' said Shona, her voice thick with exasperation. He knew he vexed her in the same way he had vexed her mother, but it was too late now for him to change.

He said nothing, simply kept on working. He felt her staring at him for a long time, then she too walked away.

* * *

Rebecca didn't bother to unpack, reasoning there would be plenty of time for that later. She also knew she would probably leave her clothes

56

folded in her case until needed and throw the dirty ones into a corner until she stuffed them in a plastic bag. Her mother would be horrified at her going anywhere in clothing with even the barest hint of a crease, but her mother wasn't there and what she didn't know wouldn't annoy her.

She was eager to speak to the Reverend Fiona McRae about her father. As the ferry had docked, she had spotted the church on a hill above Portnaseil so it wouldn't be hard to find. What she hadn't banked on was the steep climb from town to the road that ran the length of the island. Once there, however, the walk was flat and easy, although her calf muscles griped so much she wished she had used her gym membership more often. The road offered a fine view down on Portnaseil and the harbour, and beyond it to the mainland, which looked clear in the crisp autumn sunshine. At this distance from Inverness she felt her worries about the office diminish. It would all work out, she convinced herself. It would all be fine.

But that little voice in her head would not be still. A welcome. A warning. She was unsure which.

She reached the notice that informed her Portnaseil Church was part of the Church of Scotland fold, and leaned against the black iron gate to stare at the gravel pathway weaving up the hill to the building itself. Willing her calf muscles to gird up their loins, she began the trek upwards again.

When she reached the top, Rebecca paused to take in the view. At least, that's what she told herself. It was really to catch her breath and let the breeze cool her flushed cheeks. She didn't need anyone to tell her that she had a face like a well-skelped arse, as her dad used to say. She really had to do something about her fitness level. The climb hadn't been steep enough to demand Sherpa guides but it made her wonder how any elderly parishioners managed it every Sunday.

The path meandered through a graveyard that looked as though it dated back hundreds of years, with mossy stones and dark Celtic cross markers erupting from the ground in no discernible pattern. It ended at the small church building of plain grey stone devoid of any ornament. There were three large windows on the wall facing her, little more than slits, and a small belfry. The big double doors, painted green, were closed and, she discovered when she turned the large hanging oval handles, locked. She wandered around the side, her feet crunching on the gravel path, enjoying the late blooms in the lovingly tended flower beds.

She was just rounding the far corner of the building when she almost collided with a plump woman carrying an empty basket containing traces of earth and a well-used pair of gardening gloves. Here, then, was the attentive gardener. She was of indeterminate age—anywhere between forty and sixty—with the ruddy face of someone who works outdoors much of the time. They both made the expected show of surprise—exclamations, hands to chests and a few steps back. Rebecca almost laughed at their pantomime. Or was it a ritual?

'Och, lass,' said the woman, her voice dripping good humour. 'You almost put me in my grave!'

'I'm sorry . . .'

'Not to worry—I wouldn't have far to go, would I?'

The woman jerked her head behind her towards a more modern cemetery carved out of the land, a more regimented place of the dead than the Hammer horror version at the front of the church.

In the far corner two men were digging a fresh grave, one operating a small digger. The use of machinery for such an ancient art was jarring but Rebecca couldn't say why.

'I'm looking for the Reverend McRae, is she here?'

'No, lass—she's away off the island for a few days. Won't be back for a day or two yet. For the funeral.'

Rebecca wondered if it was Roddie's mother's grave they were digging.

'She wasn't expecting you, was she? Fiona, I mean.'

Rebecca shook her head. 'No, I'm over here for a few days. She's . . .' Rebecca wondered how to describe her. 'An old friend of my father's. He was born on the island.'

'Oh, is that so?' The woman was genuinely interested. 'And what's his name?'

'Connolly,' said Rebecca, feeling hope rise that this woman might've known him. 'John Connolly. He left when he was in his late teens.'

The woman was silent for a moment and then she shook her head. 'Connolly,' she repeated, turning her face away slightly. She might've

58

been trying to recall her father, but Rebecca sensed something different. 'No,' said the woman, stepping around her. 'I can't say it rings any bells, dear. Sorry for the rush, but I've got a lot to do this afternoon. I'm sure Fiona will help you when she gets back, if you're still here.'

'I'll still be here,' said Rebecca, and the woman gave her a slight smile, more out of politeness than anything else, then moved quickly along the path, her feet slapping on the gravel like ragged gunshots. Rebecca watched her go, troubled by the change in attitude. The woman had been like a ray of sunshine, welcoming, open, helpful. But she'd detected a slight change as soon as Rebecca mentioned her father's name. It was as if a cloud had passed over the sun.

* * *

Most people meeting Jarji Nikoladze for the first time thought he was Russian. Many of them continued to believe that and, even though technically they were correct, he did not think of himself as Russian. He was a Georgian and he was proud of his heritage, although he had left his homeland thirty years before, when he was ten, and was never likely to return, at least not while he was breathing. He liked Scotland. In Georgia his family had been little more than peasants but here they lived like kings. He was a tall man who kept his frame bulked out with regular exercise and close attention to his diet. His black, wavy hair was regularly and carefully cropped by one of the top stylists in Edinburgh. At the prices the man charged, he had better be one of the top stylists. Jarji was fastidious in his tailoring, nothing but the best was good enough for him. He was so clean he practically gleamed.

The same could not be said for his companion. Tamaz always looked too big for his suits and no matter how much he tried he never looked smart. He was balding but he was resolute in his attempts to disguise the fact by combing what hair he had from the back of his head forward. It fooled nobody but they were not likely to comment on the fact. His name was derived from ancient Persian and meant strong and brave. Tamaz was both of those things and had often been called upon to exercise these attributes in service to Jarji and his older brother Ichkit.

In Georgian, Jarji meant 'herald' and that was his function. He was sent by his brother to both deliver and glean news. Sometimes that entailed violence, hence the need for the particular skills of the strong and brave Tamaz. However, there was no need for any unpleasantness on this day. His visit to Stoirm was merely a formality, a way for his brother in Edinburgh to remind the man sitting across the large wooden coffee table that he had promises to keep. Henry and Jarji were old friends, but business was business, even when conducted in impressive surroundings. In Georgia Jarji would never have been allowed anywhere near such luxury. The spacious sitting room of Stoirm House had high ceilings and large windows that looked out on a perfectly mowed lawn curving down to the driveway. A mature burst of pampas grass erupted from the centre like a fountain. He had not been in this room for fifteen years but it had changed very little. The same old but comfortable upholstery; the same enormous paintings, a mixture of landscapes and family portraits. It impressed Jarji that Henry could trace his lineage back generations. Jarji could trace his only back as far as his great-grandfather, a soldier in the Red Army who died defending Stalingrad. Despite that, here he was greeted as an honoured guest, and by an aristocrat, no less. Money was a great leveller. Money and power. And a little bit of fear.

Somewhere within the house was the sound of hammering and a power drill. Renovations. The view of the garden from this room was clear but elsewhere scaffolding allowed the workers to replace windows and repair brickwork, while above them the slates of the roof were being removed and new ones slotted in.

He studied the folder on his lap, which Henry had presented to him at the conclusion of the social niceties. It contained the plans for the estate, including income and expenditure projections for the next five years and the cost of the work Jarji could see and hear being carried out already.

'As you can see, Jarji, there is nothing to cause you or your brother concern,' said Henry, his voice only barely showing traces of nerves. Jarji was used to that when conducting family business, particularly when Tamaz was standing behind him like a giant moon looking to eclipse

60

somebody's sun. Tamaz couldn't help but exude menace, his ludicrous comb-over aside.

Jarji laid the folder on the plump cushion of the couch on which he sat. He leaned forward and lifted his coffee cup. 'We have no concerns, Henry,' he said, his voice showing barely a trace of his Georgian roots, although carrying a faint American twang. He sipped his coffee. 'Ichkit merely wanted me to ensure that everything is on track. He has made a sizeable investment in this venture.'

'I've never let you down before, have I?' Henry said, giving Jarji the smile that had helped him sail through university life. 'Everything is proceeding apace.'

Apace. Only someone with Henry's breeding would use such a word. 'Good. So there are no impediments?'

'Nothing that can't be overcome.'

Jarji slowly laid his cup back on the table, sat back and languidly swung one leg over the other. He plucked at his trouser leg to make sure the crease was straight. He crossed his hands on his lap. And then, and only then, did he look back at Henry with a smile that no one would ever mistake for being good-humoured. 'So there *are* impediments?'

Henry's nervous laugh skittered from his throat. 'Nothing to worry about, I assure you.'

Jarji's smile seemed frozen. 'My friend, I do not worry. I never worry. I am famous for not worrying. Is that not so, Tamaz?'

'He never worries,' said Tamaz, his voice rumbling like the beginning of an earthquake.

'My brother, however, he is the worrier. I tell him he'll worry himself into an early grave. He worries about this venture—did you know he tried something similar a few years ago? On the mainland?'

Henry shook his head, his eyes darting from Tamaz to Jarji. 'No, I hadn't heard.'

'It is not something he likes to talk about but it ended badly. There was unpleasantness. I hope there will be no unpleasantness this time around. Memories of our previous endeavour here are also unpleasant . . .'

61

'No,' said Henry, a bit too quickly. 'There is merely some resistance from a few locals, that's all. As I said, nothing to cause concern in the slightest. They can do nothing to stop my plans—our plans—going ahead.'

Jarji's smile changed and would now cause the mercury to rise. 'That is good, old friend, that is good.'

'We have a public meeting tonight, in Portnaseil, and I'm sure it will all go well. We have planning approval in the bag, we even have a number of customers lined up for next year's opening weekend—including you and your brother, of course, as guests.'

Jarji inclined his head in acceptance. He hoped for Henry's sake that this did go according to plan. The man was from a noble family and he and his hedge fund had proved useful in the past but Jarji's brother was not a man to suffer any kind of failure, even from a man Jarji had been friendly with for over twenty years. They had become friends in university—Ichkit had insisted his younger brother receive a good British education. However, that youthful friendship and Henry's past usefulness would not protect him should Ichkit feel disappointed. He did not like to be disappointed. The name Ichkit meant 'sudden'. If there was any unpleasantness, then Henry would find out that Ichkit was well-named, for his punishment would be swift.

11

Although Rebecca had spoken to Chaz Wymark many times on the phone, she had never met him face-to-face. She knew he was two or three years younger than her, perhaps twenty-two or twenty-three, but his enthusiasm made him seem more like a teenager. When she phoned him from the hotel to tell him that she was on the island, his voice was filled with excitement, and he insisted on coming to see her immediately. He knew she had taken sick leave and she had to extract a promise from him that he would keep her presence a secret from the office. She didn't know if he was capable of it but she had no choice. This was his story, after all, and his island. She stopped to consider that. His island. It wasn't hers, despite her father being born here.

It was a beautiful afternoon and she felt like getting some air, so he told her there was a bench beside the old harbourmaster's office overlooking the harbour. She waited for him, her head tilted back to catch the rays of the sun, hoping to be lulled by the sounds of the water lapping gently against the stone jetty and the clink of cables against the masts of the boats bobbing languidly in the marina. She still felt slightly on edge, as if there was something dark looming just ahead of her. The warm autumn sunshine helped but she couldn't fully shake the sensation.

She kept seeing the face of the woman at the church darken at the mention of her father. It was just a shadow, really, and she'd tried to hide it, but Rebecca had caught it. It had troubled her as she walked back to the hotel. What had Dad been hiding all these years? What had forced him to leave, and why would people turn skittish at the mention of the family name?

She opened her eyes, looked across the harbour to where the mainland was, at this level, little more than a dark line rising from the water. Was it the woman's reaction that was bothering her, or was it lingering shame about lying to Barry? Illness was something she hated to submit to; feigning it was much worse. Maybe it was Simon? She didn't like treating him the way she did, but she couldn't help herself. He just reminded her too much of what had happened. Chromosomes, they told her afterwards. Not enough chromosomes, and the foetus hadn't developed properly. Nobody's fault, just one of those things, not that any of the medical professionals used those exact words. She hadn't done anything to endanger the pregnancy. She hadn't been drinking, she'd never smoked or used drugs, she wasn't obese. She'd even cut down on coffee. But it still happened.

There had been bleeding before, but she was told it was common during the first trimester. But then it grew worse, the pain increased, and that was it. She woke up that morning pregnant, went to bed not pregnant. One in ten mothers under thirty suffer a miscarriage, they said, as if that was supposed to make her feel better. She'd received counselling, of course, and they kept telling her no one was at fault. It was just one of those things. She was the one in ten.

When she'd first discovered she was expecting, Simon had proposed, because that was the kind of man he was. She declined because even then, when she was carrying his child, she was not certain he was the one for her. She liked him, had even told herself that she loved him, but deep down she was never fully convinced. He was handsome and he was caring and he was a good man. Her dad would have liked him, her mum certainly did, but Rebecca knew that despite their shared experience there was no future for them. Rebecca never told her mother she'd been pregnant or that she'd lost the baby. She didn't tell anyone outside the health service, apart from Simon, because it wasn't something she wished to talk about. She didn't want the pity or the sympathy. She simply wanted to get on with things: move on, nothing to see here.

But sometimes, lying alone in her bed in her little flat, she thought about what might have been. Of the baby—was it a boy or a girl? Of what it would have been like to have been a mother, to raise a child, to watch the child grow and become an adult. And on those nights, in the darkness of her room as Inverness slept beyond her windows, she wept softly.

Once she awoke to find her father sitting on her bed, watching her. Her rational side told her she was dreaming, he had been dead for two years, but it seemed so real. He didn't say anything, merely smiled that kindly smile he had, and she swore she felt him tuck a strand of hair from her forehead, the way he always used to do.

'Daddy,' she'd said, once again a little girl.

But all he did was smile. That was reassuring enough for her.

And then he was gone. She knew it was all right to grieve, to be sad, but it was also all right to carry on.

A slight disturbance in the water made her look down. The large, dark eyes of a seal were staring back at her. It pleased her. As a child she recalled her parents taking her from their home in Glasgow down the west coast for the day, to the small village of Ballantrae in the south of Ayrshire. They would walk along the beach, finding mangled branches that had been stripped raw by the water and the wind and the salt, then thrown up onto the shingle as if the sea had taken everything it needed and was done with them. They would skirt around dead jellyfish and rotting seaweed and, as they reached the far end of the beach, at a place called Bennane Head, her mother would talk of the legend of Sawney Bean and his family of cannibals said to live in a cave nearby. It was there Rebecca saw her first seal in the wild, a number of them stretched out on rocks hidden just below the surface of the water, as if sunbathing. Occasionally a head would appear, little more than a lump in the surface of the water, to regard with curiosity these strange creatures of the land, just like the one with which she was exchanging a stare now. Although this one was perhaps hoping she would throw it something to eat.

'Rebecca?'

Chaz Wymark was walking along the quayside towards her, his

camera bag slung over his shoulder. His hair was blond, his face finely tanned as only blonds seem to manage, his frame trim and fit. He was, she had to admit, pretty damn gorgeous. Enthusiasm bounced in his blue eyes and he gave her a tight hug as soon as she stood up. Rebecca wasn't much of a hugger, but she let it run its course because she didn't sense anything sexual in the young man's approach. This was the way he was—tactile, eager and boyish. He made her feel old and jaded.

'We finally meet,' he said. When he smiled he reminded her of a young Robert Redford, her mum's favourite.

'Remember, I'm not here,' she said.

The smile broadened. 'Right, gotcha. Your editor will come around.' His tone was confident. 'There's something in this, Rebecca. I can feel it. This Roddie Drummond thing is big, everyone's talking about it.'

Rebecca didn't reply. She hoped Chaz was right, but she knew she was walking a fine line. A newsroom was a collaborative area but it was not a democracy, even in the weeklies. The industry had changed but the editor's word was still law and she had broken that law. If this didn't pan out the way Chaz said it would, Rebecca would be out there looking for a new job. And in a world where any crackpot with a camera phone could call himself a journalist, jobs were hard to come by.

'I saw a seal just now,' she said, her hand waving vaguely towards the water.

'Not surprising,' he said. 'Portnaseil means "port of the seal".'

'I didn't know that.'

He looked surprised. 'I thought you were from the island?'

'My father was from the island. I've never been.'

Chaz was puzzled. 'He never brought you back home?'

'He didn't speak about the place. He left when he was a teenager and never came back.'

Chaz took this in. 'Never said why?'

She shook her head. 'That's another reason I'm here. I want to find out why. Do you know of any other Connollys on the island?'

He thought about it. 'If there are I've never met them. We can ask my mum and dad, though. But your dad would've left here long before we arrived.'

Rebecca knew Chaz's father had moved from London thirteen years before, to become one of the island's two GPs, although there was no trace of his roots in the young man's accent. He sounded island to the bone.

She sat down on the bench again. 'I'm going to talk to the minister about my father. She knew him.'

'Fiona? She's away just now, at a Church of Scotland meeting in Edinburgh.'

'I know, but she'll be back in a day or so, I've been told. I've got to start somewhere and she seems logical. But let's talk about Mhairi Sinclair. And Roddie Drummond.'

Chaz sat down beside her, set his camera bag on the ground. 'Okay, remember I'm only passing on what I've been told. This all happened two years before I got here.'

'I know. I just want some background. I've read what reports I could but I want to hear what you've heard.'

He gathered his thoughts. 'They say she was a beautiful woman,' he said. 'Stunning, is what I was told. Her mum and dad run the village store and post office, back there in the Square. Mhairi's daughter lives with them.'

'Sonya, right?'

'Yes, Sonya. She's what, sixteen now? Something like that. She was obviously just a baby when her mother was murdered.'

'But she's not Roddie Drummond's child?'

'No, her father is Donnie Kerr. Him and Mhairi and Roddie Drummond were all pals as kids.'

'So Sonya doesn't live with her father?'

'No. Donnie's had what you might call a chequered history, I'm told. Drugs. He's clean now, operates an excursion boat, takes tourists out to see the marine life in his dad's old fishing craft. Dolphin spotting, whale watching, that sort of thing. Some deep-sea fishing now and then. Takes them over to Staffa and down to Iona, too, during the summer. You'll see him tonight.'

Chaz had told her on the phone there was to be a meeting in the community hall to discuss the proposals regarding the big house and estate. The local laird was going to present his plans and had enlisted the local MP and a TV star to back him up. Chaz was going to take photographs. A telly star was always news.

'It's a shame for the girl, it really is,' Chaz said. 'She only knows her mother through photographs. I can't imagine how that must feel.'

'Where is the cottage Mhairi shared with Roddie?'

'Outside Portnaseil, a wee bit down the Spine.'

'The Spine?' Rebecca asked.

Chaz explained. 'Our only real road. It runs the full length of the island, like a spine. The cottage is a holiday home now—the island is becoming quite the attraction these days for incomers. Second homes, people retiring here. The owners got it for next to nothing, apparently. At the time it was owned by the estate, but they offloaded it as soon as they could. The fact that a violent death occurred inside doesn't seem to upset the current owners at all. It's unlikely to happen again and they know it. The island's a peaceful place, really.'

'There'd not been an incident like that for fifty years or so, is that right?'

'There's not much crime here at all. We've got police, of course. A handful of officers, working shifts naturally, and a sergeant. But there's not that much for them to do by way of violent crime.'

'Paradise, is it?'

He laughed. 'In many ways. There are problems, of course there are. Youth crime. Domestics. Alcohol abuse. Drugs.'

'Drugs?'

'Oh yes. Paradise we may be, but the islands all have their . . . erm . . . issues, shall we say. We're not immune from the pressures of modern life. Some even argue they're amplified here. Still, it's a nice place to live. I like it, anyway.'

Everywhere has its problems, her dad had once said. *You can live in the most beautiful place on earth but under the surface there is always something unpleasant.*

As the words came back to her, she wondered if he had been obliquely talking about the island. Had he dug under the surface—and found something nasty?

12

Sonya had intended to allow Gus to go all the way that night, but when it came right down to it, she backed off. She hadn't left him hanging exactly, but he still wasn't happy.

They sat in the silence of the pick-up truck, each staring through a different window. It had turned chilly out there beside the loch and they had retreated into the vehicle owned by Gus's friend Alisdair, who was off somewhere in the machair with Megan Holloway. The sliding temperature didn't seem to bother them. Megan was only sixteen, like Sonya, but she was more carefree with her favours and the blow Alisdair had brought only served to make her more liberal.

Sonya peered through the gathering dusk towards Loch an Eich-uisge and could just make out the remains of the old wooden jetty, little more than a few support beams and a couple of rotting planks. Time was, she'd been told, some local lobster fishermen used this small sea loch as a gateway to the fishing grounds in the Sound. What was left of the Stoirm fleet sailed in and out of Portnaseil, and no one specialised in lobster that she knew of. The loch itself was said to be too deep to measure, which she found hard to believe, and like every other part of the island it had its legend. It was reputed to be home to the water-horse, *eich-uisge*, which carries anyone who tries to ride it into the water, where it tears apart and eats its victim, leaving only the liver floating on the surface. Sonya didn't know why it didn't like liver but she couldn't blame it. She wasn't too fond of it either.

Gus shifted slightly beside her but she still didn't say anything or catch his eye, knowing it would be a few more minutes yet before he'd come to terms with the weakness of his flesh. Boys were so easy to manipulate, she'd found, even boys like Gus. They couldn't control their bodies at all. A few touches, a rub here, a stroke there, and it was over. Her earlier resolve to let him in had come from her anger; it had made a promise her common sense had no intention of honouring. She'd wanted to hit back at everyone for keeping secret the news that Roddie Drummond was coming back to the island. Her grandparents, Donnie— they knew and hadn't told her. She'd asked Gus and he said everyone had heard. Maybe that was why she'd ultimately decided not to shag him. To punish him, too.

She had stormed home that afternoon, her rage having grown during the rest of the school day, and demanded to know why her grandparents, Molly and Hector, hadn't told her that the man they all said had murdered her mother was coming back. They stuttered something about wanting to protect her but that didn't wash. They were islanders, they knew something like that would never be kept quiet. They should've told her.

She had never seen him in the flesh. She'd seen his photograph, though. Her grandparents didn't know that, not even Donnie knew. She had been eleven and had done an internet search. She knew what her mother had looked like, there were photographs of her all over the house, it was like a bloody shrine, but she wanted to see what he looked like. She found him on a site devoted to unsolved murders. They said her mother's case was 'unsolved', yet everyone said Roddie Drummond had done it.

She had stared at the grainy black-and-white shot, trying to find something in the eyes that told her this was the man who had beaten her mother to death. She saw nothing but sadness, and something more. It was the look of a haunted man.

And as she sat in the cab of the truck, watching the ruined jetty merge with the darkness, she resolved to ask the man who everyone said had murdered her mother if he truly was guilty.

She would know if he was lying.

Of that she was certain.

13

Johnny Newman sat on the small stage of the town hall making a studied attempt not to notice that he was being noticed. Wearing a tweed shooting jacket, tweed trousers and a tweed cap on his close-cropped head, he was the very epitome of a southern trendy trying to blend into the Highlands. He looked ridiculous, Rebecca thought, there being such a thing as too much tweed.

Rebecca knew a little about Newman, even though she wasn't in the habit of watching his TV show or any of the low-budget Brit flicks he'd made. He liked to pretend he was an Eastender born and bred, but in reality it was the Home Counties. He'd once had the accent to match, but he'd dropped it and a few consonants in favour of projecting a man-of-the-people image. Not tonight, though. Tonight he was going for lord of the manor.

The actual lord of the manor, Lord Henry Stuart of Stoirm, was by his side. He was a good-looking man, far more attractive than Newman, with dark hair laced with grey and a face that benefited from foreign suns and a careful skin regime. In his younger days Rebecca could visualise him all in black and delivering a box of chocolates to some model or other. The jawline was beginning to sag, though, and there was a weakness in his mouth that Rebecca found off-putting. There was something in his smile that she didn't like. Tall and slim, he towered over the diminutive actor, and he kept his voice low and well-modulated, unlike Newman, who wanted to make sure everyone heard his tortured vowels. Each was putting on as big an act as the other.

Rebecca made herself as comfortable as she could on the hard foldaway chair. There were about fifty of them set out in rows in the small hall, which was painted the same hard-wearing, indeterminate colour as many such venues. The walls were covered in children's artwork and public service posters—crime prevention (Lock up your homes, there's a thief about), health warnings (Get your flu jab now)—as well as notices of impending events—a ceilidh for that weekend, a play by someone she'd never heard of to be presented by the Stoirm Players, a trip for senior citizens to Inverness. A row of frosted-glass windows lined the top of the walls. The stage wasn't too high but was large enough for the am-drammers to present their plays. A large pull-down screen ran the length of the back wall to allow films to be screened. As she looked around her, she imagined picking up the hall and dropping it in any small town or village in Scotland and seeing if it looked out of place. It wouldn't.

Chaz had begun herding the platform party of Lord Henry, Newman and Viola Ramage, the constituency MP, for a group shot, so Rebecca sat by herself on the very back row of foldaway chairs. She wasn't there officially, so she wanted to keep as low a profile as possible, but Chaz had said that he expected the meeting to be attended by many of the key names in the story. In addition, the plan for the estate was a hot ticket item on the island and she wanted to have coverage of the meeting tucked away in case Barry found out she was there.

The hall was filling up, as expected. She saw Sawyer enter alone and stand at the back near the door, his eyes scanning the room. They found her and he gave a small nod of recognition. She wondered how much he'd heard of her conversation with Roddie on the ferry, and who it was he'd been having such an earnest conversation with outside the hotel.

Four young men dressed in camouflage pants and thick weatherproof jackets sauntered in as if they owned the place. They were all of a type: powerfully built, cropped hair (though one was completely bald), broad faces sporting eyes that carried the shadow of contempt for everyone around them. They leaned against the wall close to Sawyer, but there was no sign of acknowledgement. The youths laughed among themselves, pushing and jostling each other. One had fired up a cigarette, seemingly oblivious to the 'No Smoking' notice directly above his head. Just then a woman passing by said something to him and pointed to the sign. He stared at her for a beat, took a long drag, then in a leisurely manner craned round, as if to read it for the first time. His pals were watching, grins widening their faces even further. The smoker took the cigarette out of his mouth briefly, then put it back between his lips. His mates found this incredibly funny. The woman said something more, but the young man waved her away like a minor annoyance.

Sawyer stepped in at this point, said something terse and apparently forceful, because the young man plucked out the cigarette again, dropped it on the wooden floor and ground it out with his boot. He stopped when Sawyer said something further, then grudgingly stooped to retrieve the squashed remains and thrust them into the pocket of his jacket. Sawyer gave them all a well-practised policeman's glare before he took up his position again beside the door. The young men were subdued, once or twice darting glances at the former detective, but he paid them no further heed.

As she studied the locals filtering in and finding seats, Rebecca speculated which, if any, could be her cousins. She searched for traces of her father in the faces but saw none. Chaz had asked his parents but they didn't know of any Connollys. That didn't mean anything, she'd convinced herself.

One face stared back at her, but looked sharply away when their eyes met. The woman she had spoken to at the church then leaned closer to the person beside her and whispered something in her ear. Her neighbour's eyes flitted in Rebecca's direction and then darted away again. Chaz and his family didn't know of any Connollys, but Rebecca had the nagging certainty that the older generation recognised her name.

A slim young man wearing a stylish brown jacket and matching waistcoat entered and glanced around the room, as if searching for someone. He was good looking in a studious sort of way. His hair was fashionably cut, his white shirt offset by a red tie, and his denims were clearly designer. He was the epitome of smart but casual. Rebecca saw the four young men smirk and snigger and nudge each other. The young man must have heard what they were saying because he half-turned and gave them a withering stare before he resumed his scan of the room. He saw Chaz on the stage, then he found Rebecca. A little half-smile appeared on his face. He walked straight towards her and took the empty seat at her side.

'You'll be Rebecca. I'm Alan, Alan Shields,' he said, holding out a hand. 'I'm a friend of Chaz.'

Given his look, and slightly effete southern English accent, Rebecca was surprised to find his grip quite strong. 'How do you know I'm Rebecca?'

He smiled. 'Chaz told me you were a stunning redhead, so it was easy. And you're a fresh face in a sea of locals. Tourists are unlikely to be looking in on a meeting like this.'

She felt herself flush at Chaz's description.

'And here's the man himself,' said Alan.

Chaz headed their way from the stage, thumb-flicking his way through the shots on his digital camera. His face brightened when he saw Alan sitting beside her. 'So you two have met?'

'Yes, Rebecca was just as you described her.' He turned to Rebecca and lowered his voice. 'I think he's quite smitten with you.'

Rebecca felt her cheeks redden once more. Chaz gave her a shy smile. 'Behave yourself,' he said to his friend.

To cover her discomfiture, Rebecca asked, 'What's Viola Ramage's interest in this?'

Chaz looked up at the MP on the stage. 'She's an old friend of Lord Henry's.'

Alan grinned. 'Oh yes, she and his lordship are *very* good friends.'

Rebecca caught the emphasis. 'Really?'

She studied the politician with renewed interest. She was of a similar age to Lord Henry, early forties, and if politics really were showbiz for ugly people then she was the exception to the rule. Her hair retained a blonde sheen that could not possibly be natural and the lines that come with maturity actually looked good on her. She kept herself trim and obviously did not buy her clothes from the high street, unless it was one of those stores where you had to undergo a credit check just to window shop. Rebecca had covered many meetings and receptions the MP had attended and learned the woman was extremely adept at recognising those who could be of use to her and those who could not. She could size up a room with a practised flick of the eye—as she was doing right now, seeking out those in the audience who were friends and those who were not. Her eyes settled on Rebecca briefly, then moved on. The MP was so well-versed in hiding her thoughts that Rebecca couldn't tell whether she'd been recognised.

She leaned closer to Alan. 'How do you know they're *very* good friends?'

Chaz had turned his attention back to his images and answered without looking up. 'Alan works at the castle. And he likes to gossip.'

Alan affected outrage. 'I do not! I am the very picture of discretion. If I am told something in confidence it remains with me.'

Chaz didn't even glance at him. 'Then why are you telling Rebecca about Lord Henry and Mrs Ramage?'

A little smile that could only be described as wicked tickled Alan's lips. 'Because some things are too tasty to be kept secret.'

'How long has this been going on?' Rebecca asked.

'Apparently they were very good friends in uni,' Alan said. 'And they remained very good friends after she married.'

'But Lord Henry's married, too, isn't he? Some fashion designer or something?'

'And your point is, caller? Her Ladyship is hardly ever here and Mr Viola is some kind of merchant banker who doesn't like to leave his money alone too long. And of course, our wonderful MP simply has to come up here as often as she can to deal with constituency affairs, if you know what I mean?'

Rebecca smiled. This was interesting. She was not professionally interested in the extra-marital activities of the rich and shameless, but she tucked the nugget away. As her old editor would say: *You just never know what will be useful in the future.*

'Who are those young guys up the back?' she asked.

Chaz followed her gaze and she heard something rumble in his throat. 'That's Carl Marsh's moron squad.'

'Carl Marsh?'

'The estate manager, or gamekeeper if you rather. Apparently he was the one who gave Roddie Drummond a beating a few days before Mhairi's death.'

Rebecca recalled mention of previous wounds on Drummond from the newspaper reports. She hadn't found any mention of an altercation with another islander. 'Why?'

It was Alan who provided the information. 'There was talk that Carl went all Old Testament when he found out Roddie was having a fling with his wife, Deirdre.'

Rebecca considered this. 'While he was going with Mhairi?'

'No, no. I'm told he stopped the affair when he took up with Mhairi.'

Chaz frowned. 'We don't know if all this is true . . .'

'Oh, it's true,' said Alan.

'You weren't even on the island at the time.'

'But I talk to people. And I listen. And there's been a lot of talk since it got out Roddie was coming home. A *lot* of talk. And it's a fact that Carl used Roddie as a punch bag.'

Rebecca looked back at the young men. 'And that lot work for this Carl Marsh?'

Alan nodded. 'Yup. They help him on the estate, act as beaters on shooting days, generally do the donkey work. The rest of the time they're very busy being Portnaseil's village idiots. Said function they perform remarkably well. They and Carl are well-suited, and . . . Speak of the devil!'

Rebecca's attention turned to the man standing at the door. She recognised him immediately as the person Sawyer had been talking with outside the hotel. He gave the ex-policeman a curt nod. Sawyer, who was still leaning with his arms folded against the wall, acknowledged him, but nothing was said. Marsh then spotted his young helpers and began speaking to them.

He was obviously an outdoor type, very much like Sawyer, but a few

76

years younger. Rebecca placed him in his mid-forties, his hair line a horseshoe of grey clinging tenaciously above his ears and at the back of his head like moss on a tree. He wasn't tall and his sturdy frame was packed into a green combat jacket with a plethora of pockets. As he talked, he scrutinised the crowd with what looked to be a permanent scowl.

'That's him,' said Chaz. 'The woman with him is his wife, Deirdre . . .'

Rebecca hadn't even noticed her at first. She had slipped in at his back like a shadow. Her dark hair was lined with white, and her face was thin and pale, but it was her eyes that Rebecca really noticed. They were sad. No, worse than that. They were defeated. Rebecca thought Deirdre Marsh had probably been an attractive woman in her day, but it was as if something had drained what beauty she'd had and kept it for itself. Maybe that *something* was her husband . . .

By now, most people had taken their seats and were talking among themselves. Rebecca tried to tune into conversations, but she gleaned very little of interest. She thought she heard the name Roddie Drummond once or twice but may have been mistaken.

'No one from Roddie Drummond's family here?' she whispered to Chaz.

Craning round in his seat to check the faces of the audience, he nodded. 'Campbell, his dad. Back row, far corner.'

Rebecca waited a few moments, then casually glanced across the room. She saw a tall man with tough bristles of white hair that had been shaved close to his scalp. He sat alone, bolt upright and face forward, wearing a black suit and white shirt, the two seats beside him and one in front empty, as if no one wished to be near him. His expression was as tight as his haircut, the lines carved out of his weathered cheeks like crevasses on a rockface. Rebecca knew he was a car mechanic and owned Portnaseil's only garage, but he also worked a croft on the island, so he had the sturdy look of a man who had faced life just as he'd faced the elements—unflinching, unbowed, uncompromising. It was a strength she suspected he'd had to draw on many times.

The chatter of voices stilled as Viola Ramage called the meeting to order. All eyes moved to her.

'Ladies and gentlemen, thank you all for coming here tonight.' Her accent was closer to her natural Scots than the bastardised tones she used in Westminster. 'You will all be aware that Lord Henry Stuart has unveiled ambitious new plans for the estate and the island. You may not be acquainted with the extent of the changes and how they will, I'm sure, improve life here on the island.'

Way to be impartial, Viola, thought Rebecca.

'And that is why Lord Henry thought the best and easiest way to explain what will be happening is to hold this public meeting, to allow you to hear from him personally. And so, without further ado, I'd like to ask Lord Henry to come forward and outline his vision for the future of Stoirm.'

Staccato applause met the local laird as he rose from the chair and stepped to the microphone. It came from those who either supported him, were trying to curry favour, or were simply too polite not to clap.

'Thank you, fellow islanders,' he began.

Rebecca listened to the grumbles of disagreement. 'Fellow islander, my arse,' she heard a man mutter in the row behind. Rebecca stole a glance at him. He had a broad face and a thick head of brown hair, threaded with grey, curling round his ears. One of those ears sported a silver stud. He wore a denim shirt and faded blue jeans and had a thick woollen jacket draped across his knees. His face was weather-beaten and deeply lined, even though she estimated he was only in his early forties.

'Must think he's talking to his Bermuda pals,' answered a woman.

Rebecca smiled. For years, Lord Henry had spent very little time on Stoirm, preferring his London flat or his exotic hideaway.

Lord Henry ignored the grumbles. 'You all know that when I inherited the castle and the estate from my father ten years ago it was considerably run-down. My father had let the business side of Stoirm go to seed and I saw it as my duty to amend that situation ...'

'Aye, and the first thing you did was raise the rents,' said the same man, louder this time, and his words were greeted with much nodding and murmurs of agreement. He looked around, as if thanking people for their support.

'Yes, I did,' said Lord Henry. 'And it was with a heavy heart that I did so . . .'

A ripple of mocking laughter spread through the audience.

'Aye, right,' said the man again.

'Who's that?' Rebecca whispered to Chaz.

'Donnie Kerr.'

'Mhairi's ex?'

'That's him.'

'Please,' said Ramage, stepping forward again, 'if we could let Henry finish, then discussion can follow.'

Donnie Kerr stood up now, and Rebecca saw he had a strong, power-ful body under his denim shirt. He'd been something of a wreck at the time of Mhairi's death, an addict and a petty criminal. He'd obviously pulled himself together in the fifteen years since.

'I don't think we need to hear what Lord Henry has to say. We all know it,' he said, waving his arms around the room. 'We know he increased the rents right away and he's bumped them up every year since. We know him and his people have *encouraged* folk to give up their crofts on the land he wants to run the deer . . .'

'The rents were increased only in line with the Retail Price Index, as stipulated in the leases,' said Lord Henry, trying his best to remain unflappable but the smile he flashed the room seemed to Rebecca a bit forced. 'And those crofts were unsustainable. Those tenants who moved—and we're only talking three crofts here—came to me and told me that they could no longer work it. No one was forced off the land and those who wished to stay on Stoirm were assisted by the estate to find suitable homes.' There was a quiet rumble of agreement from a few in the audience, some of whom had earlier supported Donnie Kerr. Lord Henry sensed this and his smile loosened. 'Donnie, this isn't some new kind of Clearances here. These are improvements.'

'Aye, that's what the lairds said back then, too. When they moved the people out of their homes and found them suitable places on land that couldn't be farmed, or on the coast . . .'

'Where many of them turned to the sea. Your family, Donnie, among them, am I right? Your great-great-grandfather, wasn't it? Cleared from

79

lands on the mainland, and he came here? He became a fisherman, and his sons after him, and their sons.'

'Aye, he was moved to make way for sheep. But now it's deer being offered up for rich folk like your pal there who like to kill—'

Johnny Newman had been half-listening to the exchange, but now he perked up. 'Hang on a minute, mate, let's not get personal here.'

Ramage stepped in to smooth the troubled waters. 'I'm sure Mr Kerr didn't mean anything by that, did you, Mr Kerr?'

Donnie Kerr's laboured shrug signified he was far from apologetic. 'My point is, never mind soft-soaping us about the plans. We know what you're going to do. Why not simply cut to the chase and tell us what's in it for us?'

'Donnie, I think that's obvious,' said Lord Henry. 'The distillery will be up and running shortly. The estate will need new staff. There will be new jobs, new opportunities . . .'

'How many new jobs?'

His lordship hesitated. It was slight, but there. 'Well, that's yet to be determined . . .'

'I heard eight for the distillery.'

'To begin with, yes. But I hope there will be more.'

Donnie grinned and glanced at the people around him. 'You hope?'

'That's all I can say at the moment. We're speculating in a very crowded market. Do you know how many malt whiskies there are out there?'

Another voice. 'No, but I'll bet your mum and dad did!'

That brought laughter and Rebecca glanced at Chaz for an explanation. 'The old Lord and Lady were fond of a dram,' he whispered as he leaned closer. 'She drank out of one of those baby cups—you know, the ones with a lid and a raised lip?'

'Why?'

'So she didn't spill any if she dropped it. Which wasn't often because she had it strung round her neck.'

'Now, that's enough.' Ramage adopted her stern voice, one she had obviously learned from studying Margaret Thatcher news clips. 'I think we should show some respect—for the living and the dead.'

Some of the people who had laughed looked shame-faced. Donnie wasn't finished, though.

'So these jobs—minimum wage, right?'

Ramage again. 'I don't think we should discuss financial matters here—'

'Why not? That's why we're all here. We want to know what financial benefits there are for the island. We know there'll be benefits for his lordship, otherwise he wouldn't be doing it.'

The MP's voice hardened further. 'I really don't think—'

'Mrs Ramage, with all due respect, you're the constituency MP but you're not an islander. You're here because you're Henry's friend, and that's fine. Mr Telly Star there is here to bring a wee celebrity sheen to the occasion. A distraction for those who are impressed by performing monkeys . . .'

Newman was on his feet now. 'Now wait a minute, mate . . .'

Donnie Kerr ignored him. 'But the people down here?' He raised both arms and pivoted slightly, playing to the audience. 'We want to know what's in it for us.'

Viola laid a hand on Newman's arm to settle him. He sat back down, but only after giving Donnie Kerr a theatrical glare. Donnie was unimpressed.

Lord Henry tried to smile but didn't quite make it. 'I've told you, fresh opportunities. We'll be bringing new money to the island. Expanding the tourism base.'

'Expanding the tourism base?'

'That's right.'

'But they'll lodge in the big house?'

'Yes.'

'And eat there?'

'If they wish.'

'So, none of them will have rooms in the hotel here in Portnaseil?'

'Well, wonderful as the hotel is, it doesn't have the facilities that we'll offer in the new establishment.'

'Such as?'

'Well, five-star accommodation. Wifi. Food prepared by a top-class chef.'

'And the chance to slaughter innocent animals, of course.'

Henry paused, as he looked down from the stage. 'Donnie, I didn't know you had joined the anti-blood sports league.'

'I haven't. But I still don't see what benefit all this will be to the island. Your guests will arrive on the ferry—or by helicopter, because I see you're preparing a landing pad up there. They'll be met at the harbour and driven up to the big house, where they'll bide for the rest of their stay, eating five-star food and swilling five-star booze and sleeping in five-star beds. And once they've had their fill of that, and blasted a few deer and pheasies and God knows what else, they'll be driven back to the harbour and away again in the ferry. And what do we get? A few jobs at minimum wage running after them and doffing the cap.' Donnie gave the audience another meaningful glance to emphasise his next words. 'Even the workmen now are being housed in temporary accommodation on the estate. Sure, they come down to the pub and they spend money, but they'll be gone in a few months.'

'Some of them are local, Donnie, you know that.'

Donnie dipped his head to concede the point. 'Aye, some.'

Those two words hung in the air like a bad smell, as Donnie and Henry stared at each other. It was Viola Ramage who broke the silence, her smile somewhat forced. 'Mr Kerr, I assure you this will be good for the island.'

There was a sadness in Donnie's expression as he shook his head. 'No, Mrs Ramage, there's only one person this will be good for. Because, believe me, I know that Lord Henry Stuart doesn't do anything for anyone but Lord Henry Stuart.'

14

After the meeting ended, Rebecca found Donnie Kerr outside, lighting a cigarette. It was dark now, but the Square was well-lit, the yellow lights illuminating the grey stone walls of the older buildings. She was surprised at how mild the air was; she had been expecting cooler temperatures on Stoirm at this time of year. But then, as Charles had said, Portnaseil was on the sheltered side of the island. Perhaps it was colder on the seaward side. She hesitated for a second, steeling herself to approach a complete stranger. She hated doing it, had still never grown used to it, but it was part of the job.

'Mr Kerr,' she said and he turned, plucking the cigarette from between his lips.

'Aye,' he said.

She moved closer, as some people shouldered through the doors behind her. 'My name's Rebecca Connolly. I'm with the *Highland Chronicle.*'

'Oh, aye?' His eyes crinkled in amusement. 'You doing a story on that in there?' He jerked his chin towards the community hall.

'No . . .' she began, then thought better of it. 'Well, maybe . . .'

He smiled. He had a nice, easy smile. 'You don't sound very sure.'

Nerves teased the corner of her mouth and escaped in a small laugh. 'The thing is, it's not why I'm here, on Stoirm.'

'Okay, so why are you here?'

She paused. Swallowed. Wondered how he would react. 'Roddie Drummond.'

The smile died a little, along with the amusement in his eyes. 'Okay,' he said.

'I'd like to talk to you about him.'

He said nothing as he looked at her.

'Would that be possible?'

He took a long draw from the cigarette, tilted his head back to stare at the black sky and exhaled the smoke in one long breath. She waited. He hadn't told her to bugger off right away, which was always a plus. More people emerged from the hall and he lowered his head to look at them, then back to her.

'Old wounds, Miss . . . Connolly, was it?'

'You know he's back on the island?'

'Aye, I know he's back.'

'Have you spoken to him?'

He gave her a long, steady look. 'Not yet.'

'Will you speak to him?'

He didn't answer, his attention taken up by the sound of raised voices from inside the entranceway to the town hall. He stepped past her as Campbell Drummond walked stiffly from the doors, followed by Carl Marsh, his face twisted in anger. Deirdre Marsh tugged at his arm, trying to pull him back. He shrugged her off and quickened his step to catch up with Campbell as he strode away.

'Carl, please!' she screamed.

'You tell that son of yours, Drummond . . .' Rebecca could hear Yorkshire roots in his accent. 'Tell him that if I see him anywhere near my wife, I'll have him.'

Campbell Drummond didn't respond or even look in Marsh's direction. He remained silent even when Marsh caught up with him and grabbed him by the arm, pulling him round, thrusting his face closer.

'I should've done for him back then, or you should've taken him up into the hills at birth, done the world a favour.'

Campbell Drummond was clearly not afraid of Marsh. He was a good twenty years older but he looked fit and well capable of looking after himself. But he didn't respond. His face was like granite—the

84

smaller man's belligerence seemed to bounce off it. But there was a flinty quality in his eyes that was evident to anyone who looked.

Donnie tossed his cigarette to one side and slid between the two men. 'Okay, Carl, let's ease off, eh?'

Marsh allowed his attention to turn. 'Keep out of this, Kerr. You've done enough for one night.'

People had stopped in the Square to watch the scene. Chaz, Alan and Chaz's mother, Terry, stood among a number of locals, while her husband Charles headed for the three men. Marsh's moron squad were in the front, their grins malevolent now, their eyes glittering in anticipation of violence. Rebecca looked past them to the door of the police station. Surely someone was in there and would hear the raised voices. But no uniforms erupted from the door. She had no idea how many were on duty at that moment; perhaps they were all out on patrol.

'I think that's enough, Carl,' said Chaz's father, his voice calm but commanding. Marsh, though, merely gave him a sneer.

'You can keep your nose to yourself, too. No one needs medical attention. Yet. This is between me and Drummond here. And his murdering bastard of a son, wherever he is.' He faced Campbell Drummond again. 'Where is he, eh? Back in the family home, warm and safe? Eh? That where he is? The murdering little shit. You protecting him? Like Mary did?'

Campbell Drummond held Marsh's gaze but remained silent, though Rebecca saw his fists clenching. Donnie tried to pull Marsh away but the man swore at him and swung his own fist. Donnie was ready. He blocked the blow with his left arm and splayed the fingers of his right against the gamekeeper's chest to shove him hard against the stone wall of the hotel. Two of the moron squad stepped forward, the smoker one of them, but suddenly Sawyer was between them and Donnie. He didn't say anything, just stood there and stared, but it was enough to force them back to their mates.

'Go home, Mr Drummond,' Donnie said, his attention focused on keeping Marsh still. Campbell Drummond didn't move at first. He had fixed Carl Marsh with an intense glare, his fists still tightly clenched at his sides, as if he were struggling with his own violence. Then he nodded something like a thank you to Donnie, turned and walked away, his spine erect, his shoulders straight. He didn't look back.

Marsh seized the opportunity to lash out again, but the blow was wild and didn't connect. Donnie danced away and Deirdre pushed between them. 'Carl, for God's sake . . .'

'Shut up, you,' said Marsh. 'You're the cause of all this.'

He pushed himself from the wall, his eyes following Campbell Drummond as he walked briskly out of the Square towards the road. Then he straightened his jacket and strode off in the opposite direction. Deirdre watched him go, her eyes filled with a mixture of fear, sadness and rage, then she gave Donnie and Charles a fleeting smile in thanks and followed her husband.

Donnie returned to Rebecca. 'See what I mean? Old wounds.' He gazed back at Marsh as he jerked open the door of a Land Rover, climbed in and waited for his wife to catch up. The vehicle then sped out of the Square.

'Come on,' Donnie said. 'You can buy me a drink and we'll talk.'

15

Lord Henry and his party left the hall by a side door and climbed into a waiting Range Rover. Johnny Newman was still seething over the comments directed at him and he complained loudly as the vehicle headed back to the estate. Henry and Viola said nothing, allowing the actor to give vent to his artistic temperament.

'Who the hell was that bloke anyway?' Johnny asked. 'The mouthy bastard?'

'Donnie Kerr,' said Henry. 'An old friend.'

'Old friend? He didn't seem too friendly to me. He was bang out of order, going for me that way. Bang out of order. You know what I should've done? I should've gone down there and given him a slap. He was bang out of order.'

'People will come round,' said Ramage, giving Henry's hand a supportive squeeze. 'They'll see the benefits of the plan. They'll see that bringing in real, sustainable money is good for the island.'

Henry turned his hand round and threaded his fingers through hers. He gave her a smile, but it was really just for show. His mind was elsewhere, wondering how he would tell Jarji, who was staying overnight at Stoirm House, that the meeting had not gone as well as he'd hoped. He didn't know how his old chum would react. He couldn't tell Viola that, though. She knew he was doing business with the Nikoladze brothers with regard to the sporting estate. The brothers were financiers and investors—at least that's what it said on their letterhead. There was always talk of their involvement in enterprises that were something less than legal, while the original source of their millions was shrouded in mystery and no small amount of accounting legerdemain. They had never been charged with anything, but, even so, Viola ensured she remained at considerably more than arm's length from them. She was staying in a cottage on the estate while Jarji was there, which gave her some wiggle room if questions were asked. It was also easier for Henry to sneak out to the cottage than skulk around the corridors at night.

'I didn't know you'd invited the press to the meeting,' she said.

'I didn't,' Henry replied.

Newman's face grew even more livid. 'There was a reporter there?'

'Local paper only,' said Ramage. 'I can't remember her name but I saw her in the audience.'

'Which paper?' Henry asked.

'*Highland Chronicle.*'

'Christ,' said Newman, 'that means the bloody London papers could get it. You know what these bloody reporters are like, she'll smell a story she can sell—"TV star gets roasting at Highland meeting". Or it'll be bloody tweeted by the bloody paper and the whole bloody world will see it. Shit!'

Viola ignored his self-centred rant and squeezed Henry's hand again. 'It'll be fine, Henry. There's nothing she can write now that'll make any difference. All the permissions and permits are in place. Tonight wasn't even a formality, it was a courtesy.'

She was right, of course. The plans would go ahead, no matter what the likes of Donnie Kerr said. The people would accept it because they always did. And there would be benefits for all. The reporter could write what she liked . . .

He'd get someone to pull a string or two, though. Just in case.

* * *

Carl Marsh said nothing as he steered his Land Rover through the darkness towards the cottage on the estate that came with the job. The only sound was the roar of the vehicle's engine and the crunch of gears as he angrily manhandled the stick. Deirdre sat quietly, knowing better than to say anything, even though she wished he'd ease his foot off the accelerator. He knew every curve and dip in the Spine, certainly, but he was still going far too fast.

'I saw you looking for him,' he said, breaking the silence.

'You saw me looking for who?'

His lips tightened into a thin line. 'You know who.'

She decided not to engage any further. Things between them had been bearable the past few years, not happy for her part but endurable, but she still recognised the old signs. Her father had been the same and she'd learned as a child to keep away from him when the dark moods descended. As a child that was relatively easy. Not so easy for her mother, though, who more often than not bore the brunt of her father's rage. When the darkness overcame Ben Lomax, it meant pain for his wife or daughter.

Carl wasn't going to let it lie, though. 'You not going to say anything? Not even going to deny it?'

'Carl, I don't know what you're talking about.'

He spun the wheel onto the short track that led to their cottage. The headlights picked out the fence around the front garden and the gate, then the cottage itself, and prompted a cacophony of barking from the kennels at the rear, where Carl kept three dogs, two Labradors and a Spaniel. Deirdre would have let them in the house, but to Carl they were merely tools of his trade and not creatures to be pampered. He brought the vehicle to a sudden halt and threw open the door.

'You don't know what I'm talking about,' he muttered as he climbed out. Deirdre stepped down from the Land Rover and fished around for the house keys in the pocket of her woollen coat.

'Shut up!' Carl yelled at the barking dogs. They fell silent. They knew better than to defy him. They knew what would come if they did. Deirdre also knew what was coming if she didn't tread a very fine line.

She unlocked the front door, switched on the hall light, then took off her coat and hung it on one of the hooks set into the wall. She stepped into the kitchen, clicked on the strip light and walked to the sink to fill the kettle. When she turned she saw Carl standing in the kitchen doorway. He hadn't even taken off his coat. His face was blank as he stared at her, but she knew that meant nothing.

'Do you want a cup of tea?' she asked, trying to keep her voice steady.

'As if you'd interest him now,' he said, his voice heavy with disdain. 'The way you are.'

I am what you made me, she thought, but tried not to react. She couldn't react. That's what he wanted. An excuse. Keep it normal, she told herself. She had to keep it normal. She needed to calm him down. She avoided looking him in the eye because she knew from experience that could be construed as a challenge. 'Carl, do you want a cup of tea?'

'Do you want a cup of tea?' He mimicked her, his pitch higher and more nasal. 'Do you want a cup of tea?'

She didn't respond. No matter what she said it would enrage him, so she thought it prudent to remain silent. She took two mugs from a cupboard and set them beside the boiling kettle. She dropped a teabag in each, then fetched a spoon from the drawer under the sink.

He still hadn't moved from the doorway. He still hadn't taken off his coat. He watched her every move with that frozen expression.

'Well?' he said. 'You got nothing to say?'

She didn't look at him. She daren't. 'About what, Carl?' A note of weariness crept into her voice; she couldn't help it. She hoped he didn't notice.

'About what, Carl?' Mimicking her again. 'You know about what. Your behaviour tonight, is about what.'

The kettle clicked off and she poured the hot water into the cups. 'I don't know what you're talking about.'

'You hoped he'd be there. You were looking for him. Your boyfriend.'

Deirdre knew who he was talking about. She couldn't deny that. And she had hoped he'd be there. She couldn't deny that either. She also couldn't admit it. 'Carl,' she said, 'please . . .'

'Carl, please . . .' He was mimicking her again, mocking her. 'Carl, please what?'

She turned and found he had moved right up behind her. She hadn't heard a sound as he'd crossed the floor. His head was cocked to one side as he studied her with a little half-smile on his lips. She knew that smile. She knew what was coming. She'd seen the signs. She'd seen them so many times before. But not for years.

'Please don't do this,' she said.

'Don't do what, Deirdre?' His voice had changed. Before it had been accusatory, scornful; now it was conversational. 'We're talking, is all we're doing. Can't a husband talk to his wife now, is that it?'

She had the mug of tea clenched in her hand. She could feel the heat seeping through the china. The liquid was still near boiling point. If she threw it in his face now, she could steal time to get away, before it happened. Before the anger and the bitterness that was welling up within him erupted.

'Is that the way things are now?' he said. 'That a man can't even discuss with his wife the way she was looking around a room full of our friends and neighbours for a glimpse of another man? A man she fucked before?'

'I told you, Carl, nothing happened . . .'

But it had. She *had* fucked Roddie Drummond, many times. Back when she was still something a man wanted, even though Carl Marsh was already turning her into a wraith haunting her own life. She looked down at the mug, the surface of the tea shimmering in her shaking hand. It would be so easy to do it. Just a jerk of her arm and she could dodge past him and out of the cottage, into the dark, where she could hide. Escape. She had thought of it before, many times. Getting away from him, away from this island. Find Roddie, reunite with him. She had dreamed of making a new life with him on the mainland. Away from the secrets and lies of Stoirm, away from Carl and his moods and his fists. It was a dream that gave her comfort as she lay in bed beside this man she had once loved, but whom she had grown to hate, and to whom she was now totally indifferent. Part of her thought it was a fantasy, an escape, but now Roddie was back. Now was her chance. He could make her whole again, she knew it. They were both older, certainly, but if she could get away she could cast off Carl Marsh and his name to become Deirdre Lomax once again. She had been a prize before she married. Carl had, too. But that had changed.

She stared at the hot tea, willing herself to do it, to take a stand, to lash out.

'Put the mug down, Deirdre,' said Carl, softly, as if he had guessed what was going through her mind.

She found she couldn't move at all.

'Deirdre, put it down,' he said, his voice beginning to harden.

She knew what would happen if she put it down. She could tell by the way he was balancing on the balls of his feet and the way his fist had clenched. The dead look in his eyes. She knew what he would do, unless she moved first. It would be so simple, throw it right in his face, then get out.

So simple. So easy.

She put the mug back down on the kitchen surface. And waited.

16

The hotel bar was compact, with a small L-shaped counter behind which a dark-haired woman with a Glasgow accent served up drinks and flirted in equal measure. Rebecca wondered if her looks and ability to handle the chat-up lines were why she was hired, although she did seem to be smart and knew her business. The flirtatious barmaid was cliché, but it was important that she be a competent cliché. The gantry was well-stocked, with a wide variety of whiskies. The pub was doing a brisk trade and she recognised many of the faces from the meeting.

Photographs of Stoirm from the past hung on every wall. Black-and-white images of people long dead but immortalised in paper and chemicals. Men in caps and working clothes, pipes prevalent, stationed behind ploughs, herding sheep or working on boats, their faces strong and ruddy even in monochrome. Unsmiling, serious men who often regarded the camera with suspicion. Women, too, wearing long dresses and bundled in layers of wool against the elements, walking with children, working at looms, carrying laundry. Their faces were worn but many at least smiled. In one, a group of women were sitting at the harbour repairing fishing nets and laughing, as if one of them had cracked a joke.

A small flat-screen TV tuned into Sky Sports sat on a shelf high up in the corner above the door. The sound was turned down because below it a thin-faced young woman with long brown hair was strumming a guitar accompanied by a much older man with a fiddle. The woman was singing as she played, something Gaelic and melancholy.

The mixture of live music and the silent screen was typical of Scottish Highland and island life—the traditional co-existing alongside the modern. And often usurping it.

The barmaid gave Rebecca a big smile as she laid a gin and tonic and a non-alcoholic beer in front of her. She asked if it could be charged to her room.

'Sorry, hen,' said the barmaid. 'It's the hotel bar, but it's no' part of the hotel. Me and my man run this separate.'

Rebecca understood. Ash and his family were Sikhs, and although selling alcohol wasn't exactly banned by their religion, she believed, they had obviously opted not to. She paid for the drinks with a twenty, made a mental note to find a cash machine in the morning and thrust the change into the pocket of her jacket. She carried the drinks through a small open doorway to the lounge area, where Donnie sat at a tiny round table in the corner. There was no one else in the small lounge, but Rebecca guessed that wouldn't be the case for much longer. They could still hear the music and the voices from the bar, but at least they had some semblance of privacy for now.

He thanked her and sipped the beer, grimacing slightly at the taste, then sat back and stared at her as she struggled out of her jacket, one hand on the table top, his other dangling from the wooden arm of the chair.

'So, Miss Connolly,' he began.

'Rebecca, please.'

He dipped his head slightly. 'Rebecca. What can I do for you?'

She sipped her G&T. 'Roddie Drummond.'

He smiled. 'I told you, old wounds. You shouldn't pick at them—look what happened out there.'

'He's back on the island, that's news.'

He took another mouthful of his drink, then carefully laid his glass back on the table. 'Some folk would say that's the island's business.'

'People will be interested . . .'

He laughed. 'Ah, it's gone from being news to people being interested. I think there's a difference, don't you?' He didn't wait for an answer.

'Well, maybe not. You reporters never do see the distinction. Wars, political scandals, disasters—they're news. Roddie being back? That's just curtain twitching for anyone on the mainland.'

'So why did you agree to speak to me?'

He paused to think about that. 'You were at the meeting, you saw what Henry Stuart is up to. That's not been reported, not properly anyway. I'm hoping that if I cooperate a wee bit with you, you'll report that story too. A bit of quid pro quo.'

'Agreed.' She'd already decided she'd file a story on the plans for the estate. How she was going to explain her presence on the island was a problem to be solved later.

'Also, you saw what happened out there. I think things here could easily get out of hand and maybe if they know that the outside world is looking in, everyone might calm down.'

'Curtain twitching has its uses, then?'

The corners of his mouth twitched as a smile tickled. 'Everything has its uses, Rebecca. So what do you want to know?'

She dug in her large bag and produced a notebook, pen and her small digital recorder, which she held up slightly before asking, 'You okay to be recorded?'

He waved one hand in agreement while he took another mouthful of beer, his face folding with slight displeasure again.

'Can never get used to the taste of this stuff,' he said.

'So why do you drink it?'

'I'm an addict,' he said. The words were blunt, with no attempt at evasion. He had said it many times before, she felt. 'I'm not about to replace one addiction with another. And I don't like sugary soft drinks.'

He watched while Rebecca opened the notebook to a fresh page and scribbled his name and the date at the top. 'You take notes as well as recording?'

'The recording is so I can quote you accurately, the notes are for me to refer to as an aide memoire,' she explained, then clicked the recorder on. 'So, what can you tell me about Roddie Drummond?'

Donnie thought about this for a moment. 'What can anyone tell you about Roddie Drummond? He was born on the island, brought up on the island. His father is a decent man, he owns the Portnaseil garage. That man can fix anything that goes by land or sea, he's a bloody genius. His mum, God rest her, was loved around here. His sister is a braw lass, too. She married an incomer; he teaches at the school. None of them deserved what happened.'

'But what about Roddie himself?'

He sighed as he considered his answer. 'I suppose I knew him better than most. We grew up together, went to school together, got drunk together. But even then, I never really knew him. Roddie was ...' He struggled for the correct description. 'I don't know how to say it. I want to say aloof but that's not right. He wasn't a loner, he wasn't strange in any way, but he was kind of insular, you know? No, he was like a peninsula—he was connected to the rest of us, but there was a lot that was out there on his own. Part of us, but solitary.'

Rebecca scribbled down the word 'peninsula'. She liked that.

'He was always that wee bit closer to Henry.'

'What? Lord Henry Stuart?'

'Aye, only he wasn't a lord then, of course, because his old lordship was still alive and drinking. He was just Henry to us, part of our wee gang. Me, Mhairi, her brother Ray, Roddie. Well, when Henry was on the island. He was sent away to private school on the mainland. He was too good for our wee school, but come holidays—summer, Christmas— he was back, and the five of us were inseparable, I suppose you'd say.' That smile twitched again. 'The Famous Five, only we weren't quite so wholesome, unless there was a book called *Five Go Bevvying*.'

'And Roddie and Henry were close?'

Donnie considered this. 'I don't know how to put it. Roddie was always ... *in his thrall*. I don't know if that's the right word, but do you know what I mean? Roddie followed him about when he was here, like a wee dog. We used to slag him off about it, saying he was in love with Henry, but there wasn't anything like that ... well, maybe not consciously. Roddie was impressed by money, and Henry's family had most of it on the island, although at that time they were pretty much on their uppers, relatively speaking. The aristocracy having cash flow

96

problems can often be completely different from you and me being short of the readies.'

She nodded. 'And what about Mhairi?'

His eyes softened. 'She was the best of us, frankly. She was the one who kept us right.'

'You and Mhairi became more than friends.'

'Aye. I know Roddie was head over heels about her. I saw Henry looking at her too, once we were old enough to realise she was more than just one of the lads. But back then it was always her and me.' He stopped, eyes drifting slightly as he almost lost himself in the memory.

Rebecca brought him back, feeling a twinge as she said, 'She had your baby.'

'Aye. Well. I buggered that up. I became a different person and ended up being wasted a lot of the time.'

'Drugs?'

'Anything I could smoke or inject. I was a wreck.'

'What about Mhairi? Did she take drugs?'

He shook his head. 'No way. Her brother Raymond died of an overdose in Glasgow. She hated drugs. Now, drink, that was something else again. Mhairi could drink the lot of us under the table.' He sipped his lager again. 'Not while she was pregnant, though. She was a great mum. Loved that wee one.'

Rebecca scribbled down the words 'great mum', fighting her own feelings of remorse. She decided to move him away from talk of family and babies and motherhood. 'What about the night she died?'

Donnie pushed his half-empty glass around the tabletop. So far he had exuded good humour tinged with sadness, but now his face was tight with no flickering smile to ease it. He didn't speak for a few seconds, then he gave his head a little shake. 'This is harder than I thought,' he said, standing up. Rebecca felt alarm hit her—was he cutting the interview short? 'This stuff is crap, but I'll need another if I'm going to do it. You want one?'

She looked at her glass. She had almost drained it without realising, so she nodded, rifled in her jacket pocket and came up with a ten pound note. 'Here, let me pay.'

He didn't make any pretence of protesting. He took the bank note without a word and disappeared through the narrow doorway into the bar, leaving Rebecca on her own. A sprightly melody drifted in from the musicians, a jig of sorts, some of the patrons were clapping in time. It was an example of the bipolar nature of Scottish culture—one minute morose and plaintive, the next wild and carefree. She had never been a great lover of traditional Scottish music, but she found her foot tapping with the beat. Her island blood was getting in tune, she thought. Next thing she'd hear the skirl of the pipes and she'd look for an Englishman to kill. Or at least someone from another clan.

She was aware of someone watching her and through the doorway she saw Bill Sawyer sitting alone, a glass in his hand, which he raised in greeting. There was something about the man that unsettled her. Maybe it was the way he watched everything that went on around him, but then she tended to do that too. Maybe it was his superior attitude. She'd met a lot of police officers, through her dad and her job, and some of them believed they were above everyone else. Her dad had told her that it was usually the bad ones who were like that. She knew she would have to speak to Sawyer at some point, but she wasn't looking forward to it.

Her phone rang and she felt the brightness created by the gin and the music dissipate when she saw it was Simon. She debated briefly whether to answer then decided she couldn't be that heartless.

'Hello, Simon,' she said, knowing there was a hardness in her voice she really had not intended.

'Are you OK?' His voice was full of concern. She was confused at first, but then she realised he must've heard she'd called in sick.

'I'm fine, just a touch of stomach trouble,' she said, her stomach actually churning a little. *A lie is always found out,* her dad used to say, *so it's always better to tell the truth. It may be painful at first, like ripping a plaster off, but it's always for the best.* Still, she was committed now. Then she realised he might worry, given their history, so she added, 'Something I ate, maybe.'

'Where are you?'

'Home. Taking it easy.'

'I've been ringing your bell for ten minutes.'

Shit. *A lie is always found out . . .*

'Sorry,' she said, her mind scrambling for an explanation. 'I didn't hear it.'

'You didn't hear me ringing the bell for ten minutes?' He had adopted his courtroom voice, the one he used when about to skewer someone's evidence. Quiet but pointed.

'Simon, please, I'm really not feeling . . .'

'Rebecca, where's your car?'

She was thrown by the question. 'My car?'

'Your car. You usually park it in the street outside your flat. It's not there.'

Double shit. She had left it at the ferry terminal. He had her on the back foot, so she decided to go on the offensive. 'What is this, Simon? Am I being cross-examined?'

'No, I . . .'

'Because I don't like being questioned, okay?'

'Rebecca, I care about you. I'm concerned. I heard you were sick, so I thought I'd come over, make sure you're all right. But I didn't get a reply and now I'm standing in the street and your car's gone. I'm worried.'

'Don't be. I'm fine.'

There was a pause and Rebecca could hear the faint sound of traffic at his end. She pictured him standing in her street, looking up at her dark windows, the phone to his ear, his hand running through his thick brown hair, something he did when he was thinking. She'd covered court cases in which he had been involved and seen him do that while considering, or pretending to consider, his next question.

'Where are you, Rebecca?'

She considered keeping the lie going but decided against it. Time to rip that plaster off. 'Stoirm.'

'The island?'

'You know another place called Stoirm?'

As usual, when speaking to him, her words came out sharper than she'd intended. She wasn't in the least bit sorry. He'd caught her out in her lies and she was pissed off, not just at him.

'What are you doing there?'

'A story.'

'Does Barry know? I mean, he told me you were ill . . .'

Of course, Simon and Barry were pals, something with which she was never completely comfortable. She often wondered if they talked about her, if Simon shared intimate details with his best bud. Guys did that, didn't they? She knew girls did. She often wondered if Barry knew what had happened six months before . . .

'No, he told me not to come. But this is too big to miss. And I don't want him to know yet, either, Simon, so please keep it to yourself.'

'He won't hear it from me.'

Better not, she thought, and immediately regretted it. She knew Simon well, was certain he wouldn't say anything, but it was best not to get on his wrong side, just in case. She forced her voice to soften. 'Thanks, Simon, I appreciate it. This is important to me.'

Donnie reappeared in the doorway with another G&T for her, a fresh beer for himself. Behind him, she saw Sawyer's eyes were on them both.

'Simon, I need to go.'

'When will you be back?'

'I don't know.' She gave Donnie a slight smile as he placed her glass on the table and sat down again. 'Couple of days, maybe.'

'You want me to come over? We could make a wee holiday of it . . .'

'No, I'm working, Simon. I have to concentrate on it.'

'I could help . . .'

Donnie was staring at the tabletop. He was trying to appear as if he wasn't listening but he couldn't help but hear and that made her feel awkward.

'Simon, I have to go. I'll speak to you tomorrow, okay?'

'Okay.' He was disappointed. 'I lo—'

She cut him off before she heard the words. She didn't need that right now.

As she dropped the phone in her bag, Donnie asked, 'Boyfriend trouble?'

'Ex-boyfriend trouble,' she said, an embarrassed laugh rippling her throat.

He smiled. 'Relationships,' he said. 'Never easy.'

'No,' she said, wondering if he was thinking about Mhairi. 'So, tell me about that night.'

He took a deep gulp of his beer, set the glass down again, stared at it. She didn't know if he was gathering his thoughts or reconsidering his decision to talk to her. The music had changed again. The girl was back to plaintive mode, her voice sweet and solemn. No guitar this time, just the fiddle, its notes conjuring up feelings of loss. Finally, he took a deep breath and exhaled, long and slow. Then he spoke. 'As I said, I was wasted back then, out of my head on drugs.'

'What were you using?'

'Like other kids on the island I smoked a bit of weed, but when I went to Glasgow I discovered the hard stuff.'

'Why did you go to Glasgow?'

'Looking for work. Ray and me, we thought the world was our oyster, you know? It was all out there waiting for us. God knows there was nothing here. My dad wanted me to work on his boat with him but that wasn't for me. Ray's dad wanted him to work with him in the village store—did you know they owned the wee shop in the Square?'

She nodded. She wasn't looking forward to calling in there to speak to Mhairi's parents.

'We didn't find any real work, some casual stuff, labouring and the like, but we did find heroin. That was easy enough. I was never one for needles, so I was smoking at first, then I turned to snorting. But that didn't bring the high fast enough, so I overcame my squeamishness and began to inject. I was with Mhairi's brother when he OD'd. That's what made me come home. I remember watching the paramedics trying to revive him and thinking that it could've been me. Something clicked in my brain, right there, as I watched them give up, watched them shake their heads at each other. I told myself I'd had enough. That the shit

101

wasn't going to take me the way it took Ray. I thought I could beat it, you know? I thought I was more powerful.'

'But you weren't?'

His laugh was rueful. 'No. Addicts often think they're in charge but they're not. But I thought coming back to the island, away from the temptations of the big city, maybe I'd have a chance to kick it.'

'But you didn't.'

He shook his head, sipped his beer. 'There was a bloke around here by then, name of MacDonald. He'd come over from Inverness and was doing a wee bit of dealing. Nothing major, just a bit of weed and coke. But he had some heroin too.' He smiled, but he hadn't said anything funny. 'If there's one thing an addict can do, it's find a supplier, and I honed in on him like flies to shit. All thoughts of kicking it went out the window.'

'You could've got help.'

'I could've, but I didn't. I'm a Stoirm islander, you know? There's things we don't do. We don't turn on family. We don't ask outsiders for help.'

'What about Mhairi? Did you get back together?'

There was sadness in the way his shoulder slumped. 'No. She was carrying the kid when I left the island. I was gone eighteen months—that's how long it took me to screw up my life completely—and she'd moved in with Roddie. I moved back in with my father, Lachlan. He was still fishing, scratching a living out of it because he was the best sailor on the island. There wasn't anything he didn't know about the waters around Stoirm.' Donnie's eyes turned soft again as he thought of his father. 'He stood by me through it all. Defended me. Supported me. Family is everything, we stand by each other. It's an island thing.'

'Where is he now?'

'He's gone, seven years now.'

The words came automatically. 'I'm sorry.'

He acknowledged her with a slight inclination of his head. 'Dropped of a massive brain aneurism. He was only fifty-five, still a young man really, but he just collapsed down at the harbour. Gone before he hit the ground, they said. Ticking time bomb, these things, but I can't help but feel that I contributed to it.'

'And your mother?'

'She walked out when I was ten. She was from Thurso originally and never took to island life. Maybe that's where I got my restless spirit from. Dad was an islander through and through, and couldn't face living anywhere else, so they separated, eventually divorced. I still see her now and again, when I go over the water, but she never comes here. Not even for his funeral. To be honest, I don't feel any connection to her. It was always my dad, because he was always there for me. Always. It was a shock to lose him like that.'

'We all think our fathers are invincible,' she said.

Donnie looked at her, sensing some common ground. 'Your dad still around?'

She shook her head. 'Cancer,' she said. 'He was an islander, too.'

That surprised him. 'A Stoirm islander?'

'Left when he was a teenager. John Connolly.'

He tried to place the name but came up with nothing. 'Sorry, didn't know him.'

'Do you know of anyone called Connolly on the island?'

'No, but we don't all know one another intimately. We're close but not all related, despite what mainlanders think.'

Donnie fell silent, perhaps thinking about his father. Rebecca considered her dad. He was an islander, always there for her too, but so was her mother. Her childhood had been happy and free of trauma. Of course, when she'd entered her teenage years there was drama, but that was of her own making, not to mention her hormones. But overall there was a Disneyesque quality to the Connolly home. Until her father died, of course. There was nothing Disney about that. He fought it, the cancer, but it was too strong even for him. She had once thought him invincible, thought he could take anything on and best it. But she'd watched him waste away, his strong body being eaten by a pernicious, unfeeling disease.

She brought her mind back to the present. 'Can you tell me about the night Mhairi died?'

Donnie reached for his drink again and took a hefty mouthful. Then he began talking.

103

17

Donnie Kerr
Fifteen years earlier

I was climbing the walls. I hadn't had a hit all day and MacDonald had cut me off. My dole money only went so far and no one would give me work. I couldn't be trusted. My father had urged me to work with him on the fishing boat, but I thought it was just a way to keep an eye on me because there was no way I had the strength to handle the nets and old Lachlan knew that. There was no denying the sea was in my blood. It was one of the reasons I'd come back from Glasgow. I needed to be near the salt water. I needed to feel the breeze from the open ocean on my face. But there was more in my blood than the sea by then. Insects, crawling over each other as they poured through my veins to reach my brain. They were itchy little buggers and the only thing that would soothe them was a hit, just one more, just a wee taste to get sorted and then I could start getting my life together. Just one more hit and then I could fix everything, mend those fences, repair those bridges. Make my dad proud. That's what I told myself, anyway.

I'd tried to stay in my room, but the itch was too much. I'd smoked the cigarettes I'd lifted from my dad's pocket. I'd drunk as much coffee as I could, even drained what was left of the bottle of Talisker he'd had been saving for a special occasion. *Aye, Dad, good luck with that*, I'd thought as I necked it. None of it had worked, though. I still felt those insects crawling under my skin. That's what it feels like, the need for heroin. Wee ants, with feathery antennae, scratch, scratch, scratching at your veins. Crawl, crawl, crawl. Itch, itch, itch. All I needed was a wee taste, just to settle things down.

I'd searched the house for money but the old man was too canny for that by then. He'd long since learned not to leave any loose cash in the house for the insects to carry away. I had no pals left to tap. Ray was gone. One hit too many. Henry wouldn't even speak to me. Roddie—well, Roddie had stolen my girl.

Mhairi.

That's the way I saw it. Roddie had stolen her. It didn't matter that I'd buggered off and left her pregnant. It didn't matter that Roddie had been there for her when I wasn't. He'd stolen her and for that he was a bastard. Even so, I went out looking for him and Henry. They owed me something, in my mind at least. But when I found them, working on the estate—Roddie still doing whatever Henry wanted him to do—they just turned away. I was an addict. I couldn't be trusted. I'd let them down.

A storm had hit the day before. I'd felt it coming for a week, even the heroin couldn't dull that sense. It had raged in from the Atlantic and slammed against the island like it was trying to push it closer to the mainland, howling like the banshees they said lived on the mountain. It hadn't blown over completely, its tail was still swishing, leaving some blustery gusts and cold sharp rain.

The weather meant nothing to me, though. All I cared about was getting the means to scratch that itch. The way I saw it, I had no choice. If I didn't get some cash and find MacDonald, I'd be dead by morning. I knew it. The creatures coursing through my body, eating everything in sight, would consume me. As I watched Henry, Roddie and the others work I could feel the little bastards hollowing me out, using my veins and arteries as highways to every inch of my body so they could scratch and gnaw and dig.

And then the solution presented itself when Mhairi appeared.

I knew she blamed me for Ray's death. But on another level I knew she'd help me out. She'd give me something. She was always good for a tenner or so. Just a wee something. She couldn't say no, could she? We had a bond, a connection that even Roddie couldn't break. She'd had my little one, for God's sake. That meant something, surely?

Mhairi.

She was my best bet. She wouldn't see me suffer. I convinced myself of that. She had exchanged a few words with Henry and was standing alone, off to the side, watching the men work, when I approached her.

'What are you doing here, Donnie?' she asked, her voice, even raised against the wind, dull and weary.

'Mhairi, darling, I need money . . .'

She blew out her cheeks slightly. 'You always need money.'

She couldn't even look at me. She just watched Roddie.

'No, look, I really need it. Fifty quid.'

'Donnie . . .'

'Twenty, even! Please, I need it.'

'To buy drugs?'

I didn't say anything because honesty did not come easily to me back then. The drugs do that to you. 'Come on, Mhairi. I wouldn't ask if I wasn't desperate. You know me.'

She gave me a look, a not quite angry, not quite sad, then said, 'I used to. I used to know you all, but now I'm not so sure.'

I didn't pursue that. My mind was on one thing. 'Come on, Mhairi,' I said. 'Just give me some cash and I'll never ask you again. Honest.'

She thought about it. She looked so small, so beautiful. I noticed that, even in the state I was in. I always noticed that. She took one last look at the men, then said, 'I've got to go and fetch Sonya from my mum and dad.'

The guys had made it perfectly clear that I wasn't needed, so I followed her to the car. It was parked a distance away and she was already in the driver's seat before I piled in. She slammed the car into gear and pulled away. She hadn't made any move to give me money and I wasn't sure if I should mention it again. We drove on in silence. I was fidgeting, I knew it, but couldn't help myself. Mhairi didn't say anything about it. Then, suddenly, she said my name. Just Donnie, as if she was going to say more, then thought better of it. When I looked at her I could see what I thought were tears in her eyes. But they didn't affect me, all I could think of were my own needs. The drugs do that to you, too.

'So, Mhairi . . .' I said. 'About the money.'

'I'm not giving you money for drugs, Donnie. You know that.'

'It's not for drugs,' I said, but her eye roll told me she knew I was lying. After all, I was speaking. She exhaled, shook her head as if she was trying to clear it.

'Liars,' she said, quietly. So quietly I barely caught it. 'You're all liars. Every one of you.'

And when she began to cry, very gently, I found that the insects hadn't taken hold of every part of me. There was still something of the old Donnie there and I reached out and laid my hand on her knuckles where they gripped the steering wheel so very tightly. The addict was only interested in calming the insects, but Donnie—the old Donnie, the Donnie that rubbed that hand—asked, 'What's up, love?'

Her head shook again and she couldn't speak at first. She brought the car to a stop and her free hand wiped the tears from her face. 'I think I'm in trouble, Donnie,' she said.

'What kind of trouble?'

'Big trouble. And I don't know what to do.'

'Tell me, maybe I can help?'

She looked at me, her eyes searching for something in me, I don't know what. Perhaps she was looking for that old Donnie, the one she'd played with as a child, the one she'd grown up with, the one she'd loved. I wanted to tell her that the old Donnie was still here and he wanted to help, but that damned scratching was too strong and I couldn't find the words. She was trying hard to find something in my face, I could see that, but in the end too much had happened—I'd left her alone carrying Sonya, the drugs, being with Ray when he'd died, *watching* him die, being complicit in that. She had no faith in me and I couldn't blame her, even the addict couldn't blame her. The truth was, by that time the insects were on the march again and I was focused more on how to get some money out of her.

She said nothing more, merely started the car again and we drove in silence all the way back to Portnaseil. She stopped at the edge of the Square, just out of sight of the windows of her parents' home above the store.

'You'd better go, Donnie. I don't want my dad to see us together.'

I still hadn't got what I wanted, what I needed, and she knew it. 'Mhairi . . .'

She pulled her handbag from the back seat, rummaged inside and came up with two ten-pound notes. 'Take it.'

I took it. Stared at it. 'Is that all you've got?'

'It's all I'm giving you and I shouldn't be doing that. Just go, Donnie. Go and do whatever it is you have to do.'

I climbed out of the car, the money clenched tightly to prevent it from running away. I wanted to get into the hotel bar, see if MacDonald was there, see what I could get for twenty. I knew it would be enough, but it was getting late and MacDonald might've left, he might be anywhere. I would have to find him. But at the same time the old part of me rose once again to the surface. I could feel the money burning in my hands, could feel the insects scratch, scratch, scratching at my brain, but I leaned back in. 'Mhairi, you know if you need anything I'm there for you.'

Both hands were on the steering wheel and she was leaning forward over it. She gave a little sardonic laugh. 'Donnie,' she said, 'there's a first time for everything.'

She started to move before I'd closed the door. I watched the car turn into the Square, then looked at the money in my hand. The twenty quid. And all thought of Mhairi was gone. All that mattered now was MacDonald. All that mattered now was calming those little insects. All that mattered now was me.

I didn't know that'd be the last time I'd ever see her.

18

The present day

Rebecca scrolled through the text document as she sat at the table in the hotel restaurant. She'd transcribed Donnie's quotes the night before as she lay in bed, some foreign film on Channel 4 buzzing in the background. She liked noise while she worked and something with subtitles meant she wouldn't be distracted. She'd also archived the recording on her external hard drive and backed everything up on thumb drive because she lived in mortal fear of computer meltdown. Now, as she waited for someone to take her breakfast order, she read it again, this time on her tablet, which she used as yet another back-up.

If everything Donnie told her was accurate, then something had upset Mhairi. Naturally, Donnie was, as he confessed, 'climbing the walls' that night so he could suffer from false memories, but if his account was accurate, what kind of trouble was Mhairi in? There was always the possibility that Donnie was lying, of course. As Rebecca's dad always told her, *As much as we'd want them to, people don't always tell the truth. Until you know them—really know them—always bear in mind that the person in front of you is quite capable of lying through their teeth. Never accept anything at face value until you have all the facts.*

Right now, though, Donnie's words were all she had.

I'm in trouble, Mhairi had said.

What kind of trouble? What was she hiding?

She was aware of Ash wheeling towards her, so she flipped the cover over the screen and slid the tablet into the bag between her feet under the table.

'Morning, Miss Connolly,' he said, his smile wide and welcoming. 'You're an early riser, I see.'

It was only 7.45. Rebecca wanted to make an early start and had asked Chaz to collect her at half past eight.

'Are you ready for some breakfast?' Ash asked. 'We have some very nice kippers. Now there's some haddock who should've listened when told smoking was bad for their health.'

She smiled. She liked Ash. He was cheerful and it wasn't forced either. She picked the card that carried the menu from where it was wedged between the salt and pepper and studied it. She didn't normally eat that much in the morning but she loved hotel breakfasts. Apart from that, she didn't know when she'd have the chance to eat again today. She had a lot of people to try to see. And she wanted to head out to Thunder Bay first. 'I'll have the full Scottish, please. They still not letting you in the kitchen?'

'Nope!' He slapped the handles of his wheelchair. 'All I do is the meals on wheels.'

Ash gave her his smile and assured her he'd be back in a jiffy, then pushed himself away. The restaurant was empty, so she flipped the cover back on her tablet and continued reading her notes, once again honing in on Mhairi and her trouble. Donnie said she had spoken to Henry Stuart. Was it something to do with him? Or was she asking for his help? Help that couldn't be provided by her own family, or Roddie?

Ash came back with her toast and a pot of coffee on a tray perched over the armrests of his wheelchair. It looked very precarious, but he moved with such ease that she knew he'd been doing it this way for years. He said her breakfast would be ready shortly and scooted off to speak to a man and a woman who were standing in the doorway of the small dining room. He told them to sit and then cracked the same joke about the kippers. It was clear he had a routine and he was sticking to it.

The restaurant door opened and she looked up to see Bill Sawyer. Ash was heading back to the kitchen and he wished him good morning.

Sawyer didn't move immediately for a table. Instead, he regarded Rebecca, that look of private amusement she had seen on the ferry and in the bar the previous night glinting in his eyes. Then he moved directly towards her.

'You don't mind if I sit here?' he said, making it sound more like a statement of fact than a question.

Rebecca made a show of looking around at the empty tables. 'Yeah, it is a bit crowded, isn't it?'

He held out a big hand. 'Thought I'd introduce myself. I'm Bill Sawyer.'

Her parents had brought her up to be polite so she shook his hand. He didn't try to show off his strength by squeezing her fingers, which was something. 'Rebecca Connolly,' she said.

'Pleased to meet you, Rebecca,' he said. 'So what's your game?'

The directness of the question caught her by surprise. 'My game? I'm very fond of squash, but I can shake a mean dice at backgammon.' She was lying—she'd never played backgammon in her life but her first thought was farkle and she wasn't terribly sure how to explain how to play it if he asked.

He smiled. 'You a journalist of some kind?'

'Of some kind, yes.'

He nodded, satisfied with his powers of deduction. 'Well, I think you're sticking your nose where a nose shouldn't be.'

'That's the job of a journalist of some kind, isn't it?'

He inclined his head in some sort of agreement, reached for the coffee pot and poured himself a cup.

'Help yourself,' she said.

He didn't respond as he set the pot down and heaped two spoons of sugar into his cup, then some milk. He stared at the liquid as he stirred it for some time.

'Keep drilling, maybe you'll strike oil,' she said. She wasn't usually this smart-mouthed with people but the former police officer's sense of entitlement was pissing her off.

He laid the spoon in the saucer and said, 'So, what's your angle? You out to prove Drummond innocent?'

'Roddie Drummond *is* innocent.'

He sipped his coffee, looked at her over the rim of the cup. 'No, he's not.'

'The courts would disagree. He was acquitted.'

'Doesn't make him innocent.'

'And you saying he's guilty doesn't make him guilty.'

'He was found Not Proven. That's miles away from a Not Guilty.'

'It's just as far from a Guilty verdict, too.'

'No, it's not. It's when a jury thinks someone did it but they're too scared to make a decision. It's a Guilty verdict without the jail time.'

Rebecca didn't want to debate the strengths or failings of Scotland's unique third verdict, not with Sawyer. She felt it would be a waste of breath. She decided to remain quiet, even though she knew from the look of triumph in his eyes as he sipped his coffee—no, *her* coffee—that he'd taken it as an acknowledgement that he was right.

'So, what is it?' he asked. 'You anti-police?'

'My dad was a police officer.'

His eyebrows raised. 'Where?'

'Glasgow. He was a DCI.'

'Retired?'

'No, he died. Cancer.'

'Sorry to hear that.' Strangely, she felt he was sincere.

'You two get on well?'

She wrinkled her face at him. 'Why do you ask that?'

'To see if you're maybe getting back at him somehow.'

His attitude and questions were starting to annoy her. She shook her head and looked away, grateful as Ash appeared with her plate piled high with food. He laid it in front of her and said to Sawyer, 'You dining with Miss Connolly, Bill?'

Sawyer stood up. 'No, Ash. I think I've worn out my welcome here.' He nodded towards a table near the door. 'I'll be over there.'

'Full Scottish?'

'Aye, why not? I'm on my holidays.'

Ash whirled away, but Sawyer didn't make a move. He loomed over Rebecca like a deadline. 'You do what you've got to do, sweetheart. I don't know whether you really think that bastard is innocent, or if you've got Daddy issues or you just want to cause trouble. I just hope you learn the truth and print that.'

Her head snapped to face him. 'I'll glean the facts and take it from there.'

'The truth is more than a collection of facts. Did your dad never tell you that?'

He walked away, still carrying the coffee cup. She watched him go, knowing that her father had, in fact, said something similar in relation to the courts and police work. She heard his voice now. *Justice is a funny old game, Becks. The courts deal only with facts that can be proven. We deal with the truth, which often can't be proven beyond a reasonable doubt.*

* * *

The first ferry of the day to the mainland rumbled at the quay as Henry Stuart shook Jarji's hand.

'Have a safe journey back to Edinburgh, Jarji. Always good to see you.'

'Tamaz is an excellent driver,' said Jarji. 'I'm in safe hands.'

Henry glanced at the big man standing well away from them, his function merely to be seen and not form part of any conversations until invited. He had no doubt that Jarji was in safe hands.

'Take my advice, my friend,' said Jarji, still clasping his hand. 'Do not let matters here get out of control.'

'They won't, don't worry. It's just one person, really.'

'One person can be all it takes,' said Jarji. 'And I *never* worry . . .'

19

Chaz was waiting outside the hotel in his dented, well-travelled Land Rover. He leaned through the open window and looked down at Rebecca's leather boots. 'You not got any wellies?' he said, smiling.

She looked down at her feet. 'Won't these do?'

'Yes, if you don't mind them being ruined by salt water.'

Rebecca did mind that. The boots she was wearing had cost her a fortune.

'You'll find an old pair of wellies in the back—should more or less fit you,' said Chaz. 'They're my mum's.'

She swung the rear door open and saw an almost pristine pair of green wellies, a fresh pair of thick socks wedged in the top of one boot. She picked them up and carried them round to the passenger side and climbed in.

'I knew a big city girl like you wouldn't pack wellies,' he said. 'Always prepared.'

'Were you a Boy Scout?'

'Not in the way you think,' he said and left her to ponder the mystery of his words as he hauled the wheel to the right in order to U-turn from the Square.

It was another sunny day and as the beams sparkled on the surface of the calm water she found it hard to believe that the island was often the focal point for elemental sound and fury. She saw the ferry midway out on the Sound and had to shield her eyes to see whether it was

114

coming or going. It was heading for the island. BBC Radio Scotland played on the radio, the morning news show discussing the US President's response to allegations that tweeting was unpresidential. His response was, in fact, unpresidential.

Passing the church on its hillock overlooking the town reminded her of Fiona McRae and the woman she'd spoken to in the graveyard. She must've been staring hard at the church because Chaz noticed.

'It's Mary Drummond's funeral tomorrow,' he shouted over the throaty roar of the engine.

'Was Mary well thought-of in Portnaseil?'

'There's no other way to put it than beloved.'

'I don't suppose you'd know what it was like for her after the murder? When people must have believed Roddie was the killer?'

'It wasn't easy. I think Mr and Mrs Drummond went through a bad time for a year or two, maybe longer, but she was still an islander. Mary Drummond was a strong woman. She faced up to it and she won people over again. In the end, the islanders rallied round her. They're like that with their own. Incomers not so much, but if you were born here you're family.'

'How do you know all that?'

He gave her that shy smile of his. 'My dad's nurse, she's an islander. I've been gradually teasing things out of her.' His shoulders twitched slightly. 'She dotes on me, treats me like a son.'

Rebecca would guess the nurse wasn't the only woman who doted on Chaz. It wasn't just his looks, it was his whole manner. She was certain people warmed to him. 'And what about Mr Drummond? How was it for him, did your nurse say?'

Chaz let out a small laugh. 'Campbell's a different matter. He began to isolate himself from the community—well, as much as he could, given he's the only mechanic on the island, and more importantly was married to Mary. Business tailed off for a while but having a monopoly had its benefits, I suppose. Campbell, though . . .' Chaz exhaled slightly. 'I don't think Campbell ever forgave the people for the way they kind of cold-shouldered his wife for a while. He didn't care for himself. From what I hear, he was always a solitary man, but Mary was a cheery, outgoing soul. She took him out of himself.'

'And his daughter?'

'Shona? She's married now, has a child of her own, but she had a hard time, it's true. She was at school and was picked on by some of the other kids. But that passed, as it always does. Memories fade.'

'That man last night—Carl Marsh—his memory hasn't faded.'

'Aye, well, Carl's a bitter, angry man. I don't know why his wife stays with him, to be honest.'

Rebecca thought about Simon. He wasn't anything like Marsh, but she'd allowed things with him to drift too long. 'Sometimes it's easier.'

Something in her tone made Chaz give her a sideways glance. 'Sounds like experience talking.'

She smiled. 'I'm old beyond my years.'

Thankfully he left it at that and they drove on in silence, giving Rebecca the opportunity to take in the scenery. They'd left behind the straggling properties on the outskirts of Portnaseil, heading south past small inlets and larger bays ringed with sand, the calm water emerald and translucent close to shore but transforming into sapphire blue further out and then shattering into glinting diamonds where the sun struck it. Vegetation lurked under the water, dark patches of life in an alien world. The landward side was grassland and heather, dotted with a few stands of trees—Scots pine, aspen, rowan, birch and willow, the occasional interloper like Douglas fir or oak. Many of the trees had been planted by a previous Lord Stuart, she had read. He wanted more trees on the island so transplanted saplings from the mainland. The hills beyond were pock-marked with small conifer plantations and topped with heather burnished autumn brown. The mountain, Beinn nan Sìthichean, rose up into a brooding jagged peak, dominating all around. It looked like a difficult climb, but Rebecca's research had told her it was a Corbett, so while the path upwards was steep it was accessible to most. It looked magnificent against a blue sky broken by a few dusty clouds. This was more of her world than the undersea environment yet it was still not her world. She had been born in Glasgow and worked in Inverness. For all her blood roots on this island, she was an outsider—Chaz had called her a city girl—and she knew it.

The road rose swiftly and there was a sharp bend as the coastline dropped away and opened up to a rock-strewn plain stretching out to the water. She looked down and saw jagged fingers of stone pointing to the sky and others lying on their side.

'The Seven Sisters,' said Chaz. 'The legend is that they came here to wait for their husbands who had gone across to the mainland to fight. They vowed they would never leave that spot until their men returned.'

'I take it the men didn't return?'

'Well, the sisters are still there. The three witches of the mountain made it easier for them to wait, turned them to stone. They say when the men come back they will spring into life again. Loyalty—the islanders pride themselves on that.'

They zipped past the distillery and Rebecca caught sight of a new sign in the process of being hauled up on the wall facing the road, then the entrance to the big house, with a small castellated gatehouse guarding the way. She craned round to catch a glimpse of the Stuart home, but it was set too far from the road and obscured by mature trees.

'Is it a proper castle or just a large house?'

'It's a bit of both. There's an old castle there, but over the centuries bits and pieces have been added on. Frankly, it's a bit of an architectural eyesore, but I suppose Lord Henry's doing his best to spruce it up.'

They travelled in silence for a time, the radio losing the competition with the rattle of the vehicle's body and the deafening growl of the engine. Then Chaz slowed and said, 'That's where it happened.'

Rebecca studied the little white cottage set slightly above the road behind a wooden fence and gate. Its walls shone in the sunlight, the little garden was immaculate, the flowerbeds beneath the windows bare, but Rebecca knew in summer they would be filled with colour and fragrance. Looking at it now, she had trouble imagining anything dreadful having occurred there.

A little further on Chaz spun the wheel sharply to the right. 'Hang onto your hat, things will get bumpy from here on.'

She barely had time to wonder how much worse it could get when, as if to prove his point, the Land Rover bounced from the tarmac onto a deeply rutted dirt track, sending a spray of mucky water from the first of many puddles over the bonnet and up the sides. She grabbed hold of a handle above the door as the vehicle lurched to one side while Chaz corrected the wheel. Now she knew why these things were called bone shakers.

'I take it not many people drive along this road?' she said over the engine and the thump of the wheels hitting troughs.

'Not unless they have a four-wheel drive.' He smiled back at her. 'Or they have something against their suspension!'

They twisted under overhanging trees and splashed through small streams draining across the rutted track. Rebecca saw no cottages or farms, only the occasional ruined homestead, their windows empty, their roofs gone, their moss-covered stone walls seemingly growing from the land. Once families had lived here, loved here, died here. Once men and women had worked this earth. Now all that remained of them were these silent, dead buildings. And perhaps a few slabs of stone in a grave-yard like the one in Portnaseil. She had seen empty buildings many times in Glasgow and Inverness, but something about these caused a deep melancholy to settle upon her.

'Not been used since the Clearances,' said Chaz, as if reading her mind. 'The laird back then, Lord Henry's great-great-great-grandfather, give or take a great or two, had made a fortune out of kelp but that market crumbled and he saw his fortunes wane. He could've sold the island but he didn't. He'd seen what other landowners on the mainland had done, cleared the land, ran sheep . . .'

As he spoke, he jerked his head towards a cluster of sheep at the side of the road. They seemed to wait until the Land Rover was almost upon them before they skittered away into the long grass and gorse that stretched right around the track.

'He saw how those lairds had cleaned up, paid off their debts, so he had his factor move the people out. Some went to live on the coast, became fishermen. Some moved to the mainland, to the cities. Others caught a boat to America or Canada. They called it "improvement" and said it was for their own good, that the land could not sustain so many people, and maybe there was truth in that.'

'Life was hard on the land back then,' said Rebecca, repeating what her father had said years before.

'Aye, bloody hard. Long hours, backbreaking work, very little return. People starved. They died from diseases they probably shouldn't have died from. But this land was their home and had been for generations. The laird was more than just a landowner, he was their leader. But he thought more of his pocket than he did of his people and he could make more from the four-legged Highlanders than he could from rents that were never paid. He didn't even live here. He had a house in Edinburgh and he needed the money to maintain his lifestyle and to give his wife nice gowns to impress their pals.'

Chaz stopped the vehicle in a makeshift passing place and pointed to a collection of low stone walls. 'That used to be a settlement and the factor served eviction notices to every family. They refused to leave. The factor came with a company of soldiers and burned them out. Five men were arrested and thrown in jail. Their families hauled their few belongings on this track all the way to Portnaseil. That's why it's called the *Làrach nan deur*, the track of tears.'

He stared at the walls for a moment and Rebecca sensed his anger. He hadn't been born on Stoirm, but he was outraged by what had happened almost two hundred years before. Once more, the words of her father echoed in her mind: *Injustice is injustice. Time doesn't change that. What's wrong is wrong . . .*

Chaz jerked the vehicle back into gear and pulled onto the bumpy track once again. 'For a long time these moorlands were used for grouse shooting, but that played out in the 1970s. They hope the grouse will return but there's no real sign of that so far. There are a few here and there but not enough for the men to get their jollies. So they shoot pheasant, around the trees, and they can be restocked every year. All this is still owned by the estate. Lord Henry has his chums up for weekends to blast away at the birds—at anything that moves, if you ask me—and then they go back to the big house for fancy food and drink. They hire local people to serve them. Treat them like serfs, some of them. That's what he wants to expand.'

'What kind of people does he have for friends?'

'Some landed gentry. They can be okay with the staff. Showbiz types like Newman, who can be a bit full of it. But the money people, you know—market traders, hedge fund types, all mouth and braces. They're the worst. Some of them have a shocking attitude to ordinary folk.'

Rebecca thought of Greg Pullman and Edie Gallagher. His contempt had led him to a prison cell and her to an early grave. 'How do you know all this? Have you worked there?'

Chaz shook his head. 'My friend, Alan, he's in administration. He doesn't tell me everything, just enough to know that some of these people are total scum. And Lord Henry wants to bring more of them here, to expand all this . . .'

Chaz waved one hand towards the world outside the cab of the Land Rover.

'You don't approve?' she asked.

He thought about it. 'I'm happy to see more money coming to the island, as long as the ordinary folk benefit. I'm happy if there's increased employment, even if it is minimum wage, although no way do I want to see zero hours contracts but I'll bet they're in the business plan. But the killing? No, not happy with that. I don't understand it, killing for pleasure. Can't get my head around it.'

'What do the islanders think about increasing tourism, though? They must want that, surely?'

He smiled. 'The islanders have a funny attitude to tourists. They want their money but they don't like the idea of outsiders coming in and tramping all over the place. Ideally, what they'd want is for the tourists to come over on the ferry, leave their cash at the harbour and then bugger off home again.'

He slowed at a closed metal gate across a cattle grid. 'Do me a favour, can you open that and let me drive over it, then shut it behind me?'

She climbed out and stepped gingerly onto the metal slats of the grid, pulled the bolt back on the gate and swung it open. She followed its swing and waited until Chaz bounced across, the weight of the vehicle making the grid kick and grind in its pit. He stopped again to allow her to close the gate. When she turned she saw Carl Marsh watching her from the shade of a clump of Scots Pine, a shotgun tucked under his arm. He was wearing a camouflage jacket, green canvas trousers and strong leather thigh-length boots. He had a flat cap on his head. He looked like Elmer Fudd in the cartoons, all set to kill the wabbit. She looked beyond him, to the other side of the trees, and saw a blue Land Rover, larger than Chaz's short wheelbase model. She couldn't be sure, but she thought she saw someone in the passenger seat.

'And where are you two off to?' Marsh asked, his Yorkshire accent heavy with suspicion, as he walked towards them. Rebecca wondered if he should have the weapon covered, but then they were on estate land. She then wondered if he was going to order them off.

'Morning, Carl,' said Chaz, smiling through the open window. 'Taking Rebecca to see Thunder Bay.'

'Oh, aye?' The man studied Rebecca closely. Over the years she'd been scrutinised by many men. Sometimes their eyes slid up and down her body as if they were sizing her up for some kind of kinky costume. Sometimes they just focused on her breasts. She felt nothing overtly sexual in Carl Marsh's gaze but fought the urge to cross her arms just the same. There was something discomforting in the way he looked at her, as if he was probing for weak spots, something he could use to overcome her.

'And you are?' he asked.

'Rebecca Connolly.'

He squinted at her. 'Saw you at the meeting last night.'

It was a statement rather than a question, but Rebecca confirmed it all the same. 'You did. And I saw you, inside and outside the hall.'

If he was ashamed of his behaviour, he didn't show it. His eyes flicked back to Chaz, as if dismissing Rebecca for now. 'What's so interesting about Thunder Bay?'

Rebecca felt Chaz was going to somehow pander to this man, so she said, 'Do we need your permission to go there?'

There was something reluctant in the way Marsh turned back to her, as if he didn't want to talk to her at all, but his gaze was steady. 'This is estate land.'

'It's a right of way, Carl, you know that,' said Chaz, his voice reasonable.

Marsh was still staring at Rebecca. 'Aye, for now. When the new plans go through, that might change.'

'A right of way is a right of way,' said Rebecca. 'Changes on the estate can't affect it.'

'We'll see, lass, we'll see.'

'No, there's no "we'll see" about it. Tell me, Mr Marsh, have you heard of the Land Reform (Scotland) Act of 2003?' She saw by the roll of his eyes and the way his nostrils twitched that he had. She was unsurprised by his reaction, as he'd probably had it thrown at him more than once. All the same, she continued. 'Some people call it the Right to Roam, I'm sure you've heard of it.'

He clearly did not want to debate the rights and wrongs of the Act, so he asked, 'What's your interest in Thunder Bay?'

Rebecca was not about to tell him anything. 'What's your interest in my interest in Thunder Bay?'

His face tightened. 'Does this lass ever answer a straight question?' he asked Chaz.

'This lass isn't inclined to explain her reasons for wanting to travel on a right of way to see a local attraction.' Two men had now attempted to treat her like a child this morning. It normally took till lunchtime for that amount of chauvinism to rear its head.

'The Land Reform Act doesn't allow for motorised vehicles,' countered Marsh.

Rebecca didn't have an answer for that.

'Come off it, Carl,' said Chaz. 'There are four-wheel drives up here all the time.'

'Aye, as I said, for now.' Marsh was smiling now because he felt he had triumphed.

'Rebecca wanted to see the bay, that's all there is to it, Carl,' said Chaz. 'You've got to admit it's worth seeing.'

Marsh nodded, almost absently. He was still staring at Rebecca. 'They say you're a reporter.'

Shit, she thought. Her attempt at staying under the radar hadn't been too successful.

'Why are you here, on the island? Why now?'

Rebecca debated telling him the truth but decided not to. She'd seen him talking to Sawyer the day before and the chances were he had more than an inkling of the reason behind her presence on the island. She'd be damned if she would make it easy for him. 'I came to cover last night's meeting.'

He didn't believe her. No surprise there. 'And that's all?'

'What else is there?'

A slight smile. 'Have it your own way, love. But just remember, we don't like outsiders sticking their nose into island business. We have a way of dealing with people who do.'

Chaz's voice was hard when he said, 'Okay, Carl, that's enough . . .'

Marsh threw a sneer in Chaz's direction. 'And you best be watching your step, too, Chaz Wymark. There's folk around here who don't like your kind.'

Chaz gave it a beat before he said in a level voice, 'What kind would that be?'

Marsh's sneer intensified. 'Like I said, outsiders.'

Chaz barked a small laugh. 'And on what part of Stoirm will I find Yorkshire, Carl?'

Marsh's eyes narrowed as he gave Chaz the stare. Chaz gave it back. Rebecca realised this young man was tougher than he seemed.

A slight nervous laugh rose in Rebecca's throat. 'Are you threatening us, Mr Marsh?'

He didn't even look at her. 'Stating a fact, love. And you reporters like facts, don't you?' His eyes moved in her direction again. 'You want my advice? You stick to last night's meeting, report on it fairly, talk about the benefits to the island the plans will bring. Don't be talking to people you shouldn't be talking to.'

'Well, I didn't ask for your advice, but as it's been freely given, exactly who would constitute someone I shouldn't be talking to?'

'Donnie Kerr, for instance. He's trouble, that one, and a waster. He's got it in for Lord Henry, always sniping at him. Take whatever he told you with a pinch of salt.'

'Can I quote you on that?'

His lips thinned into what might have passed for a smile, if Rebecca had been feeling generous. But she wasn't. It was a smirk. 'You stay on the track until you reach the bay. Don't be raking about in the woods or on the moorland. You outsiders are nothing but trouble on the land.'

And then he turned and walked back into the stand of trees. As she climbed back in beside Chaz, she watched him reach his own vehicle. She focused on the windscreen, but she still couldn't see who had been sitting there watching their exchange.

'Pleasant sort, isn't he?' she said.

Chaz started up the engine. 'I'm surprised to see him here this morning. He usually lectures at the charm school in Portnaseil on Thursdays . . .'

20

Rebecca didn't think the surface of the track could get any worse, but to her surprise it deteriorated further as it climbed into the low hills that built towards Beinn nan sìthichean. She found herself tossed around in her seat like clothes in a tumble dryer and at one point thought she was about to be reintroduced to her full Scottish breakfast. Chaz apologised for the bumpy ride and assured her he was taking it as slowly as he could without actually stalling. She knew this to be the case but still wondered if she should get out and walk. Soon the road levelled off.

'Is it much further?'

Chaz grinned. 'You mean, are we there yet?'

Despite her bones feeling as if they were being jarred from their sockets, she smiled back. 'Yes, but I was trying to be subtle.'

He bobbed his head to the horizon. 'Just up ahead.'

She saw the thin line of a wire fence and beyond it the blue ocean. Chaz brought the vehicle to a thankful if ungraceful halt on what would have been a passing place if the track hadn't come to an abrupt end at the fence.

'The eagle has landed,' said Chaz, opening his door and sliding out.

Rebecca opened the passenger door, swivelled in the seat so her legs were dangling outside and changed from her expensive leather boots into the thick socks and green wellies. As she climbed down, a breeze on the chillier side of cool wafted across her face, while the sound of surf against rocks and a rhythmic booming filled the air. Chaz moved to the rear of the vehicle to retrieve a backpack which, judging by the hefty tripod strapped to the bottom, housed his camera gear. Rebecca took a few steps to where a thin path dipped over the edge like a lemming's runway. She stood at the rim and leaned on a fence post as she studied the narrow path cascading down the steep cliff face to the bay below. The wires stretched between the fence posts seemed to her a flimsy guard against people walking off what felt like the edge of the world. The wind was stronger here—if she stood in the wrong place it seemed more than capable of plucking her up and depositing her forcibly at the bottom of the cliff.

'Welcome to Thunder Bay,' said Chaz at her side.

The bay was an almost perfect semi-circle, the high cliffs on either side jutting out to the sea, the only way down being the dicey-looking trail to her left. Jagged rocks thrust from the foaming waters and the sea lunged against them, each assault culminating in an explosion of spray. There was a clear passage in the middle of the bay, into which the waves rushed as if they were in a hurry to reach shore, but then, once reached, thought better of it and tried to retreat again. A line of fine silver sand stretched around the inland stretch of the beach, but as it neared the water it gave way to shingle and heaps of seaweed.

'Next stop America,' said Chaz, squinting towards the horizon, where Rebecca saw a line of dark clouds.

'Is that a storm coming?'

'On the island there's either one coming or there's one just been.'

'Come on,' she challenged. 'The weather was beautiful yesterday and it's the same today. The way you islanders talk you'd think it was like a disaster movie all the time.'

He gave her a smile that was almost bashful. 'No, you're right. It's not that bad, not really. We get some beautiful weather. A lot, in fact. But when a storm comes, there are no half-measures. Feel that wind? That blows constantly on the westward side, varying degrees of strength sure, but it's there. Look at those trees . . .' He pointed to a line of squat rowans behind them, their trunks and branches craning away from the coastline. 'They didn't grow that way naturally. That's the wind for you. They bend before it but they can't escape it. The wind is part of them, shapes them. That's the island. That's Stoirm. The storms are part of what it is and islanders embrace it, make it their own. That's why we talk as if they are a constant, because they are part of us. We weather the storms. We weather life. It's an island thing.'

She took in his words. 'Pretty impassioned for an incomer.'

'I've lived here most of my life; it's all I remember. As far as I'm concerned I'm an islander, no matter what Carl Marsh says. My mum and dad are English but I'm from Stoirm, even though I wasn't born here. I love the place. I want to see the world, but Stoirm will always be my home. Does that make sense?'

As she nodded she thought of her father. He had a different view of the island.

'Do you want to walk down?' Chaz asked.

She nodded her assent.

'Okay, but watch your step. It's tricky.'

Chaz stepped past her to begin the descent and she followed. The earth beneath her feet was mainly dry, stony and hard-packed, but a few stretches of wet mud made the going tougher. She reached out to the face of the crag on her left to steady herself, keeping her eyes on her feet but now and then looking up to take in the view. Seabirds cackled overhead, their wings barely moving as they floated on the thermals. Gannets speared the water to snatch a fish in their beaks, any noise they made as they hit the surface drowned out by the surge of the surf punctuated by the booming.

'What is that?' she asked.

Chaz paused and looked back at her. 'What?'

There was another obliging boom. 'That,' she said.

He gestured across the bay. 'Fissures in the rock. Sea caves, too. Inaccessible unless you really know what you're doing or have some kind of a death wish. The water crashes in and the surrounding rocks act like an echo chamber.'

'Is that why they call it Thunder Bay?'

'Yes. Never stops, day or night, rain or shine. As long as there's the sea and the cliffs, Thunder Bay will keep thundering.'

Soon they had reached the bottom of the track and climbed over an obstacle course of fallen rocks. They paused on the silver sand to catch their breath and Rebecca took in the crab's eye view of the bay. It was, without a doubt, a spectacular location, with the cliffs rising steeply on all sides except where the white-topped waves rolled in high and proud. She followed Chaz closer to the tideline, where the salty tang of the sea mixed with the less pleasant stench of rotting seaweed. She watched the water break on the jagged rocks and fill the narrow channel.

'I take it no boats beach, or launch, from here?'

'It can be done, but you really need to know what you're doing. One slip of navigation and you'd end up on the rocks on either side and they take no prisoners. There are a few people on the island who can do it, though. Donnie Kerr, for one.' His feet crunched on the kelp. 'The Vikings managed it, too. They sailed right in and slaughtered some monks who were hiding here. They say when the wind blows just right you can still hear their screams.'

Rebecca knew that to be fanciful nonsense, but she paused to listen all the same. All she heard was the waves and the booming and the occasional screech of a gull. She followed Chaz towards the water's edge, stepping carefully on the slimy seaweed until she was close enough to feel salt water on her cheeks as it sprayed off the nearest rocks. Chaz slid his backpack off and took out his camera.

'Do you mind if I take some shots of you? I seldom get the chance to have someone to act as a focus here at the bay.'

She gave her permission with a wave of one hand and he began to snap as she studied the cliff faces in more detail, for the first time becoming aware of a myriad of nests resting on ledges and in fissures, some with birds sitting in them, their white feathers like tiny snowflakes against the grey of the rock. A few small but hardy bushes, and even an adventurous tree, bristled the face of the crags and near one she saw what looked like a large bed of heather, with no other nests nearby. She turned to Chaz and pointed. 'Is that a nest?'

He moved to her side, reaching into his bag and pulling out a pair of binoculars. 'That's where William and Kate live.'

'I'm assuming they're birds and it's not a Highland retreat for the royals.'

He focused the twin lenses on the nest. 'White-tailed eagles,' he said. 'Sea eagles. The largest bird of prey in Britain. They were extinct from early last century but they were reintroduced in a limited way in the '70s and '80s. There are a few breeding pairs on the islands now, including William and Kate. Their names change regularly, with whoever is in vogue. I expect it'll be Harry and Meghan soon.' He lowered the binoculars and scanned the skies again. 'I like to come out here regularly to check on them, make sure they're okay. They're protected, but people steal the eggs, sell them. There are people who pay good money for them, I don't know why. Some of the crofters, in particular your pal Carl Marsh, don't like them. They say they take lambs, but that's never been proved.'

Rebecca squinted against the light. 'Is there one in there now?'

'No, you'd know it if there was, even without the bins. They've got a wingspan of about eight feet.'

'Bloody hell!'

'Yeah, that's why they call them the flying barn doors.' He scanned the skies around them again. 'They must be out hunting. They eat fish and seabirds. Rabbits, too.'

'And you keep an eye on them?'

'Not just me. There are a lot of us on the island who protect them, take it in turns to keep watch. We've got a camera hidden away up there, trained on the nest, but we still like to come out and physically check. Most Stoirm islanders are proud of them.'

'Was Mhairi one of the watchers?'

'I have no idea. I mean, I assume there were watchers back then, but I've no clue whether she was one. Why? Is it important?'

She shrugged. 'I was just wondering why her last words were of this place. What did it mean to her?'

'Perhaps it was the old legend, about it being the gateway to the west for the spirits of the dead. They come here to wait for the boat to take them away. These stories were fed to the older islanders with mother's milk and some of them come here after a funeral to say goodbye. They throw the wreaths into the water and if they float out then the spirits have gone. If they wash back in, then the deceased still has business here on earth. The islanders have a saying—only the wild creatures and the dead are at home in Thunder Bay.'

Rebecca thought about this, then dismissed it. 'No, from what little I know of Mhairi she was too level-headed for that.'

Chaz snapped another frame. 'You never know. She was near death. Views change when you're about to shake hands with the devil.'

She smiled at him just as he clicked the shutter again. His speech patterns were a constant surprise. 'Shake hands with the devil?'

He looked down at the back of the camera, clicking through the photographs he'd taken, a slight laugh rippling as he did so. 'My grandfather used to say that. When you die you shake hands with the devil. Sometimes he lets go, sometimes he keeps hold and you never get free. The thing is, according to the legend, Mhairi's spirit would come here but it wouldn't leave.'

'Why not?'

He reviewed the shots he'd taken. 'She died violently and her death remains unavenged. She could be tied to the land until the person who killed her is dead.'

'Did her people come here to throw flowers into the sea after the funeral?'

'I have absolutely no idea.' He looked up at her, proffering his camera for her to see. 'That's a nice shot of you. Your face changes when you smile.'

She didn't really like looking at herself in photographs but she had to admit it was a good one. Then she realised what he'd said. 'What do you mean, my face changes when I smile? Are you saying I've got a face like a bag of nails at other times?'

He gave her the bashful look she'd seen before. 'No, not at all. It's just you have a nice smile, that's all.'

She gave him another one. 'Thank you.'

He took the camera away and busied himself with the setting, his face reddening. She wondered if he was hitting on her. Sometimes she wasn't sure about these things.

'Funny thing about my grandfather,' he said as he raised his camera and pointed it in the opposite direction—still too embarrassed to look at her, she thought. 'He was born a Catholic but never went to mass, didn't take communion, didn't go to confession. For as long as I knew him he said he was an atheist. All a load of fairy tales, he'd say. But here's the thing—when he was in hospital, in his final days, he asked for a priest.'

'There are no atheists in foxholes,' she said.

'Yeah, but my point is, maybe Mhairi knew it was the end. And maybe all the stories about Thunder Bay came to her. And that's why she said it.'

'But she'd know she would be trapped here, maybe forever.'

He shrugged and started snapping again.

She looked at her surroundings with renewed interest. Rebecca recognised Chaz's theory was a possibility as she looked around the bay, hearing the surf exploding against the rocks and the boom echoing in the caverns, as if someone was beating a big drum slowly. She felt spray hit her face and didn't find it unpleasant, not with the sun shining. On a dark night with the storms raging in from the ocean and that same spray striking flesh like sharp, tiny pellets she might think otherwise. As Chaz concentrated on his photographs, she thought about the legend. She half closed her eyes, hoping for some form of supernatural vision: a dark-haired woman standing alone at the water's edge, where the surf hissed on shingle, staring out to sea, waiting for a boat she could not board, to give her rest she could not have.

When the figure refused to manifest, she turned her back to the water and scanned the rockfaces around her, her hand raised to shade her eyes from the sunlight. She froze when she saw two people on the edge of the rim, looking down at them.

'Chaz, can you give me the binoculars?'

'Sure,' he said, unhooking them from around his neck and handing them over. He followed her line of sight as she raised them, but the two figures stepped away out of sight before she could focus properly.

'Did you see them? Two men?' she asked.

'Just as they disappeared. What's the problem?'

'They were watching us.'

'So? Could be anyone. Visitors. A couple of crofters.'

131

She shook her head, still scanning the rim for another glimpse of them. 'No, I'm certain one of them was Carl Marsh. I'm sure I saw that cap he was wearing.'

Chaz frowned, his own hand now cupped over his brow as he squinted against the sunlight. 'Wouldn't put it past him, right enough, to spy on us.'

Rebecca lowered the binoculars. 'I thought there was someone in his Land Rover when he spoke to us earlier but couldn't be sure. Now I am.'

'Carl isn't in the habit of buddying up with people. And he has no real friends that I know of. Which is a surprise, given he's such a delight.'

Sawyer, thought Rebecca. Keeping tabs on her. Had to be. She'd seen him talking to Marsh the day before. They knew each other. She wondered what the former detective feared she would find out.

A gust of wind sent a sound echoing from the rocks and then carried it away. It sounded like a scream, like someone dying in agony. Then Rebecca heard another and she saw a gull hovering above them, studying them to see if they were carrying food. She smiled to herself.

The island was getting to her.

21

Deirdre Marsh stood naked before the full-length mirror in the bedroom staring at the dark shadows on her flesh. Her body was a patchwork of bruises, her arms and ribs taking the brunt of it, and yet last night's session had not been the worst she'd ever had. Her face, though, was clear. Carl never hit her face. A tremor of pain radiated through her when she gently touched the largest discolouration, on her upper arm. That's where he had kicked her, once she was down. The first blow, immediately after she had set the mug on the worktop, had been to the stomach. When she doubled over, he swept the legs from under her and pushed her to the floor, where he kicked her once, twice, three times. She lost count after that. He was clever, though, he was oh-so-clever. The kicks were pulled, enough to hurt, enough to bruise, but not enough to do any lasting damage.

Each punch and kick had been accompanied by snarls and insults.

Look at you, look at the state of you.

Punch.

Thinking a younger man would be interested.

Punch.

It's pathetic, you're pathetic!

Punch.

You're mine.

Kick.

Always mine.

Kick.

I'll kill you before I let you go.

Kick.

Kill you.

Finally he left her on the vinyl flooring her tears failing to wash away the agony that surged through her body. He picked up his mug of tea, the tea she had made him, and left her there while he sat in the living room. The parlour, he called it sometimes. An old-fashioned word that harked back to a more delicate time. If ever there was a more delicate time. She heard the TV coming on and she visualised him sitting in his armchair, calmly sipping his tea as he watched the news. Eventually, she hauled herself onto all fours and then finally, carefully, onto her feet, hands reaching out to the sink to steady herself. She stood there for some time, her breathing harsh and stuttering, as she forced herself to take command of the pain and the rage and the shame. She could do it. She'd done it before.

And then, under the voice of the newsreader, she heard another noise.

Carl.

Weeping.

Alone, in the living room, the TV murmuring world events, the tea she had made still warm in the mug, his wife wracked with agony in the kitchen from *his* blows, *his* kicks, *his* insults. And he was crying softly to himself.

There was a time when she would've gone to him. She would've gone to him and he would've apologised and promised to never do it again. That had been early on in their marriage and she had believed him. Things would be fine between them for a while, until the next disappointment in his life, until the next time he was drunk and lost an argument in the pub, until the next time he suspected she was looking at another man. Then he would lash out, sometimes a single blow, sometimes more than one. And always he would go into a room alone and sob. In that respect he differed from her father. Ben Lomax had never regretted his violence towards his wife and daughter. To him it was natural. It was his right. Moving from her family home to be with her husband, Deirdre had believed it was the natural order things. The way it was.

Until Roddie.

She moved gingerly into their bedroom. She didn't take off her clothes, she didn't have the strength and couldn't face the fresh pain the act would cause. She lay on top of the duvet, not under, because he would come through eventually and she didn't want to be that intimate. Her dressing gown hung on the corner post of their brass bed, so she reached up to unhook it, wincing as the pain radiated from her ribs and arms, and draped it across her body. She lay on her back, dull agony a restless bedfellow who kept her from sleep. Occasionally the beams of a car's headlights crested the slight hill a little down the road and caught the window, sending the crossbars of the frame swinging across the ceiling like a flying crucifix.

She didn't know how long she'd lain there, eyes staring, her mind willing itself to vanquish the pain, to thrust it down, deep down within her, where the rest of it lived. Carl came into the room eventually, undressed silently and climbed into bed beside her. She edged a little away from him, the idea of physical contact, even through the thick duvet and her protective dressing gown, disgusting her. He didn't try to touch her, though. He kept his distance. He rolled over on his side, his back to her.

'You know I love you,' she heard him say.

She didn't reply.

'Why do you make me do it?'

Now, as she stared at herself in the mirror, she thought about his words. Did she make him do it? Did she somehow goad him into erupting? She *had* been looking for Roddie at the meeting the night before, she had to admit that, if only to herself. She had been with him, on this very bed, fifteen years before. Carl didn't know that. He might suspect it but he didn't know for certain. Other times they had taken a room in a boarding house down on the southern end of the island. Deirdre would drive down there, they would spend the afternoon together locked away in the safety of that anonymous little room, and then she came back in time to make Carl's dinner. She thought she had been so clever about it all, but Carl heard a whisper, that was all it took, a snigger behind someone's hand, a knowing look when Roddie's name was mentioned, and that was it. He never had any real proof, but he didn't need it.

She and Roddie had talked about leaving the island together, starting a new life. Sure, there was a difference in their age—she was twelve years his senior—but that didn't matter to them. She loved him and he loved her. But then along came Mhairi Sinclair. As she stared at herself in the mirror, her anger rose. *All that cow had to do was bat her eyelids at Roddie and he was off with her like a panting puppy. She'd discarded Donnie Kerr; now she was onto Roddie, and the next thing he was shacked up with that bitch. Didn't he know she was a little slut? That she'd screwed her way through all the eligible men in Portnaseil?* But Roddie had loved her since they were kids, he told her. He was sorry but it had always been Mhairi.

Mhairi, Mhairi, Mhairi. Beautiful little Mhairi, poor little Mhairi, with the brother dead from drugs and the father of her child looking then as if he was going the same way. She simply tossed that thick dark hair of hers and got everything—everyone—she wanted. She would've dumped Roddie, too, sooner or later. If someone hadn't killed her.

Deirdre carefully pulled on a blouse and jeans. She applied her make-up. She fixed her hair as best she could. She hadn't been to a hairdresser for too long, should've made an appointment in Portnaseil but couldn't. That would set Carl off again. He'd think she was doing it for another man. Especially with Roddie back home. No, she'd have to make do. She took her time because she had to look as good as she could. She knew she was trying to turn back time, but she had to do her best to recapture the woman she'd once been. When Roddie had wanted her. Before a further fifteen years of Carl Marsh had drained the life from her.

Roddie was back and she promised herself that she had taken her last beating.

She promised herself that a new life awaited her.

All she needed to do was see him.

* * *

The climb back to the clifftop was arduous and Rebecca's calves, still suffering from the day before, protested at the abuse. By the time they reached the Land Rover she was breathless and, just as she had done after her walk to the kirkyard the previous day, she vowed to attend more assiduously to her fitness levels. Only this time with added sincerity. Chaz hadn't even broken a sweat. As she sat on the baseboard of the Land Rover to catch her breath, the chill in the breeze now a blessing, Chaz handed her a bottle of water he'd fished out of his backpack. He even broke the seal for her, which was either him being polite or some kind of man thing, she couldn't tell which. She was grateful, however, because she didn't think she had the strength to twist it, let alone form words of thanks, so she took it with a nod.

Chaz placed his backpack carefully in the rear of the Land Rover, then asked, 'So, where do you want to go next?'

Rebecca took a long drink and gently wiped her bottom lip before she answered. 'Mhairi's parents.'

Chaz's eyebrows raised and he blew out his cheeks. 'Okay,' he said. 'Okay.'

He was uncomfortable with the idea. It wouldn't be easy for him. It wouldn't be a picnic for her, come to that, because of all the people to whom she needed to speak for this story, Mhairi's parents would be the most difficult to approach. She had only been in journalism for a couple of years but one thing she had learned was that it was best to make such interview requests as early as possible.

She would leave the island behind when this was all over; Chaz, however, had to stay and face these people. Stoirm wasn't *that* big that he could avoid them, she knew. 'I'd be better doing this on my own,' she said.

'No, it's okay, it's got to be done.' But she could sense he was squeezing the words out. He didn't really mean them.

'I think if two of us knock on that door it'll really put them off.'

'But they know me, won't that help?' Chaz quizzed.

'It might, it might not. The fact is, you being there might put *me*

137

off. Door-stepping is not an easy thing to do, believe me. You've never done it, I have, and I'm better on my own.' She took another mouthful of water. 'Believe me, Chaz, this is not something you want to do on your home turf.'

He nodded slowly, seeing the sense in her argument. He was relieved. His face relaxed and he looked like he'd been told the dentist was off that day. She stood up, every muscle and tendon in her legs throbbing, and opened the passenger door as Chaz rounded the vehicle's bonnet. She was contemplating the effort of lifting her leg onto the baseboard when her phone rang. It caught her by surprise. 'There's a signal out here?'

Chaz nodded. 'Broadband's crap but mobile signals can be great, if patchy.'

She dug the phone out of her pocket and checked the screen, feeling instantly a tightening in her chest that had nothing to do with her exertions. It was the office calling. She thought about not answering. She could say later she had been sleeping. She was ill, after all. At least as far as Barry was concerned. But then it might not be Barry. It might be one of the other reporters with a query about something she had left unfinished. She felt bad enough leaving them to pick up her slack, so she climbed into the passenger seat, closed the door to cut out as much of the background noise as she could and slid the button to green.

It wasn't one of her colleagues. It was Barry. She'd barely got out a hello before he went on the attack. 'What the hell are you doing on that bloody island?'

She thought about continuing the lie, bluffing it out, but that moment was passed. 'Barry, let me explain . . .'

'I told you not to go there.'

'I know, but . . .'

'But you went anyway, right?'

'Well, it wasn't exactly like that.'

Actually, it was and she knew it. What was worse, Barry knew it too.

'Bollocks, Rebecca.' Rebecca. He only ever used her full name when he was angry, which wasn't often, to be fair. In fact, she'd never heard his voice so full of rage, even though she could tell he was trying to control it. 'You deliberately defied me. I need you here—your colleagues need you here. Remember them, Rebecca? The people you work with? The ones you left to carry your load while you went off on some . . . some . . .' His fury was impairing his ability to find the right words, which wasn't like him. He found them, though. 'Some sort of personal crusade.'

'Barry . . .' she said, but he wasn't finished.

'Not only have you shown a complete lack of courtesy to everyone here, and that includes me, Rebecca, your boss, in case you've forgotten, but it's also selfish and unprofessional . . .'

She felt the words sting. 'Barry . . .' she began again.

'This isn't some bloody movie, Rebecca. You're not the maverick reporter who goes her own way and to hell with the consequences. I told you not to go and you went. This is amateur hour, this is fucking out of order . . .'

He was swearing now. Barry never swore, or at least she'd never heard him swear. From his point of view she was in the wrong and that troubled her because now she was beginning to wonder if he was right.

'Did that Wymark lad know what you were doing?'

She glanced at Chaz, who was watching her face intently, a slight frown crinkling his brow. 'No, he didn't know I was coming until I got here. He thinks you've okayed it . . .'

Barry fell silent, trying to gauge if she was telling the truth. Rebecca suspected that if he decided she was lying then Chaz would get no more work from the paper. She didn't want that on her conscience. She was relieved when Barry sighed and said, 'Okay. Right.' He paused again— she wondered if it was to take a calming breath. 'I want you on the next ferry back here.'

She didn't reply. He wouldn't like the word that came into her head.

'You hear me, Rebecca? I want you back here and at your desk tomorrow morning.'

She leaned forward in the seat, her head almost resting on the dashboard. She hated what she was about to do. She hated having to defy him again. He had called this a personal crusade and that was exactly what it boiled down to. This was personal, at least part of it, and she had to see it through.

'I can't do that, Barry.'

His voice was low and curt. 'What?'

Something dry and bitter lined her throat, so she swallowed to dislodge it. Her heart hammered in her chest. This was worse than any door-stepping assignment. 'I'm on to something here. You have to believe me . . .'

'Did you not hear me? You're not Woodward and Bernstein. This isn't the *Washington Post*. This isn't the *Sunday* fucking *Times*. We're the *Highland Chronicle*, a weekly newspaper. We report on wheelie bins and dog shit and local court stories and jumble sales, for Christ's sake. We're not built for a reporter to swan off for days on one story.'

She sat back up again, injecting as much strength into her voice as she could. 'This is important, Barry.'

'Getting your arse back here and behind that desk is important. Getting your pay once a month is important. If you don't do the first, then you'll no longer get the second, understand me?'

So there it was. She knew she risked losing her job, but she never thought he'd actually threaten it. Now that he had she felt even worse than before. Reporting jobs weren't easy to come by and being dismissed wasn't something from which you bounced back quickly. She couldn't simply submit, though. It wasn't in her nature.

'Barry, who told you I was here?' There were two possibilities. Simon. Had he simply told his mate because he'd finally taken the hint that whatever there had been between them was over and he wanted to punish her? She hoped that wasn't true, because not only did it reflect badly on a man she thought was fundamentally decent but also she was rooting for the other possibility, one that might—*might*—give her a toehold in this argument.

'Does it matter?' Barry said. 'The point is, I know . . .'

'It matters.'

He exhaled again. 'I got a call from Heather . . .'

Yes, Rebecca thought. Heather was the manager of the advertising department and she thought little of interfering in editorial matters if it meant additional revenue. The problem was, the London owners tended to agree with her, the need to protect shareholder dividends and executive bonuses being deemed more important than any news story.

Barry continued. 'They'd been contacted by the Stuart estate over there. They said you've been making a nuisance of yourself, asking questions.'

'They threatened to withdraw advertising, didn't they?'

'Not in so many words. But that was the gist, yes. It seems they have a substantial budget set aside for this new venture—and the distillery—and Heather is worried you'll scupper our chance of getting a piece of it.'

'They actually said that, that I've been making a nuisance of myself?'

'That's what Heather said. So, let me ask you: what the hell does the Stuart estate have to do with a fifteen-year-old murder?'

'As far as I know, nothing. But I did cover a public meeting last night about the proposals for the estate.'

'So? It seems it's welcomed by everyone.'

'Not quite everyone. There's local opposition.'

'There's always local opposition. They don't want trees cut down, they don't want heather disturbed, there's a newt with a "Do Not Disturb" sign on its nest. People don't like change, some just don't like progress. But I still want you back here, Becks.'

He was back to calling her Becks, which meant he'd calmed down a little. She was grateful for that but she couldn't surrender her position. She couldn't meekly go back. She knew she was tempting fate but she had to fight her corner. There was too much of her father in her to let it go.

'I can't do that, Barry.' She heard him begin to say something, but she carried on. 'I'm sorry, but this is important.'

'Important to who? You?'

'Yes, but there's also a story here. More than one. Roddie Drummond. The estate. I mean, why don't they want me asking questions? What have they got to hide? There's a suggestion that they've forcibly moved a few tenants off the land to make way for the new plans. What's that about, Barry? Have we got some new clearances going on over here?' She glanced at Chaz again, who was nodding. 'Also, Lord Henry Stuart and the dead woman were childhood friends. That didn't come out in court, as far as I know.'

'Any reason why it should? I'm sure she had lots of childhood friends who didn't get a mention in court.'

'Maybe so, but none of them have had their people phone our advertising department to apply pressure.'

He thought about that. 'I don't care, Becks. We're not set up for this sort of thing, not at the moment.'

She went on the attack. 'What happened to comforting the afflicted and afflicting the comfortable, Barry? If we don't do it, then who will? We let the big boys handle it? Is that what we're about? All the news that's fit to print, as long as it's easy?' She'd appealed to his journalistic instincts before. And failed. She was trying again. Chances were she would fail but she had to push it. 'And here's something else that wasn't mentioned back then. Mhairi said she was in trouble . . .'

'Who's Mhairi?'

'The victim, Barry. The woman who died. The young mother who was found beaten to death in her home.' She realised her tone had sharpened, so she blunted it before she spoke again. 'Something was worrying her. Something scared her.'

'How do you know?'

'Because I've spoken to a witness who didn't give evidence.' She hoped Barry wouldn't ask why Donnie didn't testify because when he heard that he had been a junkie at the time he'd do what the Crown did and reject whatever he said as unreliable. She pressed on. 'If I can get all that after one day here, Barry, think what I'll get if I stay on a few more. This is big, Barry. This is the kind of thing that wins awards. This is the kind of thing that could get a guy back to the city, if he played it right. All he needs to do is have the courage I know he has and stay the course.'

She waited for him to respond. She waited for what seemed like a long time. She had deliberately dangled getting back into the dailies because she knew that's what he wanted. This *was* a personal crusade for her, so she had to give him the motivation to get on board. Chaz watched her and she had the feeling he was holding his breath. Through the windshield she saw something move against the sky. Something big that seemed to float towards the cliffs, its long wings giving way to feather fingers.

'Okay,' said Barry, his voice low. 'Here's what we do. You take this week as unpaid leave.'

She felt relief wash over her. 'Thanks, Barry.'

'And I don't hand you your P45. But you be back here on Monday morning, come what may. And you email me a story about last night's meeting.'

She ignored the fact that if the leave was unpaid, she shouldn't have to send a story. She was getting off lightly and she knew it. As she thanked him again and the conversation ended, she watched the bird languidly beat its wings once or twice and then head gracefully over the cliff edge towards its nest.

The eagle really had landed.

22

The morning classes seemed interminable to Sonya. Her first thought had been to bunk off, but she'd never done that before and was too afraid of being caught. She knew of others who would dodge classes and head away from Portnaseil to a remote part of the coast but that wasn't for her. She liked school, she enjoyed learning. Today, though, she had something to do. Certainly it could wait until later, but she was eager to get it done.

Time dragged. Each click of the second hand on the big clock on the wall seemed to be in slow motion. Then finally it was lunchtime. She dashed out of school, avoiding both Gus and Sylvia, and headed straight for Campbell Drummond's workshop on the upper fringe of the town, keeping an eye out for her gran or granddad. It was unlikely they would be up this way, but you just never knew. Of course, there was the chance someone would spot her and tell them, but she could say she was just out for a walk at lunchtime. Why she was lingering on the roadway within sight of the workshop and the cottage beside it was a more difficult sell, so she dodged behind a hedge from which she could keep watch, hoping Roddie Drummond would come out so she could talk to him. She didn't have the courage to knock on his door; it had to appear to be an accidental meeting. She took a sandwich she'd prepared that morning from her bag and bit into it. She was hungry. She had half an hour tops, but she couldn't face classes that afternoon on an empty stomach.

A couple of cars passed as she watched, including Alisdair McGovern's Ford pick-up. He was probably heading to see his sister, who lived a mile to the north. She saw his big broad face peering out at her and he gave her a quick wave. She waved back.

A couple of off-islanders sauntered by, also heading north, obviously late-season tourists. They nodded to her and she nodded back, hoping they wouldn't start a conversation or ask directions. Thankfully, they kept on walking up the rise until they eventually vanished over the crest of the hill.

She had been waiting for around twenty minutes when Deirdre Marsh drove up in her battered little Peugeot and stopped in the yard beside Campbell Drummond's black van. The big double doors to the workshop were open and, even at this distance, Sonya could hear the clang of hammer on metal. The woman made no attempt to get out, although her head was angled towards the cottage door as if she was watching it intently. Campbell must have heard the sound of the idling engine because he appeared in the workshop doorway, wiping his hand on a rag. He frowned as he walked to the car and leaned into the driver's window. Sonya couldn't hear what was being said, but she saw Campbell briefly crane his neck to glance towards the cottage door then shake his head as he turned back to face her. He had both hands on the car door, as if he was holding it shut, but he stepped back when she pushed it open. He said something else, but Deirdre ignored him when she climbed out and walked purposefully towards the cottage.

The front door opened just as she reached it and Sonya's breath caught in her throat as she saw Roddie Drummond for the first time. He looked so different from the photograph she'd seen. Not just older but defeated. As if life had been nothing but a disappointment to him.

He said something to Deirdre, glanced at his father, who shrugged, his hands working at the rag again as if he was washing them of any responsibility. Roddie watched him disappear into the workshop, then stood aside to let Deirdre enter. He lingered in the doorway for a moment, his eyes sweeping the roadway and the countryside. Sonya eased further behind the hedge but she could still see him through the twigs. He seemed to stare straight at her for a second, then closed the door.

She waited a few minutes, the sandwich forgotten in her hand, her feelings mixed. That was Roddie Drummond. The man they all said had murdered her mother. More than ever she wanted to speak to him, to face him, but part of her, now that she'd set eyes upon him, wasn't sure it was a good idea. As it was, she was unlikely to see him, not now that Deirdre Marsh was with him.

She thrust the half-eaten sandwich away, knowing she'd grab a few minutes back at school to finish it, and then, with a final glance at the Drummond home, shouldered her bag. While she walked back towards Portnaseil, she wondered what business the gamekeeper's wife had with Roddie Drummond.

She was only dimly aware of Alisdair's pick-up cruising past her again.

* * *

Deirdre was surprised at how much Roddie had aged. His hair was thinner, his body, which she recalled as being young and firm and a joy not just to watch but to caress, had sagged. His face was fuller, his eyes not as bright. But he was still her Roddie, she knew that. After all, she was no longer the woman she had once been, but if Roddie was disappointed at her appearance, he didn't show it.

He led her into the cottage's small living room with its old but comfortable three-piece suite, an open fire with its coals lifeless in the grate, and heavy, dark furniture that had probably been in the family for generations. There were windows to the front, looking onto the courtyard, and rear, facing a small, neat garden. Radio 2 was playing in the kitchen, Jeremy Vine talking to someone about parking in the city. Other people's problems and a world away from the island.

'Good to see you, Deirdre,' Roddie said, motioning towards an armchair.

She perched on the edge of the cushion, partly because her body still ached but also because she was nervous. She'd been fine in the car, her mood almost buoyant over her sudden decisiveness. But now she was here, in this small cottage, seeing the man she'd thought about so often over the years, her certainty began to waver. It wasn't that she had been put off by the way he looked now, that didn't matter, but it occurred to her that she didn't know where he'd been all this time. For all she knew he could be married. He could have a family. She couldn't see a wedding ring, but that didn't mean anything. Perhaps he was in a stable relationship but unmarried. Until now, she hadn't considered the possibility that there would be someone else in his life.

Roddie leaned forward on the settee, his elbows on his knees, his hands clasped. 'How have you been?'

How have I been? She almost laughed. She wanted to say that there hadn't been a day she hadn't thought of him. She wanted to say that she often thought of how different her life would have been had they gone away like they'd planned. She wanted to say that when Carl made his demands, it was Roddie's flesh she stroked, his lips she kissed, it was him she felt moving inside her. These were the things she'd come here to say, but in that moment she couldn't.

'I've been fine, Roddie. And you? What have you been doing with yourself?'

A short laugh escaped his throat. 'This and that.'

They fell silent again. This was not how she had dreamt this. She hadn't expected him to pull her into his arms—she didn't know what she had expected, but it wasn't this. But what else was there? They had once been white hot with passion, but a lot of time had passed. Now it was just polite conversation.

'I was sorry to hear about your mother,' she said, amazed at how normal her voice sounded, while in her mind she was willing him to tell her how much he missed her, how much he wanted her, that he wanted to be with her.

He acknowledged with a slight inclination of his head. He stood up, obviously just as nervous as she. Somehow that made her feel better. 'Do you want a cup of tea? Coffee?'

'I'm fine, thanks.'

He sat back down again and she instantly regretted her refusal. He probably needed something to do and she would also have welcomed the distraction. The moment had passed, though. He seldom looked at her, but when he did she made sure she held his gaze. She'd heard the stories from the older folk, about the people who could make things happen with the power of thought. She knew it was all mystical bunkum but she was trying it anyway. She listened while he spoke but her mind was urging him to take her away.

'Will you be staying on after the funeral?' she asked.

He shook his head. 'Nah, I'm not welcome here, you must know that.'

'Where will you go?'

Take me with you.

'Back to the mainland,' he said.

Take me with you.

'So where do you call home now?'

He paused. 'Stayed in Glasgow for a time. I'm over near Edinburgh now.'

Take me with you.

'Is there . . .' She stumbled over her words, for this was a hard question, an important question. 'Is there someone there waiting for you?'

He gave her a look that was as surprised as it was quizzical. 'Waiting for me? How do you mean?'

'I mean, a wife, a partner, a significant other? A family?'

He understood. He even looked relieved. 'No, I'm unattached.'

She was delighted to hear that. Now was her chance. She took a deep breath, stared at the carpet. 'Do you ever think of me, Roddie?'

Take me with you.

'Think of you?'

She looked up, met his eyes. She saw it then. He *had* thought of her. She knew it. 'Of me. Of us. Of the way we were together?'

He held her gaze and she thought for a dreadful moment he was going to say he hadn't. Then his eyes softened. 'Of course I have.'

'It was good, wasn't it? What we had? You and me?'

He smiled, a small one, but a smile just the same. 'Yes, it was.'

She swallowed. This is your chance, Deirdre, you have to go for it. This is why you came. You've opened the door, time to step through.

Take me with you.

'I think about you, Roddie. Sometimes I feel I do nothing but think of you, of what we had, of what we could have been. You remember our

148

plans? To go away together? To get away from this rotten island and Carl and all the small minds? You remember?'

'I remember,' he said.

She leaned forward again, unable to keep the eagerness from her voice. 'We can still do it. It's not too late. We can leave here, start a new life. I still love you, Roddie. I know we're older, but I still feel the same. We can be together again. We can make the past fifteen years just go away, like they never happened. We can make it like it was before . . .'

She stopped. She couldn't say the name. Roddie said it for her.

'Before Mhairi?'

She nodded. 'That didn't happen, not as far as we're concerned. I know you didn't kill her, I don't care what the rest of these narrow-minded islanders think. I know you didn't. We can wipe that slate clean.'

'Just like that?'

She almost leapt to sit beside him on the couch. She didn't need to use telepathy. She was getting through to him, she knew it. She took his hand, threaded her fingers through his, the sensation of touching his flesh pleasing her. She was heartened that he didn't pull away. She was completely energised now, something she had not felt for many years. Being with Carl had sapped all the life from her, but right at this moment she felt it surging through her again. 'Yes, just like that. Wash it away. Start fresh. The two of us. Away from here.'

She wanted to say more but she couldn't find the words. It was up to him now. He sat beside her, very still, his eyes fixed on their hands and intertwined fingers. Then, slowly, gently, he disentangled them and stood up, walked to the window and looked out into the sunlight.

'Some things you can't just wash clean,' he said, his back to her, his shoulders stooped.

'You won't take me?' She thought she'd been getting to him. She thought her words had struck home. She thought he had wanted to regain what had once been as much as she. But he was rejecting her. Again.

He faced her. 'Deirdre, I can't. My life . . . is . . .' He couldn't find the words to describe his life so he merely sighed and shrugged.

'And mine is *so* wonderful,' she said, an edge now to her voice. No matter how he had lived since leaving the island, it was nothing compared to what she had endured. 'You know what Carl is like.'

He nodded, averted his eyes.

'You're really not going to take me with you?' she asked.

'I can't. You don't understand . . .'

She saw tears forming in his eyes, but she was unmoved. She'd seen men's tears before and they meant nothing. Roddie was just like Carl in the end. He'd used her, drained her. Carl kept her close because he didn't like the idea of anyone else having her. She was his and his alone. Roddie didn't even want that.

'He'll kill me, you know that,' she said. 'Sooner or later he'll go too far.'

'Then leave him.'

'That's what I want to do. But with you.' The truth was, she'd thought of it often, packing a bag, grabbing the ferry, vanishing onto the mainland. But Carl would come looking for her and find her, she had no doubt about that. He could be resourceful when he wanted to be, and when he found her it would be all the worse for her, she knew it. Seeking help wasn't an option, not to her, not simply because of the repercussions that she was certain would follow when he found out she had confided in an outsider, but also because she was ashamed of what she had allowed to continue for so long. That shame wore heavily upon her. She also didn't want to be alone, which made her even more ashamed. For years she had been told that without Carl she was nothing, less than nothing, useless, functionless. Her father had said the same to her mother and, when she grew older, to her. Sometimes the message was enforced with his fist, just like Carl. Part of her had come to believe it. The part that had lived with her father and had lived with Carl. But the other part, the part that was hers and hers alone, had only been lying dormant, waiting for this moment, this opportunity. She couldn't let it pass. Her future, the future she deserved, was standing right in front of her and she refused to give it up without a fight.

She could do this.

150

She stood up, placed both hands on either side of Roddie's face and forced him to look at her. She stood very close, almost but not quite pressing her body against his. She softened her tone. 'We can make this work, Roddie, I know we can. I don't know what your life has been like but I can fix it. We can fix it together. We were good back then, weren't we? You loved me, you said you did. I know I've thrown this at you, but we can find that again.'

Then she kissed him. He didn't try to pull away but he didn't respond either. His lips were unpliable, his hands remained at his side. Still she worked at it, her hands snaking under his arms, pulling him closer to her. But there was no response. No returning pressure, no gentle caress, no passion. Nothing. She knew then with utter certainty that she had failed. The hope that had sustained her so far withered and died. She found she couldn't look at him any more so she turned away, a finger wiping at her bottom lip. She didn't know what to do, what to say. Her emotions had raged all morning, from anticipation, to excitement, to nervousness, to joy and now disappointment. She felt tired, so very tired, and all she wanted to do was leave, to get away from this neat little room looking out to the neat little garden with some classic rock track playing in the background. She didn't want to say anything more. She just wanted to go.

She was almost through the door when Roddie said, 'I'm sorry, Deirdre.'

His voice snapped something inside her and she experienced a fresh emotion. She whirled back, the need to lash out, to wound him, strong and unstoppable. 'It's her, isn't it? You're still hung up on that slut, even after all these years. Even though she's dead. She's still there beside you.'

She saw her words had hit home. 'Deirdre . . .' he began, but she didn't want to hear anything further from him.

'Poor little Mhairi Sinclair, all the boys loved her, didn't they? You, Donnie Kerr, anyone who fell under her spell. She had you all panting after her. And she loved that, loved to play you. She was nothing but a whore.'

'Don't . . .' he said.

'Oh, I know, believe me. I know what she was like. She let Donnie get her pregnant and then she moved on to you. But even you weren't enough. I know, Roddie, I *know*! And you know what? I'm glad she's dead. I meant it when I said you didn't kill her. You didn't, you couldn't kill her. I know that. Because that would've taken balls and that's something you don't have. You always were a gutless, simpering child. And now? I don't even know what I saw in you.'

She left, her anger giving her the strength to keep her head high. But deep down she knew it wouldn't last.

23

Compared to a supermarket on the mainland, the Portnaseil General Store was small potatoes, even though the shoppers could find almost everything they needed on its shelves. Prices were slightly higher, of course, and many islanders made a monthly trip across the water to bulk buy, but if they wanted fresh bread and milk, a daily newspaper—although fewer and fewer people looked for them—or to simply replenish vital supplies, then the Sinclairs' general store was the place to go.

Rebecca peered through the window and saw a man standing at the register. He was small and his stomach bulged against his work coat, his head thatched with thick grey hair swept back from his forehead. He chatted to customers as he ran their purchases through the till, technology no longer requiring any great attention on his part, although he did keep his eye on the read-out for anomalies. Scanners may have replaced push button tills but Rebecca would lay odds that Hector Sinclair knew the price of every item on his shelves.

The shop was busy. Pupils from the high school wandered among the aisles, picking up items they knew they really shouldn't be having for lunch. Rebecca's stomach grumbled—a reminder it was that time of day. She'd eaten a hearty breakfast—far more substantial than normal—but she'd always had a prodigious appetite, even as a child. Her mother often wondered where she put it all, prompting her father to come out with another of his catchphrases: *You can't fatten a thoroughbred.*

Rebecca never fully understood the saying—she'd seen plenty of overweight full-blood Labradors—but it was one she regularly used herself.

Before he dropped her off in the Square, Chaz had told her that the family lived in the flat above the shop, which was accessed through an alleyway between the store and the old bank building. They agreed to meet for dinner in the hotel that night so she could fill him in what she'd learned.

The door to the Sinclair home was of modern PVC, with a glass panel set in the top half. Although a gauze curtain hung on the other side, Rebecca could make out a narrow carpeted stairway. She thumbed the doorbell but heard no associated buzz or ring, though that didn't necessarily mean it wasn't working. It was while she debated giving the letterbox a rattle that she saw, first, a pair of brown moccasin slippers, then legs in black trousers, then a woman wearing a shapeless, overly large blue cardigan.

Molly Sinclair hadn't aged that much in the fifteen years since her photograph had been snatched as she walked into the court building. Even her hairstyle was the same. It was short and grey then, and it was short and grey now. She was small, like her husband, but she had kept herself trim. Her eyes were sharp and wouldn't miss much, but there was a hint of sadness there too. Those eyes were wary as she studied Rebecca, as if she knew what she was going to hear, her hand clasped round the edge of the door as if preparing to slam it at any moment.

'Mrs Sinclair, I'm sorry to bother you, but my name is Rebecca Connolly. I'm from the *Highland Chronicle*.'

Rebecca's impression had been correct. The woman didn't seem surprised to see her. It could just as easily have been Donnie Kerr dropping by. She wondered if perhaps Sawyer had been here ahead of her.

'Yes,' Mrs Sinclair said, her voice flat.

'I wonder if I could talk to you about . . .'

'Roddie Drummond.'

Rebecca hesitated. Yes, someone was acting as her advance man and she suspected not in a good way. 'Well, yes, that's ri—'

'I've nothing to say.' Molly Sinclair began to close the door again.

'Mrs Sinclair, I'm not here to cause trouble . . .'

154

The woman pulled the door back once more. 'Of course you are. That's what you people do, cause trouble.' There was no heat in her voice, no rancour. For her, these were merely statements of fact. 'That's what you live for.'

'That's not my intention. The *Highland Chronicle* is a local paper and we are very sympathetic to the feelings and views of our readership.' *Christ*, Rebecca thought, *I sound like a company press release.* She made an effort to loosen her voice. 'We don't want to cause trouble for anyone. But the fact is, Roddie Drummond is back and someone is going to write about it. It's better us than some red top from Glasgow.'

Her argument was falling on stony ground because Mrs Sinclair merely sneered and swung the door towards her. Rebecca had to think of something to convince her and she needed to do it fast.

'Mrs Sinclair, I've already spoken to Roddie Drummond . . .'

It was the truth, but only barely. She *had* spoken to him, but only on the ferry and he hadn't said anything of consequence. It was the only thing she could think of under pressure and she was banking on what would be a natural antipathy towards the man who had been accused of murdering her daughter.

It worked. The door opened again and Mrs Sinclair gave her that probing look once more.

'I've heard you're here to prove him innocent,' she said.

That sounded like Sawyer. 'I'm here for the truth.'

A slight laugh coughed at Mrs Sinclair's throat, but there was no humour in her eyes. Her eyes remained sceptical but her words were all contempt. 'You won't get much truth out of Roddie Drummond.'

'That's why I'm here. To get as many sides to what happened as I can.' An old lecturer of hers had once said that everyone had their own version of events, which often came close but failed to hit the mark, so if you gathered as many viewpoints as possible you stood a greater chance of finding out what had actually happened.

'That was what the trial was supposed to do, but the truth still didn't come out.' The woman stared at Rebecca and the meld of disdain and suspicion gave way to indecision. She hooked her bottom lip with her left incisor as her fingers drummed slightly on the edge of the door. Then, with a slight sigh, she threw the door open wider and turned away. 'You'd better come in then,' she said, her back to Rebecca as she climbed the stairs. 'I know what you people are like, you won't stop until you get what you want. Even then you'll print a load of rubbish.'

Rebecca closed the door behind her and followed. It was a steep climb and it made her calf muscles grumble again. The woman, more than twice her age, went up them like a mountain goat. There was another door at the top, which led to a long hallway and a series of doors. As Rebecca was led past an open one, she glanced in and caught a glimpse of the sitting room and a glass cabinet bearing framed photographs of their dead daughter. A small utility room opposite housed a tall, grey cabinet. Molly Sinclair led her the length of the hallway and Rebecca guessed they would talk in the kitchen. She was used to that. Reporters are often interlopers in the lives of others and to take them into the centre of family life was an intrusion too far. Even Maeve Gallagher had taken her into the common sitting room of her boarding house, keeping her away from the personal space.

Molly Sinclair motioned for her to take a seat. 'Would you like a cup of tea or coffee?' she asked.

Highland hospitality. Rebecca was unwelcome but still must be fed and watered. 'Tea would be lovely.'

'I've only got Tetley. We don't go in for that posh stuff you folks drink.'

You folks. Rebecca didn't know if she meant reporters or mainlanders or anyone under thirty. She gave her host what she hoped was her most winning smile. 'That's fine. I'm not a fan of posh teas either. It should be dark and strong and not taste like perfume.'

The woman gave a curt nod, satisfied with this common ground, flicked the kettle on, then took down two mugs from an overhead cupboard. Rebecca took the opportunity to glance around. The Sinclairs lived well. The kitchen was large, bright and the fixtures modern—all mod cons, as her mother would say. The windows looked out on a back yard with a washing line draped diagonally across a patch of grass and propped up by two poles. A small shelter, housing various wheelie bins, stood beside a low fence beyond which was a stretch of long grass undulating in the breeze drifting from the Sound, a glimpse of which Rebecca caught to the right. She could see patches of sand dotted between the clumps of vegetation. Beyond the grassland stood a couple of cottages and then more open land. It was a pleasant room with a nice view. Rebecca's own kitchen in Inverness was a small square with barely enough room for a sink, a cooker and a fridge. Her view was across a tiny courtyard into another kitchen. She would often stand washing her few dishes and see the tenant opposite doing his.

Molly Sinclair carried the mugs of tea to the table, then fetched a sugar bowl and milk. No biscuits or cake. Her need to offer hospitality didn't stretch that far.

'So,' the woman said as she took a seat opposite Rebecca. 'Better get on with it.'

Rebecca took out her notebook and held up her recorder. 'Do you mind?'

Molly shrugged and sipped her tea, watching as Rebecca busied herself, noting the interviewee's name and the date on a fresh page.

'First,' Rebecca said, her routine complete, 'thank you for speaking to me. I assure you my aim here is to get to the truth, if I can, and not to embarrass or upset anyone.'

A dismissive flick of an eyebrow conveyed exactly what Molly Sinclair thought of that statement. 'What did Roddie Drummond tell you?'

'That he didn't kill Mhairi.'

A slight shake of the head, as if she couldn't believe he still insisted on his innocence. 'Well . . .' She stopped and waited, batting the ball back into Rebecca's court with a stiff look. This wasn't going to be an easy interview.

'Why don't you tell me about Mhairi? What was she like?'

Molly's face softened slightly. 'She was a wonderful lass,' she said. 'I know you'd expect me to say that, but it was true. Everybody thought so. She was kind and caring, thoughtful. Dependable.'

Rebecca was fairly certain Mhairi was not quite such a paragon. Nobody was. But it was Molly's duty as a mother to paint her daughter as Mother Theresa on steroids. And perhaps, to her, she was. 'You had a son, too . . .'

There was a slight pause. 'Yes.'

'Ray?'

'Raymond.'

'Sorry, Raymond.'

Rebecca waited for Molly Sinclair to speak but nothing further came. *Okay, down to me then*, she thought. 'Forgive me, but he died.'

Another pause. Molly's face had stiffened again. 'Yes.'

'It hit Mhairi hard, didn't it?'

'It hit us all hard.'

'Of course. But Mhairi distanced herself from Donnie Kerr after that. Blamed him for Ray's—Raymond's—death?'

'Donnie has atoned for that now. He's smartened himself up. He's made something of himself. He's been a good father to Sonya.'

'She lives with you, though, doesn't she?'

'It's better that way. Look, what has this to do with Roddie Drummond?'

'I'm only trying to get a full picture of events, Mrs Sinclair. My point is that after Donnie left to go to Glasgow with Raymond, Mhairi began a relationship with Roddie Drummond, is that right? Even though she'd had Donnie's child.'

Molly stood up suddenly. 'I think you should leave. This is a mistake.'

'Please, Mrs Sinclair . . .'

'I don't know what you're trying to infer here.'

'Nothing, I—'

'Are you trying to say that Mhairi was some kind of whore? Is that it?'

'Certainly not, Mrs Sinclair. I'm trying to say that Mhairi and Donnie and Roddie, they were all close. Since childhood, am I right? I've been told that Lord Henry was also a close friend back then.'

'I know what you were saying. Mhairi was a Jezebel, she slept with all her men friends, that they passed her around. Oh, I know what they all said about her. I know the talk. But it wasn't true, it wasn't true. She was a wonderful person, my Mhairi. She was my joy. She was my child.'

And then her carefully constructed poise cracked, a rotting brick wall

158

being pushed by flood waters. The tears seeped through and she sat back down with a wail. Her pain stabbed at Rebecca across the table and she reached out to gently caress the woman's hand, but Molly snatched it away and fished in the pocket of her cardigan for a paper tissue. As she wiped at the tears Rebecca decided to press on. Her time was limited and she had to get some answers.

'Mrs Sinclair, that night, I know Mhairi came here to collect Sonya to take her home. Do you know where she'd been?'

Molly had cradled the tissue in her hand and pressed it against both eyes. She shook her head.

'Okay. She told Donnie Kerr that she was in some sort of trouble. Did she mention that to you?'

'Please leave,' she said, her voice slightly muffled. 'Please don't ask anything more. I shouldn't have let you in. If my husband found out, he'd go off his head.'

'Why did you let me?'

'I don't know. I thought . . .' The tissue was removed from her eyes. 'I don't know what I thought. Please, just go.'

Rebecca knew she should leave. She had been asked to. She should simply pack up her gear and say goodbye. But she felt Molly Sinclair really wanted to talk. That was why she'd let her in. She had something to tell.

'Mrs Sinclair, I'm trying to help here, you must believe me. If Roddie Drummond wasn't responsible for what happened to Mhairi, then someone else was. And that person is still walking about, perhaps here on the island. I know Detective Sergeant Sawyer has been to see you . . .'

Molly didn't even attempt to deny it, so Rebecca pressed ahead.

'And I know he told you not to speak to me, that I was for Roddie Drummond and against you, but that's not true, I give you my word. I am completely impartial, it's my job to be fair, no matter what you might think about the press. I know you've probably had bad experiences but we're not all like that, believe me.'

Molly listened to the words and Rebecca felt she was getting through, so she used everything she could think of.

'My dad was a police officer, a high-ranking police officer. He believed in punishing the guilty, he did it all his life, but he also taught me that the best way to find the truth was to keep an open mind. He used to say that closed minds or fixed ideas led to injustice. Follow the evidence, not the man, he used to say. He'd seen too many police officers make the mistake of thinking that just because a suspect was dodgy then he must be guilty.'

She paused to let her words sink in. She could see the woman's resistance crumbling. She wanted to talk, most people did. They just needed the correct stimulus. Rebecca had one more weapon in her arsenal.

'My dad was an islander, did you know that? Left here when he was a teenager. So I've got Stoirm blood in my veins, Mrs Sinclair. You may not know me, but I'm not a stranger, not really, although I'm still an outsider so I can take a step back. You can't do that. No one who was here fifteen years ago can do that, not even Bill Sawyer. You need closure, the island needs closure. Maybe I can help bring that about, maybe I can't. But all I ask is that you help me try.'

Rebecca had said all she could, so she waited. The woman would either insist she left or she'd begin to talk. Nothing Rebecca could say now would influence her decision.

Molly Sinclair sat very still, her breathing ragged, her only movement her hands shredding the paper tissue and letting the fragments fall to the table's surface. The faint sound of the water whispering against the shore and the singing of the wind through the long grass drifted into the room. They were the only sounds. The waves. The wind. Molly Sinclair's breathing.

Then . . .

'What's your surname again?'

'Connolly.'

The hands stopped picking the tissue apart. There was that look again. The same one she'd seen in the face of the woman in the kirkyard. Recognition. 'What's your father's Christian name?'

'John.'

The look was still there, along with something else. A decision had been made. 'Then you'll understand the nature of secrets.'

Rebecca didn't know what she meant, but she didn't get the chance to ask anything further, for Molly Sinclair began talking.

Her voice was low, the words sluggish, as if they had been waiting too long to come alive. But after their initial breath the words began to gather in strength.

'I knew she was upset as soon as she turned up that night to collect Sonya . . .'

24

Molly Sinclair
Fifteen years earlier

At first I'd put the change in Mhairi's temperament down to lingering grief over the death of her brother, but the night she came to collect Sonya, I thought there was something more. I always knew when my girl was worried, you see, ever since she was a wee one. Her posture was normally perfect but when there was something on her mind her shoulders stiffened, her eyes lost their sparkle and her laugh, the one that brightened the house, stilled.

This was different. I knew as soon as I saw her that night that something had happened but I didn't ask what it was right away. She had been a secretive child and she'd never grown out of it. She certainly wouldn't say anything with her father sitting in his armchair watching some dreadful American TV programme while he waited to go to bed.

Hector had also changed since Raymond's death, become more introspective. Brooding, I suppose. Raymond had been his favourite—not that a parent should have favourites, but it happens. What happened in Glasgow broke his heart, Mhairi's too, for she had always been close to her brother. It had destroyed what feelings she had for Donnie Kerr. It was all sad, tragic, but what was worse was that common grief didn't lead to father and daughter growing closer. There had been a distance between them since Mhairi was a teenager, yet I never knew why. I had tried to find out over the years, of course I had, but neither of them would break the silence. All Mhairi said was that her father simply didn't understand girls, which was true, and all Hector said was that she was a disappointment to him. Her getting pregnant to Donnie didn't help matters. So whatever was troubling Mhairi would not be spoken about in his presence.

'You're late,' Hector said, without taking his eyes off the television screen, where some people were shooting guns. *Violence, too much violence*, I thought. *As if there wasn't enough of it in the world, they had to fill TV screens with it.* I didn't like the fact that Hector had two shotguns tucked away in his gun cabinet down the hall for when he and Campbell Drummond went shooting together. I was island born and raised, guns aren't uncommon, but the idea of having them in the house made me uncomfortable.

'I know, I'm sorry,' said Mhairi, but the words were directed at me. 'I was held up.'

'Where have you been?' I asked.

Mhairi paused and her eyes flicked away. 'I was down at Feshie, seeing Morag.' Morag was her friend from school. She had married a dairy farmer and moved to the south of the island. 'Not seen her in ages. You know what it's like when we get talking.'

I knew it was a lie, even before the words came out of her mouth. The pause and the looking away told me that but I wouldn't challenge her on it, not with Hector there. I followed her into her old bedroom, where Sonya was sleeping. That child was always a sound sleeper, something she'd inherited from me. Whatever gene it was that dictated sleep patterns had skipped a generation, for Mhairi was too restless a child to sleep through the night. She used to say the baby would sleep through Armageddon.

I made sure the door was firmly closed before I spoke. 'There's something wrong, isn't there?'

Even in the dim glow of the nightlight, I saw how pale and drawn Mhairi was. And there was something in her eyes that had never been there before, even after Raymond's death. I don't know how to describe it except they were haunted, as if she had seen something that had affected her so deeply she would never forget it.

'Nothing, Mum,' said Mhairi.

'No, there's something. You can't hide it from me. You never could.'

She fussed a little with Sonya's blanket. Even then the baby did not waken. 'I saw Donnie, is all it is. He wanted money.'

'Did you give it to him?'

'No,' she said, but that was another lie. I let it go again. I was convinced seeing Donnie was not what had upset her. We were all used to what Donnie had become by then, sad and disturbing though it was. What was more disturbing was the knowledge that Raymond had become a similar walking corpse. But I tried not to think about that too much. I still don't. I couldn't change it then, I can't change it now. Perhaps, had I known what our son was doing in Glasgow, I could have done something about it, but Raymond had never told me. His calls home, although they grew infrequent, were breezy. He was working, he said. He was fine, he said. But he wasn't working and he wasn't fine. And then he was dead.

I didn't blame Donnie. Hector did, but he'd never forgiven him for getting his daughter pregnant and then swanning off. Even Mhairi blamed the boy. But I never did. Not totally. Raymond had always been his own man. It had been his idea to go to the city, not Donnie's. Donnie was a follower back then, like Roddie, and although it suited my husband and my daughter to blame him, I knew in my heart that Raymond would have led the way in everything.

I watched as Mhairi bundled Sonya carefully in a warm blanket and laid her into the carry cot. The baby murmured a little but remained asleep.

'Thanks, Mum,' said Mhairi as they left the room. She didn't say goodbye to her father, who was still in the sitting room. The gulf between them was too wide for anything but necessary communication. He wouldn't have heard her anyway, for there was too much gunfire and screeching tyres on the TV.

I followed her down the stairs, still wishing she would tell me what

164

was wrong, but nothing more was said. At her car, I felt the need to make one more attempt at getting her to talk. Perhaps, in the night air, her father out of the way, she would open up, even just a little.

'Mhairi, pet,' I said, very gently, 'you know you can tell me anything. After all that's happened, you know that, don't you?'

Mhairi straightened up after moving Sonya from the carry cot into her car seat. 'Honest, Mum, it's nothing. I'm tired. It's been a long day, you know? And that drive up from Feshie in the dark takes it out of me.' The smile she gave me was forced and weak. 'Nothing to worry about.'

I still wasn't convinced. The Feshie visit was a fiction, I knew it. 'Is there trouble between you and Roddie? Is that it?'

Something then. Something in her eyes. Something that appeared and vanished like the fairies out there in the dark. Then Mhairi looked away. Another lie coming. 'No, we're fine. He's fine.'

She walked round to the driver's door, opened it. Then she stopped and seemed to freeze as she stared at the child sleeping in the back seat. I saw her face fold as tears began to well, so I moved round the car. Mhairi instantly whirled and wrapped her arms around me and held me like her life depended on it.

'Mhairi, pet, tell me what it is.' But she shook her head, sobs wracking her body. 'You've got to tell me. Whatever it is, we can sort it.'

'I'm in trouble, Mum,' said Mhairi, her voice muffled against my shoulder. 'I think I'm pregnant.'

I felt shock first, then relief, then the sensation of being here before. I thought of Hector, sitting up there watching that TV programme. He'd been disgusted with Mhairi for sleeping with Donnie out of wedlock; now it had happened again. With another man.

'But that's a wonderful thing, darling. Roddie must be very happy.'

Mhairi pulled herself away to avoid my eyes.

Suspicion filled my mind. 'You *have* told Roddie, haven't you?'

Mhairi said nothing.

I eased her back round to face me, forced her to look at me. 'Mhairi, you have to talk to me—have you told Roddie yet?'

She shook her head, her tearful eyes filled with something else. Fear? Desperation? Panic? I couldn't tell.

I took a deep breath. 'Is Roddie the father?'

Mhairi seemed to freeze, the air around us grew heavy. I knew the answer. I could see it in her face; I heard it in the silence.

'Who is the father?' I asked.

Mhairi shook her head again, not so much a refusal to answer as a means of clearing her thoughts. 'I'm not even certain I am pregnant, Mum. It's just that all the signs are there . . .'

'But if you were, Roddie might not be the father? So who might it be?'

A smile then. The one that Mhairi threw when she was finished talking about something. 'Of course it'd be Roddie. Who else would it be?'

Who else indeed, I thought, as Mhairi busied herself with little Sonya. I said nothing further as I took in this news. If she was expecting, then Hector would have to know about it sooner or later and I already dreaded having to tell him. When that day came there would be another storm and it would have nothing to do with the island's climate.

I knew I'd weather it like I'd weathered everything else. When it came down to it, Hector did love his daughter and he would stand by her. That was the island way. Family stood with family.

I had been through a lot with my children and I knew when to push and when to hold back. I also knew Mhairi was still hiding something. When she was younger she would try to throw us off some misdemeanour by admitting to something else. I couldn't help but feel that Mhairi had tried to do the same by revealing the possible pregnancy.

25

Molly stared towards the window as she remembered that night. 'I never saw my daughter again, alive or dead. I couldn't bring myself to identify the body. Hector did that. And when he came home that morning he took a bottle of malt from the shop and drank half of it before lunchtime. He doesn't drink, not like that, but that day he did. He loved her, he always had. He just had trouble showing it.'

'You didn't say any of this at the trial?'

The woman shook her head. 'There were people here who already thought Mhairi was a slut. To tell the world that she thought she was pregnant and not to the man she was living with, on top of already having Sonya to another man . . .' She lowered her eyes from the window. 'I couldn't. I couldn't do that to her. I couldn't do that to Hector.'

'You didn't tell him what she'd said?'

'I've not told anyone. Until now.'

'She wasn't pregnant, though.'

'No.'

'Mrs Sinclair, forgive me, but do you think she made that up? You said you thought she was still hiding something . . .'

'She genuinely believed she might've been pregnant, I'm convinced of that. And if she was, Roddie wasn't the father. I knew my daughter. To me she was everything, but I know she wasn't perfect. She was beautiful and she was headstrong. And she liked boys, she always had. And they liked her. No, Mhairi had slept with someone else, I know it.'

'But you've no idea who?'

'Of course I do. She wouldn't have slept with just anyone.'

'Then who?'

Molly was very still as she debated with herself whether to say. Eventually she said, 'Henry Stuart.'

Rebecca wasn't surprised. It had to be him. They'd been friends since childhood. 'Do you think Roddie could have known?'

'I don't know.'

Rebecca paused before she spoke again. 'If you had told the police about this, if you'd said it in court, then perhaps the outcome would have been different. The lack of motive was one reason why the jury returned a Not Proven.'

'That's what has tormented me all these years. I should've said something about it, but I didn't. I really thought they had enough evidence. He'd admitted it to Bill Sawyer. He was the only one with her that night. He always had a temper, that boy. Oh, such a temper. And when he was acquitted I knew I should've said. But it was too late. Even if I had spoken up, what did it prove? Nothing. No one witnessed what Mhairi told me. The post-mortem didn't show any pregnancy. And by saying something after the trial it could have just been dismissed as lies, a grieving mother trying to get back at the man they said killed her daughter. Anyway, Scotland still had that double jeopardy rule back then. Even if what I said was enough, they couldn't retry him.'

'But you've not shared this with Lord Henry?'

'I don't speak to him at all. I never took to him. There was always something ... off about him. He was polite and courteous but he was ... untrustworthy. He would come into the shop and steal things, little things, but stealing all the same. He could afford to pay for the sweets and the comics but he liked to simply take them as if it was his right. Of course Roddie took the blame. Roddie was always there at his tail and he protected his great friend. But we knew it wasn't him, so we'd let him off with it. Once we called the police, really just to throw a scare into the boy. It was all arranged with Jim Rankin. Hector and Campbell were friends back then, you see, and we didn't want Roddie to get into any trouble, not really. They're not friends now. They don't go out together drinking or shooting. Hector doesn't go anywhere now, not really. Down to the shop, of course. To church, if he feels like it. The only time those shotguns come out of the cabinet is for cleaning.'

It was no surprise that the friendship had died, Rebecca reflected. 'Mrs Sinclair, why have you decided to tell me?'

Molly considered this, trying to understand herself why she had opened up. 'Because I had to tell someone after all these years. Because you have island blood. Because I know you will not print it if I ask you.'

'Are you going to ask me?'

The woman stared directly at Rebecca. 'Yes. Use it as . . . what do you call it? Deep background. Is that right?'

It was a bit *All the President's Men* but it would do. Rebecca stared down at her notes, then reached out and clicked off the recorder. 'Here's what I can promise. I'll do my best to keep it out of any story—if there is a story. But if I feel it has to be included, then I'll speak to you first and explain my reasoning. I will not use it unless I absolutely have to.'

Rebecca knew that if she did do a story, then there was no way she could keep it out. Molly knew it too. She'd known it as soon as she began to talk. But this way she could tell herself that she was tricked. Rebecca studied her face as she nodded.

Rebecca had one more thing to ask. 'Mrs Sinclair, what did you mean when you said that I knew about keeping secrets?'

'Because of your family. The Connollys. Your father.'

'Did you know my father?'

'Not personally. He was younger than me.'

'But you know why he left the island? Do you know why he would never discuss it with me?'

A pause. 'He's never told you?'

'We lost him, a few years ago.'

'I'm sorry.' Molly's sympathy was genuine. She'd known heartbreak too.

'He refused to speak of Stoirm. You must know why.' Molly rose, picked up the empty mugs and carried them to the sink. 'Please, Mrs Sinclair. I'd really like to know.'

'I think I've said enough already.'

'You've not said anything, not about this.'

Molly began to rinse out the mugs. 'It's not my place. It's not my business.'

Rebecca felt cheated. She felt confused. And then she felt angry. 'What the hell is going on here? Why do people clam up when it comes to my father and his family?'

'Because it's a family matter. And I told you, on the island family is everything. Your father didn't want you to know, so it's not anyone else's place to tell you.' She placed the mugs on the rinsing board and turned, wiping her hands on a towel. 'It's all in the past now. Talking about these things merely gives them life again.'

'Talking about what things?'

'Things that are better off dead.'

Rebecca wanted to say more, and she would have, had Hector Sinclair not appeared in the kitchen doorway.

'Hector,' said Molly, 'this is . . .'

His face was dark and hard. 'I know who she is and she's not welcome.'

Sawyer had certainly got around. 'Mr Sinclair, I'm here to help.'

He gave her a sharp little laugh. 'Aye, right, that'll be the day.'

'Mr Sinclair—'

'Look, dear, I know you have a job to do, but you're not doing it here.' His words may have softened but his tone and expression had not. 'The coals you're raking over are best left cold, understand? No good will come of it. Our lass is dead and there's no bringing her back. Now, I'd appreciate it if you left now and please don't bother my family again. Leave us alone. Leave my lass alone. Let her lie in peace.'

Rebecca knew she would get nothing further from Molly Sinclair while her husband was around. Perhaps not even in his absence. She had said her piece. She had unloaded the knowledge she had hoarded for fifteen years and what she knew of the Connollys was not going to be shared. Rebecca had come tantalisingly close to answers, but then the island had shut her down again. She gathered her notebook and her recorder, dropped them in her bag and left. There was nothing more to be said.

* * *

Henry sat back in bed and watched Viola dressing. After all these years he had never grown tired of looking at her body. Perhaps if they had married each other he might have become used to it but as it was they saw each other only a few times a year, when he was in London or she was in the area on constituency duties. She had kept herself very trim, but then again, so had his wife, but he was never the kind of man to be satisfied with one woman. Viola had always shown she was of like mind, even at university. He suspected there might be other men, too, but that didn't matter to him. He wasn't the jealous type.

She was leaving on the late afternoon ferry so he'd ensured he got back to the house for lunchtime, so they could say goodbye in a physical way.

Their friendship meant more than sex, though. She had helped him in many ways, guiding him through the political morass when needed, beating a path through the jungle of red tape and bureaucracy. He ensured she was well compensated for her trouble, the payment disguised so as not to raise any red flags. He also valued her advice, and that was another reason he'd wanted to speak to her before she left, without anyone being able to hear. With Jarji around he hadn't had the chance, and then he'd had to spend the morning on the estate, so this was his opportunity, in the small cottage he gave her during her infrequent visits to Stoirm.

'You have to do something about that fellow Kerr,' she said, as she buttoned her blouse, looking at herself in the dressing-table mirror.

'He's one voice,' said Henry.

'One voice can become many,' she said, echoing Jarji's words earlier that morning.

Henry shook his head. 'The islanders want this development to go through. They know it's good for the island, good for the economy in the long run. Donnie's just speaking out against it because he doesn't like me.'

She turned to face him, smoothing her skirt. 'Speak to him,' she said.

'He won't listen.'

'Pay him off.'

He thought about that. 'It might work. Donnie's always struggling for cash. But he's also pretty damn stubborn and that will make him dig his heels in. That and his intense dislike of me.'

She sat down on the edge of the bed. 'What happened between you two? You used to be friends.'

'Used to be is a long time ago,' he said.

'That's not an answer.'

A vision of Mhairi Sinclair flashed in his mind. They had all been hopelessly in love with her—him, Donnie, Roddie. Other young men on the island. She was the ideal to which they all aspired. Beautiful, smart, funny, sexy as hell—and she knew it. Then she fell pregnant to Donnie, who promptly abandoned her. When he came back he was next to useless. Even so, Henry had tried to involve him in some business he had going, though it turned out Donnie was too far gone to be of any practical use. Donnie's father, Lachlan, had to step in on one particular occasion.

That night.

Henry put it out of his head. He didn't want to think of that terrible night.

'What can I say? Things change. Shit happens. The world turns.'

She gave him a reproving look. 'Henry, listen to me. You need this development. You have investors who would be somewhat less than forgiving if it fell through. You have one very vocal detractor and from what I saw last night there are others who would easily be swayed to his side. And you have a reporter on the island.'

'I've dealt with that.'

172

'The press is unreliable, Henry, and fickle. When you see her on a ferry and leaving the island, then you will know you've dealt with it. Until then, she's like Schrödinger's cat, both dealt with and not dealt with. As for Donnie Kerr, sort it and sort it now. His kind of trouble has a habit of making friends.'

26

Rebecca decided to face Sawyer down. Her encounter with Hector Sinclair had left her bruised and angry, not the least because she felt she had been close to some answers about her father. She was convinced she would've talked Molly round, but her husband's appearance had put paid to that. Sawyer had warned them in advance about her presence on the island and it had got in her way. And who else had he spoken to? She was convinced he had been with Carl Marsh earlier and had followed them to Thunder Bay. Sawyer was worried she would find something out and she was angry enough at that moment to confront him about it.

Ash was at his usual station in reception and told her Sawyer was in the bar. She found the former detective perched on a stool, a mug of coffee and the remains of a sandwich resting in front of him, reading that day's *Herald*. The barmaid was replacing a bottle of whisky on the overhead gantry. The woman gave her a smile and asked, 'What'll you have, hen?'

Even though it was just before three, Rebecca said, 'Gin and tonic, please.' Then she had another thought. 'No, make that a whisky.'

The barmaid nodded. 'Want anything in the whisky?'

'Another whisky,' said Rebecca.

The barmaid smiled. 'A double Grouse okay?'

Rebecca nodded. At that moment she felt the need for something tough and Scottish.

Sawyer's face was blank as he looked up from the newspaper. 'Hard day?'

She gave him a cold look. 'You would know.'

He swung round on his stool. 'You've lost me.'

'I find that hard to believe. I've felt your eyes on my back all day.'

Amusement glinted in his eyes. 'Is this some kind of feminist paranoia?'

Her lip curled. 'What?'

'You thinking I've been looking at you behind your back. This one of those "Me Too" situations? All men are after you, right?'

Rebecca's anger had barely been under control when she'd entered the bar; now, she couldn't hold it back any longer. 'Tell me, do you practise being a dick in front of the mirror or does it just come naturally?'

He didn't seem offended by her words at all. He said nothing as the barmaid came back with Rebecca's drink, took her money and returned with the change. Rebecca gave him another stiff look, then took a mouthful of whisky, felt it slap her tongue awake and burn all the way down. His eyes still sparkled as if they found the whole situation funny, and that pissed her off even more.

'You know exactly what I'm talking about, Detective Sergeant Sawyer.'

He corrected her. 'Former Detective Sergeant . . .'

'Yes, *former* Detective Sergeant William bloody Sawyer. You've been following me, haven't you? And when you've not been doing that, you've been warning people not to talk to me.'

He looked momentarily puzzled, but then the eyes smiled again. No, not smiled, they smirked. Rebecca had never seen anyone smirk with their eyes, but Sawyer could patent it. He took a sip of his coffee. 'The accused pleads guilty to the second count on the indictment but not guilty to the first charge.'

Rebecca took another mouthful of whisky. It hit her empty stomach like lava. 'So you're saying you didn't follow Chaz and me out to Thunder Bay this morning?'

'Not guilty, m'lud. I've seen Thunder Bay before. Don't need to see it again.'

She studied his face for any signs of a lie, but saw none. But then he would be an expert liar. 'But you did warn the Sinclairs about me.'

'I thought it only fair they know that you're intent on opening everything up again.'

'You told them not to talk to me.'

'I told them they didn't need to talk to you.'

She took another drink, a sip this time. She was beginning to calm down. If he wasn't the one with Carl Marsh on that ridge, then who was it? 'What are you so afraid I'm going to find out?'

He expelled a sharp, breathy little laugh. 'Nothing at all, darling . . .'

'I'm not your darling.'

A slight sigh, then 'Fair enough.'

She picked up her glass again, then thought better of it. The spirit was having an effect, she could feel it. Sawyer plucked a packet of dry roasted peanuts from a cardboard display at the side of the bar and dropped them in front of her. He pulled some coins from his pocket and clattered them on the bar, nodding to the barmaid. 'Get them down you,' he said to Rebecca. 'You look as if you need something in your stomach.'

Rebecca stared at the packet as if it was something unpleasant. Without looking at him, she asked, 'Why are you here?'

'You mean here on the island, or is the drink making you all philosophical?'

She looked at him then, a withering glance that told him to stop being a smart arse. He smiled, sipped his coffee. 'I came for Mary's funeral. She was a decent woman, didn't deserve a scumbag like her son. Also, you earwigged on the boat when I had my little chat with your pal Roddie. I knew he would come back and I wanted to see him.'

'To wind him up, you mean?'

'No, that's just an added benefit. Eat the peanuts. They're not poisoned.'

She didn't touch the packet. 'Why do you hate him so much?'

'Because he got away with murder.'

176

'There's no real evidence that he killed Mhairi.'

'Doesn't mean he didn't do it. Eat your peanuts.'

She took another sip, a very small one. She didn't really want it but it was there and it was a small show of defiance. 'You lied in court.'

He looked back at his newspaper. 'I wasn't believed. Not the same thing.'

She dragged a stool closer to her because she felt she had to sit down. She wasn't drunk, although the whisky was singing its way through her bloodstream; it was just that she was suddenly so tired. It had been a long day and it wasn't over. The Molly Sinclair interview, the disappointment at coming so close to getting answers about her father, Hector Sinclair's polite antagonism and the now dissipated rage against Sawyer had all taken their toll. And she was hungry. She tore open the foil wrapping, tipped out a handful of peanuts and shovelled them into her mouth. Sawyer made a show of turning the page and not looking in her direction.

'Thank you,' she said once she had chewed and swallowed.

He gave her a jerk of the head in acknowledgement. 'What are you looking for on the island, Ms Connolly?'

Answers, she thought. *About Roddie Drummond and her father.* 'The truth,' she replied.

He made a smacking sound with his lips. 'Funny thing about the truth, sometimes it's not what you want to hear.'

'For instance?'

He looked back at her again. 'I've already told you—Roddie Drummond is guilty.'

'How can you be so certain?'

'Because he told me.'

27

DS William Sawyer
Fifteen years earlier

The first time I set eyes on Roddie Drummond he was in the sole interview room of the wee police station here. Me and Gavin Burke, a Detective Inspector so new to the rank the ink wasn't dry on his new warrant card, had been sent over on the first ferry that morning. We knew a young woman had been murdered. We knew her live-in lover was found beside the body, his hands and clothes covered in her blood. It seemed to me from the off we had what the Americans would call a slam-dunk. A case barely open before it was shut.

DI Burke said he wanted to keep an open mind, but I'd been in the job long enough to know that the most obvious culprit in a case was usually the one responsible. All that mystery crap was for the telly. If a man is found standing over the body of his girlfriend, then chances are he is the one who put her on the ground, simple as. No different here.

Drummond had agreed to attend voluntarily and had signed the form to that effect. He had allowed them to take his clothes and swabs of his fingernails. He hadn't contacted a solicitor—good luck with that anyway, I thought; there wasn't one on the island and none of those bastards could get themselves over from the mainland as fast as us. Instead he'd phoned his mother, who had shown up with some fresh clothes. He didn't want to see her, though. I spotted the woman sitting at the public bar as I passed through, waiting.

Since Drummond was there voluntarily, he could leave at any time, but the island sergeant told us that he had elected to sleep in the cell. The uniform checked on him over the next few hours and Drummond hadn't slept much. He had asked how Mhairi was, but the sergeant had lied to him, said he didn't know. I wanted to go in hard but the DI wanted to take the softly, softly approach. I knew that was a mistake but I was outranked so I let the boy do what he wanted. I was confident I'd get my chance later. I'd get the truth.

We faced Roddie Drummond across the table. He looked tired. When he spoke, he did so slowly, as if he was drugged. His eyes moved from the DI to me and back again as I began the audio recording process. Drummond was nervous, he licked his lips, his eyes never settled, his hand moved restlessly on the tabletop.

When you've been in the job as long as I have, you can smell guilt, and it was wafting from him across that table like rotten meat.

Burke introduced us, then I asked for his name, address, date of birth—the usual. Drummond gave the details, as if by rote, his voice dull but his eyes alive, still darting back and forward. Once the formalities were completed, Drummond begged to know how Mhairi was. But we didn't tell him right away.

DI Burke took the lead. 'Roddie, let me first make it clear that you are here voluntarily and that during the course of this interview you can request a solicitor present or refuse to answer any questions. Okay?'

Drummond nodded, then started to ask about Mhairi again, but Burke just carried on.

'But any answers you do make will be recorded and may be used against you. Do you understand?'

Drummond blinked. 'Am I under arrest?'

I could see the guy was really spooked now. Burke said he was merely helping us with our inquiries at this stage, then checked he understood the rights and asked if he wanted a solicitor. Drummond waived his rights, I've no doubt he knew what he was doing, he said he had nothing to hide—*aye, right*, I thought—and then he demanded to know about Mhairi.

DI Burke took a deep breath. Time to hit him with it, see how he

179

reacts. 'Roddie, I'm sorry but Mhairi died early this morning. She never regained consciousness.'

Drummond stared at him, his mouth gaping as he took this in. His lip twitched, as if he was going to say something, but didn't say anything. His right hand began to tremble, his nail tapping on the table. His eyes swam. 'But . . .' he began, his words still seemingly unwilling to come. 'The paramedics were there. She spoke . . .'

'Her injuries were too great,' said Burke, his voice soft, as if he meant what he was going to say next. Maybe he did. 'I'm sorry, Roddie.'

Drummond's hand stopped quivering and his entire body was very still for a second, but then he suddenly got up and turned his back on them, resting his head against the wall. We saw his shoulders quiver, as if he was weeping quietly. I saw sympathy all over Burke's face as he nodded to me to switch off the recorder. *Christ*, I thought, *the stupid sod is buying this.*

I checked my watch. 'Interview suspended at 10.05 a.m. to allow Mr Drummond to compose himself.' I clicked the recorder off, sat back, folded my arms. Burke may have fallen for the grieving lover routine but I certainly had not. Drummond was putting on an act, I would bet my pension on it.

'Roddie,' said Burke, his voice gentle, 'you understand that we have to ask you questions, don't you? We need to find out what happened as soon as we can.'

Drummond kept his back to us, face down, forehead and both hands flat against the wall. He made no sound, he didn't move, apart from the slight jerking of his back.

'Roddie, do you want us to come back later?'

I gave the DI a sharp look. I didn't care if he outranked me, we didn't have time for this. Give this joker a break and he might decide he wants a solicitor present, or refuse to answer. I wanted to sort this pronto and get back to the mainland. Burke caught my look and waved his hand dismissively, indicating that he knew what he was doing. I doubted that very much indeed.

Drummond surprised me by pushing himself away from the wall, wiping his eyes with the sleeves of the sweatshirt he was wearing and sitting back down. Burke looked at me, his eyebrows raised in a pretty annoying self-satisfied way, as if he'd got one over one me. Aye, well—we'd see. I clicked the recorder on again. 'Interview with Roderick Drummond resumed at 10.09. DI Gavin Burke and DS William Sawyer conducting.'

Burke said, 'Okay, Roddie, let me ask you once more, do you wish a solicitor present?'

Roddie shook his head.

'For the benefit of the tape, Mr Drummond shook his head,' I said.

'Now,' Burke continued, 'why don't you tell us in your own words what happened last night?'

Roddie placed both hands on the table, laced his fingers together and squeezed so tight his knuckles shone white through the thin flesh. He took a deep, wavering breath. 'I had been out working . . .'

'Where?' Burke asked.

'On the estate. We'd had rain and a burn had burst, flooded one of the estate tenants. I was out operating the digger, shoring up the walls of the burn.'

'Can anyone corroborate that?'

'Aye, some of the lads who do odd jobs. Henry was there, the laird's son. We were all pitching in.'

'What time did you get home?'

Roddie thought about it. 'Maybe half-one, quarter to. I don't really know. Round about then.'

I knew the 999 call was logged at 1.53 a.m.

'And what did you find?' Burke asked.

The young man's hands began to shake again, his breathing grew irregular and he moved his head slowly from side to side, his eyelids blinking back the tears as he remembered. 'She was lying on the floor . . .'

'Mhairi Sinclair?'

He nodded.

'For the benefit of the tape, Mr Drummond nodded his head,' I said, my voice sounding like a bellow in relation to the low tones of the other two. But I didn't care. Burke began hitting him with questions, one after the other, fast as he could. *That's the way*, I thought, *don't give the bastard time to think.*

'Was the front door locked or unlocked?'

Roddie said it was unlocked, they never locked it when they were at home, neither him nor Mhairi. I could see he was thinking fast, maybe placing himself back into that room, determined not to make a mistake.

He said he came into the house, saw her on the living-room floor, next to the fire. It was a coal fire, Roddie said, they burned logs on it and Mhairi must've lit it when she came home. It was cold and he'd set it before he'd gone out. He dropped down beside her when he saw her, he said, spoke to her. Touched her shoulders, he thought. Held her hand, maybe stroked her face. He said he placed her head in his lap to try to clear the blood from her eyes.

Then his eyes began to drift as if he was reliving it all. He shuddered slightly, as if he was cold. I almost laughed.

Burke told him he was doing fine and repeated some of what had been said. Entering the house, the fire lit, her lying on the floor.

'Covered in blood,' I said, just as a wee reminder as to what this bastard had done. He flinched then. I liked that.

Burke asked if she was conscious.

Drummond said he wasn't sure. She was groaning, he said. She didn't say anything, nothing coherent. Maybe his name a couple of times.

Burke switched back in time, asked if he'd tried to help her. Drummond said he wiped away some of the blood, repeated he held her head and her hand.

Next question: 'Was this before or after you dialled 999?'

Drummond stopped to think about this, said he thought it was before. Then he grew more certain that he wiped the blood away before he called it in, then went back to her. That, at least, was consistent with what we had been told. The uniform who attended had done his job well. He reported that he'd observed blood on the handle of the phone.

Burke asked where the baby was during all this and Drummond seemed puzzled at first. Sonya, Burke said, Mhairi's daughter. Where was she?

Drummond said she was in her cot, asleep.

And when Burke asked if he checked on her, he paused again and I knew right there and then that the first outright lie was coming. I saw it in the wee slide of his eyes to the side and in the blink that followed. Up till then, as far as I was concerned, he'd been basically truthful, maybe not told us everything, but he'd stuck closely to what happened. Now he was going to tell us he checked on the child when he didn't. He didn't disappoint me. He said he'd looked in and saw she was fast asleep. But he hadn't done that, I knew it and he knew it. As for Burke, who knew?

We went back over things. Once you'd phoned the emergency services and checked on the child, you went back to Mhairi, Drummond? Correct?

Roddie nodded.

And you cradled her head and held her hand?

Another nod. He spoke to her and said her name. But she didn't respond, he claimed, just groaned, maybe said his name but he couldn't be sure.

Burke reminded him that he'd touched her head, her face and her hands, asked if he touched her anywhere else.

Drummond said he thought she'd stopped breathing and he didn't know what to do. He'd probably touched her shoulders, too, when he tried giving her mouth-to-mouth. He had to lay her down flat to do it. Breathing into her mouth, pushing her chest. He'd managed to dredge up something they'd shown them in school, he said, some first-aid classes. Tilted her head back, cleared her airway, breathed life into her lungs, massaged her chest. He didn't know if her heart had stopped. He admitted he didn't really know what the hell he was doing, he just did what he thought was right and it seemed to work because she started breathing again.

So according to his account, he'd pretty much touched her just about everywhere—head, hands, shoulders, throat, face, chest. So that would explain any strong contact traces, him to her, her to him. He'd thought it all through.

Burke changed tack again, asked if he'd seen anyone hanging around when he arrived home. A car, maybe, lights leaving the scene. Drummond said he saw no one.

Burke asked who would know that they weren't in the habit of locking their door when at home.

Drummond said everyone. No one locks their doors on the island.

Burke asked if they left the doors unlocked even when no one was at home.

Some people do, Drummond said, but added that they did lock their door when they were out because of Donnie Kerr. Mhairi's ex. He was a junkie and Mhairi thought he might rip them off if they left the door open when they weren't at home. He'd only do it to family. It's an island thing, he said, as if that explained everything.

Burke scribbled Donnie Kerr's name down then he asked how well regarded Mhairi was. Was she liked? Was there anyone who might wish her harm?

Drummond said everybody loved her. He said everything was all right between them. No arguments or disagreements. Nothing major. That was his exact words. Nothing major. I had a dead woman lying in a wee room somewhere who would say different if she could.

Burke moved onto Roddie himself, did anyone have a problem with him?

'Or does everyone love you too?' I chipped in.

Roddie looked at me, then paused. 'Carl Marsh.'

'And who is he?' asked Burke.

The estate gamekeeper and estate manager, Drummond explained. He had the decency to look ashamed when he told us that he'd been having it away with Mrs Marsh, prior to him shacking up with Mhairi. Marsh found out about it and gave him a hiding, warned him that it was only the beginning. Drummond took that to mean that it wasn't over. The attack was never reported to the police because it was a private matter, between two men. It was an island thing, he said again.

Burke asked him if this relationship with Mrs Marsh was still ongoing, but Drummond said it ended when he moved in with Mhairi. He claimed it was never that serious, just two people who needed people. I thought a bloody song was coming. He said Deirdre Marsh needed someone to be kind to her, because her husband wasn't what you would call a warm human being.

I asked him, 'And what about you? What did you need? Was this Deirdre Marsh just an easy shag or what?'

He just stared at me again, like he was sizing me up. 'We all need affection, don't we?' he said. 'A bit of warm human contact.'

'And she gave you that, this woman?' I said. 'Warm human contact?'

'Yes,' he said 'Until Mhairi came along.'

I gave him a wee smile. 'And then you dumped her.'

He shifted in his chair, said it wasn't like that. He loved Mhairi, had done since they were kids, but nothing had ever happened. But then it did. He said he didn't want to hurt Deirdre, she meant the world to him, but Mhairi was special. Then he looked straight at me and asked, 'Have you never had anyone special in your life, Detective Sergeant?'

I didn't answer, whether I had anyone special was none of his bloody business, and Burke began his questioning again, circling back, going over what had happened, what he did again and again. Drummond didn't waver from his version, didn't add any unnecessary detail. And Burke really was falling for it, I could tell. But I knew. Drummond was a liar. And worse, he was a murderer. And I was going to do him for it.

28

'So when did he make his confession?' Rebecca asked.

They had moved to a table away from the bar so Sawyer could tell his story. Rebecca didn't take any notes so she hoped she would remember the details. A packet of crisps and two cups of coffee had helped counteract the effects of the double whisky, so she was confident she would. She had promised she wouldn't quote him directly without his permission—what was it Molly had said? Sawyer was deep background.

'Burke left the room to check out the details of Drummond's story with the local uniform . . .'

'Jim Rankin.'

'Yes. He's dead now. Dropped of a heart attack in his garden. Poor bastard had only retired a month before. Bang, down he went.'

'That's a shame.'

Sawyer looked genuinely saddened. 'Aye, just shows you that you never know when it'll hit you. Mind you, he was a big man and his diet was none-too-healthy. I think the only exercise he ever took was pulling on his uniform. Or bending a glass to his lips.'

'Did you know him well?'

'Nah, only through the Drummond case. Never saw him again after the trial. But I heard about his death. His wife found him out there, already going cold. The poor guy should've had a new life ahead of him but it was gone, just like that. Things like that really make you think.'

She was beginning to see a slightly different side to Sawyer. He still struck her as an arrogant misogynist, and possibly a corrupt officer, but she'd seen him stare down the moron squad the night before and she could see his obvious sadness at the passing of a fellow cop, one he barely knew. She was reminded of her father again and his words popped into her head. *Even the worst gangster can love his kids or his dog. Doesn't make them any less the villain, it just makes them human.*

'So, Roddie Drummond just came right out with it as soon as you were alone?'

Sawyer smiled at the scepticism in her voice. 'Let me tell you something, darling, people do the stupidest things but they can be really clever at the same time. Burke left the room, the recorder was switched off—he didn't want me to continue the interview without him.'

'Why not?'

'In case I broke the bastard. He wanted the glory. He was a new DI, wanted to make a name for himself. He was worried I'd nick his thunder.'

'But you continued the interview anyway, without the recorder on?'

His grin widened. 'Bloody right I did. I knew it wouldn't be admissible but I wanted that bastard Drummond to know I was on to him. I told him that I was impressed with his ability to tell just enough of the truth but that I knew he'd missed bits out.'

'Like what?'

'Like he'd actually murdered that girl. That he'd beaten her to death—turned out they found tiny bits of bark in her wounds—of course I didn't know that then. He'd picked up a log and battered her to a pulp, then threw the log on the fire. All ashes by the time we got the forensic report back. So no murder weapon.'

'And what did Roddie say?'

'Nothing, at first. Just sat there, that kind of blank look he has. Like he's plugged in but the power's not on, you know? But he's fired up, right enough. It's all going on behind those eyes. Burke didn't see it but I did.

He's a clever, clever sod, that Roddie Drummond. Massive IQ, did you know that? Could've gone to uni, learned to be a genius, but he stayed here on the island.'

'Why?'

'He wanted to be near Mhairi was my take on it. He was obsessed with her. Even when he was shagging the Marsh woman he was probably fantasising about her. Anyway, I hit him with my views—that he was a lying piece of scum and he killed that girl. I told him that he could fool Burke but he couldn't fool me. I told him I'd get him, no matter what.'

'And that made him suddenly confess?'

'No. He let me talk, kept looking at me—the tears were all gone now, the trembling. All gone. Then he just smiled. That was when I knew for certain that he'd done it. Right then. When he smiled.'

'Confession by smiling? That's a new one. So when did he make the verbal admission?'

Sawyer was not put out by how unimpressed she was. He would have known she wouldn't believe him but he kept talking anyway. 'I was sick of looking at him by then so I packed up the paperwork and got ready to leave him there. I was at the door when he said it.'

Rebecca remembered the words from the coverage of Sawyer's testimony: *You'll never make it stick.*

'Hardly a smoking gun, is it? What happened to "It's a fair cop, guv'nor"?'

Sawyer leaned forward. 'Look, darling, I don't expect you to believe me. Christ, the jury didn't. Bloody advocate depute wasn't even going to lead as evidence. No corroboration. So I had to slip it in myself, on the stand.'

'And help blow your case out of the water.'

'Drummond had a clever lawyer and he made me look like a lying scumbag. Doesn't mean I *was* lying.'

'The jury didn't accept it. You screwed up.'

Sawyer looked over her shoulder as he thought about his next words. For the first time she saw something other than self-confidence in his eyes. Now she saw doubt. 'Don't you think I know that? Not in telling the court what I heard—I know what I heard and the fact that a clever lawyer made sure none of them believed me doesn't mean it didn't happen. We didn't have enough, I knew it even if the AD didn't. It was all circumstantial, his defence didn't need to try hard to argue reasonable doubt. Innocent until proven guilty, right? Well, that bastard was guilty but we just couldn't prove it. Not Proven. That's what they handed down, and in my more reasonable moments—yes, I have them—I know that's the correct verdict. He was guilty but we didn't prove it. The blood on his clothes, the contact traces on her body, even his wounds could all be explained away. He'd tried to help her, he'd held her, he'd perhaps been too rough with her throat when he tried to revive her, he already had wounds after his encounter with Carl Marsh. The only thing we had was a trace of muck and bark on his hand that was similar to samples on the woodpile but the defence argued that he could have picked that up when he was working that night, or when he set the fire. We had no motive, no eye witnesses, no other suspects, we had nothing.'

'So you made up the so-called confession to strengthen the case.'

'No. He said it. If I made it up do you not think I'd come up with something more damning? He said it.'

'Or you were smart enough to make it just weak enough to make it more believable.'

He looked back at her. The doubt was gone and that old certainty was back. 'Don't be fooled by him, darling. Roddie Drummond killed that lassie, sure as we're sitting here. And he sat in that room all those years ago and more or less challenged me to prove it.'

29

Donnie was swabbing the *Kelpie*'s deck when he became aware of a shadow falling across him. He looked up at the dock and recognised the tall figure of Henry Stuart etched against the low sun.

'Can I come aboard?' Henry asked.

At first Donnie was tempted to say no, but he merely waved a hand and the man who had once been his friend swung round the ladder and descended onto the deck. He looked around him. 'Not been on the old *Kelpie* for years. She's looking fine.'

'She's hard work,' said Donnie, although there was a hint of pride in his voice. 'Old boat, one pair of hands.' For a moment he let Henry study his surroundings, perhaps remembering happier times standing on this deck, then asked, 'What do you want, Henry?'

'We need to talk, Donnie.'

'Don't tell me, you're breaking up with me.'

Henry didn't smile. 'What's your problem with the development?'

'You know my problem. You wrap it up as a benefit to the island but we both know it'll only benefit you and your investors. Sooner or later the islanders will be shafted.'

'In what way?'

'I don't know. But I know you and I know the kind of people you're dealing with. Aye, I saw you this morning, talking to the Russian. I thought you would've learned after the last time.'

Henry's eyes were pained. 'Let's not talk about that.'

'Why not, Henry? Maybe it's time we did talk about it.'

'Is that why you've been helping that reporter?'

'Don't know about helping her. I spoke to her.'

'And what did you say?'

'Don't worry. I stuck with the party line. You're safe.'

'We're none of us innocent, Donnie,' Henry said, a hint of sadness in his voice. 'Remember that.'

Donnie knew that to be true. It was something he'd lived with all these years. Something they'd all lived with. There were times it had almost driven him back towards heroin, but he'd fought it. He was clean now and he would stay that way, even if his conscience wasn't pristine. And that conscience niggled at him now as he thought of what he hadn't told the reporter.

Of the man in a coat. A coat with a splash of red.

'This development is important, Donnie,' Henry said. 'To me, to the island. You have to trust me.'

Donnie barked out a laugh. 'Trust you? Henry, I wouldn't trust you as far as I could throw this boat. You're a user. You use people, you use this island.'

'So this is about me and not the development?'

'It's about both. I think your fancy folk will come to the estate and they'll spend their cash with you and you alone.'

'What's good for the estate is good for the island.'

Donnie snorted. 'Henry, I know you, remember? I know you don't believe that.'

Henry held his gaze steadily and Donnie thought he saw something there that he'd never seen before. He was astounded to realise it might be something very close to sincerity. 'A man can change, Donnie. You get older, you see things differently. My father used to tell me the only thing that mattered was the land and the people, and you're right, I didn't buy into that, not then. I've made some mistakes . . .'

'Mistakes that have lined your own pockets.'

Henry conceded that. 'Yes, I've made money. I've done well. But is that so wrong? When my father died the estate was on its uppers. There were debts, lots of them. I could've sold the place easily, cleared them off that way. There was a Saudi prince with his chequebook in his hand,

Donnie, ready to pay over the odds. I didn't sell. I cleared the debts myself. Because the estate is part of my family, part of my heritage. I realised that. The estate is the island, Donnie, and we all need to work together to preserve it. That's why I'm doing this.'

Donnie stared at him, tried to gauge whether he really was sincere. He still saw the young boy he played with and laughed with. That young boy had been capable of lies, just as they all were, but Henry had always been more adept. He often skated free of trouble, not just because his father owned most of the island but also because he was able to deflect blame so very easily.

'It's about planning for the future, Donnie. There's always more money needed here, more expenditure, more work. That's what this plan is all about. We need to make the estate pay its way. It needs to be self-sufficient.'

'You know what worries me, Henry? It's that you'll get all the cake and the island will get the crumbs.'

Donnie saw that his words had hurt but he didn't care.

When Henry spoke, his words came out carefully. 'What if I promised you that you would get a slice of that cake?'

Another explosive laugh. 'You bribing me, Henry?'

'A business proposition. You don't stir up trouble, I'll guarantee you a decent income. You wouldn't need to scramble for customers, Donnie. They'd be served up to you on a plate. A silver plate. My clients will have wives and partners and many of them won't want to partake of the sport on offer. Sure, the new spa will have its attractions but days out on the water, seeing the dolphins and the whales, will be something different for them.'

Donnie sat down on the starboard gunnel and considered this. It would be a godsend financially. It would get him out of the hole, no doubt about it. Guaranteed customers with considerable disposable income. He looked over the side at the water, watched the surface undulate softly against the *Kelpie*'s keel, felt each slight lift and dip as it rode the gentle swell. He had come to know every inch of this boat. He had come to love it and would do anything to keep it. He tilted his head to the sky, saw a tissue of cloud drifting from the west. He looked back at Henry, who was waiting for his answer.

'I'll take my chances, Henry. My own chances.'

Henry looked genuinely disappointed, but Donnie knew he wouldn't try to change his mind. They had been old friends, they knew each other very well. Just as Donnie knew that Henry put himself first, Henry would know that once Donnie had made a decision that was it. He was stubborn to the point of self-destruction. That was his way.

Henry merely nodded then turned and climbed back up to the dock. There was nothing more to be said between them. Donnie climbed the ladder halfway to watch him walk across the quayside to where Carl Marsh waited in his Land Rover. He saw Henry shake his head and say something as he climbed into the passenger seat.

Donnie stepped back onto the deck and returned to the gunnel. He tilted his head back, let the weak sun play on his face and felt the faint pounding in his ears that told him the weather was going to change.

30

Rebecca had suspected that Chaz was flirting with her a little that day and there was a part of her that had responded. He was a couple of years younger but he was easy on the eye, talented and good company. She had also learned he was compassionate and cared about his adopted island home, although he wasn't blind to its failings. What she had gone through in the past year—the baby, Simon—meant she wasn't interested in any kind of relationship but she found she was not averse to spending more time with him. As she rattled out a report on the public meeting and emailed it to Barry, she found she was looking forward to seeing him again. That meant there was more than a twinge of disappointment when she arrived in the dining room to see him sitting at the table with his friend Alan. She kept her smile in place, though. She'd become adept at that in recent months.

Chaz stood up as she approached and gestured towards his slim, sallow-faced companion. 'Alan's joining us, hope that's okay.'

'I hope I'm not some kind of third wheel on this little bicycle built for you two,' said Alan, his eyes smiling.

Chaz blushed and flicked his napkin at his friend. 'Behave.'

Rebecca could feel her own face warming up, so she covered it by studying the menu. 'So what do you do at the big house, Alan?'

'Oh, as little as possible,' he said, with a languid wave of his hand.

'Don't listen to him,' said Chaz. 'He practically runs the place.'

'I've told you a million times not to exaggerate, Chazer. I'm an administrator, that's all.'

'And what does an administrator on an estate like that do, exactly?'

'Paperwork, mostly. Show me a pile of paperwork and I'll administrate the utter hell out of it.'

She could tell he really didn't want to talk about his role in the estate. 'So you work with Carl Marsh?'

Alan's lips pursed. 'Mmm, indeed I do. *Lovely* man. Somewhere there's a party wondering just what the hell happened to its life and soul.'

Ash wheeled over to them and took their order. Chaz and Alan both ordered chicken, Rebecca went for the fish. As she watched Ash glide effortlessly towards the kitchen, she said, 'Does anyone know why Ash is in a wheelchair?'

'Car accident is what I heard,' said Chaz. 'Back in Glasgow.'

'Not as simple as that,' said Alan.

'We don't know that's true,' said Chaz, giving his friend a warning look.

'I got it from Lee-Anne.'

Chaz's face wrinkled dismissively. 'Lee-Anne's a fantasist.'

Rebecca asked, 'Who's Lee-Anne?'

'Seasonal worker,' said Chaz. 'She lives over on the mainland but comes to the island during the summer, works as a waitress in the hotel and up at the big house when there's a need.'

'And what did she say happened?'

'That Ash and his friends in Glasgow went up against some racist thugs,' said Alan. 'Ash came off worst. One of them drove his car right at him, pinned him to a wall. His family moved up here as soon as he was able to travel.'

'No racists on Stoirm then?'

'Oh yes, there are racists everywhere. Hatred is universal. There are no geographical barriers to narrow, bitter little minds.'

Rebecca sensed that he was speaking from personal experience. He had kept his voice light but there was an acidity to the words.

Chaz was still unconvinced. 'Lee-Anne also said that George Clooney once gave her a lift from Inverness to Wick.'

Alan gave the younger man the kind of look a schoolteacher gives an unruly pupil. 'Who's to say that gorgeous George didn't offer a young lady a lift?' He looked back at the menu, even though he had already ordered. 'Anyway, just because she tells the occasional story doesn't mean everything she says is a lie, Chaz.' He smiled at Rebecca. 'But that's Stoirm for you. Stories and lies, with the truth hiding somewhere in between.'

Alan's words made her think about Mhairi and Roddie. She'd learned a lot since her arrival on the island and, coupled with what she'd researched beforehand, she was having difficulty separating fact from fiction.

'Speaking of which,' began Chaz, 'what did you get out of Molly Sinclair?'

Rebecca hesitated, and Chaz correctly guessed why. 'I trust Alan. He's on our side. He's a gossip but that comes in handy sometimes.'

Alan slapped Chaz's arm with the back of his hand. 'Hey!'

Chaz smiled, waiting for Rebecca to talk. So she did. She told them what Molly had said, she outlined her conversation with Sawyer. She threw in details from Donnie Kerr's interview. She filled in what blanks she could from the research she had done. They listened, occasionally dropping in a question or asking for clarification. They paused when Ash brought the food, but if he noticed he didn't seem to mind. Perhaps he was used to it. As she talked, more diners filtered in. Hotel guests, an elderly couple who Rebecca thought she'd seen at the public meeting, a group of four people in casual clothes who talked about their boat in loud voices, saying they had heard there was weather moving in and they'd need to get back to the mainland in the morning, making her assume they had docked at the harbour for the night. And all the while, in addition to their questions, Chaz and Alan kept up their own banter, joking with each other, occasionally launching playful slaps and punches.

Rebecca ate her food as if she hadn't eaten for days, which is how she felt. It had been a long time since breakfast and a packet of peanuts and some crisps only went so far. If she hadn't been talking so much she would've had her plate clear before her dinner companions had unfolded their napkins. She told Ash to put the food on her bill, shushed the protestations from the two men, and they all retreated to the bar. Two of Carl Marsh's moron squad were there, manspreading around a couple of the small round tables while watching football on the TV. They stared at the three of them as they entered and Rebecca heard Alan tut loudly.

'Speaking of small, bitter minds . . .' he said.

Chaz eagerly volunteered to get the drinks in, so Rebecca and Alan moved into the lounge area, which was empty. Once they had made themselves comfortable, and to fill in the awkward gap left by the absence of the one person that linked them, Rebecca asked, 'So, how did you end up on Stoirm, Alan?'

'Shipwreck,' he said. 'Washed ashore like David Balfour in *Kidnapped.*' He smiled. 'My parents finagled the job for me. Perhaps you can tell I'm not from these here parts. My father is one of those legendary figures—"something big in the city"—and when I left university, neither Oxford nor Cambridge, to his eternal chagrin, he feared I would wander aimlessly like a gypsy and get myself into all sorts of trouble. And he was probably spot on. So he prevailed upon Lord Henry to give me a position up here shuffling paper around. And it turns out I have an aptitude for it.'

'It's more than just shuffling paper around, surely?'

'Oh yes, there's email, too. I'm a secretary, Rebecca, a noble profession, to be sure, but still little more than a serf at the beck and call of my superiors.'

'You don't enjoy it?'

'I hate it. But it brings in a modest stipend. I have a nice little flat above a nice little garage that was once a nice little stable. It's far enough away from the big house to give me the illusion of independence. And as superiors go, Lord Henry isn't bad.' He looked up as Chaz appeared from the bar with three glasses perched precariously in a triangle in his hands. 'And, of course, the island does have its compensations . . .'

Compensations. That would be Chaz. She had picked up the signals during dinner, now she knew for certain. Alan and Chaz were involved. So much for Chaz chatting her up—and it explained his curious comment about being a boy scout. *Not in the way you think.* For her part, there was disappointment but also relief. She really wasn't ready. She didn't know when she would be, but she knew it was too soon.

Alan's disdain for the moron squad suggested that he had experienced their bitter little minds in action, for they would be far too manly to accept a homosexual in their midst. As Chaz carefully laid the drinks on the small table and they each took their own, she wondered if he had suffered at their hands, too.

'So, Jessica Fletcher,' said Alan, 'where exactly are we with the case?'

Rebecca thought about it. 'The only thing we can say for certain is that Mhairi Sinclair was murdered. The only person in the frame at the time was Roddie Drummond. He said he found her badly beaten and tried to help. Donnie had seen her earlier that night and she told him she was in trouble. That trouble was that she thought she was pregnant and Henry Stuart was the father . . .'

'No surprise there,' said Alan, his voice low. 'Let me tell you, he's had more women wafting through the corridors of that house than draughts. And there are a lot of draughts.'

'Does his wife know?' Rebecca asked.

'Of course she knows, but she ignores it.' He dropped his voice even further. 'Apparently she's prone to a little bit of extra-marital herself. *Very* fond of a sausage supper, if you know what I mean? Can't say I blame her.'

That earned another flick of Chaz's fingers, but there was a laugh in his voice as he said, 'Behave yourself.'

'Where was Roddie Drummond that night?' Alan asked.

'Working on the estate, fixing a flood. Sawyer said they checked his alibi and it was substantiated, from Henry on down.'

Alan's eyebrows raised. 'Henry was with him?'

'Apparently. The police spoke to him and he said he was with Roddie and the others doing the repairs. Donnie said he was there, too; he was supposed to help but he was too wasted. Why?'

He wiggled his fingers. 'I've never known his lordship to get his hands dirty, is all.'

'It was fifteen years ago. He wasn't lord of the manor back then. People change.'

Alan was unconvinced but he didn't argue the point.

'That doesn't mean Roddie didn't kill Mhairi when he got home,' Chaz said.

'Whose side are you on?' Alan asked.

'Just playing devil's advocate.'

'Chaz is right,' said Rebecca. 'We've got to be open to everything. But there's no tangible evidence that he *did* kill her, despite Sawyer's best efforts to the contrary.'

Rebecca was aware of movement at the doorway and she saw two more of the moron squad peering at them as they passed. One nudged the other and said something, nodding in their direction as he did so. The other laughed and said in a loud voice, 'Hope they disinfect they glasses. Wouldn't want to catch something off them.'

Chaz tensed and looked about to rise, but Alan laid a hand on his arm to keep him in place. His face was expressionless, as if he had heard such taunts so often before and was well used to them. Without even turning round to see if the two idiots were still there, he leaned on the table, his chin propped up on the heel of his hand. 'So, what other suspects do we have?'

Rebecca sat back, gathering her thoughts. 'Carl Marsh, to begin with. He was angry at Roddie. And he was supposedly out that night, God knows where.'

'Probably off killing something, but Mhairi? Bit of a stretch,' said Chaz.

'Perhaps he didn't mean to kill her. He's got a temper, we know that, so maybe he just got carried away. Then there's Deirdre, of course.'

'Ah, a woman scorned,' said Alan, obviously enjoying playing amateur detective.

'Exactly. She was at home alone, according to reports. She might've decided to go and have it out with Mhairi for stealing her toy boy. Again, maybe things got out of hand. I don't think this was a premeditated murder. I think it just happened.'

Chaz and Alan both nodded in agreement. Then Chaz said, 'Then there's Henry.'

Alan held up a hand. 'Now, hang on. Henry may be many things—although I'm still unsure he would be out there in dead of night with his sleeves rolled up—but he's not a killer.'

Chaz shrugged. 'She thought she was expecting. Her mum thought Henry could be the father. His dad was still around back then and there was no way he'd want that kind of scandal. From what I hear he was a decent old codger, though a bit of a snob. The last thing he'd want is to have his boy liaising with a village girl.'

'Liaising,' Alan said, hiding a laugh behind his hand. 'He's *liaised* with a lot worse, let me tell you.'

Chaz looked at Rebecca, inclining his head towards his friend. 'See what I mean about being a gossip?'

Alan began to protest, but then shrugged. 'No, I can't make any sort of denial work. I do like a bit of scandal.'

Rebecca smiled, enjoying their banter. 'We don't know if Mhairi had told Henry, though. And we can't rule out Donnie Kerr either. He was out of his head on drugs back then. Mhairi had been his girl, then she went off with Roddie. Who knows what was going on in his mind?'

Chaz and Alan fell silent and Rebecca wondered if they were pondering, for the first time, the notion that a murderer had been living among them all these years. She threw them another thought. 'But then there's the good old-fashioned opportunist. A stranger, a visitor, who broke in and things turned nasty.'

They nodded but she knew they weren't buying that theory. The killer was an islander. If it wasn't Roddie, it was someone they knew. Perhaps someone they liked.

It was an uncomfortable thought.

31

Gus McIntyre was tense as he sat next to Sonya in the parked car. She had convinced him to drive to the Drummond workshop and cottage and he had finally agreed. He was a few months shy of his seventeenth birthday but had been driving the old Vauxhall his father had bought him for almost a year. Sonya was still plucking up the courage to knock on the door. Outside, night had fallen with such a suddenness that it had unnerved her, even though she was used to the island and its ways. She remembered the old tale her grandfather used to tell her about the night, that it was caused by swarms of blackbirds flying out of Beinn nan sìthichean and blocking the sunlight. Certainly raven-wing clouds had been gathering since early afternoon and were now folded over the moon and the stars. Occasionally headlights pierced the darkness from the north. They'd see them long before the vehicle made an appearance, the twin beams raking the sky, giving the feathery underside of the clouds some substance, before they'd flare through the windscreen, bathing them in bright light, then passing. When the vehicles came from Portnaseil, the lights would first flash in the rear-view mirror, then light up the interior before zooming on to float at speed over the road ahead and the hedgerows on either side before cresting the hill and vanishing. Each time lights glinted from either direction she and Gus would jump apart as if stung, for she knew there was no way he was going to spend this amount of time out here without getting something out in return. That something was still only fervent kissing and desperate groping, though her anger of the previous day was long gone so it wasn't quite so fervent on her part as it had been at the loch.

Her grandmother had told her about the visit from the reporter and it had annoyed her. This was nobody's business, certainly not the bloody papers. She wasn't surprised her grandmother had spoken to the woman, though. Sonya had always suspected she had wanted to tell her more about the night her mother had died but her granddad prevented it. He didn't like to speak of Mhairi and would dismiss her queries with a gruff excuse. *It's all in the past, Sonya.* She hoped that her grandmother would tell her something, now the floodgates had opened, but it was as if talking to the reporter had emptied her. She waved away Sonya's pleas to know more, saying she had already said too much and had only spoken because there was a chance the reporter would try to speak to Sonya. There had been a coolness between her grandparents that evening and Sonya knew it had been caused by the journalist's visit and whatever Molly Sinclair had told her. She had discussed all this with Gus—she had to talk to somebody— and he had agreed with her. This was island business and had nothing to do with mainlanders. That reporter should just go home and leave them alone.

'Somebody should make her go,' Gus had said, his fingers brushing at the hair over her ear before he leaned in for the first kiss of the evening.

She let him kiss and tongue and nibble. She let him touch and fondle and grope. She responded. But her mind was always on the reporter, while her eyes seldom left the cottage door. As her fingers threaded through the short hair at the back of Gus's head, she wondered if she would ever steel herself to stand at that door, to knock on that door, to wait for that door to open and to see Roddie Drummond standing at that door.

And then, the door opened.

And Roddie Drummond was there.

She pushed Gus away and peered through the windscreen. She could just make him out in the soft light cast through the curtains and the bulb above the doorway. He was wearing a long wax coat and a hat and was standing in the courtyard, as if taking the air.

Gus narrowed his eyes to sharpen his vision. 'Is that him?'

Sonya didn't reply. She watched Roddie, as he stood motionless for a few moments. Was he trying to decide what to do? She expected him to move towards his father's transit van, but he thrust his hands in the pockets of the coat and began to walk towards them.

'You going to speak to him then?' Gus asked.

Again, she didn't reply. He turned onto the road and walked towards Portnaseil, slowly, as if still unsure of his direction. As he came level on the opposite side of the road he studied the car parked on the grass verge. Sonya resisted the urge to duck down to avoid being seen. She didn't move. She stared at him through the glass and his eyes caught hers.

Shock filled his face and he froze. His mouth fell open, as if he was about to say something, but then closed again.

'Now's your chance,' said Gus. 'Speak to him—that's why we're here, isn't it?'

Roddie didn't move and neither did Sonya. They stared at each other, separated by the window glass and the breadth of the road. And something else. As if standing between them was her mother, the woman she closely resembled.

'Drive,' she said, her voice hoarse, suddenly not wishing to be here. She needed to be somewhere else, anywhere, just not here on this stretch of island road with the clouds merging above them and the breeze whispering to the ghosts of the past who lurked in the darkness. 'Drive!'

Gus turned the key and the engine roared. He hit the pedal so hard the Vauxhall jerked forward, its rear wheels churning at the grass verge, and they took off down the road. She twisted in her seat to look through the window behind her. Roddie was still standing there, watching them roar off. Then the darkness swallowed him.

* * *

Donnie Kerr stood on the stone harbour above the *Kelpie* and stared up at the black sky. He felt pressure in his temples and something heavy hung in the air. He could hear a hiss on the surface of the water, as if the air was telling it to limber up. No one else would hear it, only him. He looked down at his boat as it bobbed restlessly on the slight swell. It had been a slow day, only two customers, but when the storm struck there wouldn't even be that. That was the season well and truly over, he decided. It hadn't been the best but it sure as hell wasn't the worst.

He breathed in a deep lungful of night air, felt a coppery tang on his tongue. Tomorrow, the next day, it would hit and hit hard. He gave the boat another look, satisfied himself that it was well battened down and would easily ride out the weather in the sheltered harbour. He had come to love that boat, something that would have surprised his younger self. It was the only thing standing between him and unemployment, but his affection came from something deeper. He was an islander and the boat was part of the island and its life. That was a lesson his father had tried to teach him, that Stoirm was more than simply the place he had been born, it was something that lived in the blood and the heart, but he had scoffed. His natural sailing skills and his affinity for the elements were things he had tried to deny and even escape. If heroin can be seen as an escape.

He knew the decline in the fishing industry had deeply affected his father, not to mention the decline in his son. Lachlan had scraped through, though he had taken risks that he shouldn't have, going out in seriously rough weather, ignoring quotas occasionally, actively breaking the law in order to keep his head above water. Donnie was certain the stress of those years, when he himself took solace in drugs, had taken such a toll that his father's body just gave up.

The unseasonably warm air was not unpleasant as he walked along the harbour towards the Square, even though it was the herald of something that would be the opposite. He thought about Henry's offer. He thought about his own bills. He was getting by, but only just. He could have accepted the bribe, for that was what it was, and life would be easier. But he couldn't—it would mean he was bought and paid for. He could not become part of Henry's pursuit of profit, not again. He'd ride out any financial tempest somehow, just as the *Kelpie* would ride out the storm.

Seeing a figure on the edge of the Square, he stopped dead. He couldn't make out who it was but that wasn't what sent the shock tingling from the nape of his neck to his back, arms and fingers. It was the coat and the wide-brimmed hat. He had seen it before, years before.

That night.

It hadn't been a junkie's fever dream. It had been real.

It was the same one, he knew it. As he drew closer he saw the splash of red on the shoulder, faded now but still there.

He quickened his step and the figure turned. Donnie was on the harbour side of the Square and the man was on the far corner at the bottom of the road leading to the Spine, but even at that distance he could make out who it was.

Roddie.

Donnie began to run. He had intended confronting him after Mary's funeral, there being something distasteful about doing so while his dead mother was still above ground. Once Mary Drummond was lying warm in the island earth, then he would speak to him.

Roddie heard him approach and looked his way briefly, recognition clear on his face, then he turned away again to head back up the incline towards the Spine, disappearing beyond the range of the Square's lights. Donnie's feet pounded on the concrete and he reached the roadway in seconds. He paused in the shadow created by the hotel and the bar and peered up the incline, his eyes very quickly adjusting to the darkness, but there was no sign of Roddie. Where the hell had he gone? Donnie held his breath and listened for footfalls but heard nothing. He sighed and turned back towards the Square, his mind spinning. The coat. The hat. The splash of red. It was real. All real. He forced himself to remember. The years and his condition at the time had caused his memory to fragment and shatter until what was left were shards that sliced behind his eyes. The wind. The rain. The figure in the roadway outside the cottage. A tall man, taller than Roddie. Not Roddie. Most certainly not Roddie. Then, who?

The realisation hit him just as he reached the rear corner of the pub, where the emergency exit opened out. So lost was he in trying to piece together the broken glass of his memory that he was unaware of the furtive movement and the dark shape breaking free of the shadows. He sensed the attack and tried to turn, but he was too late and the figure too fast. Something harder than a fist slammed into the side of his head. Bright lights danced before his eyes as the pain rocked through his skull and he staggered, dimly aware of something long and slim swinging up again and cracking across his left cheek, snapping his head to the right and taking the rest of his body with him. Then another blow crashed across his ribs and he slumped to his knees. He tried to raise his fists but he had no strength. Another hard crack across his face sent him spiralling to the ground.

He lay on his belly. He tried to move, his right cheek scraping against the gravel on the roadway. A pair of booted feet stepped into his line of vision. A foot was raised, he saw the treads on the underside of the work boots, then it was rammed into his face with such force that it put his lights out for a few moments.

Consciousness flickered briefly and he saw Roddie standing a few feet away, looking down at him, his eyes wide. Then Donnie's vision began to swirl once more. He was sucked down and down and down, to where the world was cold and silent and deep.

32

Lord Henry stood at the window of the small office, as if studying the rain spattering against the glass. The weather had broken during the night and the new day awoke to leaden skies with darker smudges promising worse was to come. The black clouds matched his lordship's black suit. His funeral suit. For this was when they were to lay Mary Drummond in the ground.

Alan Shields stared at his employer and did his best to hang on to his temper. The man hadn't actually come out and accused him of anything, but there was an inference draped over his tone that he didn't like. Lord Henry paid his wages, but he was not going to sit still while he was being damned by inflection.

'I really think you should spell out what you're accusing me of,' he said, his voice flat as he fought for control.

They were in Alan's office in the big house, a cramped little room with the single window looking out onto the courtyard. Despite Chaz's expansive comments regarding his duties, in reality he was fairly low on the estate's totem pole. His facility with numbers meant he dealt with payroll and, by extension, personnel, but to call him human resources would be giving the term an elasticity that it did not actually possess. He'd called himself an administrator but even that was giving his position nobility. He was a clerk, a paper pusher, a lowly functionary. If anything proved that his employment was little more than a favour on Henry Stuart's part for a friend with deep pockets and the ear of many in the city, it was the fact that he shared this little room not only with the cleaner, whose accoutrement cluttered up the corner behind the door, but also with reams of printing paper and materials, all of which lined the shelves behind his desk. In his more honest moments, Alan wondered if his father, who had arranged the job, also financed not only his wages but also his room and board. His father loved him, he was a decent man, and he so desperately wanted his son to feel valued. The truth was, Alan would've jacked in the whole thing if it hadn't been for Chaz. He'd tried to get him to leave with him, head to a city somewhere, live together, make their way together, but Chaz needed the surety that he had something to go to. A job. A reputation.

His lordship seldom looked Alan in the eye. Perhaps to do so might serve to recognise him as some sort of equal. However, this time he was watching something in the courtyard, so Alan quietly craned upwards in his chair to look over the sill to see Carl Marsh, a flat cap on his head, talking to one of his moron squad. Alisdair something, Alan thought. He had never bothered to learn their names because that would give them a humanity they didn't merit. He and Chaz had both suffered too much verbal abuse from each and every one of the little shits.

'I'm not accusing you of anything, Alan,' said his lordship. 'I merely asked if you discussed any estate business with that reporter last night. You were seen having dinner with her in the hotel. Along with your friend.'

There was a curious emphasis on the word *friend*, as if His High and Mightiness really wanted to say *fuck buddy*. Chaz was more to Alan than a roll about in bed, which they had done quite energetically the night before, thank you very much, and the word 'friend' was too anaemic for how he felt about him. As for who had tattled the tale of him being with Rebecca, that could only have been one of the moron squad. Perhaps the one outside talking to Marsh.

'She didn't ask anything about the estate,' Alan said.

Carl Marsh had completed his conversation and was striding

across the courtyard, deep lines gouging his cheeks. Alan sensed that whatever the youth had told him, he didn't like it.

Henry continued to watch his estate manager as he said, 'Then what did you talk about?'

Alan saw no reason to lie. 'Roddie Drummond. That's why she's on the island.'

Henry digested this. 'So, she's not here about the development?'

'She didn't mention it.'

Henry turned, this time meeting Alan's eyes. As they stared at one another, Alan saw his employer was debating how trustworthy he was. *Good luck*, Alan thought. *I've been lying with considerable fluency since I was a teenager. Try discovering you're gay when your family is filled with red-blooded men who like to hunt, shoot, fish and play sports in which men touch each other frequently but in what they see as an acceptable fashion.*

'And what can you tell her about Roddie Drummond?' his lordship said, still watching Alan closely.

'Absolutely nothing. He was merely the subject of conversation at the table.'

'Was I mentioned?'

'In what regard?'

Henry's jaw clenched as he tried to retain his own temper. For himself, Alan had relaxed and was enjoying himself. He and his employer had never warmed to each other. Lord Henry was uncomfortable with Alan's open homosexuality, and Alan didn't like his lordship's bare-faced avarice. Or his womanising. God knows Alan was no prude, but Lord Henry's sexual adventures made *Fifty Shades* look like Enid Blyton.

'In regard to Roddie Drummond, Alan,' said his lordship, his voice tense.

'Only that you were all friends as children.' Alan didn't mention the fact that he had bedded the dead woman too. Chances were Lord Henry wouldn't remember. No one could remember that many names. 'And that you gave Roddie an alibi for the night of the murder.'

That got a reaction. Lord Henry was adept at hiding his true feelings but Alan saw a little tremor run across his brow. 'Alibi?'

'He was with you that night, digging ditches.'

Henry paused to take this in, as if he couldn't remember where he'd been that night. Then he said, 'Yes, that's right. And your, em, friend Chaz Wymark, he's helping her in this investigation?'

'He is.'

Henry nodded, turned to the door. 'Thank you,' he said and left the room.

Alan smiled as the door closed. Something told him his days were numbered on the estate. He couldn't say he would be sorry to see it go.

* * *

Henry walked the corridors of the house, his mind turning over what little he'd learned. That little gay bastard wasn't telling him everything, he was certain. But what was more annoying was that the bloody reporter was still on the island. He had been with Carl Marsh when she visited Thunder Bay and she'd shown far too much interest in that part of the island for his liking. The pressure on her newspaper hadn't borne fruit. As Viola said, the press is unpredictable and fickle but he really thought appealing to their balance sheet would do the trick. Well, he'd show them he meant it. He'd cancel all advertising immediately and he'd suggest to friends in Inverness they do the same. That would bring the bastards to heel.

But the alibi, that was the real problem. He had a vague memory of what he'd said back then, but would it hold water now?

33

Deirdre's Marsh's body jolted in shock when her husband all but kicked the front door of their cottage open. He had left only an hour before to begin his day but here he was back again, his face as dark as the clouds. She was in the hallway and he lunged at her as soon as he saw her. She tried to get away but he grabbed her by the hair and dragged her into the kitchen. It was always the kitchen, never any other room. Always the kitchen with its easily cleaned vinyl flooring.

She yelped in pain as he gave her a ferocious tug and propelled her across the room to slam into one of the chairs circling the kitchen table. She tripped and fell to the floor. He loomed over her, his eyes hard and cold, his fists—those fists—clenched tightly at his sides.

Deirdre held up a hand as if to ward off a blow that had not yet been swung. 'Carl, what . . . ?'

'You were seen, slut.'

His words came in a harsh rasp, as if anger had scraped the surface off them, revealing something raw and ugly. At first she didn't understand, just a brief moment that furrowed her brow. 'Seen? Wh—' Then the realisation sliced her words.

'That's right,' he said. 'Don't deny it because you know it won't do any good. *Cow.* You dirty . . .' He kicked her, his boot catching her on the thigh. 'Adulterous . . .' He kicked her again, his aim higher, and she whooped for air as she doubled over. 'COW!' The third kick landed squarely on her chest and drove what little breath was left out of her

211

lungs. She gasped and sprawled on the floor, hands scraping for purchase, but her nails merely slipping on the smooth surface. Bile rose into her throat and she tried to cough it up but couldn't.

He stepped away and she thought—hoped—it was over, but he was only pausing to take off his wax jacket.

This one was going to be bad, she knew it.

* * *

When Rebecca went down for breakfast, she learned from Ash that Donnie Kerr had been found in the roadway unconscious. It had all happened after Chaz and Alan had left and she'd gone up to her room. The way he'd heard it, some bloke had rushed into the bar just before closing, said there was a guy outside needed help, then rushed out again. The bar was empty and by the time the barmaid had understood what had been shouted the guy was gone—but Donnie was bleeding on the road.

'He'd been given a right doing,' said Ash, shaking his head. 'Never heard anything like this, not here.'

'Where is he now?' Rebecca asked.

'The hospital. Doctor Wymark was called in. Seems he's still out of it. He got a right going-over. Lucky he's not dead, apparently.' Ash shook his head. 'This doesn't happen here. There are fights, aye, punches thrown, but not like this. We had the local police in here. Terrible, terrible.'

'Does his family know?'

'Donnie has no one, apart from the Sinclairs and Sonya. I think they've been told.'

Rebecca's first thought was to head to the hospital, but they wouldn't tell her anything, let alone let her see him. Ash left to fetch her breakfast and she looked up to see Chaz heading her way. He looked very smart in a black suit and tie. They would both attend Mary's funeral, but she would keep a respectful distance from the actual mourners. Chaz had known the woman and he was entitled to be there, but she was an outsider.

212

He dropped his wet umbrella beside the table and sat down. 'You heard about Donnie?'

'Ash told me. What does your dad say?'

'He's still up there and Donnie's in a coma. Dad is worried there might be brain damage. Whoever did it beat him with a metal fence post and then took their boot to his head.'

'Do they know who?'

He shook his head. 'Not a clue. Pauline didn't know who the guy was that raised the alarm. Never seen him before, she said.'

'Pauline?'

'Behind the bar. She runs it.'

It could be a visitor, but Rebecca's first thought was Roddie Drummond. She didn't know why. A gut feeling.

* * *

Sonya sat at her father's bedside, the sounds of the small hospital seeming to converge on his tiny room. The ping of the monitor measuring Donnie's vital signs was loudest, but outside the door she could hear her gran and granddad talking in low voices to Dr Wymark. Beyond them was a TV playing some stupid daytime programme. She stared at Donnie's face. They had cleaned him up and dressed his wounds but his skin was waxen. He had always looked so healthy, so full of life. Now he looked dead.

He was breathing on his own and they said that was a good thing. He wasn't dead. But he wasn't alive, either. Not really. Not the way he should be.

The hospital was small, Dr Wymark had said, facilities were limited. He'd have to be taken to the mainland, to Inverness, for specialist treatment and they'd need to call in a helicopter. They wouldn't let her go with him, so she was spending what time they had now.

She held his hand, wishing his fingers would tighten and squeeze, just like she'd seen in films, but they remained loose. They were warm but lifeless. Like sticks, sitting in the palm of her right hand. She wiped away tears with her free hand. She'd heard people say that even if you were in a coma you were still aware of what was going on around you. She'd asked Dr Wymark and he'd said he didn't know. No one really knew.

She leaned in closer to the bed and whispered in Donnie's ear. 'If you can hear me, let me know somehow.'

She waited. The bleep of the EEG was like a clock ticking.

'It's me. Sonya. Your daughter. Your wee lass . . .'

He'd call her that now and again, knowing it would get a rise out of her. It was okay when she was little but she was grown up now, she was a woman. She'd always called him Donnie; it seemed strange to call him Dad, even though she knew he was her father. He didn't mind. He hadn't been much of a father when she'd needed one, when she was younger, but he'd tried to make up for it. She knew that.

Tears tumbled from her eyes and she let them fall. She wasn't going to let go of him, not now. He'd come back to her, she was certain. He wouldn't go, not like this, not like her mother.

She glanced at the open door, saw her grandparents still outside with Dr Wymark, so she lowered her voice even further. Donnie would still hear her, if he could.

'This is all that reporter's fault. Her and Roddie Drummond. They caused this. Things were just fine and then they had to come and spoil it all.' She swallowed. 'But I'll get her. I'll get them both. I promise you, I'll . . .'

The EEG suddenly started to ping furiously and Donnie's body began to tremble, then convulse with such violence that his hand snatched itself from between hers. She screamed and shot out of the plastic chair just as Dr Wymark rushed in, closely followed by a nurse. Sonya backed against the wall, watching them as they attempted to stabilise him. She heard them speak, their words calm but urgent, but she didn't understand what was being said.

Dr Wymark glanced at her and said to the nurse, 'Please take her out of here.'

Her gran moved quickly, wrapped her arms around her and tried to pull her from the room, but Sonya rooted herself to the spot, unable to look away as her father bucked and shook on the bed, his eyelids

214

fluttering open and shut, open and shut, the whites of his eyes flashing each time.

'Dad!' she screamed, the word wrenched from her. 'Dad! Dad! Dad!'

* * *

Deirdre curled up on the kitchen floor, feeling the blood trickling from her scalp onto the vinyl. She was numb. He had kicked and punched and kicked her again, each assault accompanied by a snarl filled with hatred. She had never seen him so bad. And this time he did not weep in the front room. He did not go away on his own to wallow in the guilt as it crept up on him.

She carefully straightened one leg, then the other, and though she could feel the numbness thawing she felt the pain scream. She moved her arms, the agony screeching through her. Nothing was broken, she was sure, and although she had been groggy she hadn't passed out, which she assumed to be a good thing. She was badly hurt, she knew that. Her fingers, hands, arms trembled as she tried to rise, but she didn't have the strength to battle through the pain. She'd found such strength before but this time it evaded her, so she lay on the floor and let the ache take over her body, knowing it would pass. Even though it was bad this time, the worst she had ever experienced, it would pass. She was in agony and she was bleeding, but she was alive and it would pass.

Carl had stamped out of the kitchen, muttering expletives. She had heard her name and Roddie's. She had followed his footsteps along the hallway and into the small cupboard where he kept his shotguns locked away in a tall green locker. She heard the clang of the door as it was thrown back and then he stormed out of the cottage. He hadn't taken his jacket with him, she noticed, and the rain was really coming down. She could hear it battering off the roof. He'd catch his death out there, she thought. Then, despite the pain and the anguish that kept her lying on the cold floor, she smiled. Catch his death. She should be so lucky.

She decided to attempt to move again. She didn't think she could stand, but she could try to crawl. She hauled her upper body onto her elbows and forearms, each tiny movement raising a cacophony of hurt,

215

and she paused, Sphinx-like, for a few moments, gathering her strength and her resolve. She didn't know how long she had before he came back. She knew he would come back; he always did. And if he returned with the intent of starting on round two, she planned to be ready for him.

Taking a deep breath and almost crying from the shock, she started to drag herself towards the kitchen door.

34

Rebecca huddled under her umbrella against the rear wall of the church. The mourners who had defied the weather to say goodbye to Mary Drummond stood around the grave at the far corner of the graveyard. It was quite a turnout and indicative of how well regarded the woman was that even the glowering clouds and darting rain couldn't keep people away. There was a forest of umbrellas, mostly black, like dark mushrooms sprouting in the dampness.

Roddie, dressed in a long black coat, stood with his father and his sister Shona, who Rebecca recognised from the harbour the day she arrived. At her side was a man she assumed was her husband and a girl of about eight or nine years. The child was the spitting image of her mother, Rebecca noted. There was a slight gap around this family grouping, just as there had been around Campbell at the public meeting, but Rebecca couldn't say whether it was through respect or the toxicity that seemed to cling to Roddie. Shona and her daughter sheltered under a single umbrella held by her husband, while Roddie had one to himself. Their father spurned any kind of shelter: Campbell was stiff and erect as he stared at the coffin that had been lowered into the grave, his hands clasped in front of his black woollen coat as if he was praying. Shona was crying and her brother had surreptitiously reached out with one hand and clasped hers to offer comfort.

Fiona McRae had made it back to the island and was standing at the head of the grave, solemnly reading the poem by Henry Scott Holland, 'Death Is Nothing At All'. The lines told them that Mary had only slipped away into the next room. The Reverend may have believed that but Rebecca didn't. There was no next room. There was only this room, this world, and what people left behind.

Rebecca now fully remembered seeing the minister at her father's funeral, when she and her mother had been standing at the door of the crematorium while people walked by, shook their hands, mouthed condolences. It's a curious form of torture for all concerned, the post-funeral line-up. Friends, relatives of her mother but none from her father's side, police colleagues, neighbours, even a couple of crooks her father had arrested, had all walked that line, their faces solemn, their voices hushed as if they were fearful they would waken the dead. But the dead were beyond being disturbed. Their flesh was but ashes, their bones ground up, poured into an urn to be presented to the grieving. What had once been living and breathing was dust; what made them what they were was gone. There was no next room. There was no great beyond. There was only an eternity of nothing. Those who had gone lived only in memory and that was fleeting and faulty.

Fiona McRae had been one of the people who solemnly walked the line to Rebecca and her mother. A shake of the hand, a sorry for your loss, then she was gone. Watching her now as she intoned the words of the poem, Rebecca promised herself she would talk to her that day. She had questions about her father and she had to have answers. There had been too many looks that were like half-finished sentences. She felt sure the minister would have the answers she needed.

She saw Bill Sawyer and Lord Henry Stuart in the crowd, a few other faces that had become familiar during her stay, including the woman she'd met on this very spot. Was it only two days ago?

Dr Wymark wasn't there; he had duties at the hospital, where she'd heard Donnie had taken a turn for the worse. Terry Wymark was there, though, looking stunning in black, as she stood beside her son. No Alan, though. He'd told Rebecca that he detested funerals. She couldn't blame him.

The clang of the gate at the bottom of the steep path reached her ears. A latecomer, she thought, but whoever it was had missed it all.

The funeral party was breaking up, the mourners drifting away from the grave. Even Roddie and his sister's family were edging back. Only Campbell remained. He was drenched. Rebecca could see that even from this distance. He was in the same position, head bowed, hands clasped, a few feet and an eternity away from his wife. Did he buy the whole next room thing, she wondered?

A cry of alarm made her look to her right. Carl Marsh was striding towards the mourners, his boots splashing in the rainwater gathering in the gravel, his thick woollen jumper and his bare head soaking wet, the shotgun in his hands held at waist height. His attention was fixed on Roddie Drummond. He marched across the grass and the paths and the graves, coming to a halt within six feet of his target and raising the weapon to shoulder level.

'Drummond, you wife-stealing bastard!' he screamed.

Roddie saw him then, his face liquid with fear. His body steeled itself to flee but he had nowhere to run. To his credit he pushed Shona aside, just as her husband snatched the child out of the line of fire. Campbell snapped out of his reverie and looked up, his eyes at first dreamy but then solidifying into something more of this world when he saw Marsh and the weapon.

Bill Sawyer was the first to move, edging forward, his hand out. 'Carl, put the gun down . . .'

'You go to hell,' said Marsh without looking at him.

Sawyer took another step and Marsh swung the barrels of the shotgun in his direction.

'Take another step and I'll send you to hell myself. I mean it.'

'Carl!' snapped Henry. 'Have you lost your mind?'

Marsh's eyes flicked towards his employer, then he jerked the weapon back in Roddie's direction. 'All due respect, your lordship, but this is none of your concern. This is between me and this murdering bastard. I should've done this years ago.'

A handful of mourners ran for the gate, their panicked voices floating among the raindrops. Suddenly, the downpour was thunderous, drilling at the ground and the people on it, but those who remained were oblivious. All eyes were fixed on the drama in front of them.

Henry took a step closer. 'Carl, I don't know what's happened but—'

'I'll tell you.' Marsh cut him off. 'He's not back a day and he's had my wife, my Deirdre, in his bed. That's what's happened. She was seen, yesterday, at his cottage. Not even back a day. Not even a single bloody day!'

Sawyer and Henry both looked at Roddie, but all he could do was shake his head. It was left to Campbell to answer. 'That's not true, Carl . . .'

Marsh sneered. 'You would say that, he's your son. What is it they say on the island? Family is family and everything else is just everything else. That right? You all do it, all you bloody islanders. Stick together. Protect each other. Lie for each other.'

Roddie finally found his voice. 'Deirdre came to see me, I won't deny that. But nothing happened. We just talked, that's all. Just talked.'

'You expect me to believe that? After what happened before, between you and her? I started a job back then, when I battered lumps out of you . . .' Marsh steadied the stock of the shotgun against his shoulder, lowered his eye along the barrel. 'Today I'll finish it.'

Campbell stepped in front of his son. 'You'll need to kill me first, Carl.'

'Get out of the way!'

Campbell didn't move.

'For God's sake, Carl,' said Lord Henry. 'Don't be a bloody fool!'

Marsh kept the shotgun trained on the Drummonds. 'I'll take you, too, if that's what you want.'

'You'll have to,' said Campbell, his voice very calm.

'And me.'

Shona's voice, her face streaked with tears as she moved to stand in front of her father.

He pulled her aside, kept himself between his children and the shotgun.

Marsh, his cheek pressed against the wooden stock, smirked. 'See what I mean? You all stick together, even when he's a dirty, murdering wife-stealer. Family, it's all family . . .'

Then Sawyer placed himself in the line of fire. 'I'm not family, Carl. God knows I've got no great love for Roddie Drummond, but this . . .' He held up both hands. 'This isn't right.'

'It may not be right, but it's fitting. He should've been put down before—it would've saved everyone a lot of grief. He should've been taken up into the hills, like the old days, at birth. Drowned up there. That lass would still be alive. My wife would still be my wife.'

Fiona McRae had moved closer to the line of fire and Carl finally noticed her. 'This doesn't concern you, love. This is to do with the flesh and the blood, not the soul. Once this is done he'll be your business, but not before.'

'My concern doesn't begin and end with the afterlife, Carl,' she said, still moving, not to the group in front of Roddie but towards Marsh. 'And even if it did, you're placing your own soul in jeopardy here.'

He laughed, a bitter, snarling sound. 'Don't preach to me, love. I'm not one of your flock. I'm not a believer. Save it for that hypocrite there.'

Fiona kept moving. 'Carl, I know you're not a believer, but Deirdre is. She never misses services, you know that. Do you think this is what she wants?'

'I know what she wants. She wants that one'—he jerked the barrels and the sudden movement startled Fiona, but she kept moving slowly towards him—'between her legs. She's made that plain. But I've taught her a lesson about that. She won't make that mistake again. But just in case . . .'

Fiona's eyes narrowed. 'What kind of lesson, Carl?'

He didn't answer her.

'Carl, what kind of lesson did you teach your wife?'

'That's no concern of yours.'

Fiona edged closer. 'Where did you get the blood on your hand, Carl?'

Marsh twisted the shotgun to the right so he could study his left hand, the one that gripped the weapon's forearm. Rebecca leaned to her left to see for herself the smears of blood, wet from the rain.

Still moving, slowly and carefully, Fiona asked, 'Whose blood is that, Carl?'

He didn't answer, but the barrels of the gun dipped slightly. There had been a change in his body language. Whereas before he'd been tense and erect, now his back had curved, his shoulders had drooped. He had been angry and resolute when he arrived but now there was something else. Although she didn't have a clear view of his face, Rebecca felt she knew what that something else was. Shame.

Fiona was directly in front of him now, the barrels level with her chest, but she ignored them. There was an edge to her voice now. 'Where's Deirdre, Carl?'

The rain drummed in the silence that followed. Sawyer had eased to the side and was almost casually making his way closer to Marsh. Rebecca scanned the faces of the remaining mourners. Some were terrified. Some were blank, as if they didn't fully understand what they were witnessing. Others were hard and knowing. They didn't need to be told where Deirdre was or whose blood was slowly being erased by the torrent.

Fiona knew she wasn't going to receive an answer. Her tone softened. 'Put the shotgun down, Carl.'

Marsh didn't move.

Sawyer sidled ever closer, picking his way through the gravestones.

Fiona poured some grit back into her voice again. 'Carl, you're not going to shoot anyone, certainly not the person you want to shoot. Look . . .' She jerked her thumb behind her, to where Roddie was shielded by his father and sister. Marsh raised his head to gaze over her shoulder, seeing them as if for the first time. 'This will not change anything, Carl. This will not change the past or fix the present. All it will do is ruin the future. Put the shotgun down, Carl. Let's all get out of the rain.'

She raised her hand as if to take the weapon but Marsh took a step back, the barrels rising again. This time she didn't flinch. 'You don't want to do this, Carl, not really. I know you don't . . .'

His brittle laugh cut through the hiss of the rain. 'That's where you're wrong, love. I really do.'

He stepped around her and steadied the weapon again, his finger on the trigger. It was a quick, fluid movement but Sawyer was close enough now to reach out for Carl, though he saw him and swung the shotgun in his direction. Fiona was also in motion. She ducked under the barrels to catch Carl in a rugby tackle, forcing his body backwards and the weapon upwards just as the trigger jerked. The blast shot harmlessly into the air. They slipped on the wet ground, Carl still holding the weapon but Fiona on top, forcing it hard against his chest. Sawyer reached them and wrested the gun from Carl's hands.

Fiona stood up and wiped the mud from the front of her robe, then waved to the Drummonds to leave. Roddie bundled Shona away, but Campbell lingered, giving Carl, still lying on the ground, a long look. Then he followed his family from the graveyard. Those mourners who still hung around filtered towards the gate with them. Chaz and his mother seemed to be waiting for Rebecca to move, but she gestured for them to go on ahead. She wanted to stay for a while.

Sawyer checked the shotgun was safe but still left it cracked open as he crooked it over his arm. He stooped to haul Carl up from the ground.

'Stupid bastard,' he said.

Lord Henry shook his head at his estate manager but said nothing as he, too, walked away.

Sawyer had a wry smile on his face. 'I think that means you're fired, pal.'

With no weapon in his hand and the object of his hatred now out of sight and heading down the pathway towards the gate, Carl Marsh seemed deflated. His shoulders were hunched, his eyes cast downwards. Rebecca could almost feel sorry for him.

If it wasn't for the blood on his hands.

Fiona hadn't forgotten about that either. Her voice was cold when she spoke. 'What have you done to Deirdre, Carl?'

It looked at first as if he wasn't going to answer, but then he said in a dull monotone, 'She's at home.'

Sawyer's voice was harsh. 'You weren't asked where she was, you were asked what you did to her.'

Marsh seemed to think about this before he raised his eyes to Sawyer. 'What any man would do. I taught her a lesson.'

Sawyer glanced at Fiona and gave her a little nod. Then he gripped Marsh firmly by the shoulder. 'Come on, then. Let's go see . . .'

It had looked as if the fight had gone out of the estate manager, but he had either been faking or it suddenly returned, for he moved very fast, twisting himself free and slamming the former police officer firmly with both hands on the chest. Sawyer lost his footing and tumbled back, landing hard on the gravel path that ran between two rows of graves. Fiona reached out but Marsh swiped her hand away and darted off, his feet slapping hard on the gravel. Sawyer swore once, and powerfully, but then he was on his feet, still holding the shotgun as he pursued Marsh out of the graveyard.

Fiona watched them go, her face concerned, then she saw Rebecca standing against the wall and her expression changed to one of surprise.

'Rebecca?'

35

Carl Marsh pushed his way through the stragglers at the church gate, ignoring their protests. One of the men tried to grab him but Carl landed a punch and he fell back. Pain jarred along his arm from his knuckles but he ignored it. They already ached from the lesson he'd taught Deirdre so a little more made no difference.

He heard Sawyer call his name as he hurtled down the steep path behind him but he paid no heed. His Land Rover was parked at an oblique angle on the road, the door still lying open, so he threw himself into the driver's seat and fired up the engine. He slammed and locked the door just as Sawyer reached him and jerked at the handle.

'Carl, for Christ's sake!'

Marsh barely looked at him as he reversed at speed, then spun the wheel to the left and gunned the engine to surge forward again. The shotgun clattered to the ground as Sawyer held onto the passenger door handle and hauled himself onto the narrow footplate. Sawyer clung on as the Land Rover bulleted down the Spine, trying to open the door and slapping at the window glass with his free hand. Marsh ignored him. He drove directly at a crowd of mourners walking towards Portnaseil. They scattered and the damp air was filled with curses.

Someone would call the police, he knew, if they hadn't already. He'd seen the look between Sawyer and the minister when they'd asked about Deirdre. He had to get home, but first he had to get rid of his unwanted passenger.

Marsh swung the wheel sharply to the right and then back to the left and Sawyer lost his already precarious grip, flew off and hit the tarmac hard. In the wing mirror, Marsh watched him roll over and over before he came to rest. He didn't get up. Marsh smiled and scanned ahead of him, hoping to see Roddie Drummond and his family, vowing he'd take them all if he did, but he knew it was a long shot. He'd seen the car at the church gate when he arrived and knew they'd be at the community hall by now, where food and drink waited for the mourners. The police would think that's where he was headed and would be waiting.

But he wasn't going into Portnaseil. He had a job to finish.

* * *

Rebecca raised her umbrella to let the minister shelter from the rain, although it was too little, too late. Between standing at the graveside, then trying to talk down Carl Marsh and grappling with him on the ground, the woman was soaked through. Nevertheless, it seemed the thing to do.

'Rebecca, what are you doing here?' she asked.

'Roddie Drummond.' It was all Rebecca had to say. Fiona opened her mouth in a silent 'Ah' and gave her a slight nod. 'Also, I wanted to see you.'

'Me? Why?'

Rebecca paused. 'I need to know about my father.'

The minister didn't ask what she wanted to know. Neither did she look surprised. 'What did he tell you?'

'Nothing. That's why I'm here. I have to know.'

Fiona looked out to where the grey sky merged with the grey sea and the wind whipped the crests of the waves white. There was no evasion in the look. It was as if she had been expecting Rebecca to turn up on her doorstep one day, but now that it was here she wasn't quite ready.

'Tomorrow,' she said. 'Come to the house.'

'I might not be here tomorrow,' said Rebecca. 'Once Roddie

Drummond leaves the island I have no story, no reason to be here. And he only came back for the funeral.'

Fiona squinted at the clouds, growing darker every minute, looked around at the trees waving in the wind and then back out to the Sound again, where the swell rose and fell. 'There'll be no ferries till this blows over, believe me. And it'll get worse before it gets better. No one is going anywhere. Tomorrow. Right now, I need to get to Deirdre Marsh.'

* * *

Carl Marsh spun into the short driveway outside his house and jumped from the driver's seat, leaving the engine running. He bellowed Deirdre's name as he charged through the open front doorway and into the hall, where blood speckled the faded rug. He glanced into the kitchen but his wife wasn't there. He followed the trail to the rear of the cottage, glanced into the cupboard where he kept his gun locker, saw he'd left the door open. Careless, he thought. Not that it mattered now. He poked his head into the room he used as a small office but she wasn't there either.

'Deirdre!'

His voice boomed through the silence of the house. *Where the hell was the unfaithful bitch!* 'Deirdre! Come here now!'

This time she answered, her voice faint and only one word. 'No.'

The front room. The parlour. She'd moved herself in there. Well, he was damned if he was going to go to her. 'Deirdre, you come out here, and I mean right now.'

'No,' she said again.

He moved back down the hallway. He didn't rush—each step was unhurried, almost leisurely. Someone would be here soon, but he had a little time. He wanted to give her the chance to obey his command, even though his anger rose with each silent step. His knuckles brushed the wall between him and the front room, as if he could somehow feel her presence through the brickwork. 'Deirdre, you'd better do as I say . . .'

'No.'

Just that one word. No.

Thoughts spun through his mind. *She thinks she's being defiant. She thinks she's being assertive. I'll show her what she really is. Nothing. Less than nothing.* 'If I have to come in there and get you, it'll only make things worse, you know that. I haven't the time for this—get your arse out here!'

'No.'

His jaw clenched. His fists tightened. *If that's the way she wants it, then fine. It will only be the worse for her and she knows that. I'll show her, this time. Really show her.*

He kicked the door open. She was standing against the far wall, her forehead pressed against the plaster as if it was holding her up.

'Come over here,' he ordered, but she didn't move. 'You fucking bitch, I said come over here.'

He strode across the floor, but before he reached her she turned and he saw the rifle in her hands and he remembered the open locker door. He stopped short, looked into her eyes, saw that she was quite calm.

'No,' she said once more.

And then she pulled the trigger.

36

The wind howled around the Square, and even though it was only late afternoon it was darker than it should have been. Rebecca, Chaz and Alan sat in the bar. Rain rattled against the opaque windows and occasionally the lights flickered.

'Do you think the power will go?' Rebecca asked.

'If it gets any worse,' said Chaz.

'Will it get worse?'

'Very likely.'

Fiona was right. The ferries were confined to port. The storm blowing in from the west had enveloped the entire island and, even though the harbour was relatively calm, thanks to Portnaseil's sheltered location, turned the Sound into a restless, undulating blanket of grey. It didn't look that bad to Rebecca, far from a death trap for vessels, but what did she know?

They had each fallen silent again and Rebecca stared at her gin and tonic while Alan spun his almost empty glass of wine on its stem. Chaz, as always the designated driver, was on the sparkling water and his long glass was empty.

'Well,' said Alan, breaking the silence, 'that's been an eventful day.'

Deirdre Marsh was in custody, locked away in the small cell at the police station across the Square. She hadn't said a word since she had been found by Fiona sitting in an armchair beside her husband's dead body, the rifle with which she had blown a hole in his chest draped across her lap. She'd first been taken to the hospital, where Chaz's father had treated her injuries. Bruises, contusions and lacerations. Carl had managed to inflict the maximum damage again, without breaking bones or damaging organs. It didn't make it any less painful.

No one seemed to mourn the passing of Carl Marsh.

Bill Sawyer was not so lucky. His tumble from Marsh's Land Rover had been a bad one and he'd dislocated his right shoulder and shattered his right shin bone, a shard thrusting through the flesh. He was in hospital but was in no danger.

Donnie Kerr had almost slipped away during a seizure, the doctor said. He should've been airlifted to the mainland but the storm had prevented the helicopter from taking off, let alone reaching the island. They would do what they could but thankfully he had stabilised and was strong and fit. Dr Wymark was hopeful he'd pull through.

There was little appetite for the funeral party in the town hall, so what mourners were left had drifted off. From the shelter of the hotel's reception, Rebecca and Chaz had watched the black-clad locals get into their cars or walk home, their bodies bent against the growing wind and the driving rain. Ash said that his mother and brother had catered the affair and there was a lot of food going to waste. It was a shame.

In the lane that ran to the Sinclairs' door, the moron squad stood, some smoking, all huddled into their jackets. None of them had hoods because they were manly men and a bit of weather was nothing to them, testosterone being a wonderful umbrella. There was a new face, though, a young man Rebecca hadn't seen before, and he had a thick parka with the hood up. His testosterone level needed a bit of waterproofing, it seemed.

When Alan joined them and they moved into the deserted bar, they found that Ash's family had spread out some of the food left over from the funeral. Pauline said it was free for whoever wanted it so they ate some of the sandwiches while Alan told them about his chat with Lord Henry and his belief that his days of gainful employment on Stoirm were coming to an end.

'What will you do?' Rebecca asked.

Alan looked at Chaz. 'That depends, doesn't it?' Chaz looked slightly uncomfortable, so Alan explained. 'I want us to leave, Rebecca, but the bold boy here isn't ready to go.'

'It's not that,' said Chaz, convincing no one. 'I mean, where would we go?'

'Anywhere. London, Glasgow, Edinburgh, Timbuktu. There's a big, wide and wonderful world out there, my boy, and it's waiting to be discovered. New lands to conquer—and I want us to do it together.'

Chaz stared at his empty glass. Rebecca understood. It was a big step. She remembered what it was like leaving home but at least she had been heading to a job in Inverness.

'Chaz, baby,' said Alan, pressing his point, 'what's the point in staying here? Do you like being the only gays in the village?'

'No, but . . .'

'But you're frightened, right?'

Something flickered at the side of Chaz's mouth and Alan knew he was right. He reached out and laid his hand on top of his lover's. 'There's no need to be frightened, not as long as we're together. You and me, kid, top of the world, ma.'

The flicker turned into a smile. 'That world blew up at the end.'

Alan waved his words away. 'A mere technicality.'

Then they fell silent again, but Alan kept his hand on Chaz's. Rebecca saw Chaz turn his over and their fingers intertwine. She thought it was a sign that Chaz had made a decision. She hoped so. Everyone deserved to be happy, even though not everyone got what they deserved.

Later, as Rebecca headed to her room, she glanced through the hotel door and saw that darkness had fallen fully. Chaz and Alan would go home to change and then meet her later for dinner. She left them, the bar's only customers, Alan still trying to convince Chaz that they could have a life together off the island.

Alone in the small lift, Rebecca turned over the day's drama in her head. Alan was right—it had been eventful. But in the end she was still in the dark about everything. She had the Carl Marsh story—she could talk about him turning up at the funeral with the gun, but not about what he done to his wife. She had been charged with murder and, even though she wouldn't appear in court until they could get her back to the mainland, details relating to her shooting her husband were *sub judice* and could not be reported beyond saying that it had occurred. There might be an argument that anything relating to Carl was equally off-limits, but that was an envelope she was willing to push. Barry might think differently, but that would be up to him. She'd write it up, send it and let him worry about the legalities. That's what he got the big bucks for.

Her phone rang as she stepped out of the lift into the corridor. She glanced at the screen and sighed.

'Hello, Simon,' she said, rooting around in the pocket of her coat for the room key.

'Is everything okay over there?' he said, his voice concerned, and she felt a tingle of shock. Had the news got out? Had someone on the island called the nationals? 'They say the ferries are off.'

Relief washed through her, even though she knew it wouldn't be long till word did spread. She had to get something filed right away. 'Yes, the weather has closed in here.'

'Is it bad?'

'It's wet and blustery but it's no Hurricane Bawbag,' she said.

'But the ferries . . .'

'The ferries go off if a whale farts, I'm told. It's nothing to worry about, Simon. I'm fine. The hotel isn't going to collapse around me.'

Once again, her tone was sharper than she'd intended and, once again, she regretted it immediately. She turned the key in the lock, opened the door.

'I thought you'd be back by now,' he said.

'Tomorrow maybe, more likely the day after.'

There was a slight pause. 'I miss you,' he said.

She knew he expected her to reciprocate, but she didn't. 'I've got things to do, Simon. I need to file some copy and then have dinner. I'm meeting a couple of people . . .'

'Who?'

She leaned against the door frame, her foot wedging the door open. For some reason she didn't want to continue this conversation in her room. What was that about? Was it too intimate a location to speak to a man she'd already been intimate with? 'Just Chaz and his friend Alan.'

'Chaz? The young photographer?'

'That's right.'

'And who's this Alan?'

She thought she heard a note of jealousy in his voice. 'They're gay, Simon. Alan is Chaz's boyfriend.' Her tone became more pointed again. 'Look, I have to go. I've got work to do. I'm fine. Everyone's fine. The island won't blow away.'

'I just thought . . .'

'Simon . . . I'm going.'

She hung up before he could say anything further. She slumped in the doorway, guilt at being so terse robbing her of strength. She was aware of hurried footsteps behind her but before she could turn someone slammed against her and propelled her forward. She whirled round as the person followed her and closed the door. Deep shadows filled the room with only a little light creeping through the gauze curtains from the Square, but she was acquainted enough with the layout to step further away from her assailant without tripping over anything. As her eyes became accustomed to the gloom she could make out a motionless figure against the door, as if blocking any attempt to escape. Whoever it was, he was big and stocky and she could hear his harsh breathing.

'Who the hell are you?' she asked, pleased her voice was relatively steady despite her heart hammering at her chest.

'You caused all this, cow,' said a voice. Young. Local. Male. 'You shouldn't have come here.'

'Caused all what?'

'You and that Roddie Drummond, coming here, stirring it up.'

She backed up a little bit further until she felt the edge of the bed press against her thigh. She slowly reached out and switched on the bedside lamp. The young man blinked back at her but didn't move. She sensed that now he was here he didn't really know what to do. He was a good-looking boy, maybe in his late teens, wearing a bulky parka, jeans and boots. She realised she'd seen him before, standing in the rain with the moron squad.

'Who are you?' she asked.

He shook his head. 'Doesn't matter.'

'What do you want?'

He swallowed, looked around the room, as if surprised to find himself

233

there. 'You need to be stopped,' he said. 'You're hurting people, causing trouble. People don't want you here, nosing around, stirring it all up. What happens on the island is the island's business.'

His body language suggested he was now regretting this course of action, so she decided to keep him talking. 'So what are you going to do? Beat me up?'

He couldn't look her in the eye so she couldn't tell if that had been his plan and he now thought better of it, or if she had put the idea into his head. She looked around for something to defend herself with, should he decide on the latter. The bedside lamp was the nearest object, but the fact it was plugged in wouldn't help her. He didn't seem to be making any moves towards her, so perhaps he really was beginning to think he'd made an error of judgement.

'Even if you do, you think it'll make a difference?' she said. 'I've already learned a great deal and shared it . . .'

He looked back at her then, as if she'd reminded him of something. 'What do you know?'

'A lot,' she bluffed. She still knew very little and all she had sent over the water was a report on the public meeting, but she hoped her lie would make him realise how stupid he was being. She guessed he'd been fired up to do this by the moron squad, who would be furious over the death of their boss. Someone mourned Carl Marsh's passing after all.

His wandering eyes lighted on her laptop bag propped up against the hefty dark wooden wardrobe in the corner and he darted towards it. She realised what he was doing just a little too late, for he already had it in his hands before she got to him. He pushed her hard on the chest and she stumbled back against the bed as he wrenched open the door. She threw herself after him, catching him in the doorway, trying to reach the strap of the bag to snatch it back, but he managed to shrug her off, then jerked his elbow into her chin, knocking her almost off her feet, before he took off down the hallway.

'Give me that back!' she shouted, ignoring the jarring pain, but he didn't even look back. She hadn't expected him to suddenly stop and meekly return the bag, but the words were out before she knew it. He was already most of the way down the stairs to the ground floor before she pushed her way through the door. She prayed she didn't lose her footing as she took the steps two at a time, one hand momentarily grabbing the banister for support. As she shouldered her way through to the ground level, she saw Ash at the front door, looking out into the Square. He looked back at her as she darted across the reception area.

'Miss Connolly, what's going on? I just saw Gus McIntyre running out . . .'

'He stole my laptop,' she said.

He was surprised. 'Gus? He's a nice lad.'

'Yes, a nice lad who stole my laptop.'

As she stepped outside, she heard Ash say something about calling the police. She knew she should wait for them but she needed that laptop back. And she didn't like being a victim.

The Square was deserted. The wind whipped at her clothes and shrieked around the stone buildings like a squadron of harpies. The street lights swayed slightly and the rain washed across the pools of light like insects with a purpose. Where would he have gone? He wouldn't head for the harbour, there was nowhere else to go after that, unless he had water wings and a death wish. She ran along the front of the hotel and the bar, the sound of her footsteps lost in the screech around her, until she reached the road that led to the Spine. The lights from the Square died here, leaving a thick, inky darkness filled with the groan of the elements. There was no point in going any further. The young man would be well away by now, she knew that.

A nice lad, Ash had said. Maybe he was, but Rebecca was angry. She was angry at Gus, angry at herself, angry at this whole bloody island. Her laptop was gone, all her notes. Everything she had stored. Yes, the boy would be arrested pretty quickly but he'd have plenty of time to destroy everything. She didn't know how computer literate he was but all he'd need to do was throw it in the Sound, let the water and the salt do its worst.

Shit.

She stared into the darkness again, the wind tugging at her hair and her clothes, the rain hitting her like a cold shower. She suddenly felt stupid, standing there in the darkness being battered by the weather, so she turned to head back to the warm hotel.

Gus was standing a few feet away from her, her laptop bag dangling in one hand at his side. She froze, shocked by the sight of him. She hadn't heard him approach so she reasoned that if he meant her any harm he would've done it by now. He said something, too quietly for her to hear over the howl. She took a few steps closer and he didn't back away. 'What did you say?'

He looked away. 'You shouldn't have come here. Why did you come?'

'It's my job.'

He thought about this and she fixed her eyes on the laptop bag. She was close enough to reach it now, but was she fast enough to get it from him before he took off again? He was a strong lad and she wasn't sure she would be able to win it back.

He looked up again, saw the direction of her gaze and looked down, as if he'd forgotten it was there. He held it out. 'I'm not a thief,' he said.

She took the bag from him and slung it over her head so that the strap was safely wrapped diagonally across her body. He might change his mind, she thought, and that way there was little likelihood he would remove it. 'You could've fooled me,' she said.

He looked hurt. 'I just need you to stop.'

'I'm not going to, Gus.'

He flinched when she used his name. He hadn't expected that. She thought she saw his eyes fill with liquid. She hadn't expected that.

'It's just . . . Sonya,' he said. 'I wanted to do something for Sonya.'

'She's your girlfriend, right?'

He nodded, then shook his head. 'I think so. I don't know. We're . . .' He tried to think of the words. 'I don't know what we are. We . . . mess around. I like her. I want there to be more but she holds back.'

He was a good-looking boy, he could probably have his pick of the island girls. Rebecca wondered if Sonya *was* special to him.

'You wanted to impress her?'

He shrugged. 'Something like that. I'm sorry. I wasn't thinking

236

straight, what with Donnie. All this today. It's . . . big, you know? Hard to cope with.'

'And the moron squad wound you up?'

He was puzzled. 'The what?'

'The guys I saw you with earlier. Carl Marsh's lads.'

He understood and looked even more ashamed of himself. 'I shouldn't have listened to them. Alisdair's okay, but when he gets with the rest of them . . .' His words tailed off with a shrug. 'They said you had to be punished for what happened to Carl. They blame you and Chaz Wymark. They said you all had to pay.'

A chill rippled down Rebecca's spine. 'Gus, where are they now, Alisdair and the rest of them?'

Another shrug. 'I don't know. Why?'

She didn't answer. She was already rushing past him back towards the hotel.

37

Chaz could feel the wind buffeting the side of his Land Rover, even in this sheltered section of the Spine. Alan had Classic FM on the radio, an operatic piece by Puccini. Alan loved Puccini and had been trying to teach Chaz more about classical music. He liked some of it, even some opera, but he remained firmly a contemporary music guy. Still, he put up with it because Alan liked it. That's what partners did.

Partners. He'd never actually thought of Alan in that way. They were pals, sure, lovers certainly, but he'd never thought of it as something stronger. Until tonight. Until Alan said he might leave the island and he wanted Chaz to go with him. The thought of losing him had stabbed at him. He didn't want Alan to go, but knew he had to. There was nothing for him on the island; his flat came with the job, and if he stayed there was no work, so he wouldn't be able to rent. Chaz's parents fully accepted their son's sexual orientation, but would they be happy for him to sleep with Alan under their roof? The islanders were funny. Alan's comment about the only gays in the village wasn't accurate; there were others. But on the island it was all kept under the radar. The younger islanders were more open-minded, but there was a thread of distaste among a few of the older locals. Most tended to accept it, or at least ignore it in a live-and-let-live way, but there were a few who were unforgiving. He knew his dad had lost patients when it became known that Chaz was gay. They insisted on seeing the other doctor and travelled the length of the island to attend her surgery. One patient had said she didn't want to be examined by a man who had filth in his blood, as if Chaz's father was carrying some kind of contaminant that had infected his son. So if Alan moved in with them, what would other patients think?

And then there was the moron squad. They were young but they never missed an opportunity to make their homophobia known. Sometimes it was a goading comment, other times a smirk and kissing noises as they passed. Once they even slashed Chaz's tyres. He knew it was them. They were the only ones stupid enough.

Alan was singing along to the aria, his eyes closed. Chaz shot him a look and smiled. Alan couldn't sing a note but he liked to try. Chaz loved that about him.

He turned his attention back to the road, compensating slightly when a hefty gust caught the side of the vehicle. Partners. Love. He hadn't analysed their relationship until now. He'd just let it happen. Neither of them had used the word *love*. Yes, the sex was good and they were relaxed in each other's company. They could even sit silently together without ever feeling the need to begin a meaningless conversation. They were compatible, a matching set. But now, with the prospect of Alan leaving, he knew he had to make a decision. A commitment was necessary and even though he had hesitated, he now knew, deep down, what the answer would be.

He stared through the windscreen, the wiper swiping furiously at the rain. He didn't need daylight to know where he was; he'd driven this road since he was a boy, his father beside him, road regulations being customarily flouted on the island. There wasn't that much traffic, even on the Spine, and Chaz couldn't remember the last time there was a crash.

He'd miss the island. He'd miss its funny little ways and the fact he could turn a corner and find a new bit of history or mythology. He'd miss the way the past still lived in the stone and breathed in the hills. But it was time to move on. Time for the next great adventure . . .

Headlights filled his rear-view. Some idiot had them on full beam and the reflection seared his eyes, so he twisted the mirror away slightly. Whoever it was behind him was really travelling and was right on his tail. It was another Land Rover, he could tell that. Then they turned on an array of spotlights on top of the cab and the interior of Chaz's vehicle exploded with light. Even Alan, whose eyes had been closed, became aware and twisted round in his seat, one hand raised to block the harsh glare.

'What the fu—' he said.

And then they felt the first bump. It wasn't much more than a nudge, but it was clear the vehicle behind had hit them. It pulled back then and Chaz gently depressed the brake, hoping they would pass by, but the big 4x4 barrelled towards them and bumped their rear once more. The Land Rover lurched forward and both he and Alan jerked backwards with the force of the blow. Chaz fought with the wheel, as it wiggled out of control.

The vehicle behind fell back again. The lights receded, so Chaz hit the accelerator and sped on, eyes darting to the rear-view. The vehicle had slowed and its lights vanished when he topped a rise in the road and dropped down the other side.

'Who the hell was that idiot?' Alan asked, his voice shaking.

Chaz didn't answer. He had a suspicion. Only the moron squad would be reckless enough to do something like that. They'd probably been getting themselves all hopped up on something since the news of Carl Marsh's death. They idolised that man, Chaz never understood why. On the other hand, birds of a feather . . .

And then he saw the lights again, first the glow growing stronger as their Land Rover neared the top of the hill and then the full eruption as it careered towards them once more.

'Dear God,' he said softly.

He thought they were going to really slam into them this time, but why? What the hell was this all about? He rammed his foot down and surged ahead. The wind was stronger on this stretch of road and he felt it try to snatch control from his grip. He turned the wheel against it, kept the nose steady, glanced in the rear-view, saw they were almost upon them and they were faster and they were heavier: he had felt that with the first bump. But there was nothing he could do, nowhere he could turn to avoid them: on the right was a ditch between the road and open moorland stretching to the hills, on the left was a narrow verge that dipped sharply to the rocky coastline.

'Chaz,' said Alan, just as the vehicle steamed directly behind them, its lights burning, its engine the roar of an angry beast.

'I know,' said Chaz.

Then, just as Chaz braced himself for a ferocious crunch, it veered to the right and overtook them, the driver pumping the horn. They saw a couple of blurred faces grinning at them and heard whooping and jeering as the long wheelbase Land Rover dodged ahead of them. It veered in their path then zoomed ahead, the horn still blaring, until it rounded a bend and was obscured by foliage at the side of the road.

The tension eased from Chaz's body and his grip on the steering wheel relaxed. He realised then that his knuckles ached from squeezing so hard.

'Bloody idiots,' said Alan, his voice trembling from the tension.

'That's why we call them the moron squad,' said Chaz, shooting Alan a look. There came a smile in return, and though a pale ghost of a thing, a smile all the same. Chaz flashed his own back.

But then the smile died. Alan sat bolt upright and screamed his name as his hands shot out in front of him to slam against the dashboard. Chaz looked back to the road—he'd only looked away for a second— and he saw the other Land Rover ahead of them. He jerked the wheel and veered into the other lane, but the vehicle began to move as he drew level with it and swiftly picked up speed to run alongside. He glanced past Alan and saw the grinning face of the driver. The boy actually waved, as if saying hello. Chaz rammed his foot down on the accelerator to try to pull ahead but the idiots maintained their speed. The road twisted and turned as they neared the section overlooking the Seven Sisters. The needle edged up to sixty, which was as fast as Chaz dared go, even on a road he knew well. *The idiots, the absolute bloody idiots!* Both engines screeched as they jockeyed for position.

Chaz took his foot off the gas to let them push ahead. It would allow him to tuck himself in behind them. But the driver was ready for that and he did the same. Chaz hit the pedal, hoping he could gather enough velocity to surge beyond, but they matched him again. And then, just as they swerved neck-and-neck around a bend, he saw a set of lights coming towards him.

For a brief moment he didn't know what to do. The speeding vehicle beside him didn't give an inch, the lights ahead were hurtling his way.

He heard Alan say his name, quietly, almost a whisper, perhaps even a prayer.

He hit the brakes too hard. The Land Rover skidded on the road, slick with rain, mounted the verge and took off into the air before it plunged towards the rocks, the noise of its engine now the shriek of a terrified creature. Alan screamed his name once more as the jagged edge of one of the Seven Sisters rose sharply in the headlights.

38

A young police officer was waiting at the hotel, having been alerted by
Ash about the theft of the laptop. Rebecca hurriedly explained that she
had it back, no harm done, and brushed away his questions.

'We need to find my friends,' she said.

'Miss, we need to deal with this report of a theft.'

'No, you need to listen to me.' Her voice hard with urgency. 'My
friends may be in trouble. There are people out there who may do them
harm.'

The police officer smirked. 'Miss, are we not being a wee bit dramatic
here? What kind of harm?'

That pissed her off. 'No, I'm not being dramatic. My friends Chaz
Wymark and Alan Fields are under threat from the mor—' She stopped
herself in time. 'From the young men who work for Carl Marsh. You
know who Carl Marsh is, don't you?'

His face hardened at her tone. 'Miss . . .'

'You need to listen to me. And you need to stop calling me Miss. My
name is Rebecca Connolly and you need to take me to find them.'

He stared at her for a moment, his eyes searching for something that
would guide his next decision. Thankfully, he found the right thing.
'I've a car behind the station. Which way would they go?'

She peered now at the road ahead, hoping for a glimpse of lights, but
the darkness beyond the sweep of the headlights was unbroken. The
constable was a decent driver but Rebecca could feel the tug of the wind
as he concentrated on his steering.

It was the rear lights they saw first, just a glimpse as they hit the top of a hill, lying on the rugged shoreline to the left, then the police car's beams picked out the dim outline of the Land Rover wedged against one of the Seven Sisters. Rebecca was out of the car before it had even come to a complete standstill. She ignored the cries of the police officer telling her to wait, she barely registered the woman standing beside a dark-coloured hatchback, her mobile phone in her hand, already calling for help. She slid down the steep drop and stumbled around the jagged boulders, her feet in turns scraping and slipping on the slimy rocks, the constable still calling to her to stay away, that it could be dangerous, but all she wanted to do, all she needed to do, was get to the Land Rover. Chaz's Land Rover. Music blared from the radio, something operatic, something sad and tragic and moving. The engine turned and clicked while steam from the crushed bonnet floated into the falling rain. The 4x4 had slammed into the tall column of rock and sat at an oblique angle, its rear passenger wheel perched on a smaller clump of rock. The passenger door hung open and she climbed up onto a boulder to peer in, her footing precarious thanks to the rain, salt water and seaweed.

Alan was hanging in his seatbelt, but he was conscious. He didn't even look at Rebecca, as her head appeared over the edge of the Land Rover's floor. He had Chaz's hand clasped between both of his as he whispered to him.

Drip

Rebecca moved slightly, hanging onto the door for support, and saw Chaz was unconscious behind the wheel.

Drip

Alan kept whispering as he raised one hand to brush Chaz's hair away from his forehead.

Drip

Liquid hit metal. Blood, draining from Chaz's wounds. A steady, rhythmic drip, like the ticking of a clock, like the clicking of the engine. Rebecca stared at the young man, so motionless, so pale, the wheel against his chest, skewered by the shard of bodywork that pierced his side.

244

'Chaz,' she said, and then couldn't think of anything else.

Alan didn't look round. He kept saying something as he fixed Chaz's hair. She couldn't be certain but she thought he was telling the young man that he loved him.

She could hear the police officer on the radio, his voice urgent as he called for an ambulance.

'Help's coming, Alan,' she said, feeling she had to say something. 'Everything will be okay. Help's coming . . .'

Alan didn't acknowledge her. He ran the back of his hand gently down Chaz's face and made a soft shooshing sound. When he spoke, he did so without turning, his voice gaping with pain. 'Look what they've done, Rebecca. Look what they've done to my beautiful boy . . .'

She stared at him as the rain fell and the aria ended and the ticking in the engine slowed and died.

39

The clock ticked.

It sat on the tiled fireplace, an old-fashioned wooden clock, its rounded top sloping out to wings. Its face was plain, there was nothing ornate about it. Rebecca wondered if it had come with the manse or if it was some kind of family heirloom. But its tick was clear and strong and steady.

Very little sound reached her as she sat beside a warm log fire in this cosy little book-lined study in the rear of the house. Just the clock, rhythmically ticking time into oblivion, and the underlying crackle and hiss of the logs burning in the grate. She could hear the wind, of course; that had been a constant since the day before. It hadn't seemed to have grown in intensity, though. It was now a backdrop to the island, shrieking and howling over land and water, surrounding the stone-built manse and probing for weakness in slate or render. But the building was a strong one: it had withstood such attacks before, and it would survive this one.

But inside the room, there was, above all, the clock.

Tick

Tick

Tick

The sound sent her mind flicking to the night before, perched on that slimy rock, the wind plucking at her clothes, the sea singing somewhere in the dark. The Land Rover's engine winding down. The aria on the radio. Alan's voice, talking softly to Chaz.

Tick

Tick

Tick

The blood dripping steadily onto the vehicle's bodywork. The sound of car doors closing. Lights flashing. Voices calling out.

Tick

Tick

Tick

Time passing. A second, a minute, an hour, a day, a life. All in a moment. A single heartbeat becomes many, throbs for a time, then stills.

Tick

The clock's heart wouldn't still. Even if it did, someone could bring it back to life with a twist of a key.

Tick

You couldn't do that with a human heart. Not her father's heart. His heart was still and no one could wind him back. Carl Marsh. Mhairi Sinclair. Gone. Still. The child Rebecca had carried, that had been growing inside her. The clock ticks, once, twice, three times. No longer. Life goes on. The ticking continues. They were all lost in the silence between the ticks.

The door opened and Fiona McRae came in carrying a tray with a cafetière of coffee and cups. Cake, too. Chocolate. Life goes on. Coffee goes on. Chocolate is eternal. Rebecca thought of Maeve Gallagher and her tea ritual and her own clock, silent, dead. *God, was that really only a few days ago?* So much had happened since then. So many ticks of the clock. So many spaces in between. The dead space.

Fiona set the tray down on the little table between them and sat in the winged leather chair opposite. Under the tray, Fiona had been holding an old leather book, which she slid down beside her. She didn't make any moves to pour as she stared at Rebecca, concern etched heavily on her kind face. She was pretty, Rebecca noted. She'd probably have been a very pretty young woman. She would've had to be to attract her father, for he was a handsome man. Except towards the end, when the disease ate at his once strong body and blunted his once sharp mind. One tick of the clock and he was gone before the next.

'Have you heard how Chaz is?'

Fiona's voice startled her, even though she was looking right at her.

Her mind had been lost in the ambient sounds; the human voice seemed momentarily alien.

'He'll live, thankfully,' she said. 'The wheel had pressed against his chest but he was wearing a thick jacket, which helped. His ribs took some punishment. The bit of metal didn't hit anything major. He'll be off his feet for a while, may have to walk with a stick for a time.'

Fiona smiled. 'That's a relief. With all that's happened in the past day or so we didn't need another tragedy.'

Rebecca fell silent, the ticking of the clock filling her mind. She watched the second hand counting the day down. Chaz hadn't fallen between the ticks. Chaz had beaten time. And she was thankful. Life went on.

'Rebecca, are you sure you want to do this today?'

She focused on Fiona, saw her kind face was furrowed with concern. Rebecca nodded. 'I have to know,' she said.

Fiona poured two cups of coffee from the cafetière. She cut two slices of cake, laid them on small plates. She placed one in front of Rebecca and set the cup beside it. She picked up her own cup and sat back, sipped, watched Rebecca closely. There was silence between them for a while. Except for the wind outside, moaning like a ghost. And the clock.

Tick

Tick

Tick

Rebecca waited, her mind still too numb to ask any questions. That young man, Gus, had said she had caused this. All this violence and death. Had she? She didn't think so, couldn't bring herself to think so. She didn't make Roddie Drummond come back home. She hadn't forced Carl Marsh to abuse his wife all these years. She had no hand in Donnie Kerr being beaten up.

But Chaz . . .

He was targeted because of her. If she hadn't come to the island, he would never have been involved. He would not be lying in the hospital. His mother would not have been put through the shock of hearing about what had happened and the fear of losing her only child. Alan, although spared any lasting injury, would not have had to consider life without the man he loved, would not have had to consider the space between the ticks.

'I'm leaving on the first ferry out of here,' she said. 'I never want to see Stoirm again, to be honest.' She paused, looked directly at Fiona. 'But I need to know.'

Fiona sipped her coffee, placed the cup carefully on the saucer in her hand and set them both down on the table. She sat back, crossed her legs, laid her forearms on the arms of the chair. The index finger and thumb of her right hand rubbed together, as if feeling the width of some invisible fabric.

Tick

Tick

Tick

Finally, she spoke. 'That's what your father said to me, the day he left. That he never wanted to see Stoirm again. He kept his word.'

'So will I. But first I need to know. Why did he leave?'

Fiona was very still, just the finger and thumb swirling against each other.

'Your father's family came here from Ireland over a hundred and fifty years ago,' she said. 'The Connolly clan, they liked to call themselves, and they were part of a small religious group called the Blood of Christ. Three families came over originally, the Connollys, the Devlins, the Cloughertys, but they were all known as the Connolly clan. A few more followed. Nowadays they'd be called fundamentalists but even that doesn't cover how strict their views were. Basically, the word of God was the law and they adhered to it. Stoirm islanders always had one foot in Presbyterianism, the other in Paganism, and over the years they've tolerated New Agers and Wiccans but the Blood's views were too strong even for them. Still, they were accepted as long as they kept to themselves up in their little clachan in the hills, which is what they did. I suppose you'd call them hillbillies in a lot of ways. There were stories, of course, of strange rituals, but frankly that was just stuff and nonsense. Fairy tales to scare the children over here on the east side of the island. Stoirm is fond of its stories. They were staunch Christians and they were a strong family unit, even compared to Stoirm families, whose bonds are all but unbreachable. Their views were extreme but there weren't any sacrifices or blood rituals. That was all rumour.'

'My father wasn't religious,' Rebecca said, her voice sounding hollow even to her.

'No, he wasn't. Their views tempered over the years. At first they married only one another—Connolly married Devlin, Devlin married Clougherty, Clougherty married Connolly and so on—but that couldn't continue. Time passes.'

The clock ticks, Rebecca thought.

'Things change. There was more contact with the outside world, or at least what outside world there was on Stoirm back then. Some people drifted away from the clachan, settled in other parts of the island, married outwith the clan. The Blood of Christ was watered down, you might say, with the blood of Stoirm, and frankly it was all the better for it. They abandoned the Blood's tenets, adopted something more . . . flexible, shall we say? But your father's family? They stayed true to their faith. Their numbers dwindled but there were still a few of them in the clachan. Even so, time took its toll and by the time your father came along, they still had their faith but they weren't as deeply entrenched in it as their parents and grandparents.'

'So what turned my father against them? Against Stoirm?'

Fiona looked down at the untouched chocolate cake as if it was the answer. 'There's an old joke about the kirk. Why does it not approve of having sex standing up? Because it may lead to dancing.' Fiona didn't smile. Neither did Rebecca. She wasn't sure she would again. 'Morality, Rebecca. You must know that for centuries women weren't allowed to do many things. Up until the late 1960s I couldn't have been ordained as a minister for word and sacrament. Women were oppressed for many, many generations and I'm ashamed to say that the kirk was in the forefront of that oppression. There was an old law, centuries ago, in the seventeenth century, against Concealment of Pregnancy, and it remained in force for decades. Basically, if a woman hid the fact that she was pregnant and the child was stillborn, or died at childbirth, the woman would be held guilty of murder. The father, if he knew, was blameless. It was only the woman who was responsible. I suppose it was an anti-abortion law but like many laws it was open to abuse. If the woman was married, then there was no need to conceal the pregnancy but if she was unmarried? There was huge shame to illegitimacy then. If the woman revealed it, she was liable to all kinds of public rebuke, especially at the hands of the Church. She could be shunned, ridiculed, cast out. To an extent, a little of that attitude still exists here on Stoirm.'

Rebecca thought of Mhairi Sinclair. *I know what they think of her*, her mother had said, *that she was a whore*. She'd had one child to one man, and feared she was pregnant to another, while living with a third.

'The law changed, of course, but the shame was still there. Abortion wasn't as freely available. And the flesh is what the flesh is, so there were still unwanted pregnancies. Certainly, arrangements could be made. The woman could go into hiding until the pregnancy reached term and the child taken away for adoption. We have no idea how many such cases there were. Sometimes they would go to the mainland and a trip to a back street abortionist. The woman didn't always return.'

'Fiona, what has this got to do with my father?'

'The Connolly clan weren't immune from illegitimacy.'

'So, was my father illegitimate, is that it? Is that the big secret?'

'No, your grandparents were legally wed and he was born two years after.'

'Then what?'

Fiona breathed in deeply. 'There's a saying here on the island: *They should've been taken up into the hills at birth*. It means that someone should never have been allowed to live.'

Carl Marsh had said that twice about Roddie Drummond. It had registered with her but she hadn't given it too much thought.

'Your great-great-grandmother, Roberta Connolly, was a strong, highly motivated woman. She was strong in her faith, strong in her views and strong in her convictions. To her, a child born outwith wedlock was an abomination, a thing of the devil. They say she fell pregnant herself when she was seventeen to an islander. No one knows what happened to the child, or even if it's true. But whenever any of the clan fell pregnant out of wedlock and a marriage wasn't on the table, it was her they turned to.'

Rebecca felt something cold grasp at her stomach. 'What was she, an abortionist?'

Fiona shook her head. 'No. Well, not quite. I'm not going to debate the morality of abortion, I'll have my view, you'll have yours, we may agree, we may not. But what Roberta did? Well, perhaps it was worse. The pregnant woman went to live with her in what remained of the clachan. We're talking early twentieth century here, the clan had dispersed even further, the Blood of Christ was all but a memory. Those confined women would remain with her until they gave birth.'

Fiona stopped speaking. Outside the wind threw itself against a window somewhere, rattling it like a demand for entry. The ice in Rebecca's belly was solid and she recognised it for what it was. Dread. Her mind had jumped ahead of Fiona's words. When they came, they came with a whisper, as if Fiona didn't want the elements to hear. 'They say that Roberta took the new born babies and . . . disposed of them.'

Fiona's eyes began to fill with tears. Rebecca could tell this was painful for her, even though it had happened more than a hundred years earlier and she didn't know any of the people personally. Rebecca already knew the answer to her next question, but she needed to ask. She had come this far. The dread could not stop her.

'I take it you don't mean she put them up for adoption?'

Fiona took a long time to answer and all Rebecca could hear was the wind whirling and the rain tapping its bony fingers on the window. The clock on the mantelpiece, always the clock.

Tick

Tick

Tick

'No,' Fiona said finally. 'Roberta had a more direct way of dealing with the girls' shame. They say when she helped deliver the child, she had a bucket filled with water at her feet. It didn't take a lot of water, not for a newborn. It would've been so very easily done. Seconds, really.'

252

Seconds. Like the clock. Like the ticking of the clock. All done. A life over before it had begun.

Rebecca soaked this in. In her mind she saw a bare little room and a table. She had no idea what Roberta Connolly looked like but she saw a big woman, severe, standing between the opened legs of a young girl on a tabletop. A metal bucket at her feet, waiting.

She thought of her own unborn child. That had been a twist of fate, a fault in chromosomes. This was purposeful. This was cold and calculated. The horror of it tingled at her spine. Something else. Shame. It was her ancestor who had done it, her blood. In that moment she knew something of how her father felt.

'And the islanders knew this was going on?' she asked.

'They knew, but they didn't talk about or acknowledge it in any way. This island has its secrets, Rebecca, and the people keep them. Only the older folk know of it now, people my age and upwards, and it's never, ever spoken about. The past haunts the present on Stoirm, but it must never taint it. To talk of it gives it life. By not talking about it, the shame of it will die. But back then it was accepted. And even condoned.'

'And my father found out about it?'

Fiona gave her a slight nod. 'Yes, he did.'

'How? If no one talked about it, how did he find out all that time afterwards?'

Fiona hesitated before she answered. 'Roberta kept a journal. He found it.'

Rebecca's eyes flicked to the spine of the leather book wedged between Fiona and the arm of the chair. 'Is that it?'

Fiona's breath escaped in a long sigh as she retrieved the book and held it in both hands, as if she was afraid it would get away from her. 'I don't know why she kept a record of sorts. She doesn't go into great detail but it's clear from the language what she was doing. Perhaps it was her way of expunging her guilt. Perhaps she thought it important that these small deaths, these little lives with no names, be recorded. Perhaps she was proud of it. I really don't know. Anyway, your father found it among some old things and he read it. He was, what? Seventeen, eighteen? But he was so disgusted with what his family had done, what they had known about, what the whole island seemed to have known about, that he left. He told me he couldn't live here any more, knowing what had gone on back then, what had been allowed to go on. He gave it to me the day he left. Now it's yours.' She held the book out to Rebecca. 'If you want it.'

Rebecca stared at the dark leather volume. She knew why her father had refused to even talk about Stoirm, but there would be more detail in the book. She could learn about her family, where she had come from. She saw herself reach out to take the book, felt its coolness on her fingertips, saw herself opening the cover and carefully turning the yellowing pages, deciphering a spidery hand filled with dates and names and religious indignation and horrible, spiteful, bitter thoughts. She saw all that without ever actually taking the book from Fiona's hands.

She didn't need the book to tell her where she came from. She already knew. She wasn't a Connolly from Stoirm. Her life began with John and Val. Mum and dad. She was a product of their love and their care. She was a part of them and they were part of her. It was also true that whoever had gone before also lived within her. All his adult life her father had carried guilt that was not his to carry. She knew part of that guilt would now remain with her. It would join her own. Those little lost souls would be with her forever. She didn't need a tangible reminder.

Tick

Tick

Tick

'Burn it,' she said.

Fiona seemed satisfied and immediately threw the book into the fire. They both watched in silence as the flames began to singe the old paper and curl the edges of the cover. The paper erupted into flame and smoke but the leather merely blackened. Within a few minutes the words written down so long ago were at one with the smoke. There seemed nothing more to be said, so Rebecca stood up to leave.

'Your father was a good man,' Fiona said as she rose.

'He was,' said Rebecca.

'He tried all his life to make up for what Roberta did.'

'I see that now.'

'I think he more than made up for it, don't you?' The minister stared directly into Rebecca's eyes, as if she had divined her earlier thoughts. 'It wasn't his debt but he repaid it, in full and with interest. You owe nothing, Rebecca. You are not Roberta. The book is gone, the slate is clean. Understand?'

Rebecca nodded and said her goodbyes. They hugged. In another world Fiona might've been her mother. In another world that book and what it recorded would never have existed. But in this world Fiona was just her father's old girlfriend and that book was now ash and blackened leather. The words were gone and the smoke was gone, but what they recorded was still there, hanging in the air around her. And within her.

On the roadway back to Portnaseil, the wind whipping at her coat, she stopped and stared across the island to the hills in the west. Somewhere up there, hidden in the wet mist and standing firm against the storm, was what was left of the clachan. Somewhere up there, perhaps, was a table with old, forgotten dark stains upon it. And perhaps a rusting metal bucket lying on its side in a corner.

A noise drifted towards her through the wind and the rain that beat on her face and her hair. A little cry, something pitiful, something alone out there in the open land. It could have been a sheep or a bird. But to Rebecca it sounded like something else.

A child's cry.

A child not meant to live, its single, heartrending wail the first and last it ever made.

A cry that would be carried by the wind and echo forever around the island.

The cold feeling in her gut erupted and she bent double, her retching joined by deep, shuddering sobs.

40

The girl standing in the reception area fidgeting and pacing like a bird trapped in a windowless room was familiar but not because Rebecca had met her before. She had seen photographs of someone who looked like her. Right away she knew the girl was Sonya Kerr. Even with the dark smudges under her eyes, her hair flat and lifeless and her skin pallid, Rebecca could see Mhairi's features come to life.

'Someone to see you, Miss Connolly,' said Ash from behind the desk, darting a finger towards Sonya, who stopped pacing to give Rebecca a stare that was a mixture of curiosity and defiance.

'Sonya?' said Rebecca and saw the look turn to surprise.

'You know me?'

'No, but I know who you are. You look like . . .'

'My mother? I know. They all say that.'

The girl not only looked but also sounded worn out. Rebecca could sympathise. She felt like someone had pulled out a stopper somewhere and drained her. 'What can I do for you?'

'It's Donnie . . . my dad.'

Rebecca closed her eyes briefly. *Don't let him be dead*, she thought.

'He's conscious now,' said Sonya, sending a wave of relief washing through Rebecca's weary body. 'He wants to see you.'

Rebecca was glad Donnie was back in the land of the living, but she was done. 'Sonya, I'm tired and I'm wet and I'm sure you know last night was—' She sought the correct word. 'Difficult. For everyone. All

I want to do is have a hot bath and put on some dry clothes and sleep for a few hours, hopefully get off this island soon.'

'He's got something to tell you. About my mother. About the night she died.'

Rebecca told herself she didn't care, that she couldn't take any more of Stoirm and its secrets.

'Please,' said Sonya, a note of desperation creeping in. 'He really wants to talk to you and I promised I'd bring you. I've got a friend outside with a car, we'll take you right now.'

Rebecca told herself that as far as she was concerned all of this was over.

Sonya's eyes hardened. 'You caused all this. You came here and caused all this. The least you can do is hear what my dad has to say. He's in that hospital bed because of you.'

That's not true, Rebecca wanted to say, but she was too exhausted to debate the point. All she could say was, 'Okay.'

She was at the exit to the small car park before Sonya realised she'd won the argument. Gus was sitting in a beat-up old Vauxhall Vectra and he gave her a shame-faced look as she climbed in the back. Sonya climbed in the passenger side. 'This is my friend Gus,' she said.

'Pleased to meet you,' said Rebecca.

Gus didn't say anything. She hadn't told the police it was Gus who had made the visit the previous night. He had been stirred up by the moron squad, most of whom were now safely tucked up in the police cells for what they had done to Chaz and Alan, although Ash told her one was proving elusive—*He's taken to the heather*, was how he put it. On another day that phrase would have made Rebecca smile, but not that day. Some of the island's limited police manpower was beating that heather in the south of the island. He had nowhere to go and they'd flush him out sooner or later.

Nothing further was said during the short drive to the hospital. The rain, propelled by the wind, splattered the windshield and hit the roof with such force it sounded like someone was playing a drum. Rebecca found herself looking across the moorland, staring at the hills, greyed and smudged by the rain, and thinking about Roberta Connolly and what she had done. Sonya had her face turned towards the window, as if she was staring at the hills too. Did she know about the Connolly clan? Fiona had said only the older generations knew, but had Molly told her? Probably not. It was something the islanders wanted to die and, as Fiona said, talking about it just gave it life.

Gus brought the pick-up to a halt outside the double glass-doors of the small hospital. 'I'll take you to him,' he said.

'You're not coming?' Rebecca asked Sonya.

The girl shook her head. 'He told me and my grandparents already. He wants you to know, too.'

Rebecca searched her face for some kind of hint but saw nothing. Sadness, maybe, but at what she didn't know. 'You're wrong, you know,' Rebecca said.

'About what?'

'About me causing all this. This would've happened whether I came to the island or not.'

Sonya looked away again. She didn't accept what Rebecca had said. She had to blame somebody and Rebecca was the easiest target. And Roddie Drummond. But Rebecca would bet a year's salary that the girl had never met him.

Gus held the door open for her, polite compared to their last encounter, and then veered to the right. 'I take it Sonya doesn't know about last night?' Rebecca asked.

He shook his head. 'It was my idea. I told you. And I'd do it again.'

'Good to know,' she said.

Another few paces, then he said, 'She wanted something done but Donnie, her dad, had some kind of seizure and they almost lost him. At least that's what she thought. She blamed herself for thinking about doing something about you, for saying it out loud. She thought that he'd heard her. So I did it without her knowing.' He stopped at a set of double doors. 'He's in the second room on the right.' Rebecca thanked him and pushed the nearest door open, but stopped when he spoke again. 'Why didn't you tell the police about me?'

'How do you know I didn't?'

'Because I'd be in the cells with the other guys.'

'Well,' said Rebecca, stepping through the doorway, 'the day's not over yet.'

* * *

Bill Sawyer was in a chair beside Donnie's bed, a pair of crutches propped against the arm. His right arm was in a sling, his right leg, poking through a blue dressing gown, was bandaged from ankle to thigh.

'Should you be up on that?' Rebecca asked.

'It's not that bad,' he said.

'I heard you broke it.'

'You heard right. Not got far to travel anyway.' He jutted his chin towards the other bed in the room.

Rebecca looked at Donnie, still hooked up to machines but relatively bright-eyed, despite the bandages around his head. His face was mottled by bruising, and what skin she could see was wax. When he spoke his voice was rough, as if someone had taken a cheese grater to his vocal cords.

'Thanks for coming,' he said.

She kept her voice as light as possible, although she didn't feel that way. 'Who could resist the invitation of a man who came back from the dead.'

He gave her a smile, which was on the weak side of wan, but it was Sawyer who spoke. 'You might as well know that I've advised Donnie not to speak to you.'

'There's a surprise,' she said, pulling a plastic chair from behind the door closer to the bed. 'Did you see who jumped you? Was it Roddie?'

Donnie gave a very slight shake of the head, movement still being painful. 'It wasn't Roddie. He was around, but he didn't do it. It was one of Carl Marsh's boys . . .'

'I've brought Donnie up to speed on everything that's happened,' said Sawyer. 'Terrible shame about that young lad. I'm glad he's all right, that could've ended very badly.'

Rebecca said nothing as she concentrated on dousing the tears burning at her eyes. She wouldn't cry, not in front of Sawyer. 'Why did you want to see me, Donnie?'

Donnie gave Sawyer a look. Sawyer gave him a shrug. 'You've got her here now. You know what I think, but it's up to you.'

Donnie's eyes swivelled back to Rebecca. 'I didn't tell you everything when I told you about that night. The night Mhairi died.'

He waited for her to say something. 'Okay,' she said, finally.

'I couldn't tell you everything, not then. But now, with all that's happened, it's time to set everything straight. The truth is, I didn't meet Mhairi on the estate. There was work going on but not on the estate, as such.' He paused, took a breath. 'We met at Thunder Bay.'

41

Donnie Kerr
Fifteen years earlier

I was standing alone on the beach when Mhairi arrived. I'd been side-lined, pushed away like an annoying child. I was pissed off with them because I knew it meant I wouldn't be paid—and I really needed that money. I'd blagged a lift to Thunder Bay with them, hoping I'd be able to pitch in and get some readies so I could get to MacDonald and get myself set up. But Henry had told me to keep out of the way, that he didn't need some useless junkie buggering things up. So I backed away from them. The lights of the *Kelpie* burned through the darkness, the wind hitting me off the water and plucking at my hair and my clothes. It screamed around the bay like an echo chamber. The *Kelpie* navigated the narrow channel towards the shore, where the RIB was waiting. The seas were high but not too bad; my dad at the helm meant the boat would ride them with ease. This was the tricky bit, the transfer, but the channel was relatively calm and even in my agitated state I knew it would go without a hitch.

Roddie was in the RIB, along with a couple of Russians. I didn't know how they would communicate—those guys didn't have a word of English and Roddie sure as hell couldn't speak Russian. But the Russkies seemed to know what they were doing, so maybe hand signals were enough. All they had to do was keep the RIB steady anyway, and help the cargo off the *Kelpie*. Henry Stuart was at the water's edge with Jarji, his pal from university, and the hulking brute who followed him around. I don't remember his name. They were all watching the water intently. None of them saw Mhairi, her torch swinging left to right as she threaded towards them down the cliffside path. I saw her, though. *She shouldn't be here*, I thought, and it crossed my mind to warn them, but then, why the hell should I? They were cutting me out just because I was sick. I should've been on that boat—that was my job, to sneak the *Kelpie* out of the harbour and navigate out to sea—but when that bastard Jarji saw earlier in the day I was hurting I was out in the cold.

That was when Henry had a conversation with my dad, Lachlan. I wasn't present for that, but I could guess what had been said. I knew money would have been offered and refused. Threats would have been made. Sure, veiled threats, because Henry wasn't a thug, but threats all the same. Hints. Inferences. Reminders that the men Henry was working with were not averse to meting out violence.

Lachlan didn't like what I had become involved with but he also knew that if he didn't help then I would be in even further trouble, so he agreed to take the *Kelpie* out, meet the freighter on the open sea, pick up the cargo and bring it back via Thunder Bay. No one visited Thunder Bay at night and certainly not when the weather was closing in. There were no houses overlooking it. No one to see what was being landed. Except the sea birds, tucked up in their nests high in the cliffs. And the spirits of the dead, waiting to be taken into the west.

If you believed that sort of thing.

That got me thinking about the cargo. It was being taken to the West, too. But not to a better life.

I didn't know if Mhairi had seen me standing alone on the sand, but if she had she ignored me and headed straight to the lights at the shoreline. Her hair, caught by the wind, streamed back from her head like long, black ribbons. I remember it clearly. She strode across the beach as if the slimy seaweed and rocks weren't there. She was always sure-footed, always pretty agile. As kids we would leap from rock to rock down near the Seven Sisters. As often as not, me and Roddie and Henry would end up sliding into the pools of salt water that nestled between them, but Mhairi always kept her feet dry. That was when I first began to fall in love with her, aged eight. I can still see her face as a child, laughing at us boys as she perched on a jagged boulder, her toes digging into fissures in the rock. A ballet dancer on points.

Mhairi marched straight up to Henry and said something. I saw her pointing out to the *Kelpie*, which was alongside the RIB now and unloading the cargo. Powerful lights flashed in the hands of the men on the dinghy, illuminating the young women being helped down the ladder, their faces bleached by the beams, their eyes wide in fear. Some clutched bags, others had suitcases or backpacks. They took the hands of the men in the RIB and sat where they were told. I saw my dad helping them over the side with words of encouragement. His eyes, though, would have told a different story. I knew he would be fighting revulsion. I also knew he would never, ever speak of this night again. Not to me. Not to the police. He was doing this to protect me, his son. Family was everything on Stoirm. Part of me knew that and believed in it. The part that hadn't been eaten away by insects.

Mhairi whirled on Henry now and he was pulling her away from Jarji and the big Russian. She was tearing into them all—I could tell by her body language, even though the sound of her voice was faint above the wind and the waves. Her arms were waving like knives, forwards and back again, from the sea to Henry's face. They were quick, slicing motions. Her head was so animated it was as if she was trying to head-butt him. And, knowing Mhairi, that was exactly what she wanted to do. Henry's hands came up as he tried to defend himself, to explain, but I knew any lies he came up with would mean nothing to her. She knew him too well. She knew us all too well.

The RIB's outboard roared as it headed to shore, the cargo transferred, and the *Kelpie* was edging back to sea. My dad would sail around the north of the island and be back in Portnaseil before first light. Mhairi was still laying into Henry when she suddenly stopped and froze. I knew what she'd seen and part of me had been waiting for that moment.

She'd picked out Roddie's face on the RIB. Almost immediately he saw her too. He'd been too busy to pay attention to what was happening on dry land. His face glistened with shock when he spotted her.

Seeing Roddie must have been too much for her. She turned and ran back across the beach. Jarji moved to Henry's side and said something but Henry shook his head. I saw Jarji give his big pal a look and knew something was brewing. I took off after Mhairi at that point—but only for selfish purposes, not to protect her. The insects were scampering in my blood and I knew she was my only hope of getting something out of the night. She was moving fast, though, heading up that trail as if it was nothing, while I puffed and scraped my way after her, sometimes almost on all fours, my hands grasping at the mud for purchase.

I called out her name but my voice was lost in the roar of the wind. I could see her torch beam jiggling ahead and the dark shape of her body as she moved easily upwards. I called again. This time she heard me and stopped, turned.

'You're here, too?' she shouted. Even as the wind fragmented her words I could feel the disappointment.

'Mhairi . . .'

She'd turned before I'd hardly got out her name.

I pushed myself to catch up with her, struggling to breathe but determined not to give in. I needed to talk to her. I needed her to help me. The crawling under my skin actually helped propel me upwards because I told myself she was my only chance of making it stop. I kept going, hoping she would wait for me at the top.

As I finally hauled myself to the head of the track I saw her standing at the edge, her torch off, staring down at the beach. I looked down with her, saw the RIB had beached and in the flashing torch beams picked Roddie out beside Henry and his friends. They were looking up at the cliff top. I knew they couldn't see us standing up there in the darkness, but something in the way they huddled together, looking in our direction, felt precarious, sinister. For the first time I realised we were working with dangerous people.

I became aware of Mhairi's soft sobs. 'Mhairi . . .' I tried again.

She held up a hand to silence me. 'Donnie, don't . . .'

I didn't know what to say anyway. Standing on the cliff edge, looking down on the beach and seeing the scene through Mhairi's eyes, as the cargo was guided out of the RIB. No, not cargo—they were women, young women, Eastern European women, believing we were helping them, believing we cared. The need for drugs still roiled in my system, but the little part of me that was still Donnie Kerr, the man who had loved Mhairi, felt ashamed for being part of this trade. I turned to where three Range Rovers were parked, awaiting to take the cargo—the *women*—to the empty cottage on the estate where they'd stay for a few days. Mhairi's little car was sitting at an angle in front of them.

'We'd better be moving,' I said.

The fire in her eyes had died and now there was only sadness and confusion. 'Why, Donnie?' she said. 'Why are you all involved in this?'

I couldn't answer at first. I didn't know how it had all come to this either. What was I doing there? I didn't know really.

I watched Roddie and the big Russian break away from the others and head across the beach. They were little more than shadows but I knew it was them.

I looked at her—I felt hollow inside. 'What other reason is there, Mhairi?' I said. 'Money.'

She turned towards me. 'To buy drugs?'

I didn't say anything. I didn't need to.

'And Roddie?' she asked me.

Roddie was no different from the rest of us, I told her. She thought he was, but he wasn't.

The two dark figures were making their way to the path up the side of the cliff, so I said we had to go. She let me lead her to the car. She backed it up a few feet, turned and began to bounce her way back towards Portnaseil.

I remember staring at her face in the weak glow of the dashboard. 'How did you find us?' I asked.

'Carl Marsh.' That made sense. Marsh wasn't involved but there was every chance he knew something was going on and he wouldn't miss out on the chance to hurt Roddie in any way he could. Letting his girl-friend know what Roddie was involved in was too good to miss. 'I'd been looking for Roddie,' she said. 'And Henry . . .'

'Why?'

She ignored me, of course, she was so angry. 'What the hell are you all thinking?' she was shouting. 'People trafficking? Bringing women here, to Stoirm . . .'

They were going to the mainland over the next few days, but that made no difference to her.

Her sarcasm when I tried to explain was like a blunt instrument and it beat me into silence. 'Do you know what happens to them now?' she ranted. 'What those friends of yours make them do? The life they lead?'

The truth was, I hadn't thought about it. Roddie had come to me in Glasgow and told me that Henry had work for me at home. Something that would pay well. I'd seen Roddie a few times in the city and had even helped him with bits of work for Henry and his Russian friends. But Roddie hadn't told them that I was using quite as heavily as I was. As soon as that bastard Jarji saw me, I was out and my dad, by default if nothing else, was in. I had known what the cargo was but I didn't care. All I thought about was the pay day. But that had been snatched away from me.

The little car lurched and bumped on the rutted track. I wanted to suggest she slow down but I didn't know how that would be received. I stole another look at her face. The anger was still there, an anger I knew so well.

It struck me that I needed to tell her what she was involved in now. It was serious. 'You know you can't say anything about this, don't you?' I ventured. 'These blokes that Henry's involved with, they're not the kind of blokes you want to mess with, you know?'

She said nothing, just kept driving in the faint light. I saw her mouth was a thin little line, her jaw clenched tight. The only thing that was loose was a single tear that broke free and trickled down her cheek.

When I look back, I hardly know myself. I should have stayed with her. I should have kept her safe. But all I wanted was money. I asked her for some cash when we reached the Spine—it took me that long to pluck up the courage.

I was desperate.

But I should have been with her that night.

42

The present day

Rebecca listened to Donnie. Her gut had told her this wasn't for publication, so she hadn't taken out her notebook or recorder. Donnie was telling her only because he felt she had to know, and probably to appease his own conscience. After all this time, how would she make any of this stand up sufficiently to go to press? She couldn't accuse a peer of the realm of being involved with people traffickers without proof, and the word of a former addict who could be seen as having an axe to grind wouldn't be enough. Even if he would be willing to repeat it outside this little room, which she sensed he wouldn't.

And as she listened she knew that the truth about Mhairi's death and the reason her father left the island were tied in a way. It was all about protecting family. It was all about keeping secrets.

Mhairi was looking for Henry to tell him she thought she was pregnant. Her mother told no one at the time to protect her daughter, who was already seen as . . . what was it Molly had said? A Jezebel. Carl Marsh had maliciously steered her to Thunder Bay, where she would discover that her current lover was involved in smuggling young women, no doubt destined for brothels on the mainland. Donnie Kerr was earmarked to borrow and sail the *Kelpie* but his drug addiction had put him out of the game, so his father was pressed into service. Lachlan had said nothing to protect his son. Donnie had never told this story before because it would blacken his father's name.

Family.

Secrets.

'After that, everything was just about as I said before,' said Donnie, his voice hoarse and weak now. 'Mhairi gave me money, dropped me off in the Square, went to fetch little Sonya from her parents' house.'

'*Just about* as you said before,' Rebecca said. 'Was there more?'

Donnie looked at Sawyer again, who said, 'You've gone this far, might as well tell the rest. If you'd told me all this back then, things might be different now.'

'Aye, like you'd believe a strung-out junkie. Anyway, it didn't fit your preferred version of events.'

Sawyer shrugged. 'Tell her, Donnie.'

Donnie took another deep breath, closed his eyes as if mustering his strength. 'I told you that I didn't see Mhairi again after she dropped me off and that was the truth. I went into the hotel bar but MacDonald wasn't there. I had this cash burning through me, and I knew he lived in a wee flat above the bank, so I banged on his door. There was no answer. Turned out the guy was on the mainland that night, but I didn't know it. So there I was, money to spend but nothing to spend it on. I was feverish and jittery and all those little creatures were having a party under my skin.

'But I kept thinking about Mhairi and her face when she saw Roddie on that RIB and the way she was so sad and so frightened and so angry all at the same time. And I wanted to help her, I didn't know how, but even in the state I was in I wanted to be with her and get her through this. She'd said she was in trouble, but I didn't know if she meant because of what she'd seen or if there was something else.'

Rebecca briefly considered telling him about Mhairi's pregnancy fears but decided against it.

'So I decided I'd go to her cottage, make sure she was okay. Or at least I think I did.'

'You think you did?'

'You've got to understand what I was like.' He swallowed, licked his lips, reached to the bedside cabinet for the glass of water. Rebecca moved round the bed and handed it to him. He took a long drink, thanked her, then his head sank back onto his pillows again, his eyes closed. 'You have to understand my state of mind then. I was out of it, I had no idea what was real and what wasn't sometimes. I'd see things, hear things, things that weren't there. Shadows on the moors would become creatures. The wind would become voices. The stories that we're all told on the island would take root in my mind, become real. For a long time I wasn't sure about this, couldn't be sure if I was imagining everything, including going back to the cottage. For years I didn't know if I'd just thought about going back or if I dreamed I'd gone back or if I'd actually gone there. I remembered the wind battering at me as I walked. Or did I? I seem to remember throwing up a couple of times but couldn't tell you if that was on the road or wherever. Everything I saw, thought I saw, would come like wee lightning flashes of memory.'

'So what is it you think you saw?'

Donnie opened his eyes and his gaze was steady. 'I didn't get as far as the cottage,' he said. 'I was a wee bit away, I could see Mhairi's car, but then I heard someone walking along the road behind me. Again, you've got to understand what I was like, what people thought of me. I was a junkie and I couldn't be trusted. I was out on the Spine in the middle of the night so I must've been up to no good, probably going to tan somebody's house. So I nipped off the road, hid in the hedgerow.'

'Who was it?'

'I couldn't see his face. He had on a wide-brimmed hat and one of those long wax coats, you know the type with the sort of cape over the shoulders? Real outdoor gear. He was just a shadow moving in the dark sort of thing. He walked right past me, straight to the cottage. He went up to the door.'

'And did he go in?'

'I don't know. I decided to head back home then. I was feeling really ill and by that time I'd decided that I was more important than anything Mhairi was going through.'

'But you don't know who it was?'

He took a breath. 'Not then. I think I do now. Those coats, the good ones, they're hard-wearing. They can last years if they're properly taken care of. The thing I remember was this splash of red on the shoulder.'

'Red? Like blood?'

He shook his head. 'No, nothing like that. Paint, maybe. A big red patch on the left shoulder of the cape.' He thought about it again. 'Woke up the next morning in my own bed—well, came to, more like. Didn't know if it was all real. Until the other night when that bloke jumped me. Just before I passed out I saw the coat again, and the hat. Saw the red mark on the shoulder, fainter now but still there. Roddie was wearing it.'

Rebecca let that sink in. 'So Roddie was wearing it the night Mhairi died?'

He shook his head. 'No, I'd been with him, remember? He wasn't wearing that, he was wearing a thick sort of parka. I remember telling him that if he fell overboard it would drag him down. He changed into a yellow oilskin before he got into the RIB.'

'So who do you think it was?'

'I think the only person it could have been was Campbell Drummond. Roddie's dad.'

43

The wind had dropped considerably by the time Rebecca left the hospital and turned towards the Drummonds' cottage. The Sound still had a serrated grey look that matched the sky, but the rain had stopped, at least for the moment, although oily clouds trailed dark tendrils towards a mainland that was lost somewhere in the murk.

She thought about Donnie's new information. She had asked Sawyer if he was going to report any of this, but he said too much time had passed, none of it could be corroborated, and anyway, it was all off the record. Then he gave her a kind of distant look. 'Things have a way of sorting themselves out over here.'

She didn't know what he meant by that, but she did know that she was back on the story. She didn't want to be, but this was something she had to see out.

A familiar figure emerged stiffly from the Drummonds' courtyard and headed away from her towards Portnaseil. Hector Sinclair glanced back at her when she called out his name, but he didn't acknowledge her or even slow. He maintained a steady pace, his body language resolute, anger evident in every step.

That didn't look good.

She had broken into a run by the time she reached the courtyard. The door to the cottage was open but she hesitated at the threshold and called out Roddie's name first, then, 'Mr Drummond?'

The short hallway led to an open doorway through which she could see a tall fridge/freezer and the corner of a kitchen unit. A narrow

271

staircase stood to her left while a door opened to the right; she presumed to the cottage's sitting room. She was uncertain about entering without an invitation, but the open front door worried her. Did islanders really leave their doors unlocked in the twenty-first century? She turned her attention to the workshop doors. They looked firmly locked. Whenever she had passed before there had been a black transit van with DRUMMOND MOTOR ENGINEERS etched on the side. The courtyard was empty.

She leaned back into the hallway, called out once more. No answer. No sound at all. Rain began to drip on her shoulders again and that was the clincher. Bugger it, she thought, as she stepped over the threshold and cautiously pushed open the door to the sitting room.

Campbell Drummond was sitting at a table of dark polished wood. He was wearing the black suit he'd worn at the funeral. Or maybe it was another one, considering the drenching he'd had. He was sitting in a chair, his body half turned away from the table, as if he'd recently slumped there, his right arm resting on the top, his hand holding a framed photograph of his wife. It was the same image that had been used on the funeral's order of service. She was young in the shot. Alive. A woman frozen in time. Rebecca wondered if that was the way Campbell Drummond always saw her. Not in the next room but there, beside him. He must have heard Rebecca enter but he didn't acknowledge her presence. He was lost somewhere in the space between that chair and the portrait in his hand.

'Mr Drummond?'

His head lifted slowly in her direction. He wasn't startled, he wasn't shocked, but he seemed to drift back to reality as he focused on her.

'My name is Rebecca Connolly, Mr Drummond.' She paused to see if anything registered but his face remained blank. If he knew who she was, he was hiding it well. 'I'm a reporter with the *Highland Chronicle*. I'm doing a story on your son.'

His eyes didn't move from her face. His expression could've been carved from stone.

'I'd like to talk to you about the night Mhairi Sinclair died,' said

Rebecca. 'You were seen, Mr Drummond, outside the cottage she shared with your son.'

The stone crumbled then, just slightly, but Rebecca guessed that was quite a show of emotion for this man. He gave her a little nod, as if he'd been expecting her. She thought of Hector Sinclair and the look on his face as he took each angry step towards Portnaseil. He'd been here. He'd thundered out of this little house and was now heading where? Home? Or somewhere else?

'I knew this would happen,' he said eventually, his voice sad and weak. 'As soon as I heard Roddie was coming back, that he was coming home, I knew it would come to this. I knew that somehow it would all come out.' He looked back at her again. 'I take it the police will be here soon?'

She shook her head, moved closer. 'No police.' Then she surprised herself. 'This is an island thing.'

He simply nodded. That was something he understood. Then he remembered something. 'Connolly, Connolly. You're her, aren't you? The daughter of the Connolly who left?'

'John Connolly. His name was John.'

It made sense to him. 'Then you understand the island and its ways.'

'No,' she said truthfully. 'Frankly, I don't. To be honest, all I want to do is get off this place and back to where things make sense. Or some semblance of sense. I don't understand this need for secrets to be kept, even when people have died. When babies have died. My father kept the secret of his family, took it to his grave, and I don't understand that.'

'Blood secrets,' he said softly. 'They are the most important to keep.'

That's bollocks, she thought. But she didn't say it. She didn't want to risk antagonising him in any way. She'd come here for answers. She knew why her father had left the island. Now she wanted the rest. 'Mr Drummond, did you kill Mhairi?'

He looked back at her, shock carved on his face. 'Kill her? No! No, I would never do that. She was a beautiful lass, a beautiful lass. She was family, near as.'

'But you know who did?'

The shock was gone, replaced with sadness again, as if he didn't wish to know what he knew. He said nothing for a time. Rebecca balanced on the arm of the chair closest to him and waited. He stared at the photograph and reached out to tenderly touch the glass.

'I should've said something back then, but I couldn't, it would've killed Mary. Maybe it did, somehow, in the end. Not knowing. Wondering if her boy was a murderer.' His fingers rested on his wife's face, then slid away and he looked over to Rebecca. 'That damned coat. I'd forgotten I had it. Forgotten I'd even pulled it on that night. I've worn it maybe twice since . . .'

44

Campbell Drummond
Fifteen years earlier

It was my wife Mary who sensed there was something troubling Mhairi. It was nothing the lass said, nothing she did, just a feeling there was a storm raging inside her. Mary knew people. Over the centuries there were those born on the island with the sight, *an dàrna sealladh*, who could see events that had not yet occurred. There were those who were in tune with nature—Donnie Kerr was one. Then there were those like Mary who could sense thoughts and feelings sometimes before the person even knew they had them. The *fey*, they call them on Stoirm. Mary knew something was troubling that lass.

Mary loved Mhairi. We both did.

We'd been distraught when she fell pregnant to Donnie, not in a moralistic way but because we knew Donnie was not the one for her. It had always been Roddie in our eyes.

When we saw them together, even as little ones, we knew they were a fit, just as Mary and I were. I was a quiet man—I can be brusque, I suppose you'd call it, but Mary was vocal and open and likeable. But we fitted and we knew similar good fits when we saw them. Roddie lit up whenever Mhairi was near and they were so relaxed in each other's company. She wasn't like that with Donnie or Henry. Only with Roddie.

Mhairi had come looking for Roddie that night. She hadn't seen him most of the day, she said, and she'd been told he was with Henry, but she didn't know where. I had seen Carl Marsh in the bar earlier. I'd never liked the man, even though he and Hector had often gone out shooting with me, but I told Mhairi that if Roddie was with Henry, Carl was the man to know where. She thanked me and headed back to Portnaseil in her little Metro.

'It's a wonder that wee car isn't lifted off the road in this weather,' Mary said to me as we watched her back out of the courtyard.

I remember looking to the sky, listening to the wind. It wasn't that bad. I'd certainly known worse and tried to reassure Mary. But as she closed the door I knew she was worried.

For the next few hours she barely said a word and that wasn't like her. Finally, I asked her what was wrong and she told me that she felt something was troubling the lass. I tried to dismiss her fears, but if I am honest even I had seen something in her eyes. A dark shadow had been cast over them and lingered.

The present day

Molly Sinclair had tried to stop her husband from leaving the house again, but he wouldn't listen. He hadn't said anything when he'd returned from seeing Campbell Drummond, but his silence spoke volumes. She hadn't seen him so angry. No, she had. When Roddie Drummond was acquitted. He'd sat around the house for days, saying little, the anger burning inside him. There had been a chasm between him and Mhairi, but she was still his daughter and he was grieving. He had calmed down after a time, but the fires still kindled somewhere, deep down. Now they raged again.

'What did Campbell say, Hector?'

He didn't answer. She'd heard him come up the stairs and she stood in the hallway, watching him open the door to the small room. She knew what was in there and she took a few faltering steps. When he came back out again she saw what he was holding and she felt something grab at her throat. She could guess what her husband had been told.

She wanted to reach out, to turn him to face her, but she feared his anger would make him forget himself.

'Don't do this, Hector,' she pleaded.

Still not a word spoken. He didn't need to say anything.

'It won't bring Mhairi back.'

He paused and slumped against the door frame, as if he was suddenly very tired. She reached out and laid her hand gently on his shoulder. 'This isn't the way, Hector. Tell the police. Let them deal with it.'

He jerked his shoulder from under her hand. 'Like they did last time? Great job they did.' He straightened and moved down the stairs.

She reached out to grab him but he was already gone. 'Hector! Please!'

The front door slammed.

Molly leaned against the wall of the stairway and let the tears come.

Campbell Drummond
Fifteen years earlier

Well, once Mary started talking there was no stopping her that night. She badgered me to find Roddie and Mhairi and ensure everything was all right. I tried to make little of it all, but there was no convincing her. I had known, as soon as my wife started, that I would be heading out into the weather sooner or later. Why I tried to convince myself otherwise, I don't know.

I dug out my Australian Bushman's coat. I didn't wear it much even then, not with the red paint all over the shoulder.

I'd lain the coat over a chair, a pot of paint open on a shelf above it, and the inevitable happened. No amount of scrubbing got it all out; white spirit merely left a milky stain which in some ways was worse than the red, so I tended to wear the coat only at night, or when I was working the croft. The wide-brimmed hat I pulled on was waterproof and the leather cord tucked under my chin would keep it in place. I'd always hated a hood; funny how these details seem so clear looking back. I haven't thought of that for years. Hoods muffle the world around me. I didn't hear the voices like Mary did but I did like to hear the sounds of the island, even the wind and the rain.

Roddie had taken the van that night so I was facing a walk down the Spine to their cottage. I didn't mind, really. I was an islander and the elements were part of me.

The present day

Hector Sinclair was an islander and the elements were part of him. The buffeting winds trying to catch the solid shell of his grocer's van held no fears for him. He'd driven through worse and for less reason. He ignored the mechanical protests of the suspension as he bounced off the Spine and onto the muddy, rutted trail. He glanced at the passenger seat, at what was resting on it.

He was an islander. They had tried things the mainland way before. But now it was time for the island way.

He looked ahead and made a sharp adjustment to the steering as the van slumped into a trench and muddy water splashed across his windshield. The little van wasn't built for this kind of terrain, but he didn't care. The engine whined as he pressed his foot down to force the wheel out and back onto the track.

The track that twisted off into the grey air ahead.

The track that ended at Thunder Bay.

Campbell Drummond
Fifteen years earlier

I'd always prided myself on keeping fit. I ate well. Working on the croft gave me plenty of exercise. I didn't smoke or drink to excess. So the walk to the cottage beyond Portnaseil didn't take me long, even with the wind whirling and jostling around me as if it was trying to hold me back. I wasn't *fey* but even I began to feel something force its way into my subconscious. I tried to ignore it but the feeling grew stronger with each step, as if there was a dark malevolent being gathering strength in the darkness ahead.

As I was getting closer I thought I saw someone scamper off the road near the cottage, just a glimpse of movement, but by the time I reached the spot I could see nothing. I looked towards the cottage and should've been relieved to see Mhairi's little Metro pulled in at the gate, but I wasn't. As I moved closer I saw its sides were splashed with mud, though of course that meant nothing really, not on a night like that one. The Spine was often covered by a film of muck, often silage, dribbled by the farm containers dragged regularly along it.

Further down the road I saw a fancy four-wheel drive pulled off to the side. I knew most of the vehicles on this part of the island but I wasn't familiar with this one. I could see muddy splashes on its doors too. While I was puzzling over this, voices reached me from inside. Even as I stood on the road. I eased the gate open and climbed the path that rose towards the front door. The voices were louder. Mhairi's voice and my son's. They were angry voices.

I heard her scream, 'How could you do it?'

Then Roddie, his voice lower, trying to calm her down.

I didn't know what Roddie had done and I thought about knocking, but then I decided against it. Roddie was my son but Mhairi, to all intents and purposes, was Roddie's wife. It was not my place to interfere in their business. If there is one law of nature it is that couples fight. Mary and I had butted heads many times over the years and we were still together, still a fit. Roddie and Mhairi were a fit. The main thing was everyone was safe. Mary's feeling had been wide of the mark this time.

I moved away from the door and carefully swung the gate closed behind me. Let them fight. Let them yell the heat out of whatever had happened. In the morning, they would be calmer and they would talk it over, whatever it was. I would tell Mary that they were both back home, safe and sound, but not mention they were arguing. She would worry. She would interfere. That was her way.

As I walked back towards Portnaseil, I wondered again whose

four-wheel drive it was. It was a mystery. But there was nothing I could do about it on a dark and windy night. I told myself I'd find out in the morning.

The present day

Rebecca stared at Campbell Drummond, her mind reeling. Even though she had half-expected to hear it, she was stunned by what he had been hiding all these years. Roddie had lied. He had been with Mhairi before she died. They had been fighting.

Despite her attempts to remain impartial, a part of her had wanted Roddie to be innocent, had wanted him to be the victim of a ruthless police officer's lies. That desire had begun to wane when Donnie told her about Thunder Bay; now it seemed to evaporate completely.

Roddie had killed Mhairi. Roddie hadn't found Mhairi already injured.

'Why didn't you tell the police this?'

He was looking at his wife's photograph again. 'I couldn't do that to Mary. Tell her that her son was a murderer?' His head shook slowly. 'No, I couldn't do that. I just couldn't.'

Secrets.

Family.

Blood.

It was an island thing.

As her mind processed the new information, another thought struck her. 'Mr Drummond, did you tell Hector Sinclair this?'

Campbell nodded. 'It was time he knew. Time for all this to end. None of it can hurt Mary now.'

Rebecca recalled the man's face as he'd stomped past her. That was not the face of a man who was going to let this lie.

'Where's Roddie, Mr Drummond?'

'He took the van. He's gone to say goodbye to Mhairi one last time. He said he was leaving on the first ferry and he wouldn't be back.'

'He's going to her graveside?' Rebecca asked.

Campbell shook his head solemnly. 'No, he'll go to the bay. The grave is where her mortal remains lie. The bay is where her soul still waits.'

Stories. Secrets. Tradition.

Life.

Death.

Her voice was heavy with sarcasm. 'It's an island thing, right?'

But it wasn't, not really. Everything she had learned that day was an island thing. Donnie had kept the secret of what had happened at Thunder Bay that night to protect his father, even after his death. Campbell had kept the secret of what he knew that night to protect his wife from the truth. And, even if he didn't admit it, to protect his son. But now they had both broken that pact with the island. They were talking about it. They were giving the past life. Her father had been more of an islander than he knew. He had kept the secret of the clachan.

'Did you tell Hector where Roddie was?'

He was back looking at Mary's photograph. Lost again.

'Mr Drummond,' she said, her voice sharp, and he phased back to her. 'Did you tell Hector Sinclair where Roddie was?'

His eyes filled with tears and the hand that held the framed snapshot began to tremble slightly. 'There's only one end for blood secrets.'

45

Roddie Drummond didn't hear Hector Sinclair behind him. He'd been standing at the water's edge, his eyes closed, feeling the wind finger his hair and the spray striking his cheeks like bitter tears. His ears were filled with the rhythms of the bay. The surf. The crash of wave against rock. The beat of the current in the caves.

He didn't know what he'd expected to find here. Some kind of closure, perhaps. Or forgiveness. Or perhaps the glimpse of a familiar face etched against the spray and the surging waves. A figure, waiting for release.

Mhairi.

He missed her so much. He missed her every day. If he could turn the clock back he would change everything. He wouldn't have come with Henry to the bay, wouldn't have been embroiled with the Russians, and none of it would have happened. He would still be with her, he knew that. They would've raised Sonya and had their own kids. They would have been happy.

He took a deep breath, tasted the salt on his tongue, felt the clean, pure island air fill his lungs. He wished it was enough to purge his soul of the toxins created by his life, of the things he had done, of the people he had worked for. Of the feelings of loss and remorse.

Guilt.

When his mother died he knew he had to come back to the island. He owed her that much. But he knew returning would open up wounds that had barely scabbed over. The hurt was never far away. The hurt and the shame for what he had become. The Russians had looked after him. They had hidden him from Sawyer—a change of name, a paper trail so convoluted no average cop could follow it. In return he worked for them. Bringing goods into the country. Transporting goods. Selling goods. People, drugs, weapons, drink, cigarettes, pirate DVDs, pornography. Anything on which they could turn a profit. He did whatever they asked, whenever they asked, out of fear and in order to make a living. He didn't care very much what he did. As far as he was concerned he had died that night fifteen years ago, along with Mhairi.

Someone said his name and he opened his eyes. Turned. Saw Hector Sinclair and the shotgun at his shoulder. Roddie should have been terrified but he wasn't. He should have felt the need to run, to hide, just as he had the day before, when Carl Marsh had threatened him. But he didn't. Instead, inexplicably, he felt something like calm.

'You killed my lass,' said Hector.

'No,' was all Roddie said.

'Don't lie. The time for lying is over. You killed my Mhairi.'

'No,' Roddie said again.

Hector obviously didn't believe him. The shotgun didn't waver as he took a step closer, then another. Roddie stared into the twin barrels, still feeling no fear. He was tired. Tired of running, of hiding, of lying. His life, since he left the island, had been one of daily dread and mistrust, but since he'd been back he'd felt something else begin to steal over him. Something he hadn't felt for fifteen years.

Peace.

Maybe this was where it was all meant to end. Not on a desolate piece of waste ground or in some dingy back alley in Glasgow, but here, in Thunder Bay, on the island.

Home.

'Then who?' Hector said, the shotgun aimed directly at Roddie's face. 'If not you, then who? Tell me what happened. Tell me what happened that night.'

Roddie closed his eyes. He didn't want to talk about it, to relive it. But Hector was Mhairi's father and he deserved to know the truth.

46

Roddie Drummond
Fifteen years earlier

Mhairi was screaming at me. Every word seemed to be stoking the fury in her eyes. I tried to calm her down, aware of another presence in the room, listening to every word, watching every move. Waiting. Mhairi's eyes frequently darted towards him, standing in the doorframe, as she raged.

I'd seen her face set tightly when she'd arrived home to find us waiting for her, but she'd said nothing until she'd put Sonya to bed. Then she came into the living room and her fury uncorked. She didn't care who could hear her. Her words were for him, too.

'How could you be involved in such a thing?' Mhairi's voice had changed. The anger still snarled, but something else had joined it. Disappointment. And that was harder to bear.

'You don't understand,' I told her, one hand reaching out to her, but she stepped out of reach.

'You're bloody right I don't. I don't understand any of this. Drugs and crooks and people-smuggling. Ray dying. Donnie as good as. You and Henry involved in this . . . business. No, I don't understand,' she ranted.

'It's just this once,' I assured her, glancing at the figure in the doorway. 'Henry agreed to help his friend, that's all. And he asked me to give him a hand. The money's good, Mhairi, and we can use it, you know that . . .'

Her eyes flashed again. 'The money? The money's good? What about those women? What's good for them?'

I couldn't answer that. I'd ignored the truth of what Henry and his friends were doing—only concentrated on the benefits for him. And Mhairi, of course.

'You can't tell anyone, Mhairi,' I had to say. It was important she knew.

'You expect me to keep quiet? You expect me to be part of it all?'

I saw our guest's head raise slightly at this. Could tell the atmosphere was changing.

I didn't know how much English Tamaz knew, but I suspected enough to understand what was being said. I had to make Mhairi understand.

'You're not part of this, I am,' I said. 'You just need to keep it to yourself. You can't tell anyone.'

Her laugh was brittle. 'Secrets. More secrets.'

'Mhairi, listen to me. You don't understand how important it is that you say nothing about this.'

She followed my glance to Tamaz, studying him as if he had just arrived, even though we had been waiting for her to return with the child. 'And what happens if I don't?'

Tamaz stared back at her, his expression inscrutable.

I dropped another log into the grate; it had been well-seasoned and the fire was hot, but I felt the need to do something. The bark began to smoulder immediately. I had set it earlier that evening and Tamaz had ordered me to put a match to it while we were waiting for Mhairi. The big man felt the cold. That surprised me.

I turned and looked at Tamaz again, the reflection of the flames dancing in his pupils the only sign of life I could see. The big Russian could have been a statue, he was so still.

'Mhairi, please,' I begged. I was starting to feel a little frightened by now. She didn't reply. The look she was giving Tamaz was one I had seen many times. It was a challenge, a dare.

Tamaz still bore his blank expression but I knew he was the last person in the world she should be goading. Sonya made a noise in the bedroom. A little moan as she slept. Tamaz heard it.

'Go see baby,' he said, but when Mhairi moved to pass him he stepped in her way and pointed at me. 'No. You go see baby.'

I didn't move. Sonya moaned again. It's just a little moan, I wanted to say. She does it all the time. But I didn't speak. Tamaz stared at Mhairi. He looked calm.

'Roddie?' I could sense confusion in Mhairi's eyes.

'She won't say anything,' I told Tamaz. I moved to stand between the big man and Mhairi.

'Go see baby,' Tamaz repeated in his monotone, as if he was bored.

Sonya had fallen silent again. 'She's fine,' I said, the words trembling. 'Let's just relax here, okay? All of us relax.' I held my hands out, one in Mhairi's direction, the other towards Tamaz. 'Mhairi, tell him you won't say anything about what you saw.'

For a moment I thought she was going to continue to defy him, but then I saw fear overcome her outrage. She looked to the floor.

'Everything's fine.' I smiled at Tamaz with a confidence he most certainly did not feel. 'We'll go back, tell them everything's fine. No worries, okay?'

Tamaz didn't move. He looked at me, blinked, then switched to Mhairi. She raised her eyes again and I saw quiet defiance.

Tamaz gave her a curt nod. 'Go see baby.'

'Tamaz, mate, the baby's fine, she just . . .'

Those flat, emotionless eyes slid back towards me. 'Go see baby. Or I go see baby. You choose.'

'Don't you go anywhere near her,' Mhairi screamed, launching herself at the big man, but he merely folded his huge arms around her and pinned her against him. She struggled but wasn't strong enough to break free.

Tamaz looked at me again. 'Go see baby.' His voice was even.

My heart thudded in my chest. I couldn't move. I couldn't say anything.

'Do it now,' Tamaz shouted.

I caught Mhairi's eye. I wanted to tell her it would be all right. I wanted to tell Tamaz that I was staying right where I was. I wanted to be man enough to protect the woman I loved. I wanted to be the hero of my own story . . .

I slid past the Russian and moved into the bedroom. It was dark and it was cool and Sonya was sleeping soundly.

I should have gone back into the living room. I should have done the right thing. I should have been there.

I closed the bedroom door, sat on a small stool beside Sonya's cot, stroked her head and spoke softly, soothingly, fearful I would wake her up, but needing to make some kind of noise to block out the sounds from beyond that closed door . . .

47

The present day

Hector Sinclair listened in silence to Roddie's words, the shotgun still pressed hard against his shoulder, the barrels sure and steady. He spoke only when Roddie told him about leaving his daughter alone with that man.

'You could have stopped it.'

Roddie had told himself that for fifteen years. He should have stayed. He should have done something. The truth was, even if he had, there was nothing he could have done. Tamaz was a big man and he had killed before, Roddie was certain. He could have called for help but before anyone arrived it would all have been over. Roddie might also have been dead. And perhaps even Sonya. He did not think the big Russian would baulk at killing an innocent child.

He didn't say any of that to Hector. The silence between them was filled by the tide hissing on the shingle.

'You could have told the police the truth,' said Hector.

That was not possible either. As Roddie had cradled Mhairi's head on his lap Tamaz had made it very clear: speak and it would be bad for his family. His mother, his father, his sister. They would suffer.

But Roddie didn't say anything of that to Hector either. There was nothing he could say, not now.

The waves crashed against the rocks.

'You didn't kill her then,' said Hector, lowering the weapon.

Roddie shook his head.

'But you were there.'

Roddie nodded.

'And you did nothing to stop it.'

Roddie couldn't deny it. The barrels of the shotgun were aimed at the seaweed between them and Hector's attention was focused beyond the rolling waves of the channel to the open ocean, as if he was searching for a boat to come and take them both away.

The water boomed in the caves.

'She was my lass,' Hector said, something fluid catching at his voice. 'She was my lass and I loved her. Through it all, I loved her. I distanced myself as she grew older because I thought she was ...' He stopped, swallowed. 'I thought she was a whore. Too much time spent with you and the rest of the boys. You weren't with her for nothing. You were boys, she was a girl. She must've been giving you all something. That's what I thought, that's what I believed. And then she had Sonya and I knew it was true.' His eyes welled and he tried to shake the moisture free. 'But it wasn't true. It wasn't, not really. She was my lass and I loved her, but I never told her that. Never.'

Roddie watched the older man's body curve slightly, as if he was bending against the wind. The fingers wrapped around the shotgun loosened and his eyes, still seaward, were unfocused now. Time between them had stopped. The sea still surged, the wind still blew, the boom still echoed round the bay, but for them there was nothing but the memory of a beautiful girl who neither of them had loved enough to save.

Roddie had felt at peace here on the island. Now he felt strangely free. At last he had told someone the truth. The truth will set you free, they say. He felt the weight of the lies he told back then lift from him to be carried off into the wind. He raised his head, saw the clouds sailing towards the land and beyond them a glimpse of wispy blue. Something large and dark floated above him, its wide wings languidly catching the air currents.

For a brief moment he thought the boom was just the water pounding into the caves but then something slammed into his chest with a searing white heat and he found himself flying backwards to land with a splash in the surf. He didn't feel much pain, not after the initial blow. The cold water ebbed and flowed around him, his life draining from him to mix with the bay. He stared at the sky, searching for the sea eagle, finding it soaring high above, large and wild and free, and wondered what it felt like to be *that* free.

Maybe he would find out.

Then he saw her face, leaning over him. Her beautiful face, untouched by age, her black hair curling down towards him. He raised a hand to touch her, but she was just out of reach. As it always seemed to be: when they were children, when she was with Donnie, even their time together had been too short. Perhaps now they could be together.

We will never be together.

He heard her voice, even though her lips didn't move. He looked beyond her to her father, who was weeping uncontrollably, the shotgun still at his shoulder. Roddie understood. He would never leave Thunder Bay now. His death would be a mystery, another secret. Never spoken of. He would take Mhairi's place as she moved into the west. He was responsible for her death: he hadn't wielded the weapon but he was to blame. She could rest now, and he would stay. It was as it should be.

He died then, his body lying in the surf, the waves of the Atlantic rolling in and catching his head, wafting it back and forward, as if he was nodding his assent to something that only he could hear.

The waves rushed in and retreated. His head drifted with them.

Back and forward.

Back and forward.

Back . . .

48

Rebecca stood on the quayside waiting for the signal to board the ferry. A knot of foot passengers clustered around her. She thought about those women, all those years before, coming to this jetty in ones and twos, their minders keeping a close eye on them. Donnie had explained that they had been lodged in an empty cottage for a few days, then taken across to the mainland and on to the cities. What had been going through their minds, Rebecca wondered, as they stared across the Sound to the mainland? Did they think they were heading for a better life? Did they know what awaited them? And where were they now? Their arrival on the island marked the beginning of something and it may not have been pleasant. Rebecca felt the same way. Her suitcase leaned at a lopsided angle against her leg, its wheel finally having detached itself as she'd bumped across the Square. She couldn't help but see it as a metaphor for her time on Stoirm. The wheel had come off her life too, in a way.

She had visited Chaz that morning. Alan was there and they had chatted for a while. Chaz was weak, but he managed to smile and even laugh. Alan helped, with a constant barrage of bitchy comments. Chaz would be fine, she knew. They would both be fine.

She bade goodbye to Donnie, and even Sawyer. No one mentioned Roddie Drummond and what had happened at Thunder Bay. His death would remain a mystery, at least to the police. Natural justice had been served. It was an island thing.

As she left the hospital she spotted a familiar figure heading in from the car park.

'Lord Henry,' she said, bringing him to a halt in the entrance. She saw him trying to place her and coming up short, so she helped him out. 'Rebecca Connolly.'

As recognition seeped in, his eyes became guarded. 'I'm sorry, but I've nothing to say to the press. I'm here to visit an old friend.'

'Not sure Donnie is all that interested in seeing you.'

He tried to brush past her, but she wasn't letting him off that easily. 'After all, you're responsible for putting him in here.'

That pulled him up. 'I had nothing to do with what happened.'

'Not directly, but we both know it was your people who did it. Perhaps not on your explicit orders, but when you unleash a man like Carl Marsh, who knows what might happen?'

That careful look came back. 'I don't know what you're talking about.'

'I think you do. I think you told Marsh to stop Donnie from causing any further trouble over your development plans. I think you gave him free rein.'

He dismissed her with a wave of a hand. 'You can't prove any of this.'

'No, I can't,' she conceded and let him turn away before she spoke again, her words coming out before she even knew it herself. 'Just as I can't prove anything about Thunder Bay fifteen years ago. The night Mhairi died.' He faced her again and she saw a shard of fear piercing the earlier wariness. That pleased her. 'Oh, don't worry yourself. I can't print anything. But I know why she said "Thunder Bay" before she died.'

He studied her, trying to gauge how much she really knew. Finally, he spoke, but something in his tone suggested he was merely reassuring himself. 'You don't know anything, Miss Connolly.'

She paused just long enough to let it sink in that she may, indeed, know quite a lot. 'Maybe not,' she said. 'Questions will be asked. Not by me, because I have no evidence and, anyway, I don't know anything.'

His eyes searched her face for some clue that she was fishing. She remained as impassive as she could. He took a step closer, dropped his voice. 'You're playing a very dangerous game, Miss Connolly.'

A tingle of fear hit her for the first time. She had wanted her moment with him, to somehow puncture that arrogant air of his. And she had. She had seen it in that tiny flicker of his eyes, in the tightening of his jaw, in the darting lick of the lips. It had been a spur of the moment decision to confront him and she hadn't properly thought it through. Whoever these Russians were, they wouldn't baulk at the thought of killing a journalist. She took a moment to reason it out, then said, 'Not really. Other people also don't know what I don't know. And it's already gone beyond them. The word is out, and if something unfortunate was to happen to me, they will know. So, unless you and your friends are willing to go on a killing spree and draw even more attention, then my advice to you would be to keep your head down and your arse up.'

She turned away, her knees weakening. She could feel his eyes boring into her back as she walked towards the doors and she hoped she could get out with her head held high. This had been a mistake, a big mistake, but she had to bluff it out. What she said wasn't quite true—it hadn't gone further than Donnie, Sawyer and her. But she would pass it on to as many people as she could—old friends of her dad's, Barry and his contacts, perhaps even a lawyer or two—just to keep herself safe. Sawyer had already said he would steer it to his former colleagues. In the end, though, she knew nothing would happen to Lord Henry or his old chums. As Sawyer said, there was no proof, just the word of an ex-junkie who was strung out at the time. Lord Henry would work that out for himself.

Even so, she was almost in the open air when he couldn't help himself. 'I'll sue, if you do print anything.'

She stopped. Turned. Forced a smile. 'Of course you will. That's why people like you win. That's why you always win. Because you have the money and the connections to make sure everything is locked down tight. But blood stains, your lordship. And you're steeped in it.'

They stared at each other for what seemed like a long time, then she walked away.

Now, standing on the quayside, she smiled. Fear aside, she had to admit it felt good. Of the five childhood friends, he was the one who had emerged unscathed and he was the one who least deserved to. The perturbed look on his face had gone some way to make her feel almost better about her visit.

'Will you come back?' Fiona McRae's voice startled her and she turned to see the minister smiling at her.

Rebecca gave Portnaseil another look, her smile fading. 'No,' she said, 'I don't think so.'

Fiona accepted the finality. 'The past is a living thing here on Stoirm. The past we talk about, that is. But once you get on that boat and you reach the mainland, it's all just stories.'

'And the past we don't talk about?'

Fiona laid her hand on Rebecca's arm. 'It's dead. Gone. Never happened.'

She thought about Lord Henry again. She thought about Hector Sinclair and Roddie Drummond. She thought about her father and Roberta Connolly. 'I wish it was that simple.'

'It is, if you want it to be. Don't let the past ruin the present and haunt the future. You had no hand in it, you are not to blame. I tried to tell your father that, on this very spot. That's why he never spoke about it, Rebecca. He wanted it to die and so must you. Sometimes you just have to let the past die.'

The ramp clanged down and the foot passengers began to move. Fiona gave her a hug. 'If you ever need to talk ...' They promised to meet up in Inverness for lunch. Maybe they would. Maybe they wouldn't. The future, unlike the past, is not certain.

Rebecca dragged her one-wheeled case down the ramp and onto the ferry, hauled it up the steep stairway to the lounge, where she found a seat looking away from the island. She didn't want to see it again. She looked across the Sound at the dark-blue bulk of the mainland. She'd be back home soon enough, she told herself. She'd write up something to keep Barry happy, ask enough questions to put Lord Henry's plans in doubt. But perhaps not. She couldn't write everything she knew about Stoirm and its many little deaths. There were secrets to keep.

Her mobile rang and she glanced at the name on the screen. Simon.
She reached out to answer, then stopped.
Sometimes you have to let the past die, Fiona had said.
She let it ring.

ACKNOWLEDGEMENTS

I've stated before that authors don't work in a vacuum when creating a book and this one is no exception. Although the actual writing is a solo effort—one person alone at the keyboard, except for their insecurities—there is a host of people figuratively at their back, or virtually at the other end of a cable.

Special thanks go to Denzil Meyrick for his unswerving support and guidance. Also to those authors who read this in its various stages: Caro Ramsay, Lucy Cameron, Theresa Talbot, Michael J. Malone and Neil Broadfoot. Thanks for putting in the time, and your advice was not just welcome but spot on. As well as Neil, I also have to give a shout out to the remaining members of the Four Blokes in Search of a Plot team—Gordon Brown and Mark Leggatt—who are always on hand for a word or a choice insult. The Tea Cosy of Inspiration also had a role to play.

Gratitude also goes to Jenny Brown, who graciously spent time with me and gave me pointers both before and after the first draft was completed.

Thanks to Alison Rae and all at Polygon for seeing the value of the book and to my editor Debs Warner for keeping the tale on track. And catching my errors. Also to designer Chris Hannah for what I think is a stunning cover.

I am indebted to Iain MacPherson for his assistance with the Gaelic phrases and David Kerr for his local knowledge. Also to Stephen Wilkie and Dr Sharlene Butler for their help.

And then there are the book bloggers and booksellers and librarians, without whom we could not function. The list has grown considerably over the years and space here is limited, but you all know who you are and I appreciate everything you do, not just for me but all authors.

To festival organisers who have invited me to attend—thank you so much. And please have me back.

Similarly, friends who have supported me, shared posts, attended events and generally kept me something approximating sane, thank you. Again, you know who you are, and I won't list for fear of missing someone out, but you are all important to me.

MYSTERY SKELTON
Skelton, Douglas.
Thunder Bay.
01/29/2020

Family
Comforts

Family Comforts

Rebecca Wilson

For Nina –
my inspiration, my joy,
my comfort

Contents

Introduction

Breakfast & brunch

Quick comforts

Midweek meals

Weekend winners

Slow cooker superheroes

Something sweet

Family comforts

Comfort food to me is the embodiment of home. That warm, cozy feeling you get when you are in a familiar environment, surrounded by the people you love, eating food that makes you feel happy.

In this book, you will find my tried-and-tested wholesome family recipes, which fill me and my family with joy and happiness. When feeding a large (or even a little) crowd, you want to choose recipes that are guaranteed to go down well, so you've come to the right place. Pick from easy breakfasts or tasty family brunches, super simple and easy recipes that can be ready in no time, to family meals that really bring everyone around the table.

I love to use my slow cooker to make my life a little easier, by quickly prepping the base of the dish in the morning and letting it simmer away all day long, filling my house with inviting smells while I look forward to eating later. And let's not forget the puds! My Nina and I have such a sweet tooth so I like to create recipes that are naturally low in sugar, then I can have an extra slice or two!

I have developed every recipe to be suitable for the whole family, from grandma and grandpa coming around for Sunday dinner, to your newly weaning baby at 6 months of age. Every recipe can be enjoyed together, which not only helps your little ones become confident foodies, but it makes our lives just that little bit easier – win, win, win!

WHY EAT TOGETHER?

Growing up, we always ate around the table together with my mother and siblings, all talking and enjoying food with one another. However, it wasn't until I had my daughter Nina, three years ago, that I realised why this is so beneficial. Not only does it save you time by cooking just once, it helps to ensure that every member of your family, including you, has the opportunity to sit down and enjoy a good meal together.

But most importantly, it helps teach our children the physicalities of actually eating, chewing and developing cutlery skills, and contributing to forming positive attitudes towards food and nutrition as they grow older. Offering a wide variety of tastes and textures, while eating together to show your little ones how much you're enjoying the meal, helps children to grow older with reduced tendencies of being fussy with their food. They're watching you, learning from how you eat, and how happy and positive the meal experience is for you – this makes our little ones want to join in and model our behaviours.

And finally, sitting around the dinner table prompts conversation not only with your older children but with the little ones too. It's a fantastic opportunity to help children develop their speech and communication skills. It truly is my most favourite part of the day, so I hope you enjoy these meals with your family just as much as I do.

Adapting the recipes to suit your diet

If you have specific dietary requirements, whether dairy-free, gluten-free, egg-free, vegan or vegetarian, there are ways to adapt the recipes in this book to suit your family's needs. Look out for the * symbol next to the ingredients in the recipes to see which ones you can substitute. Here, I have listed some foods that you can use as substitutes – unless it is specifically stated in the recipe, choose whichever one works best for you. And always check product packets for hidden ingredients you may not be aware of.

DAIRY-FREE COOKING

Butter For most recipes, you can replace butter with dairy-free spreads (these are better for baking), or with coconut or olive oil.

Milk You can substitute milk for plant-based alternatives in all recipes. Soy, pea and oat milks are all a suitable swap from 6 months onwards, and you can introduce nut and hemp milks for children over 2 years old. However, avoid substituting with rice milk as this is not suitable for children under the age of 5 years. Try to choose a milk that is fortified with extra vitamins to ramp up your nutritional intake.

Cheese There are many dairy-free cheeses on the market these days, shop around and find ones which you like the taste of and melt well. It is best to choose a cheese alternative that is fortified with B12 and other vitamins, if possible. Alternatively, in most recipes you can just leave out the cheese or swap it for nutritional yeast flakes (about 1 tablespoon replaces 40–50g/1½–1¾oz of cheese), however, be mindful that in both cases this may reduce a little of the moisture content in the finished dish.

Dairy cream, cream cheese and yogurt In most supermarkets you will find plant-based alternatives to these products. If you do struggle to find anything, use an alternative that is a similar texture to what you are trying to replace. For example, you could replace Greek yogurt with plant-based yogurt or plant-based cream cheese thinned down with a little plant-based milk. Don't be afraid to experiment and make the recipe suit you.

EGG-FREE COOKING

If egg is the main ingredient in a recipe, for example in an omelette, it is not always possible to replace with an alternative option and so it may be best to choose another recipe in this case. However, when egg is used to bind ingredients together, such as for pancakes, flax and chia eggs are a great substitute. Be mindful that they do not expand and rise like a hen's egg would, so the results will be a little different, however, they do work to keep the ingredients together and add a little extra moisture to the recipe. To make 1 replacement egg, follow the instructions below, before adding to your recipe.

Chia egg Stir 1 tablespoon of chia seeds with 2½ tablespoons of warm water and set aside for 5 minutes.

Flax egg Stir 1 tablespoon of ground flax seeds with 3 tablespoons of warm water and set aside for 10–15 minutes.

Egg replacers In recent years, it has become much easier to purchase egg replacers in supermarkets. Look out for either powdered versions or products in the fresh fridge aisle. These are used predominantly in baking.

Egg wash alternatives When a recipe calls for an egg wash, this is to give a little sheen to your bake, especially pastry. Use plant-based milk as a substitute (soy, almond or coconut milk works best), or aquafaba – the liquid that comes in a tin of chickpeas.

NUT-FREE COOKING

When a recipe calls for peanut butter or crushed nuts, there are some options you can take depending on your specific allergies. If possible, opt to substitute for nut-free butters like tahini, sunflower, or specific nut-free butters, which now exist on the market. You could also leave out the nuts altogether, however, please note that nut butters, may be added as a binder or for extra moisture, so the end result may differ slightly.

GLUTEN-FREE COOKING

Gluten is the name of a protein found in wheat and some other grains. If you lead a gluten-free diet, there are plenty of alternatives. In most cases, plain (all-purpose) or self-raising flour can be replaced in like-for-like quantities with shop-bought gluten-free variations. Also, look out for gluten-free baking powder, soy sauce, Worcestershire sauce, mustard and stock cubes, as some of these products may contain traces of gluten. While oats don't contain gluten, they are often processed in factories with other grains that do, so always look for oats marked as 'gluten-free' to avoid any cross contamination.

MEAT REPLACEMENT IN RECIPES

Veggies You can generally replace meat with either firm vegetables like mushrooms or butternut squash, or meat-replacement products. Just be mindful that meat-replacement products often contain added salt, so factor this in when serving to little ones. They are also usually low in fat, therefore, it is important to replace this lost fat with other forms of higher calorific foods like avocado or nut butters, especially when serving to babies, as little ones need those extra calories to help them grow.

Tofu This is an excellent meat replacement. Use the correct firmness and follow the instructions on the packet to incorporate it into the recipe. Soft silken tofu is a good substitute for thick cream in desserts or to add at the end of cooking soups, while firm tofu is great to breadcrumb to turn into nuggets or stir through pasta or noodle dishes.

Be mindful that there are hidden traces of meat and fish in some foods like Worcestershire sauce, which usually contains anchovies, so try to find vegetarian options or leave these ingredients out. Some cheeses use animal rennet in their production, however, there are plenty on the market that are vegetarian, and this will be displayed on the packet.

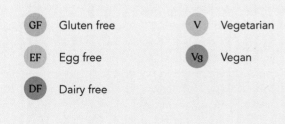

GF	Gluten free	**V**	Vegetarian	Whenever you see a * next to the letters in the recipe symbols,
EF	Egg free	**Vg**	Vegan	this indicates that the recipe can be adapted to suit this
DF	Dairy free			dietary requirement. Please take care and turn to this section for possible alternatives.

Things to remember when feeding your baby

The recipes in this book can be served to every member of your family, including babies from the age of 6 months. Here are a few tips to make your family meals enjoyable even for the littlest ones.

SALT

Every recipe has been specifically developed to be low in salt and sugar so that they are safe for little ones to enjoy, but still delicious for us adults too. You can find specific instructions in the recipes where moderation for babies is advised. Remember also that some shop-bought products, especially seasonings like soy sauce and stock cubes, can be very high in salt, so always opt for low-salt varieties when cooking for little ones.

The use of salt in seasoning our own food as adults is a habit that develops as we grow older, and not everyone has the same salt tolerance. Please do feel free to season your own food once the family meal has been dished up, or your little one's portion has been removed from the pan. Adapt recipes with extra chilli, pepper or spice if you feel like it – make your food your own, it's there to be enjoyed!

As a guide, refer to the below:

Babies under 12 months should have less than 1g of salt per day (0.4g of sodium).

Toddlers aged 1–3 years can have a maximum of 2g of salt (0.8g of sodium).

Children aged 4–6 years are allowed 3g of salt per day (1.2g of sodium).

Children aged 7–10 years can have a maximum of 5g of salt per day (2g of sodium).

Children aged 11 years to adulthood can have a maximum of 6g of salt per day (2.4g of sodium).

SUGAR

There are no set guidelines to how much sugar little ones should be consuming, but the general rule is as little as possible. So to make the recipes in this book suitable for all, including our youngest taste testers, we need to impart that sweet taste from more natural sources. One of the best ways to do this is to use fruit as a natural sweetener. Banana works really well and is delicious in most cases, however, sometimes it does have quite a strong taste which isn't desirable in every bake. Using apple purée is a great alternative, and the easiest way is to purchase shop-bought baby food pouches, which are 100 per cent apple with no added sugar. You can also use any sweet baby food fruit pouch such as mango, prune or pear, as long as there are no added sugars or cereals. You can, of course, make your own fruit purée by boiling skinned and chopped fruit with a splash of water until softened, then mash or blend to form a purée.

A note on honey: In some recipes, I have also used honey as a natural sweetener. However, please note that it is unsafe to offer honey to children under the age of 12 months as there is a risk of botulism. Honey is also not suitable for those following a vegan diet. Instead, replace the honey with maple syrup or leave out all together.

FINGER STRIPS

One of the most important things is to ensure you are serving the food in an appropriate shape for your little one. The best way to do this is to cut everything into finger strips, using your forefinger as a general guide. This isn't a specific size, it is purely to ensure that your little one can pick up the food easily and feed themselves. When a baby can both hold a portion of food in their hand and bite off mouthfuls, this is at a manageable size for a baby. This is why it is important you do not place food in your baby's mouth and allow them to figure it out for themselves.

NO TEETH?

It is a common misconception that babies need teeth to eat finger foods. In fact, their gums are hard enough to chew and process food from 6 months of age. Some babies do not grow their first teeth until they are over a year old, and in most cases the back molars (chewing teeth) usually do not come in until little ones are around 18 months old plus. This would be too long to wait to serve finger foods, and you run the risk of delaying the opportunity to develop their eating skills.

TO AVOID CHOKING

Concerns about choking can be the scariest part of offering finger foods to a baby. However, it is important to offer a wide variety of tastes and textures from the beginning of weaning to help your little one learn this important eating skill. Try not to let this worry you too much, or hinder your family eating experience, and remember there's a huge difference between gagging and choking. To minimise the risk, serve food in an appropriate shape for your little one's age, avoiding all hard, round food, like whole nuts or grapes. Crush nuts into very small pieces or offer as a nut butter, and cut grapes into quarters lengthways. Whole blueberries must be cut in half or squished before serving, however, foods like peas and sweetcorn kernels are too small to be a choking hazard so these can be served whole. Generally, anything larger than a

pea, and smaller than a golf ball should be modified in shape to make it safe for a baby. The age in which you can relax these rules varies on your little one's ability to chew food and their age.

As a general guide, small blueberries can stay whole from around 2 or 3 years of age but whole nuts shouldn't be served under the age of 5. Some more examples here:

- Toast – cut into finger strips

- Hard-boiled egg – cut into quarters lengthways

- Raw apple – from 6 months, grated; from 12 months, cut into thin slices; from 2 years, eat whole depending on their chewing skill development

- Avocado – cut into wedges; for younger babies, leave some of the skin still attached to aid with grip

SPOON FEEDING

If you prefer to lead a spoon-fed approach when first starting to wean your baby, this is completely fine and entirely your decision as a parent. Every recipe in this book can be blended down, with a little extra water or milk (cow's, plant-based or baby's usual milk) to your desired consistency. This enables you to still eat the same meals together, teaching your little ones healthy eating habits. Read more on the benefits of eating together on page 6.

Don't forget you can absolutely combine both weaning methods and offer finger foods alongside puréed foods while you gradually increase the consistency and texture for your baby.

For more information on how to begin weaning, pick up a copy of my first book *What Mummy Makes*, which takes you through the first stages of weaning in more detail.

Useful ingredients and equipment

There are a few ingredients that I always have in stock, no matter what, and as soon as I've used them up, they go right back on my shopping list. These are the ones that add such comforting flavour or texture to my cooking that I find myself drawn to them all the time. Likewise, my hero accessories – not entirely essential, but they do make cooking easier and more fun!

HERO INGREDIENTS

The ingredients I couldn't be without:

- Garlic-infused olive or rapeseed (canola) oil

- Low-salt stock cubes

- Low-salt soy sauce

- Mushroom powder

- Vanilla extract (not essence)

- Ground cinnamon

- Fruit purée pouches

- Cheddar and smoked Cheddar cheese

- Smoked paprika

- Dried mixed herbs

- Panko breadcrumbs

- Peanut butter – 100% peanut

- Cornflour (cornstarch)

HERO KITCHEN ACCESSORIES

For making life in your kitchen that little bit easier:

- Thick, non-stick aluminium foil is great for roasting anything, saves your trays from lots of burnt bits, and reduces that tedious clean up time.

- Non-stick baking paper – not to be confused with greaseproof paper, which is not non-stick. Pick the right paper to line your cake tins with, to avoid disappointment after all your baking efforts.

- If you can find it, foil-backed non-stick baking paper has the qualities of a non-stick lining, with foil which bends and moulds easily so you can raise the sides to trap in juices. It also conducts heat well to help with creating the desirable crispy bottom.

- Hand stick-blenders and food processors save huge amounts of time, and open up your cooking and eating experience to a wider range of tastes and textures.

KITCHEN ESSENTIALS

If you're a newbie to cooking, here's a little list of kitchen items to get you started:

- Good set of kitchen knives – a small paring knife for chopping foods like fruit, a large chef's knife for cutting meat and large vegetables, plus a serrated bread knife for cutting anything with a crumb – try to buy the best your money can buy and keep them as sharp as you can

- 2 chopping boards, one for cutting vegetables and fruit and another for cutting meat

- Tin opener

- Rolling pin

- Digital weighing scales

- Potato masher

- Wooden spoons

- Rubber or silicone spatula

- Non-metal fish slice

- Colander or wide kitchen spider strainer tool

- Non-metal whisk, or rubber-tipped metal whisk

- Large non-stick frying pan – 28cm (11in) or larger

- Set of lidded saucepans

- Set of varying size non-stick, low-sided baking trays, but if you only buy one, get a tray that is as large as your oven will hold – this means your food will have more flavour and cook more evenly as there will be more room to spread it out on the tray

- Box grater

- Mixing bowls – minimum one small and one large

Food prep tips and tricks

There are useful tips for speeding up prep in the kitchen that will save you time and make the whole cooking process a little easier. To begin, it may seem like one of the simplest of things, but reading the recipe in full before starting to cook will save you from making a lot of mistakes down the line.

CUTTING, CHOPPING AND COOKING

A sharp knife is the most important place to start. It might sound contradictory, but it is actually much safer to use a very sharp blade than a blunt knife. It means the blade will glide into the food you are chopping rather than slipping and possibly cutting yourself. It is also much less effort to chop up that onion or tomato at a quicker pace. So my first tip is to invest in a knife sharpener – I personally prefer to use a sharpening steel rod, but there are lots of different products out there – find the one that works best for you.

Set up a little waste bowl near your chopping board for any veg skins or general rubbish accumulated during cooking. This keeps your work surface clean and tidy and helps you feel in control of your cooking space, plus it makes the clean up once you finish cooking much more manageable.

Let little ones help with chopping by using scissors to cut up foods that are soft and break easily, like herbs or bread.

Skipping some steps in vegetable preparation can help if you're short on time, and this can even help you create healthier meals too. When prepping fruits and vegetables like potatoes, carrots, parsnips, kiwis and apples, quite often the skin is edible and full of nutrition. Just give them a good wash and they're ready to cook or eat.

Boiling a pan of water can be sped up! Ensure you start with a very hot pan before you put the liquid in – just watch out for steam and spatters. To really speed up the process, boil a kettle of water before adding it to a hot pan. This also applies to pan-frying: unless stated in the recipe, always add ingredients to a frying pan once the pan is hot so that the food will start to fry straight away, rather than slightly stew in its juices at a lower temperature – the results will be so much more delicious.

Grating an onion means that the finished dish won't be full of onion chunks that could be disliked when serving to little ones. You can, of course, dice the onion as small as you can, but an easier way is to utilise your box grater.

To make the process much easier and less messy, start with chopping off the dry top of the onion, but leave the root still together, then cut in half through the root and remove the dry skin from the outside of each half. Hold the flat side of the onion against a box grater, so that you are holding all the layers together and coarsely grate. Once you have the motion, you may find it easier to look away slightly for a moment at a time to avoid any juices causing those onion tears. Arguably, the easiest way of all is to use the grater function on a food processor.

To dice an onion, cut it in half and peel it, keeping the root still attached. Place the onion, cut-side down on your chopping board and with a large sharp knife level with the board, cut 2 or 3 slices through the side of the onion, almost touching the root. You can hold the blade vertically and cut thin slices around 5mm (¼in) wide through the top side of the onion half pointing towards the root, but ensuring you do not cut through the root. Rotate the onion so it sits landscape in front of you, and cut it into slices, 5mm (¼in) wide. Because of all the other cuts you have made, these final slices will cut the onion into very small cubes.

How to prepare garlic: There are many ways to prepare garlic, and usually a recipe will suggest which method is best to use as different methods give varied flavour outcomes. Here they are explained:

Sliced Peel the whole garlic clove by topping and tailing and removing the dry skin, then thinly slice into small rounds.

Minced Slice peeled garlic cloves, then bunch up the slices and run your knife over the garlic many times in different directions until the garlic has been chopped into very small pieces. Use your finger to carefully scrape the garlic from the side of the blade and chop again to try and get the pieces all the same size.

Crushed There are a few ways to do this one. You can use a garlic crusher or you can mince the garlic and then crush it by pressing it down under the flat side of the blade of your knife with one hand until the garlic turns into a paste. If your little ones are old enough, adding a touch of salt at this stage helps break down the garlic to crush it quicker.

Grated Use a very fine grater, lemon zester or hard-cheese grater to grate peeled garlic, this breaks it down into small,even-sized pieces.

To peel a boiled egg, tap it on a hard surface to initially break the shell, then gently roll it with the palm of your hand to crack it all around. Be sure not to press too firmly and squish the egg inside. Now, either under running water or in the cold pan filled with water, peel the egg – the water helps the shell come away easier and takes away the need to sit and pick off lots of tiny pieces of shell.

BAKING

The best tip I can give you when baking is to invest in some digital scales. Accuracy is key when baking, as a touch too much or too little of an ingredient can really affect the outcome of your finished bake. Here are a few tricks to help when baking at home:

Lining a cake tin: Do this before you have made up the batter. Liberally grease the base and sides of the inside of your cake tin with any fat, but preferably butter. For extra assurance that the base will come away easily, it's best to line the bottom with non-stick baking paper.

For a round cake tin, take a piece of baking paper that is slightly bigger than the circumference of your tin. Fold the paper in half and in half again the other way. Then fold it in half once more, into a triangle shape this time, ensuring there is one point where all the folded creases meet. Hover this folded paper triangle over the base of your tin with the point over the centre of the circle. Mark where the outside edge of the base comes to on the paper and use a pair of scissors to cut down the triangle to size, so that when you unfold the paper it is in a circle shape that should fit perfectly inside the tin.

For a square or rectangular baking tray, cut one long strip of baking paper that is wide enough to lay flat in the base of the tray and up the two opposite sides without any creases or folds. Press the paper into the tray, letting the grease keep it in place, then trim down any excess paper so that there is only 1–2cm (½–¾in) sticking up at each side – you'll use these as handles to remove the finished bake from the tin later.

To ensure your bake comes out as intended, here are a few do's and don'ts:

- When starting to bake, I find it best to gather all of the ingredients you need and have them on your work surface in front of you. This ensures you don't forget anything and get that sinking feeling when the cake goes in the oven.

- Always use the correct butter temperature, if the recipe calls for softened butter, ensure you do not use cold, hard butter as this won't give the same outcome. If you need to soften butter quickly, cut it into small cubes and place on a plate. Fill a separate large bowl with very hot water from the tap to heat up the bowl, remove the water, dry quickly, then place that hot bowl upside down over the butter, after 5 minutes, the butter should have softened. You can also soften cubed butter in the microwave on a low heat setting, but be very careful to not melt the butter, as this will also alter the recipe. Soft butter should feel very squishy when pressed and slightly melt with the warmth of your finger.

- If a recipe calls for self-raising flour or baking powder – these are raising agents which are activated when mixed with wet ingredients. Therefore, as soon as you have combined any raising agent with the wet ingredients, work quickly to get your bake in the oven to maximise the effectiveness of the agent.

- When baking anything that you want to rise in the oven, like a cake, it is really important to not open the oven door for the first 50–70 per cent of the cooking time, however tempting it may be. Even if in doubt, don't open the door as you will run the risk of some hot air escaping and the bake not rising properly.

- To achieve a light and airy finish to your cakes, sift your dry ingredients into the cake batter – in particular ingredients like flour, baking powder and cocoa powder. If it looks clumpy, sift it.

- If you find your bakes aren't rising, check the expiry date of your ingredients. It's very easy to have a tub of baking powder sitting in your cupboard for a while, but if it's out of date, it won't work properly.

Breakfast & brunch

Start your day right with quick family meals that help ease you into those chilly mornings.

Rebecca's strawberry breakfast pastries

These naturally sweet fruity cheesecake pastries are super quick to whip up – and your home will smell like a French pâtisserie!

GF*
EF*
V
Vg*
DF*

🍴 Makes 6 large or 12 small pastries ⏱ Prep 10 minutes, Bake 20 minutes ❄ Freezable

about 200g (7oz) strawberries, hulled

140g (5oz) full-fat cream cheese or thick Greek

yogurt*, plus extra if needed

1 tsp vanilla extract

1 x 375g (13oz) sheet of ready-rolled puff pastry*

1 egg* (or milk*)

1 tbsp icing sugar (optional)

(*See pages 8–9)

Preheat the oven to 200°C fan (220°C/425°F/Gas 7).

In a small mixing bowl, mash 80g (2¾oz) of the strawberries with the back of a fork until fairly smooth – a few lumps is totally fine. Stir in the cream cheese and vanilla until well combined. You want a nice thick paste which holds its shape well; if the mixture feels too runny, add more cream cheese until thickened up because if the mixture is too loose, it'll end up running off the pastry when baking, resulting in a sloppy mess.

Unroll the pastry sheet and cut it into 6 or 12 squares. The shape depends on the dimensions of the pastry sheet, so you may end up with rectangles, or you can cut them into triangles too. Transfer the pastry to a non-stick baking tray and gently score a 1cm (½in) border around each pastry edge, ensuring you don't cut all the way through.

Spread about 1 tablespoon of the cream cheese mixture onto each pastry, keeping inside the border. Slice the remaining strawberries into 3mm (⅛in) thick slices and arrange them on top of the cream cheese mixture, again keeping inside the border.

Whisk the egg and brush over the pastry borders. Try not to let too much egg drip down the sides of the pastry as this will prevent a high, flaky rise. Bake in the preheated oven for 15–20 minutes until the pastry has puffed up and is golden. Add an optional dusting of icing sugar for an extra treat, if you wish.

Cut into strips to serve to little ones with some fruit on the side.

Love your leftovers Pastries will keep for 2 days in the fridge. To enjoy leftovers at their best, reheat in a hot oven for around 5 minutes or until piping hot, keeping an eye on them so they don't catch. You can also freeze these pastries for up to 1 month, either before or after cooking. To bake from frozen, pop in an oven set to 180°C fan (200°C/400°F/Gas 6) and cook for 20–25 minutes from raw, or for 7–12 minutes for cooked frozen pastries. Be sure to keep a good watch as they will catch easily around the edges if reheating cooked pastry, but be mindful to bake until piping hot throughout.

Simple swaps You can use pretty much any fruit you like – raspberries and blueberries work really well. Ideally choose a soft fruit, however if using a firm fleshed fruit like apple, grate it into the cream cheese then thinly slice for the top. You can also prep the pastries the night before, up to giving them the egg wash, then keep in the fridge to pop in the oven in the morning for a well-deserved lie in!

Peach chia jam

Use the natural sweetness of canned peaches to your advantage to make this moreish jam, perfect for topping toast, filling sandwiches or for flavouring yogurt and smoothies.

GF

EF

V

Vg*

DF

⏲ 1 generous jar's worth (about 400g/14oz)   ⏱ Prep and cook 20 minutes

1 x 415g (14¾oz) can of
  peaches in fruit juice (not
  syrup)
4 tbsp chia seeds, preferably
  white

1 tsp vanilla extract
1 tbsp honey* (for over 1s)
  or maple syrup (optional)

Add the peaches, including the juice, to a blender, along with 100ml (3½fl oz) of water. Blend until super smooth, then transfer to a medium-sized saucepan.

Set the pan over a medium–high heat and, while it comes up to temperature, add the chia seeds, vanilla and honey or maple syrup, if using. Simmer for 5–10 minutes until the jam is well thickened and coats the back of a spoon.

Take off the heat, and transfer the jam to a heatproof bowl or spring lidded jar. The jam will continue to thicken as it cools. Once completely cold, cover the bowl (or seal the jar) and store in the fridge for up to 2 weeks.

Top tip Turn to page 208 to see how to turn this jam into delicious peach melba tarts.

Blueberry semolina

Technically a pudding, but seeing as it's so low in sugar, there's no reason why this delightfully comforting bowl of goodness can't be served for breakfast!

⏱ 1 adult and 1 little ⏱ Prep and cook 10 minutes ❄ Freezable

EF

V

Vg*

DF*

150g (5½oz) frozen blueberries
500ml (17fl oz) milk*
1 tbsp honey* (for over 1s),
  maple syrup or golden
  caster sugar (optional)

1 tsp vanilla extract
90g (3¼oz) fine semolina
(*See page 8)

Put the frozen blueberries in a microwavable bowl with 1½ tablespoons of water, cover and heat for 3 minutes until the blueberries have fully defrosted and are very soft.

Meanwhile, heat the milk in a medium-sized saucepan along with your sweetener of choice, if using, and the vanilla extract.

While it comes up to heat, measure the semolina into a separate small bowl, ready to add to the milk. Take the blueberries out of the microwave and use the back of a fork to break up the fruit a little more

Once the milk is starting to steam, you can see small bubbles forming and it feels very warm when you hover your hand over the liquid, quickly tip in the blueberries. Immediately, to avoid the milk splitting, take a whisk in one hand and the semolina in the other and sprinkle the semolina into the milk, whisking continuously to avoid the mixture lumping. The milk should thicken straightaway. Stir and allow it to cook for a further couple of minutes until it reaches your desired consistency. Thick is best in my opinion, but bear in mind it will thicken further as it cools. If, by chance, your milk looks to be separating, sprinkle in some extra semolina and stir continuously until it thickens and comes back together.

Decant into serving bowls and enjoy as is or with a dollop of yogurt and more fruit on top.

Love your leftovers The semolina will keep for 2 days in the fridge, or freeze for 2 months. Defrost and reheat with an extra splash of milk until piping hot throughout.

Cinnamon breakfast buns

Start the day with the smell of comforting cinnamon wafting through your home and these warm, soft-in-the-middle little cinnamon rolls ready for everyone to enjoy.

⏓ Makes 12 buns ⏱ Prep 20 minutes, Bake 18 minutes ❄ Freezable

120g (4¼oz) unsalted butter*, very soft, plus extra for greasing
1 tbsp golden caster sugar (optional)
1½ tbsp ground cinnamon
1 tsp vanilla extract

200g (7oz) Greek yogurt*, plus extra to drizzle
300g (10½oz) self-raising flour, plus extra for dusting
1 tsp baking powder
(*See page 8)

Preheat the oven to 190°C fan (210°C/415°F/Gas 6–7) and grease a large baking tray with a little butter.

Put 80g (2¾oz) of the soft butter in a small bowl, along with the sugar, if using, and a tablespoon of the cinnamon. Stir and set aside.

Put the remaining butter in another bowl with the rest of the cinnamon, the vanilla extract and the yogurt. Mix until the butter is combined with the yogurt, then add the flour and baking powder and combine to form a dough.

Tip the dough onto a floured work surface and bring together to form a ball. Try to knead it as little as possible to avoid overworking the dough – a more rustic look results in softer buns. Pat it down with the palm of your hand, then roll out into a rectangle as neat as you can get it, about 8mm (³⁄₈in) thick. Spread the cinnamon butter all over the dough, going right to the edges and ensuring it's an even thickness throughout. From one of the shorter edges, roll the dough up into a sausage, then cut it evenly into 12 discs.

Place each spiral onto the prepared baking tray, cut-side up and touching each other, to form three rows of four spirals. This way, they will rise together and create a softer batch bake. If you prefer a crispier texture, separate the buns out. Pop the tray in the preheated oven and bake for 15–18 minutes until the dough has puffed up and is golden on top.

Drizzle with yogurt and serve with fruit for breakfast, or try the cream cheese frosting on page 30 for a delicious alternative!

Love your leftovers These cinnamon buns are best served warm, so reheat any leftovers in the microwave for 15 seconds to enjoy warm and soft. They will keep for 2 days in an airtight container, or freeze for 3 months.

EF
V
Vg*
DF*

Fruit and nut breakfast bars

Soft and fruity, these no-added-sugar bars are perfect for all ages to enjoy as an easy-grab breakfast at home or on the go. They are fab for packed lunch boxes too!

GF*

EF

V

Vg*

DF*

🍴 Makes 10 bars   ⏱ Prep 10 minutes, Bake 20 minutes   ❄ Freezable

60g (2oz) soft dried prunes
70g (2½oz) dried apricots
   (preferably unsulphured)
200g (7oz) porridge oats*
80g (2¾oz) cornflakes or rice
   crispies

60g (2oz) nuts, finely chopped
   (or ground for under 1s)
2 x 90g (3¼oz) pouches apple
   purée (see page 10)
50g (1¾oz) almond butter (or
   peanut or cashew butter)

2 tsp vanilla extract
100ml (3½fl oz) milk*
100g (3½oz) unsalted butter*
   or coconut oil, melted,
   plus extra for greasing
(*See pages 8–9)

Preheat the oven to 190°C fan (210°C/415°F/Gas 6–7) and grease a 20cm (8in) square brownie tin. Cut a strip of non-stick baking paper and use it to line the base of the tin, with a little paper overlapping two of the edges. This is so that you can easily remove the bake from the tin once it's cooked.

Chop the prunes and apricots into about 1cm (½in) dice – no need to be precise about this, just keep running the knife over the fruit so that you have lots of small pieces.

Put the chopped dried fruit in a mixing bowl, add the rest of the ingredients and give it a good stir.

Tip the mixture into the prepared baking tin and level out the top with the back of a spoon.

Pop the tray in the preheated oven and bake for 15–20 minutes until you can see the edges are starting to take on a little colour.

Using the two paper handles, transfer to a chopping board and leave to cool for 5 minutes before cutting into 10 bars.

Love your leftovers Store the bars in an airtight container for 4–5 days, or freeze for up to 3 months. Defrost at room temperature or blast in the microwave for 60–90 seconds.

Love choccy? Try adding in a handful of chocolate chips for the older kids!

Apple and courgette breakfast muffins

V

DF*

These are a real winner. Whip up a batch in the morning and you'll have delicious muffins ready for a few days' worth of breakfast and snacks for the whole family.

⅛ Makes 12 muffins ⏱ Prep 15 minutes, Bake 18 minutes

spray cooking oil (optional)
1 small courgette
1 red eating apple
3 medium eggs
2 tsp vanilla extract
180g (6¼oz) melted unsalted
  butter* (see page 8)
1 x 90g (3¼oz) pouch apple
  purée (see page 10)

70g (2½oz) fruit sugar or
  golden caster sugar
  (optional for young babies)
300g (10½oz) self-raising flour
1 tsp baking powder
2 tsp ground cinnamon
1 tbsp demerara sugar, for
  decoration (optional)

Preheat the oven to 170°C fan (190°C/375°F/Gas 5) and line a deep 12-hole muffin tray with non-stick paper cases. Spray with cooking oil if your cases aren't non-stick.

Grate the courgette and apple on the coarse side of a box grater. Then, a handful at a time, squeeze out most of the liquid and add the pulp to a mixing bowl.

To the courgette and apple pulp, add the eggs, vanilla, melted butter, apple purée and fruit sugar, if using. Whisk until well combined, then sift in the flour, baking powder and cinnamon. Gently stir and fold the flour into the wet ingredients until there are no lumps, but avoid overworking the mixture.

Divide the batter between the 12 muffin cases and, if you wish, sprinkle a tiny amount of demerara sugar on top to give the tops a little sweetness and crunch.

Bake for 16–18 minutes until well risen and baked throughout. To check, insert a knife into the centre of a muffin – if it comes out clean, they're done. Leave to cool a little on a wire rack before serving.

Love your leftovers Store the muffins in an airtight container for 3 days at room temperature. They are delicious reheated – pop in the microwave for 60 seconds or in the oven for 10 minutes. Alternatively, freeze for 3 months and defrost at room temperature, or microwave for 2 minutes until piping hot throughout.

Top tip If you would like to transform these muffins into a delicious dessert, I urge you to whip up some cream cheese frosting. Mix 3 heaped tablespoons of unflavoured soft cream cheese with 1 tablespoon of maple syrup. Smother a generous teaspoon of the frosting onto the top of a muffin and dig in!

Baked fruity French toast fingers

GF*
EF*
V
Vg*
DF*

If you have some day-old, turning-stale bread, this recipe is a perfect way to use it up. Traditional eggy bread vibes made super simple by baking in the oven, so no need to stand at the stove flipping – this way everyone gets warm eggy bread to enjoy together.

🍴 2 adults and 2 littles   ⏱ **Prep 10 minutes, Bake 17 minutes**   ❄ **Freezable**

melted butter* or oil, for greasing
6 slices of bread* of your choice (brioche works best), approx 2.5cm (1in) thick
1 large overripe banana

3 medium eggs* (see note below)
1 x 90g (3¼oz) pouch of unsweetened fruit purée (see page 10)
2 tsp ground cinnamon

2 tsp vanilla extract
60ml (2fl oz) milk*
(*See pages 8–9)

Preheat the oven to 180°C fan (200°C/400°F/Gas 6) and line a large heavy baking tray with non-stick foil, greasing it with a touch of cooking spread or melted butter.

Cut the bread into 5cm (2in) wide strips (a regular slice of bread will cut into 3 strips) and set aside while you make the egg mixture.

In a large wide-bottomed bowl, mash the banana with the back of a fork, then add the eggs, fruit purée, cinnamon, vanilla and milk, and whisk well using a balloon whisk.

One at a time, dip the bread fingers into the egg mixture, ensuring that they are fully covered and you can see no dry bread. Transfer to the prepared baking tray, ensuring they are spaced apart and not touching each other as this will help them cook evenly.

Pop the tray in the oven to bake for 15–17 minutes. If you have time and remember, flip the eggy bread over using a large fish slice and spray the top with a little more cooking oil – but don't worry if you're getting the kids sorted, it'll still be yummy without. You'll know they're done when the sides of the bread are starting to turn a dark brown and the bread feels dry rather than wet to the touch.

Serve with yogurt for dipping and your choice of fruit.

Love your leftovers The toasted fingers will keep for 2 days in the fridge, or up to 2 months in the freezer. Reheat from frozen in an oven set to 180°C fan (200°C/400°F/ Gas 6) for 10–12 minutes, or in the microwave for 60 seconds until piping hot.

Egg free? Replace the eggs with 200ml (7fl oz) of a milk of your choice, whisking well with the other ingredients. Soak the bread and place on a very well-greased baking tray, as without the eggs it may be more prone to sticking. Bake as above.

Eggy bread sarnies

There is something very comforting about turning a regular old sandwich into an eggy bread sarnie. Crispy eggy coating on the outside with soft sarnie fillings starting to ooze and melt from the heat of the pan – what a treat!

⫯⫯ 1 adult or 2 littles   ⏱ **Prep and cook 10 minutes**   ❄ **Freezable**

2 slices of bread*
1 large egg*, beaten (or see
   opposite)
a little fat for frying (butter*,
   or sunflower, olive or
   coconut oil)

FILLING COMBOS:

Peanut Butter and Jam
a small handful of fresh
   raspberries, mashed with
   a fork
1 tbsp smooth or crunchy
   peanut butter

Peanut Butter and Banana
1 tbsp smooth or crunchy
   peanut butter
½ banana, mashed with a fork

Cheesecake
1 tbsp cream cheese* mixed
   with a drop of vanilla extract
sliced strawberries and a small
   handful of blueberries

Cheese and Chutney
30g (1oz) Cheddar cheese*,
   grated
2 super-ripe plums, skin and
   stone removed and mashed

Pizza
tomato purée mixed with a
   little black pepper and a
   pinch each of dried mixed
   herbs and smoked paprika
30g (1oz) Cheddar cheese*,
   grated

Tuna Cheese
1 tbsp Greek yogurt* (or
   mayonnaise for older kids)
½ small can of tuna, drained
30g (1oz) Cheddar cheese*,
   grated
freshly ground black pepper

(*See pages 8–9)

Make your sandwich as usual; if there are two wet ingredients, spread one on each piece of bread, then sandwich together.

Whisk the egg in a wide flat-bottomed bowl that's large enough to fit your bread in. Dip the whole sarnie into the egg, turning it over so the entire sandwich is soaked in egg.

Add a little butter or a drizzle of oil to a non-stick frying pan over medium heat. Cook the sandwich, flipping it over after 2–3 minutes, until the entire outside is golden.

Love your leftovers The cooked eggy bread sarnie will keep in the fridge for a day, or freeze for up to 2 months. To reheat, place the frozen eggy bread sarnie on a baking tray and bake in a hot oven for 5–8 minutes, or until piping hot.

Egg free? Mash a banana well and drizzle in a little milk to loosen the consistency (this acts as your egg replacement). Soak your sandwich in the liquid, then fry over a low heat for a little longer than above as the sugar in the banana is prone to catching if you cook on a higher heat. This method works best for the sweet filling options.

Turn over to see how they look

Lemon and poppyseed sheet pan pancakes

GF*

EF*

V

Vg*

DF*

Save time in the morning by quickly whipping up this scrummy pancake batter and baking as one large sheet in the oven instead of standing and flipping each pancake at the stove top. Delicious as is, you could also serve it dipped in a little yogurt, or drizzle over some honey for you and your children (if over 1) for a delicious, comforting combo.

2 adults and 2 littles Prep 10 minutes Bake 20 minutes Freezable

250g (9oz) self-raising flour*
finely grated zest and juice
   of 1 unwaxed lemon
2 medium eggs*
30g (1oz) poppyseeds

1 tsp baking powder*
1 tsp vanilla extract
150g (5½oz) Greek yogurt*
2 tbsp honey* (for over 1s)
   or maple syrup (optional)

80ml (2½fl oz) milk*
40g (1½oz) unsalted butter*,
   melted
(*See pages 8–9)

Preheat the oven to 190°C fan (210°C/415°F/Gas 6–7) and line a 25cm x 35cm (10 x14 in) baking tray with non-stick baking paper. (If your tray is a little larger, that will be fine too.)

Put all the pancake ingredients in a mixing bowl and stir until just combined. Avoid over beating as this will make the pancakes tough.

Pour the batter onto the baking tray and gently spread out until it is an even thickness throughout – it should be around 1cm (½in) thick.

Pop the tray in the oven and bake for 15–20 minutes or until the top of the pancake has turned golden, it's slightly springy to touch and there is a wonderful smell of lemon in your kitchen.

To serve, use a pizza cutter or sharp knife to cut the large pancake into little squares, and serve with your favourite pancake toppings, with fruit on the side.

Love your leftovers The baked pancakes will keep for 2 days in an airtight container in the fridge, or freeze (with parchment paper between each piece) for up to 3 months. To reheat, pop in the toaster until a little crisp on the outside and fully defrosted and piping hot inside, or you can blast it in a hot microwave for 60–90 seconds from frozen.

Gingerbread waffles

Soft, fluffy, warmly spiced waffles that will make you all smile! Use the same batter to whip up pancakes instead, if you wish.

EF*

V

Vg*

DF*

🍴 2 adults and 2 littles   ⏱ Prep and cook 20 minutes   ❄ Freezable

1 overripe banana
1 x 90g (3¼oz) fruit purée
   pouch (eg. apple/mango,
   see page 10) or another
   banana
2 medium eggs*

1–2 tbsp coconut or golden
   caster sugar (optional)
1 tsp vanilla extract
100ml (3½fl oz) milk*
150g (5½oz) self-raising flour
1 tsp baking powder

2 tsp ground ginger
2 tsp ground cinnamon
1 tsp mixed spice
unsalted butter* or cooking
   oil spray, for greasing
(*See pages 8–9)

Plug in your waffle maker so it starts to heat up while you make the batter.

Put the banana in a large bowl and mash well using the back of a fork. Try to make sure there are no large lumps of fruit.

To the mashed banana, add the fruit purée, eggs, sugar, if using, vanilla and milk and whisk well. Now sift in the flour, baking powder and spices and stir to combine until you see no lumps.

Add a half teaspoon-sized knob of butter to each waffle grid – which should be piping hot by now – and use a silicone pastry brush to distribute it and evenly grease the waffle grids. This will prevent sticking and give the outside of each waffle a nice crust.

Pour 2–4 tablespoons of the batter into each waffle mould, depending on the size of your waffle maker. Close the lid and cook for 3–4 minutes, or until the batter is fluffy on the inside and has formed a lovely crust.

Serve your waffles with yogurt, fresh fruit and an optional drizzle of maple syrup or honey* (for over 1s).

Love your leftovers Waffles can be stored in an airtight container at room temperature, or freeze for up to 3 months. Reheat in the toaster, oven or microwave from frozen until piping hot throughout.

No waffle maker? You can also cook the batter in a frying pan to make pancakes to stack up, or pour it into a lined baking tray and bake as a sheet pancake, as on page 38.

Cherry and chocolate baked oats

GF*

EF*

V

Vg*

DF*

What a way to start the day... a chocolatey oaty batter, topped with convenient frozen cherries, then popped in the oven while you make yourself a coffee and get the little ones ready for the day. Perfect for those cold mornings where you just need a comforting hug of a breakfast.

⏲ 2 adults and 2 littles   ⏱ Prep 10 minutes, Bake 30 minutes

a little butter* or olive oil,
  for greasing
2 ripe bananas (or 180g/6¼oz
  apple purée, see page 10)
130g (4½oz) rolled porridge
  oats*
2 tbsp unsweetened cocoa
  powder, sifted

1 tsp baking powder*
350ml (12fl oz) milk*
1 tsp vanilla extract
2 medium eggs*
1 tbsp maple syrup (optional,
  you can use honey* for over
  1s), plus extra to serve

a handful of frozen pitted dark
  cherries
1 tbsp finely chopped nuts, or
  flaked almonds for over 2s
  (optional)
(*See pages 8–9)

Preheat the oven to 190°C fan (210°C/415°F/Gas 6–7) and lightly grease a 1–1.5 litre (35–52fl oz) ovenproof ceramic or glass dish. The smaller the dish, the deeper the baked oats will be.

Add the peeled bananas to the dish and mash well with the back of a fork. Add the oats, cocoa powder, baking powder, milk, vanilla extract, eggs and maple syrup, if using. Give it a good stir, then level the mixture out, ensuring there are no oats creeping up the side as these will crisp up too much and make cleaning the dish later difficult.

Scatter over the frozen cherries (no need to defrost) and the nuts, if using, then pop in the oven. Bake, uncovered, for 20–30 minutes until the oats feel firm to the touch and the cherries have released some of their juices. Allow to rest for 5 minutes to firm up and cool down a little before serving as is or with plain yogurt and fresh fruit. If you have a really sweet tooth, add an extra drizzle of maple syrup to your portion.

Love your leftovers The baked oats will keep for 2 days in the fridge. To reheat, decant into a smaller dish, then add a splash more milk and reheat in the oven at 190°C fan (210°C/415°F/Gas 6–7) for 10–15 minutes. Or reheat in the microwave for 60–90 seconds until piping hot.

Sweet swap The frozen cherries add a beautiful tart contrast that pairs well with the sweet oats, however, you can use drained canned cherries if you fancy a sweeter taste.

Breakfast cranachan

Cranachan is a traditional Scottish dessert usually consisting of whipped cream, fresh raspberries, oats and whisky. This version replaces the cream with yogurt, and skipping on the whisky means that it is suitable for the whole family, but I won't judge if you start the day with a little swig!

🍴 2 adults and 1 little   ⏱ Prep and cook 15 minutes

30g (1oz) unsalted butter*
100g (3½oz) porridge oats*
  (see page 9)
2 tbsp honey (or maple syrup
  for under 1s), plus extra if
  needed

150g (5½oz) raspberries,
  plus extra for topping
250g (9oz) Greek yogurt*
(*See pages 8–9)

Melt the butter in a large frying pan and add the oats and the honey or maple syrup. Allow the oats to toast, stirring often, for around 5 minutes until they start to slightly catch on the edges and smell delicious.

Take the pan off the heat and transfer three-quarters of the oats to a large mixing bowl. Stir to break up them up so that they cool more quickly. Leave the remaining oats in the frying pan, off the heat, ready for decorating the finished cranachan.

While the oats cool for a few moments, prep the raspberries by putting them in a little bowl and mashing with the back of a fork. If your fruit is super tart, you can add a touch of extra honey or maple syrup, if you wish.

Measure the yogurt into the bowl with the oats and stir to combine. You're now ready to assemble!

Spoon alternate layers of the raspberry and the yogurt and oat mixture into small glasses or bowls so that you create a pretty layered look. Sprinkle over the reserved oats as a crunchy topping and finish with some extra fresh raspberries.

Love your leftovers Uneaten cranachans will keep for up to 2 days in the fridge.

Top tip You can also ripple the raspberries into the yogurt mixture and freeze in ice cream moulds for a delicious frozen yogurt ice pop.

Easy breakfast pizza

Pizza for breakfast? Yes, please – especially when it's as easy as this. This makes one pizza, so just scale up the quantities as needed.

GF*
EF*
V*
Vg*
DF*

🍴 1 adult or 2 littles ⏱ **Prep 10 minutes, Bake 8 minutes**

2 tortilla wraps*

1 heaped tbsp tomato purée (paste)

a pinch of dried mixed herbs

a small handful of fresh spinach

1 pork sausage* (see below)

15g (½oz) Cheddar cheese*, finely grated

1 medium egg* (optional)

freshly ground black pepper (*See pages 8–9)

Preheat the oven to 200°C fan (220°C/425°F/Gas 7).

Place a tortilla wrap on a large baking tray. Spoon a little of the tomato purée into the centre and spread out with the back of a spoon, then layer the second tortilla on top. Spread the remaining tomato purée over the top of the second tortilla wrap, leaving an empty border around the outside. Sprinkle over the herbs and a little black pepper.

Using a large knife, finely chop the spinach as you would fresh herbs, then sprinkle the spinach over the tomato purée.

Score a line down the side of the sausage, if using, and peel away the skin. Break the meat into chunks, the smaller the better, and arrange on top of the tortilla, leaving the central section clear for the egg later. Sprinkle the grated cheese over the top, again avoiding the middle.

Crack the egg, if using, into the centre of the tortilla. Place the tray in the oven to bake for 7–8 minutes until the sausage is browned and cooked and the white of the egg has turned opaque. If you can, keep an eye on the bake to avoid the yolk setting too.

Love your leftovers This dish is best served fresh, but any leftovers can be kept for a day in the fridge and reheated in the oven for about 4–5 minutes until piping hot.

Are you a good egg? If you want to serve this to your little ones with the egg yolk still a little runny (the yummiest way, in my opinion!), make sure you follow official advice and in the UK buy eggs which are British Lion stamped as they meet the highest standards of food safety.

Note Some sausages can be a little salty, so if you are serving to kiddos under 1, either remove some pieces from their portion, replace the sausage for pork mince, or leave out all together.

Kedgeree

With mildly spiced rice, eggs and smoked fish, my version of this classic is a little quicker than usual because us parents need to save as much time as possible in the morning!

GF*

EF*

DF

🍴 **2 adults and 3 littles**   ⏱ **Prep and cook 25 minutes**   ❄ **Freezable**

about 200g (7oz) basmati rice
a knob of butter* (about 25g/1oz)
1 tsp garlic-infused oil
2 spring onions (scallions), finely sliced

2 garlic cloves, minced
1 tbsp mild curry powder
1 tsp ground ginger
1 low-salt vegetable or chicken stock cube*
4 medium eggs* (optional)

300g (10½oz) skinless, boneless smoked haddock (preferably undyed)
snipped chives, to serve
freshly ground black pepper
(*See pages 8–9)

Fill the kettle and set to boil so it's ready for when you need it.

Fill a standard mug nearly to the top with the rice, taking a mental note of the fill line in the mug. Put the rice in a fine sieve and rinse under the tap until the water runs clear.

Set a very large lidded non-stick frying pan over a medium–high heat and add the butter and oil. Add the spring onions and garlic and fry for 1 minute or so to release their flavours. Add the curry powder, ginger and a grinding of black pepper and fry for 1–2 minutes, then add the washed rice and crumble in the stock cube. Stir to coat the rice with the spices and cook for a further 2 minutes.

Now, using the same mug you measured your rice in, fill it up to the same fill line with water and tip it into the pan. Do this again so that you have added two parts water to your one part rice. Stir and set the lid on the pan. Lower the heat to a gentle simmer and cook for 10 minutes – don't take the lid off!

Meanwhile, if you are adding eggs, bring a separate pan of water to the boil. Add the eggs and cook for 8 minutes. Once done, run the pan under a cold tap and allow the eggs to sit in the cold water for 5 minutes.

While the rice and eggs cook, cut the fish into big bite-sized chunks. Once the rice has had its 10 minutes, give it a little stir, rest the fish on top of the rice, then gently stir it into the rice. Place the lid back on and cook for a further 5 minutes, or until the fish is firm, flakes easily and is fully cooked.

Once the eggs are cooked, peel them (see page 16 for tips) and chop into quarters. When the fish is cooked, give it all a very gentle stir, being careful to not break up the fish, and add the eggs. To serve, pile into bowls, sprinkle with a few chives and enjoy!

For babies under 2, serve 1–3 chunks of fish depending on their age, as smoked fish has a tendency to be a little salty. If you wish, you can take a piece of fish and mash it into the rice to distribute the flavour. When serving little one's portion, give it a once over to double check there are no bones.

Love your leftovers This is best served fresh, however, leftovers should be chilled within the hour, refrigerated and eaten within 2–3 days, or can be frozen for up to 2 months. Defrost fully in the fridge, then reheat until piping hot throughout in a frying pan or in the microwave. You may need to add a splash more water to replace any lost moisture.

Quick comforts

All the recipes in this chapter can be made in 10–25 minutes. From throw-together pasta dishes that are ready in the time it takes to boil the pasta, to soups which only take a moment to prepare, delivering simple, cosy meals to enjoy together.

Rebecca's broccoli fritters

A quick, nutritious lunch or dinner packed full of goodness, and a real winner for all.

⑪ 2 adults and 2 littles ⏱ Prep and cook 20 minutes ❄ Freezable

50g (1¾oz) Cheddar cheese*
½ head of broccoli
100g (3½oz) self-raising flour*
100ml (3½fl oz) milk*
2 eggs*

1 tsp baking powder*
sunflower oil, for frying
freshly ground black pepper
(*See pages 8–9)

Using the coarse side of a box grater, grate the cheese and broccoli, discarding the stem. Put them in a large mixing bowl along with the rest of the ingredients and season with a little black pepper. Mix well to combine, but ensure you don't overwork the mixture.

Preheat a large non-stick frying pan with a little drizzle of oil over a medium heat. Spoon heaped tablespoons of the mixture into the frying pan, spreading out into neat circles using the tip of the spoon. You will need to fry these in batches of three or four, depending on the size of your pan. Cook the fritters for 2–3 minutes, flip and cook for a further 2 minutes, until the outside has browned nicely and the inside is piping hot and fluffed up. Repeat to cook all of the batter.

Alternatively, pour all the batter onto a large baking tray that has been lined with non-stick baking paper and use a spatula to evenly spread the mixture to around 1cm (½in) thick. Ensure it is the same thickness all over without a hump in the middle. Bake at 180°C fan (200°C/400°F/Gas 6) for 15–20 minutes until it's golden on top and is not too gooey inside; it should be a little soft, but there shouldn't be any raw mixture.

To serve, cut the fritters into strips for little ones and serve with plain yogurt for dipping.

Love your leftovers Fritters will keep for 2 days in the fridge, or freeze for 3 months. Defrost and reheat by blasting the fritters in the microwave for 60–90 seconds, flipping halfway through, until steaming and piping hot throughout.

Speed it up Use a food processor to whizz up the broccoli and cheese before adding the other ingredients to make a batter in an instant!

Cheesy parsnip bites

These savoury scones have a delicious sweetness from the parsnips that pairs really well with cheese. Delicious on their own, with a little cream cheese, cured meats for the older folk, or a little dollop of jam works perfectly too! A real all-rounder.

GF*

EF*

V

Vg*

DF*

🍴 **Makes approx 25 bites** ⏱ **Prep 10 minutes, Bake 15–20 minutes** ❄ **Freezable**

3 medium parsnips, peeled and coarsely grated (approx. 180g/6¼oz grated weight)

85g (3oz) smoked Cheddar cheese*, grated

1 tsp dried mixed herbs

1 tsp garlic granules

1 tsp smoked paprika

1 tsp baking powder*

250g (9oz) self-raising flour*

100g (3½oz) Greek-style yogurt*

100ml (3½fl oz) milk*

1 small beaten egg* or a little

more milk*, to glaze (or more cheese*)

1 tbsp sesame seeds (optional)

freshly ground black pepper

(*See pages 8–9)

Preheat the oven to 190°C fan (210°C/415°F/Gas 6–7) and line a large baking tray with non-stick baking paper.

Put the parsnips, cheese, herbs, garlic granules, paprika, baking powder, flour, yogurt, milk and a pinch of black pepper in a large mixing bowl and stir with a wooden spoon until starting to clump together. Tip the contents out onto a clean work surface, then gently and briefly knead together to form a ball of dough.

With the palm of your hand, press out the dough until you have a rough circle around 2cm (¾in) thick. Use a large sharp knife to roughly cut a criss-cross pattern, so you have lots of little dough bites around 4cm (1½in) square. If you have little taste testers under one, cut the dough into finger strips so it's easier for them to hold – the exact shape is not important, so go as rough or as neat as you can be bothered.

Transfer the bites to the prepared baking tray, spacing them at least 2.5cm (1in) apart. Brush the top of each bite with a little beaten edd or milk using a pastry brush, then sprinkle with sesame seeds. Alternatively, skip the egg and sesame seeds and add a tiny amount of extra grated cheese to the top of each bite.

Bake in the preheated oven for 15–20 minutes until the parsnip bites have risen well and turned a golden brown colour. Once cooked, they should tear in half easily and be light and fluffy inside.

Love your leftovers The bites will keep for 3 days in an airtight container at room temperature, or freeze for up to 3 months. Reheat in the oven for a few minutes until piping hot, or bake from frozen for approximately 10 minutes until piping hot throughout.

Hidden veg cheese on toast

Creamy, cheesy, soft in parts and crispy in others, this winter warmer will give everyone smiles all round. It's my take on a Welsh rarebit but with added goodness!

GF*

EF*

DF*

🍴 Makes 4 toasties ⏱ Prep and cook 15 minutes ❄ Freezable

1 small parsnip
4 chestnut mushrooms
15g (½oz) unsalted butter*
4 slices of bread*
1 tbsp cornflour (cornstarch)
180ml (6fl oz) milk*

1 tbsp Worcestershire sauce* (optional)
1 tsp English mustard* (optional)
110g (3¾oz) Cheddar cheese*, grated (if substituting,

choose a good melting cheese)
(*See pages 8–9)

Peel the parsnip and grate it using the fine side of the box grater, discarding the central core. Grate the mushrooms too. Add the parsnip and mushrooms to a frying pan along with the butter and sauté the veg for around 5 minutes until soft.

Meanwhile, line a large baking tray with non-stick foil. Preheat the grill to high and toast the bread until a pale brown colour.

Once the veg is cooked, add the cornflour to the pan and cook for a further 2 minutes, stirring often. Add the milk to the pan, along with the Worcestershire sauce and mustard, if using. Cook for a further few minutes, stirring continuously, until the sauce is very thick. Remove the pan from the heat and add two thirds of the cheese, stirring until melted.

Divide the mixture between the four pieces of toast, spreading it out to reach the edges. Sprinkle over the remaining cheese and grill until the tops have turned a lovely dark golden brown colour and the cheese sauce is bubbling.

Cut the toast into triangles and serve with a side salad or fruit. For little ones, opt for finger strips, which are easier to hold. Ensure it has cooled down, as the topping will be very hot straight from the grill.

Love your leftovers These cheese on toasts are best served immediately, however the cheese sauce can be kept in the fridge for up to 3 days, or the freezer for 3 months for when you want to make cheese on toast in a hurry. Alternatively, add a splash more milk to the cheese sauce and stir through pasta for a yummy quick mid-week meal.

Curried tuna and spinach toasties

This one might not sound like it's for you, but I urge you to give it a go. Creamy tuna, with a few extra greens, all laced with comforting spice flavourings – a total winner!

GF*

EF

DF*

🍴 **Makes 2 toasties** ⏱ **Prep and cook 15 minutes**

a large handful of fresh
   spinach
1 x 110g (3¾oz) can tuna in
   spring water, drained
1 tsp garlic granules
1 tsp mild curry powder
4 heaped tsp cream cheese*

60g (2oz) Cheddar cheese*,
   finely grated
4 slices of bread*
20g (¾oz) unsalted butter*,
   softened
freshly ground black pepper
(*See pages 8–9)

Put the spinach in a sieve and pour hot water from the kettle over the leaves – this will wilt them instantly. Use the back of a spoon to push out as much liquid as you can, then tip the block of spinach onto a few pieces of kitchen roll to squeeze out as much water as you can. Transfer the spinach to a chopping board and run a large sharp knife over it to cut it into very small pieces.

Put the chopped spinach in a mixing bowl, add the drained tuna, garlic granules, curry powder, cream cheese, Cheddar and a little black pepper and give it a very good stir. Divide the mixture into two and spread over two pieces of the bread, right up to the edges. Top each slice with the other dry slices of bread to make two tuna sandwiches.

Place a large frying pan over a medium heat to warm up. Spread the top of each sandwich with a little butter, ensuring you reach edge to edge. Place the sandwiches in the frying pan, buttered-side down, then quickly spread butter over the other side before the pan gets too hot to have your hands near. Fry the toasties for 3–4 minutes on each side, until crisp and golden on the outside and the cheese has turned all melty inside.

Cut in half, or into finger strips for little ones, and serve with a side salad. Best served immediately.

Love your leftovers The toasties are best served fresh, however, any leftovers can be stored in the fridge for up to 24 hours. Reheat in a frying pan until the cheese has melted again and the filling is piping hot throughout.

Easy baked prawn baguette

GF*

EF*

DF

This has all the satisfaction of the popular prawn toast from your local takeaway, but it's a much healthier alternative – plus it's a lot easier to make! Just try stopping the "mmms" at your table.

🍴 2 adults and 2 littles ⏱ Prep 10 minutes, Cook 11 minutes

2 spring onions (scallions)

1 large garlic clove

1 tbsp low-salt soy sauce*

1 tbsp cornflour (cornstarch)

190g (6¾oz) fresh raw prawns (shrimp) or defrosted raw frozen prawns (shrimp), peeled and deveined

1 medium egg*

1 large part-baked baguette*

80g (2¾oz) sesame seeds

garlic-infused olive oil spray

freshly ground black pepper

(*See pages 8–9)

Preheat the oven to 200°C fan (220°C/425°F/Gas 7) and line a large baking tray with non-stick foil.

Roughly chop the spring onions and garlic, then add to a small blender pot along with the soy sauce, cornflour, prawns, egg and a little black pepper. Whizz until the mixture is smooth.

Cut the baguette in half lengthways. Using the back of a tablespoon, spread half the prawn mixture on the cut side of each baguette half, ensuring you reach the edges. Smooth the mixture out so it's an even thickness all over.

Sprinkle half of the sesame seeds into a mound on the baking tray, then press a baguette half, prawn-mixture side down, into the seeds so that they all stick to the wet mixture. Try to use all the seeds on the tray, ensuring they all stick to the baguette. Repeat with the rest of the sesame seeds and other baguette half. Arrange the prawn baguettes, prawn-side up, on the baking tray and fill in any gaps on the top of the prawn mixture that doesn't have any sesame seeds stuck to it. You want the entire top to be a layer of seeds.

Spray each baguette half liberally with the garlic-infused oil, then bake in the preheated oven for 9–11 minutes until the crust has crisped up and the top feels firm to the touch, with the sesame seeds taking on a little colour. The prawns will no longer be translucent in colour and will feel firm once cooked.

Cut the baguettes into triangles or finger strips, and serve with some yogurt for little ones and sweet chilli sauce for the big kids to dunk into.

Love your leftovers Best eaten straight away, however leftovers will keep for a day in the fridge.

Loaded broccoli crumpets

Even though crumpets work brilliantly here, you could use this yummy mixture on top of toast, English muffins or mini tortilla wraps. You can also swap the broccoli for grated and drained courgette or carrot. A versatile and quick family lunch to feed your hungry crew.

⧊ Makes 3 crumpets ⏱ Prep 5 minutes, Cook 12 minutes

3 crumpets*
2 large broccoli florets
1 tbsp tomato purée (paste)
2 tbsp cream cheese*
1 tsp garlic granules

30g (1oz) smoked Cheddar
   cheese*, finely grated
freshly ground black pepper
(*See pages 8–9)

Preheat the oven to 200°C fan (220°C/425°F/Gas 7) and line a large baking tray with non-stick foil or baking paper.

Slice the flowery ends off the broccoli florets, reserving the stalks for another meal. Run your knife over them to finely shred the broccoli into very small pieces – this way it will cook quickly and combine with the rest of the toppings better.

Put the broccoli in a small bowl and add the tomato purée, cream cheese, garlic granules and a little black pepper. Mix well, then spread over each crumpet, making sure you go right up to the edge. Place them on the prepared baking tray and top each one with a little grated cheese.

Bake the crumpets in the preheated oven for 10–12 minutes to cook the topping, melt the cheese and heat through.

Serve with a side salad or soup to dunk into. Cut into finger strips to serve to little ones.

Love your leftovers If you have any crumpets left over, keep these in an airtight container in the fridge for 2 days. Reheat in a hot oven for 5 minutes, or until piping hot throughout.

Broccoli and mushroom pasta soup

A super quick and versatile dish loaded with veg, and with lots of options on how to serve to varied tastes in your family.

GF*

EF

V

Vg*

DF*

🍴 2 adults and 2 littles ⏱ Prep and cook 15 minutes ❄ Freezable

1 head of broccoli
2 medium all-rounder
  potatoes or 4 new potatoes,
  washed and sliced into 1cm
  (½in) chunks
150g (5½oz) button or
  chestnut mushrooms, wiped

clean and halved
2 low-salt stock cubes*
  (chicken or vegetable)
1 tsp dried porcini mushroom
  powder (optional)
150g (5½oz) dried pasta* (any
  shape you like)

60–80g (2–2¾oz) Cheddar
  cheese*, grated, to serve
freshly ground black pepper
(*See pages 8–9)

Cut the broccoli into florets and finely chop the firm end of the stem. Add to a saucepan along with the potatoes and mushrooms. Crumble over the stock cubes and add a good grinding of black pepper along with the mushroom powder, if using.

Pour boiling water from the kettle into the pan to just cover the veg (this will be roughly 800ml/28fl oz) – any more and the soup will be too watery. Put a lid on the pan, leaving a little gap at one side or resting the lid on a wooden spoon to allow a little steam to escape. Bring to a boil, then reduce the heat slightly and allow it to boil for 10–15 minutes until the potatoes are soft throughout.

Meanwhile, in a separate pan, cook the pasta according to the packet instructions.

Once the veg is cooked, blend until super smooth using a stick blender, or in a liquidiser in batches. Be careful – it'll be hot.

To serve, pour the soup into bowls and add a few big spoonfuls of pasta to each bowl to soak up the soup. Add a little mound of cheese to the centre of the bowl and allow it to melt into the soup: it's a game changer! Alternatively, mix a little of the soup in with a portion of pasta so that the soup acts like a pasta sauce, with some grated cheese on top. This option is great for fussy eaters. Adults, you can serve with pasta, or bread on the side for dipping, along with a sprinkling of salt on top of the soup. Try adding a few dashes of hot sauce for an extra kick.

Love your leftovers Allow leftovers to cool and store in the fridge, covered, for up to 3–4 days, or freeze for 4 months. Reheat until piping hot throughout.

Lemon pea pasta

Need a last-minute dinner idea for a busy midweek meal? Try this silky pasta dish with zingy lemon, which cuts through the buttery richness. It's a total crowd pleaser!

GF*

EF

V

Vg*

DF*

🍽 2 adults and 1 little   ⏱ Prep and cook 15 minutes   ❄ Freezable

200g (7oz) dried pasta*
1 unwaxed lemon
2 fat garlic cloves
120g (4¼oz) frozen peas
40g (1½oz) unsalted butter*
a drizzle of garlic-infused
    olive oil

a small handful of your
    favourite cheese*, such as
    Cheddar, finely grated
freshly ground black pepper
(*See pages 8–9)

Bring a large pot of water to the boil and start to cook the pasta according to the instructions on the packet.

Meanwhile, zest half of the lemon and, using the same zester, grate the garlic cloves. Run a knife over the zest and garlic to ensure it's super fine and set aside until needed.

Five minutes before the pasta is cooked, add the frozen peas to the water.

Now set a large frying pan over a medium heat and gently melt the butter with the garlic oil until runny and starting to foam slightly. Keep on a medium heat so the butter does not burn.

Add the zest and garlic to the butter, along with a generous grinding of black pepper and allow to cook for a minute before squeezing in the juice of the zested lemon. Cook for a further 30–60 seconds, then use a spider strainer to transfer the cooked pasta and peas from the saucepan to the frying pan. Don't worry if a bit of water comes along too – you want some liquid to loosen the sauce. Add the handful of cheese and a little dash more of the pasta cooking water, if needed. Toss and stir to melt the cheese and you're done. Serve immediately.

Love your leftovers This dish is best served fresh as pasta has a tendency to overcook when reheated. However, if you don't mind this, store in an airtight container in the fridge for up to 2 days and reheat in the microwave for 2–3 minutes until piping hot throughout.

Make it baby friendly For little taste testers, choose a nice longer pasta shape like rigatoni or fusilli so that they can hold the pasta in their hands. If your little ones are over three, pasta shells are fab for this recipe as the peas like to sit inside all the nooks and crannies.

Creamy turkey gnocchi

A speedy midweek meal that provides winter warming comfort when you're craving a bit of stodge.

GF*

EF

DF*

⏲ 2 adults and 2 littles   ⏱ Prep and cook 12 minutes

500g (1lb 2oz) turkey mince
   (7% fat)
a drizzle of olive oil
1 large courgette (zucchini)
500g (1lb 2oz) gnocchi*
1 low-salt chicken stock cube*

2 garlic cloves, minced
3 tbsp crème fraîche or
   mascarpone cheese*
20g (¾oz) Cheddar cheese*,
   grated (optional), plus extra
   to serve

freshly ground black pepper
(*See pages 8–9)

Add the turkey mince to a large frying pan with a little oil and start to cook on a high heat, breaking it up a little with a wooden spoon.

Grate the courgette and squeeze to remove most of the moisture before adding the pulp to the turkey. Season with a little black pepper and allow to cook for 5 minutes. If the pan is filling up with lots of juices, this will stop the mince from browning nicely and it will boil instead. So to remove it, tilt the pan slightly and use a large spoon to scoop most of the excess liquid into a small bowl. You can discard this or add it to the gnocchi water while cooking to give it extra flavour, if you wish.

At this stage there is 5 minutes left of cooking, so set a large saucepan of boiling water from the kettle on a high heat, add the gnocchi and the juice from the mince, if using, and cook according to the packet instructions. Some take longer than others, so time it so that the gnocchi will be cooked by the time the sauce is done.

Back to the turkey, crumble in the stock cube and cook for a further 4 minutes, stirring often. Soon it should start to catch on the edges and you'll see some crispy brown bits – perfect!

Add the garlic to the pan and cook for 30 seconds, then add the crème fraîche or mascarpone, a ladle of the gnocchi cooking water and the cheese, if using, stirring well so that the sauce combines. Once the gnocchi floats, scoop it out and add it to the sauce, tossing well. Serve immediately with a little extra cheese on top.

For little ones under 2, cut the gnocchi in half lengthways, or into quarters if they are particularly big. You can also blend up the gnocchi with a little milk and stir through the mince if you wish.

Love your leftovers Any leftovers will keep for 2 days in the fridge. Try adding it to a baking dish with an extra splash of milk, topping with grated cheese and baking in a hot oven for 15–20 minutes until crispy on top.

Courgette and chorizo carbonara

Just a small amount of chorizo in this dish takes it to a whole new level. With added courgette for extra veg, this is a quick and easy family favourite.

🍴 2 adults and 1 little ⏲ Prep and cook 15 minutes

160g (5½oz) dried spaghetti*
45g (1½oz) chorizo*, skin
  removed and cubed
  (optional, see tip)
1 large courgette (zucchini)

3 medium eggs (British Lion
  stamped – see page 47)
80g (2¾oz) smoked Cheddar
  cheese*, finely grated, plus
  optional extra to serve

20g (¾oz) unsalted butter*
freshly ground black pepper
(*See pages 8–9)

Set a large pan of water on the hob and bring to a rolling boil. Add your pasta and cook according to the packet instructions.

Meanwhile, put a large non-stick heavy-based frying pan over a high heat and allow to heat up while you finely chop the chorizo. Add the chorizo to the pan and let it cook while you coarsely grate the courgette. Gather the grated courgette in your hand and gently squeeze it to remove half of the liquid before adding to the pan. Allow the courgette and chorizo to fry until the veg is softened and the flavoured oil from the chorizo is released.

While they cook, crack the eggs into a large mixing bowl and add the grated cheese. Whisk the eggs well with a balloon whisk, then take a standard builder's mug and scoop up enough pasta cooking water to half fill the mug. While whisking the eggs with one hand, slowly drizzle the hot water into the bowl, whisking continuously. This tempers the eggs, meaning they are less likely to scramble when you add them to your sauce later.

Once the courgettes have softened and there is no liquid sitting in the pan, add the butter and a little black pepper. While the butter melts, fill your mug up again with more pasta cooking water and set it aside in case it's needed later. Then drain your pasta and add to the frying pan.

Remove the frying pan from the heat and toss the pasta so it's coated in the veg and chorizo. With tongs or a spoon in one hand, pour the cheesy eggs into the pan, stirring and moving the pasta continuously to stop the eggs from scrambling. Add a touch more of your cooking water if you feel the sauce needs loosening slightly, then serve immediately with an extra grating of cheese on top if you wish.

Love your leftovers This dish is best served fresh out of the pan but you can keep cooled leftovers for a day in the fridge, however you do run the risk of scrambling the eggs when reheating.

> **Note** Chorizo can be salty, so give little ones under 12 months just a small piece to try. Also note that some varieties contain cow's milk.
>
> **Top tip** To make this dish vegetarian, swap the chorizo for a tablespoon of garlic-infused oil, and add 1 teaspoon of mild smoked paprika to the pan along with the courgette.

Child-friendly beef stronganoff

GF*

EF*

DF*

Tender, succulent strips of beef in a creamy mushroom sauce. This recipe includes grated mushrooms, which melt and hide in the sauce making it safer and easier for little ones to enjoy.

🍴 **2 adults and 2 littles**   ⏱ **Prep and cook 15 minutes**

200g (7oz) pasta of your
   choice*
1 small brown onion, peeled
200g (7oz) chestnut
   mushrooms
1½ tbsp garlic-infused oil

1 low-salt beef stock cube*
300–400g (10½–14oz) sirloin
   steak
1 tbsp cornflour (cornstarch)
200ml (7fl oz) crème fraîche*
1 tsp Dijon mustard*

a small bunch of fresh flat-leaf
   parsley, chopped, to serve
freshly ground black pepper
(*See pages 8–9)

Set a large pan of water on the hob, bring to the boil and get the pasta on to cook according to the packet instructions.

Quickly start on the sauce. Using a box grater, grate the onion and mushrooms, discarding the central stalks. Add the veg pulp to a large frying pan with 1 teaspoon of the garlic oil. Stir and sauté over a medium-high heat for 3–4 minutes until the veg is softened. Crumble in the stock cube and add a touch of black pepper.

Meanwhile, trim off the excess fat from the side of the steak and slice it into 1.5cm (⅝in) wide strips. Add to a bowl with the cornflour and toss so that all sides of the meat are coated in flour.

Once the veg is soft, use a spatula to push the onion and mushrooms into a small mound on one side of the pan. Move the base of the pan so that where the veg is sitting is no longer over direct contact with the heat below. Add the remaining oil to the empty side of the pan, then scatter in the beef in an even layer. Fry for 2 minutes, flip and fry again for a further 2 minutes until browned and just cooked – be careful not to overcook the beef which will make it chewy.

Add the crème fraîche and Dijon mustard to the pan, along with one ladle of the pasta cooking water, and stir to combine everything.

Strain the pasta, reserving a touch of the water, and add the pasta to the pan. Stir well, and if it feels too thick, add a touch more of the pasta cooking water to loosen the sauce. Serve immediately with a scattering of chopped parsley.

Love your leftovers Stroganoff is best eaten fresh from the pan. However, leftovers will keep for 2 days in the fridge. Reheat with a splash of extra milk in a frying pan or in the microwave until bubbling and piping hot throughout, but be careful not to overcook the beef.

Aubergine pesto

GF
EF
V
Vg*
DF*

Stir this through freshly cooked pasta, as pictured, or use it to top a pizza or toast. It's also great on a jacket potato, or as a dip on the side of chips or sliced flat breads.

🍴 **Coats pasta for 2 adults and 2 littles**　⏱ **Prep and cook 12 minutes**　❄ **Freezable**

2 medium aubergines
　(eggplants)
2 large garlic cloves

2 tbsp garlic-infused olive oil
juice of 1 lemon
50g (1¾oz) Cheddar cheese*

(see page 8), finely grated
freshly ground black pepper

Peel both aubergines, then slice into 1.5cm (⅝in) cubes. Put them in a saucepan and pour in enough boiling water from the kettle so that the aubergines are half covered. Put the lid on and cook for 5 minutes. Stir and cook for another 5 minutes without the lid on.

Meanwhile roughly chop the garlic, then add it to the saucepan along with the oil, lemon juice and a little black pepper and cook for a further 3 minutes. Now the aubergines should be really soft. Add the cheese and blend until smooth using a stick blender, or decant into a food processor to blitz.

Love your leftovers The pesto will keep for 3 days in an airtight container in the fridge, or for 3 months in the freezer. To defrost, either place in the fridge overnight, or pop in the microwave for 2–3 minutes, stirring often until piping hot.

Broccoli pesto

GF
EF
V
Vg*
DF*

Quick, nutritious and delicious!

🍴 **Coats pasta for 2 adults and 2 littles**　⏱ **Prep and cook 10 minutes**　❄ **Freezable**

1 head of broccoli, cut into
　florets
2 large garlic cloves, whole
a large handful of fresh
　spinach

finely grated zest of ½
　unwaxed lemon and juice
　of the whole lemon
50g (1¾oz) Cheddar cheese*
　(see page 8), finely grated

3 tbsp garlic-infused olive oil
60g (2oz) cashews or pine nuts
　(optional)
freshly ground black pepper

Set a large pan of water on a medium–high heat, bring to the boil and cook the broccoli and whole cloves of garlic together for 5–6 minutes or until soft. Drain well and add to a food processor along with the spinach, lemon zest and juice, grated cheese, oil, cashews or pine nuts, if using, and a little black pepper. Add half a ladle of the broccoli cooking water, then whizz until super smooth. You may need to add more water if the pesto looks too thick – keep adding and whizzing briefly until you have a silky smooth sauce.

Stir the pesto through cooked pasta before serving with a little grated cheese.

Love your leftovers The pesto will keep in the fridge for 4 days, or freeze in ice cube trays to use as and when you need it. To use, add a few cubes to a small bowl with a little extra water and microwave on high for 2–3 minutes or until piping hot.

Creamy spinach and garlic fish gratin

GF*

EF

Quick and easy to whip up, this flavourful dish is perfect for sharing. Serve with a loaf of crusty bread to dunk into the sauce.

🍴 2 adults and 2 littles ⏱ Prep 5 minutes, Bake 20 minutes

2 handfuls of fresh spinach
150ml (5fl oz) double (heavy) cream
2 large garlic cloves, finely grated
150–200g (5½–7oz) raw prawns (shrimp), peeled and deveined

about 300g (10½oz) boneless, skinless white fish, such as haddock, monk fish, cod or basa
50g (1¾oz) smoked Cheddar cheese, grated
20g (¾oz) breadcrumbs* (see page 9)

a drizzle of garlic-infused oil
freshly ground black pepper

Preheat the oven to 220°C fan (240°C/475°F/Gas 8) and find yourself a large rectangular oven dish, measuring about 30 x 20cm (12 x 8in).

Put the spinach in a sieve or colander and pour boiling water from the kettle or very hot water from the tap over the spinach to wilt it. With the back of a spoon, squeeze out as much liquid as you can, then tip the block of wilted spinach onto a few sheets of kitchen paper and squeeze to soak up as much water as you can.

Put the spinach on a chopping board and finely chop, then scoop it up and transfer to your oven dish. Pour in the cream and add the garlic and a little black pepper. Give it a really good stir before adding the prawns. Chop the fish into bite-sized chunks and add those to the dish too. Stir to coat the fish in the cream mixture, then sprinkle over the cheese and the breadcrumbs and drizzle a little oil on top to help it all crisp up.

Bake in the preheated oven for 15–20 minutes until the prawns have turned pink, and the fish is white and flakes easily.

Serve with crusty bread and a side salad for an easy relaxed meal, or it's delicious with mashed potato and veg so the cream soaks into the mash.

For little ones, either serve the fish in chunks for baby to feed themselves, or chop it up small and serve on a spoon.

Love your leftovers This dish is best served fresh, but leftovers will keep for a day in the fridge. Reheat in the oven until piping hot throughout.

Top tip You can use single (light) cream, rather than double, if you'd prefer to make it a little healthier. Although it may split slightly during cooking, it will still taste delicious.

QUICK COMFORTS

Smoky paprika and fish soup

GF*

EF

DF

Silky smooth tomato soup, deeply flavoured with paprika, garlic and peppers and succulent chunks of fish. This is perfect served with a big chunk of crusty bread for dunking.

🍴 2 adults and 2 littles   ⏱ Prep and cook 30 minutes   ❄ Freezable

1 tbsp garlic-infused oil
1 brown onion, roughly diced
3 garlic cloves, sliced
1 tbsp tomato purée (paste)
2 tomatoes, quartered
1 yellow pepper, deseeded
  and roughly chopped
500g (1lb 2oz) tomato passata
  (strained tomatoes)

1 tsp golden caster sugar
  (optional)
1½ tbsp smoked paprika
1 tsp sweet paprika (optional
  – you can use extra smoked
  paprika instead)
1 low-salt chicken or vegetable
  stock cube*

350g (12oz) fresh or frozen
  fish pie mix
freshly ground black pepper
1 lemon, cut into wedges,
  to serve
crusty bread*, to serve
(*See page 9)

Put the garlic oil and onion in a large, lidded saucepan and sauté for 3–5 minutes, or until soft. Add the garlic and tomato purée and cook for a further 2 minutes.

Now add the tomatoes and pepper, along with the passata. Fill the empty passata packet half full with water and swill around, then tip it into the pan. Add the sugar, if using, paprikas and a little black pepper, and crumble in the stock cube. Allow it to come up to the boil, then simmer for 10 minutes, or until the pepper starts to soften.

Remove the pan from the heat and carefully blend the soup using a stick blender. You can leave it chunky or blend to a smooth purée, whichever you wish.

Now add the fish, stir and put the lid on the pan. Put the soup over a medium heat and simmer for a further 10 minutes for fresh fish or 15 for frozen, or until the fish is cooked through, piping hot and flakes easily.

Serve in bowls with a generous squeeze of lemon juice on each serving, and a chunk of crusty bread to soak up the soup on the side.

Love your leftovers The soup will keep for 2 days in the fridge, or freeze for 1 month.

Water-fried chicken

GF*

EF

DF

It'll feel like an odd process to pour a load of water into your fried chicken pan, but trust me, the results are phenomenal – the juiciest, most flavourful piece of chicken you'll ever eat! My Nina loves it!

🍴 3 adults and 2 littles   ⏱ Prep and cook 25 minutes   ❄ Freezable

4 tbsp plain (all-purpose) flour*
  (see page 9)
8 skinless, boneless chicken
  thighs
1 tbsp sunflower oil
freshly ground black pepper

Put the flour on a plate, season with a little black pepper and mix briefly. One at a time, coat the chicken pieces really well, ensuring that the flour covers every part of the meat.

Heat a large, non-stick, heavy-based frying pan over a medium–high heat and add the sunflower oil. Once hot, place the chicken pieces in the pan, unrolled and flat, ensuring they don't overlap and the chicken is sitting snugly in the pan. Fry on each side for 3–5 minutes until starting to turn a little brown – they won't be cooked through at this stage.

Once the chicken is sealed, pour in about 250ml (9fl oz) water, or enough to come just under halfway up the sides of the chicken pieces. Now let it simmer away until all the water has evaporated, this will take around 5–10 minutes. There's no need to turn the chicken, so you can put the pan on the back burner and get on with other meal prep during this time.

Once most of the water has evaporated, the chicken will be fully cooked throughout. When there's the smallest amount of liquid left in the base of the pan, you can flip the chicken back and forth and allow it to crisp up and colour on each side for 2 minutes. Use a spatula to scrape the thick crispy chicken juices from the bottom of the pan onto the fillets – this is all really yummy flavour. The chicken will gain colour very quickly, and then it's ready. Take the pan off the heat and allow to rest for 3–5 minutes before serving.

Serve with rice or potatoes and salad or veg. This chicken is great in wraps or tacos too! For little taste testers, cut the chicken into finger-sized strips so it's easy to hold.

Love your leftovers The chicken will keep in the fridge for 2 days and is delicious cold in sandwiches, but to reheat place back in the pan with an extra splash of water to avoid it drying out.

Note This will work with all cuts of chicken, with or without skin and bones, but thighs give you the juiciest outcome. If you choose cuts with bones in, cook for an extra 5 minutes or so to cook through fully.

Peanut butter chicken curry

A creamy, rich and nutty sauce coating succulent pieces of chicken. You can swap the meat for butternut squash or chunks of tofu to make this dish meat free.

GF*

EF

DF*

⏱ 2 adults and 2 littles, plus leftovers ⏲ **Prep and cook 25 minutes** ❄ **Freezable**

2 tsp garlic-infused or
   sunflower oil
500–600g (1lb 2oz–1lb 5oz)
   skinless, boneless chicken
   thighs, cut into 1cm (½in)
   wide strips

2 tsp mild curry powder
2 tsp smoked paprika
1 medium white onion
3 small garlic cloves
15g (½oz) unsalted butter*
1 x 400ml can coconut milk

4 tbsp peanut butter (smooth
   or crunchy)
2 tbsp low-salt light soy sauce*
1 low-salt chicken stock cube*
juice of 1 small lemon
(*See pages 8–9)

Preheat a large, non-stick, heavy-based frying pan over a high heat and add the garlic infused oil. Add the chicken in a thin, even layer, trying not to overlap the meat too much. Wash your hands quickly, then sprinkle over 1 teaspoon each of the curry powder and paprika, reserving the rest for the sauce. Stir well, shake the pan so the chicken falls into an even layer, then leave it to cook for another 3–4 minutes before stirring again. Cook for a further few minutes until the chicken is just cooked through and has gained some lovely colour on the outside. Leaving the pan alone will help the chicken to catch at the edges resulting in a deeper flavour.

While the chicken cooks, top and tail a whole onion, removing the dry outer skin. Using a box grater, coarsely grate the onion. Flip the box grater around then peel and finely grate the garlic cloves.

Once the chicken is cooked, spoon it into a bowl and set aside while you cook the sauce. Reduce the heat to low and add the butter to the frying pan along with the onion and garlic pulp, ensuring there isn't any hiding inside the grater. Now add the remaining curry powder and smoked paprika.

Sauté the onion and garlic until softened, scraping up any of the crispy chicken bits from the base of the pan. Once the onion is translucent and any excess moisture has evaporated, add the coconut milk, peanut butter and soy sauce and crumble in the stock cube. Give it a good stir, or whisk if that's easier, and cook for 3–4 minutes until the sauce has come together well. Add the chicken to the sauce, ensuring you add any resting juices too, then squeeze the lemon juice into the pan. Stir well and simmer for 5–10 minutes on low until you're ready to serve.

This dish pairs really well with rice or flatbreads to soak up the delicious curry sauce.

Love your leftovers Any leftovers will keep well for 2–3 days in the fridge, or freeze for up to 3 months. Defrost and reheat in a saucepan over a medium heat until bubbling and piping hot throughout, adding a touch more water if needed.

Love your slow cooker? This dish would be easy to prepare in the slow cooker – add all the ingredients (except the oil and butter) and cook on LOW for 6 hours. Stir and serve as desired.

Midweek meals

Taking between 30–45 minutes to make, these easy recipes are perfect to rustle up midweek to give smiles all round after busy family days.

Easy baked Scotch egg muffins

GF*

DF

Scotch eggs are one of my all-time favourite comfort foods, and one of my cravings when pregnant with Nina. However, traditionally they can be a bit fiddly to make with lots of different steps. Try this super simple version to achieve a take on the classic. They are healthier too, being baked rather than fried!

🍽 **Makes 6** ⏲ **Prep and cook 30 minutes**

cooking spray, for greasing
about 50g (1¾oz) panko
    breadcrumbs*
1 small courgette (zucchini)
180g (6¼oz) pork mince
    (12% fat) or sausage meat*
    (see note opposite)

1 low-salt chicken stock cube*
6 small eggs
freshly ground black pepper
snipped chives, to sprinkle
    (optional)
(*See page 9)

Preheat the oven to 200°C fan (220°C/425°F/Gas 7) and spray 6 of the holes in a non-stick metal muffin tray with cooking spray. Add a teaspoon of the breadcrumbs to the base of each hole.

Coarsely grate the courgette and squeeze out as much excess liquid as you can before adding the pulp to a small bowl.

Now, add the pork, a little freshly ground black pepper, 4 tablespoons of the breadcrumbs (around 30g/1oz) and crumble in the stock cube, ensuring there are no large lumps. Using your hands, squish the mixture together to combine well, then divide into 6 equal balls.

Working with a ball of mixture at a time, roll it in your hands so the outside is smooth, then pat down to a fat patty. Place the patty in the muffin mould, flat side down. Either using your fingers, a small glass or the end of a wooden rolling pin, press the mixture into the mould so that it forms a cup shape with sides that are around 5mm (¼in) thick. Don't worry if the meat mixture comes up higher than the sides of the mould, this is fine – just try to keep the top neat and smooth to avoid small pieces browning quicker than others.

Once you have shaped all 6 portions into neat cups, sprinkle a teaspoon of breadcrumbs into each – this will soak up any excess cooking juices. Pop the tray in the oven and cook for 12 minutes.

Once the 12 minutes is up, take the tray out of the oven. If you feel the meat has expanded, grab the end of the wooden rolling pin and press the centre of the meat cup down to give you a larger space for the egg to fill.

Crack an egg into each cup. Don't worry if a little of the white spills over onto the edge, as you can trim your Scotch egg cups after baking. However, if your eggs are too large, you can crack the yolk into the cup and reserve a little of the white in the shells to avoid overfilling each cup.

Continued on page 88

Continued from page 87

Top each cracked egg with a light sprinkle of breadcrumbs, some black pepper and a final few sprays of cooking oil spray.

Place the muffin tray back in the oven and cook for another 9–10 minutes, or until the egg white has fully set and the tops have browned a little.

Allow to rest for 5 minutes before running a dinner knife around each Scotch egg cup and releasing it from the muffin tray.

Sprinkle with a few snipped chives, if you like, and serve with salad for a delicious lunch at home, or at a family picnic.

Love your leftovers The Scotch egg cups will keep for 2 days in the fridge. They are delicious eaten cold, but you can also reheat in the oven for 5–10 minutes or until piping hot throughout. Egg white goes rubbery in the freezer, so it's best to eat these delicious treats fresh.

Note Sometimes it can be tricky to find small eggs these days, so buy a mixed-size pack and choose the smallest eggs in the bunch. If you can only buy pork mince in larger quantities, try using the leftover mince for the Hidden-veg-packed Sausage Pinwheels recipe on page 98.

Too salty? Little tummies cannot handle too much salt, therefore opt for pork mince, rather than sausage meat, if serving to babies under the age of 1, and refer to page 10 for guidance on salt intake for your little one.

Baby-friendly baked falafels with mango salsa

GF*
EF
V
Vg*
DF*

Super soft on the inside and seeded on the outside, these falafels, pictured overleaf, are also mildly spiced and help expose little ones to a real variety of tastes and textures.

🍴 12 falafels ⏱ Prep 10 minutes, Bake 35 minutes ❄ Freezable

1 large yellow onion
2 x 400g (14oz) cans chickpeas, drained and rinsed
3 garlic cloves, grated
a handful of fresh parsley
a handful of fresh coriander (cilantro)
1 tbsp garlic-infused olive oil
2 tsp ground cumin

2 tsp ground coriander
3 tbsp plain (all-purpose) flour*
1 tsp baking powder*
4–5 tbsp sesame seeds
garlic spray cooking oil
freshly ground black pepper

For the cucumber dip
10cm (4in) piece of fresh cucumber

1 garlic clove, finely grated
4 heaped tbsp Greek yogurt*

For the mango salsa
1 ripe mango
1 heaped tbsp pickled red cabbage
1 tbsp chopped parsley
1 small lemon
(*See pages 8–9)

Preheat the oven to 200°C fan (220°C/425°F/Gas 7).

Grate the onion on a box grater and add the pulp to a food processor pot, squeezing out most of the juice as you transfer the onions over. Add all the remaining ingredients, except the sesame seeds and oil, and whizz until smooth.

Put the sesame seeds in a small bowl ready for rolling. Now take a tablespoon-sized portion of the mixture, drop it into the seeds, then pick up and roll into a ball – as you shape lots of seeds should stick to the outside of the falafel. Once covered, roll the ball into a sausage shape (this helps little ones to hold it more easily), but if you prefer to shape into patty rounds, feel free to do this. Place the falafel onto a baking tray and repeat until all of the mixture is shaped. If you wish, you can shape enough falafels for your little ones, then add a teaspoon of salt to the remaining mixture before mixing and shaping the adult portions. Spray each falafel a couple of times with the cooking spray and bake for 30–35 minutes until golden on the outside, but still soft on the inside.

While the falafels bake, whip up the dip by grating the cucumber on a box grater. Squeeze out most of the moisture before adding to a bowl along with the rest of the ingredients and a little black pepper.

For the salsa, peel and chop the flesh off the mango around the central stone. Slice the the fruit into centimetre cubes and add to a bowl along with the pickled cabbage, parsley and the juice of half of the lemon. Mix and set aside.

Serve the falafels with the salsa and dip together with couscous or flat breads, for the perfect at home takeaway. For babies under a year, cut the falafels in half lengthways to expose the soft inside and make them easier for little fingers to hold.

Love your leftovers Falafels will keep for 3 days in the fridge; reheat in the oven, wrapped in foil so they don't dry out, for 5–10 minutes until piping hot. Or freeze for 3 months; reheat from frozen in the same way, but add an extra 5–10 minutes to the baking time. The salsa and dip are best served fresh but will keep for a few days in the fridge.

Easy broccoli cheese nuggets

These nuggets, with roasted broccoli vibes, are deliciously soft on the inside and crisp on the outside. A delicious way to get the kiddos to eat their greens.

GF*

EF*

V

Vg*

DF*

⸙ Makes 12–14 nuggets ⏱ Prep 10 minutes, Bake 22 minutes ❄ Freezable

a medium–large head of
  broccoli, cut into florets
50g (1¾oz) self-raising flour*
90g (3¼oz) Cheddar cheese*,
  grated

1 medium egg*, beaten
about 4 heaped tbsp panko
  breadcrumbs*
garlic spray cooking oil
(*See pages 8–9)

Preheat the oven to 190°C fan (210°C/415°F/Gas 6–7) and line a baking tray with non-stick baking paper.

Steam or boil the broccoli until soft and tender – cook for about 5 minutes if boiling and 7–8 minutes if steaming. Drain the broccoli and tip into a large mixing bowl, then, using a potato masher, try to break down the broccoli as much as possible. If you wish, you can run a knife over any larger bits. Add the flour, cheese and egg to the bowl and mix well to combine.

Pour the breadcrumbs into a large flat-bottomed bowl. Scoop a tablespoon-sized portion of the broccoli mixture in your hands, tip it out onto the breadcrumbs, and shape into a small round nugget shape, turning it over in the crumbs so that all sides get coated. Transfer the nugget to the prepared baking tray and repeat until all the mixture has been shaped. Give each nugget a squirt or two of garlic-infused oil, then flip over and spray again. Place the tray in the centre of your preheated oven and bake for 18–22 minutes until the breadcrumbs have turned golden and crisp.

Serve with oven chips (see page 164) and veggies, or fill a wrap or sandwich with a few of these morsels.

Love your leftovers Nuggets can be kept in the fridge for 3 days, or frozen for up to 3 months. Reheat or defrost in a hot oven for 5–8 minutes from fresh, or approximately 15 minutes from frozen, or until piping hot inside.

Simple swaps Substitute the broccoli for cauliflower in the second step, cooking for 6 minutes if boiling and 8–9 minutes if steaming.

Salmon spinach parcel

Crispy flaky pastry surrounding soft and succulent baked fish, with an easy spinach and cheese filling – a classic made easy!

GF*

EF*

DF*

🍴 2 adults and 1 little   ⏱ Prep 15 minutes, Bake 25 minutes   ❄ Freezable

2 big handfuls of fresh spinach
1 garlic clove, crushed
3 tbsp soft cream cheese*
25g (1oz) Cheddar cheese*, grated
a small handful of fresh

flat-leaf parsley, finely chopped (optional)
½ x 375g (13oz) ready-rolled puff pastry sheet*
240g (8½oz) skinless, boneless salmon (you can ask your

fishmonger to remove the skin, if you'd prefer)
1 egg*, beaten (or a little milk*)
freshly ground black pepper
(*See pages 8–9)

Preheat the oven to 190°C fan (210°C/415°F/Gas 6–7).

Put the fresh spinach in a sieve and pour over hot water from the kettle to wilt the leaves. Using the back of a spoon or ladle, press out as much liquid as you can. Put the lump of wilted spinach on a few pieces of kitchen paper and press to drain as much liquid as you can.

Place the dry spinach on a chopping board and very roughly run a large sharp knife over it to finely cut it up. Put the chopped spinach in a medium-sized bowl and add the garlic, cream cheese, grated cheese, parsley and a little black pepper. Give it a very good mix.

Unroll the pastry sheet halfway across and cut down the side of the roll. Ensure to cut through the baking paper too, leaving it in place under the pastry you are using. Place the remaining pastry in an airtight bag and save in the fridge for another recipe.

Place the pastry in front of you on a work surface – the left half will be the bottom of the parcel and the right half will be the top. Spread half of the cream cheese mixture onto the left side of the pastry, leaving a 2.5cm (1in) border. Then, using a piece of kitchen paper, pat the salmon dry before placing it on the cream cheese mixture. Spread the remaining cream cheese mixture over the top of the salmon.

Beat the egg and, using a pastry brush, apply a little egg around the edge of the pastry. Using the paper to help you if you need to, fold the right-hand (bare) half of the pastry over the filling to form a parcel and gently press the edges together with the sides of your hands. Use a fork to crimp the cut edges of the pastry together, then transfer the parcel – still on its paper – onto a large baking tray.

Using a sharp knife, gently score a criss-cross pattern into the top of the pastry, but be careful not to cut all the way through the pastry. Cut a slit (about 2.5cm/1in long) in the top of the pastry – this helps excess steam to escape. Put the tray in the preheated oven and bake for 20–25 minutes until the pastry has puffed up and has turned a lovely golden brown and the base is crisp and golden too.

Slice into 5cm (2in) wide strips to serve to adults, or 2.5cm (1in) strips for little ones. Serve alongside salad or vegetables, and rice or potatoes. Delicious with oven baked chips too!

Love your leftovers This is best eaten fresh, but leftovers will keep for a day in the fridge and can be frozen for up to 1 month.

Waste not Try the Peach Melba Tarts on page 208 to use up the other half of your pastry sheet.

Tuna and broccoli cheese muffins

Protein, carbs, dairy and veg all in one delicious little muffin. The perfect lunch or snack for when you're on the go.

EF*

DF*

🍴 12 regular muffins   ⏱ Prep 10 minutes, Bake 25 minutes   ❄ Freezable

4 large florets of broccoli
1 x 105g (3½oz) can of tuna
   in spring water, drained
170g (6oz) self-raising flour
1 tsp baking powder
125g (4½oz) unsalted butter*,

melted, plus extra for
   greasing
3 medium eggs*
60ml (2fl oz) whole milk*
½ tsp mustard powder
   (optional)

½ tsp smoked paprika
   (optional)
120g (4¼oz) Cheddar
   cheese*, grated
(*See page 8)

Preheat the oven to 180°C fan (200°C/400°F/Gas 6) and grease a 12-hole non-stick muffin tray well with butter.

Grate the broccoli on a box grater, whizz in a food processor or finely chop – you just want the broccoli pieces to be very small so that they cook evenly in the muffins. Add the broccoli crumbs to a mixing bowl along with the rest of the ingredients. Mix until the batter is just combined, then divide it between the 12 holes of the prepared muffin tray, using a tablespoon and teaspoon to scrape the batter into each hole.

Place on the middle shelf and bake for 20–25 minutes until puffed up, golden on top and an inserted knife comes out clean. Allow the muffins to cool in the tin for 10 minutes before gently prizing them out of the tin and transferring to a cooling rack.

Love your leftovers Store leftover muffins in an airtight container in the fridge for 3 days, or freeze for up to 3 months. Reheat in a hot oven for around 5–10 minutes until piping hot, or blast in the microwave for 40 seconds. You can reheat straight from frozen by adding an extra 5 minutes to the oven time or by microwaving for around 2 minutes until piping hot throughout.

Simple swaps You can swap the broccoli for wilted, drained and chopped spinach; or grated and squeezed carrot and courgette (zucchini) would work perfectly too.

Hidden-veg-packed sausage pinwheels

GF*

EF*

DF*

Full of extra veg, but you would not know, these pinwheels are seriously moreish. Perfect with mash for dinner, on a buffet table or as a picnic delight!

🍴 Makes 12 ⏱ Prep 25 minutes, Bake 20 minutes ❄ Freezable

1 small carrot
1 small courgette (zucchini)
1 medium parsnip
300g (10½oz) pork mince
 (5–12% fat) or sausage meat*
 for over 1s (see page 91)

2 tsp smoked paprika
1 tsp garlic granules
50g (1¾oz) Cheddar cheese*,
 grated
40g (1½oz) dried breadcrumbs*

1 x 375g (13oz) sheet
 ready-rolled puff pastry*
1 egg* (optional)
freshly ground black pepper
(*See pages 8–9)

Preheat the oven to 200°C fan (220°C/425°F/Gas 7) and line a large baking tray with non-stick foil.

Lay a clean tea towel on your work surface and place a box grater in the centre. Coarsely grate the carrot, courgette and parsnip, then remove the grater, lift up all four corners of the towel and gather the veg into a tight ball. Over the sink (lots of juice will come out!), twist the tea towel around so that all of the juice is squeezed out of the ball of veg. Tip the veg pulp into a large mixing bowl, and add the meat, paprika, garlic granules, cheese, breadcrumbs and a grinding of black pepper. (You'll mix it in a moment.)

Get the puff pastry ready by unrolling it on your work surface, keeping it on the paper it comes wrapped in. Using one of your hands, squish the filling mixture together to incorporate all the veg into the meat. Taking handfuls of the filling mixture at time, place it onto the pastry and gently smush it over to cover the entire sheet so you can barely see the pastry underneath. The meat mixture will be approximately 1cm (½in) thick.

With the pastry sheet sat landscape in front of you, start at one of the long edges and fold 2.5cm (1in) over – this is the start of your spiral. Now, use this ledge to gently push and roll the spiral up so you're left with a long pastry sausage shape. If it helps, lift the paper underneath the pastry to help you roll it up.

Now to cut the pinwheel shapes. Using a large serrated knife, tap all 11 marks of where you're going to cut the pastry to make 12 evenly-sized pieces. Find the central point and mark the sausage in half, then mark each half into 3 pieces. Finally, mark each of these pieces in half. You can now cut the pastry roll into 12, placing each pinwheel on the baking tray with the spiral pattern facing up. Ensure you arrange the pinwheels on the tray at least 5cm (2in) apart so they have enough space to cook evenly. If you would like to, egg wash the sides of the exposed pastry, but this step isn't necessary. Place the tray in the top half of the preheated oven and bake for 15–20 minutes until the meat has firmed up and the pastry is golden and flaky.

Love your leftovers Pinwheels will keep for 3 days in the fridge, or freeze for up to 3 months. To reheat, place in the oven for 10–12 minutes or until piping hot throughout. They can be reheated from frozen too for approximately 15 minutes, but keep an eye on them – once defrosted they will catch easily.

Cheese and onion pasties

This is honest, humble food that takes me back to my childhood – crispy, flaky pastry encasing a soft, warm cheese, potato and onion filling. These pasties are much simpler than you would expect to prepare, and will leave your house smelling very homely.

⚒ Makes 4 pasties   ⏲ Prep 15 minutes, Bake 22 minutes

unsalted butter* or oil, for greasing
225g (8oz) potatoes (Maris Piper or a good all-rounder)
1 brown onion

120g (4¼oz) Cheddar cheese*, grated
1 tsp Dijon mustard* (optional)
1 x 375g (13oz) sheet ready rolled puff pastry*

1 egg*, beaten (or milk*)
1 tbsp sesame seeds (optional)
freshly ground black pepper
(*See pages 8–9)

GF*
EF*
V
Vg*
DF*

Preheat the oven to 190°C fan (210°C/415°F/Gas 6–7) and grease a large baking tray or line it with baking paper.

Peel and dice the potatoes into 2.5cm (1in) cubes and put them in a microwaveable bowl. Add a splash of water, cover and microwave for 4 minutes until the potatoes are cooked. (You can also cook them on the hob, if you prefer.) Drain and mash the potatoes as well as you can.

Add the mash to a large mixing bowl and flatten it out so it cools more quickly. Now, peel a whole onion and coarsely grate it (see page 15 for tips on how to do this). Try to squeeze out a little of the juice before adding the pulp to the potatoes along with the cheese, mustard, if using, and a little black pepper. Mix well using a rubber spatula and set aside.

Unroll the puff pastry and cut the sheet widthways into four short strips. Working with one pastry strip at a time, brush a 2.5cm (1in) border with the beaten egg around the edge of each strip – this will help to seal the pastry into a parcel.

Divide the potato mixture into four. Take one portion in your hand and form it into a fat, flattish sausage shape. Place this on the bottom half of the pastry strip, then fold the bare top over the filling and seal the edges, using your hands to press the pastry around the filling. Using a fork, press the three open edges together, crimping it about 2cm (¾in) from the edge – this will give a pretty pattern and help avoid any leakages. Transfer to the baking tray, then repeat with the other three pasties.

Brush the beaten egg over the tops of the pasties, then using a sharp knife, cut 3 slits into the top of each; this lets the steam escape and avoids the pasties exploding in the oven.

Sprinkle the sesame seeds over the pasties, if using, and bake in the preheated oven for 17–22 minutes, or until the pastry has puffed up and is golden.

Love your leftovers These pasties will keep in the fridge for 3 days, or freeze for up to 4 months. They are best defrosted at room temperature, then reheated in the oven for 10 minutes, or until piping hot throughout.

Courgette and tomato tart

Flaky puff pastry, creamy cheese and wafer thin veggies that turn soft and delicious when baked.

GF*
EF
V
Vg*
DF*

🍴 2 adults and 3 littles   ⏱ **Prep 10 minutes, Bake 25 minutes**   ❄ **Freezable**

1 medium–large courgette (zucchini)

3–4 cherry tomatoes

1 x 375g (13oz) sheet of ready-rolled puff pastry*

2 garlic cloves, crushed

¼ tsp dried mixed herbs

4 heaped tbsp mascarpone cheese*

40g (1½oz) Cheddar cheese*, grated

1 tbsp nuts (almonds, pine

nuts and hazelnuts work best, optional)

2 tsp olive oil (preferably garlic-infused)

freshly ground black pepper (*See pages 8–9)

Preheat the oven to 200°C fan (220°C/425°F/Gas 7) and set a large, heavy non-stick baking tray on your work surface ready. To make extra sure you avoid a soggy bottom to your tart, find another baking tray and place it upside down on the middle shelf in your oven to heat up while the oven comes to temperature. This will help cook the base of the tart a little better.

Using a sharp knife, slice the courgette into wafer-thin discs. Slice the cherry tomatoes, too, cutting them across the equator so that the seeds stay attached inside.

Unroll your puff pastry and, using a large dinner plate as a template, cut out a very large circle. Alternatively, cut the pastry into smaller rectangles to make individual tarts. Transfer the pastry to your baking tray and, using a sharp knife, gently score a line around the edge of the pastry, 1cm (½in) from the edge. This will allow the crust to puff up nicely.

Add the garlic and herbs to the mascarpone cheese, mixing well to combine, and spread it over the puff pastry, keeping inside your scored border. Place the courgette slices on top, followed by the tomatoes. Sprinkle the grated cheese over the veggies, followed by a little grinding of black pepper.

Put the nuts on a chopping board, or in a pestle and mortar, and chop or bash into very small pieces. If serving to little ones under 3, it's important to ensure the nuts are no larger than ½cm (¼in) in size. Scatter the nuts over the top of the tart. If you're unsure, avoid sprinkling the nuts on one half of the tart and serve this side to your little ones.

Now, drizzle a little oil over the top of everything and, using your fingers or a pastry brush, apply a thin layer to the exposed pastry too. Place the tray on top of the upside-down hot tray in the oven and bake for 20–25 minutes until the pastry has puffed up on the edges, the base is golden brown and cooked all the way through to the centre, and the cheese has turned a little golden on top.

Love your leftovers The tart will keep for 3 days in the fridge – enjoy it hot or cold. To warm, place in the oven for 5–10 minutes until piping hot throughout. This tart will also freeze for up to 3 months; reheat from frozen in an oven set to 200°C fan (220°C/425°F/Gas 7) for 10–20 minutes until completely defrosted and piping hot. Keep an eye on it, as the pastry will catch easily.

Comforting chicken soup with bread dumplings

GF*

DF

Feeling a little under the weather, or just need warming up on a cold wintery day? This soup will do the trick!

🍴 **2 adults and 2 littles**   ⏱ **Prep and cook 40 minutes**   ❄ **Freezable**

4 chicken thighs	**For the dumplings**
2 large carrots, peeled	6 slices of white bread*
2 celery sticks	2 medium eggs
1 low-salt chicken stock cube*	½ tsp dried mixed herbs
1 bay leaf (optional)	freshly ground black pepper
1 tsp dried mixed herbs	(*See page 9)

Remove the skin from the chicken thighs, but leave the bone in – this will give flavour to the soup.

Put the chicken in a large saucepan. Roughly slice the carrots on a diagonal into large chunks, then slice the celery to the same size so it's easier to remove when serving if little ones prefer not to eat this. Add the veg to the pan with the chicken and cover everything with about 1 litre (35fl oz) of boiling water. Crumble in the stock cube and add the bay leaf, if using, and mixed herbs. Stir and let the soup simmer for 15 minutes.

Meanwhile, make the dumplings. If the crusts on your slices of bread are really tough, remove them; however, if they are soft, it's fine to keep them on. Slice the bread into 1cm (½in) cubes, or as small as you can. I find the easiest way to do this is by cutting the slice into lots of long thin strips, then slicing small chunks off the strips. Alternatively, you can whizz up the bread in a food processor.

Put the bread in a bowl, along with the eggs, herbs and a little black pepper. Give it a really good stir and get your hands in to squish the bread into the egg to help it soak up as much as possible. Allow to stand for a minute before rolling the mixture into golf ball-sized balls. You may need to cup the mixture in the palm of your hands to squeeze it together into balls, but once you get the dumplings in the pan, they will hold together.

Once the soup has had 15 minutes, add the bread dumplings and cook for a further 15–20 minutes until the dumplings feel firm to the touch.

Once the dumplings are ready, remove the chicken from the soup, then pull the meat from the chicken bones and add it back to the soup. Serve in bowls, together or deconstructed for little taste testers. You can serve the broth in a cup if you wish, and the dumplings in halves or quarters. Adults, feel free to add salt to your portion.

Love your leftovers The soup will keep for 2 days in the fridge, or freeze for 2 months. Defrost and reheat in a saucepan or microwave until piping hot throughout.

Top tip Use the leftover bones from your Sunday roast chicken instead of thighs here, to make your meals stretch even further.

Sesame-crusted chicken bites with tahini yogurt dip

GF*

EF

DF*

Succulent soft chicken coated in a moreish sesame crust, these are chicken nuggets on a whole new level!

⚒ 2 adults and 2 littles, plus leftovers   ⏱ Prep 15 minutes, Bake 20 minutes   ❄ Freezable

6 skinless, boneless chicken thighs
50g (1¾oz) plain (all-purpose) flour*
50ml (1¾fl oz) milk*
1 tsp sesame oil (optional)
70g (2½oz) panko breadcrumbs*

50g (1¾oz) sesame seeds
30g (1oz) Cheddar cheese*, finely grated
freshly ground black pepper
garlic-infused oil spray

For the dip
4 tbsp Greek yogurt*

1 tbsp low-salt soy sauce*
1 garlic clove, crushed
juice of ½ lime
1 tsp tahini (sesame seed paste)
freshly ground black pepper
(*See pages 8–9)

Preheat the oven to 200°C fan (220°C/425°F/Gas 7) and line a large baking tray with non-stick baking paper.

Unroll the chicken thighs and slice widthways into 2cm (¾in) wide strips. Add the chicken to a bowl or sealable food bag, then add the flour, milk and sesame oil, if using. Give it a really good mix so that every part of the chicken is covered in the floury batter.

In a separate large bowl, combine the breadcrumbs, sesame seeds, cheese and a little black pepper and mix well with your fingers to ensure the cheese is mixed with the breadcrumbs.

With one hand, take a piece of chicken and place it in the breadcrumb bowl. With your other dry hand, cover in the breadcrumb mixture and transfer to the baking tray. Repeat with all of the chicken, keeping one hand for the wet chicken and the other for the dry breadcrumbs. This way you don't end up with a big sticky mess.

Give each piece of chicken a few squirts of garlic-infused oil, then bake in the preheated oven for 20 minutes, or until golden on the outside and the chicken is cooked through.

While the chicken cooks, make the dip by adding all of the ingredients to a small bowl and mixing well.

Serve the bites with the tahini dip, salad and wraps, or veg and potatoes. For little ones, cut the chicken bites in half lengthways to expose the soft flesh inside.

Love your leftovers These bites are delicious cold in a sandwich. Keep in the fridge for 2 days, or freeze for 3 months. Unbaked nuggets can also be frozen, then cooked from frozen for approximately 25 minutes, or until the inside is piping hot.

Jacket potatoes

A family staple in my house all year round. There are many ways to cook jacket potatoes, but what is the best way for you? Here are some options.

Firstly, choose nice large baking potatoes. Wash them well and if they're particularly dirty, give them a little scrub with a potato brush.

Pat dry with kitchen paper, prick five or six times all over each potato to allow steam to escape and avoid exploding, then rub them with a touch of olive or garlic-infused oil. Now you're ready to cook in your desired method (see below).

Oven – this way gives the crispiest skin

Place the potatoes on a baking tray large enough for the potatoes to have plenty of room. Bake at 170°C fan (190°C/375°F/Gas 5) for 70–90 minutes, depending on the size of your potatoes. No need to turn them, so you can pop them in the oven and forget about them until they're done.

Microwave – this is the quickest option

Place the potatoes on a large microwaveable plate and cook on high for 5 minutes. Turn and cook for a further 3–6 minutes or until an inserted knife slides in easily.

Microwave and oven – best of both worlds

If you just can't live without that crispy baked potato skin, then once the microwaved jacket potatoes are fully cooked, place on a baking tray and bake at 200°C fan (220°C/425°F/Gas 7) for 10–20 minutes, turning once, until the potatoes are crisped to your liking.

Slow cooker – for prepping ahead

Alternatively, wrap each pricked and oiled potato in a square of kitchen foil and place them in a slow cooker, in a single layer, and cook for 4 hours on HIGH or 7–8 hours on LOW. This is a great option if you want to have an easy dinner ready for when you get home.

To serve, cut the potatoes into quarters, keeping the base still attached, and add a dollop of butter, dairy-free spread or one of the following two delicious topping mixtures to the centre. For little ones, cut the warm potato into finger strips, or mash with the back of a fork.

Turn over to see how they look

MIDWEEK MEALS

Lemony tuna

GF

EF

DF*

A really quick topping for easy lunches with minimal effort but maximum flavour.

🍴 Fills 2 large jacket potatoes   **⏱ Prep 5 minutes**

1 x 110g (3¾oz) can tuna in
    spring water
75g (2½oz) mascarpone cheese
    or soft cream cheese*

25g (1oz) Cheddar cheese*,
    grated
30ml (1fl oz) milk*
1 small unwaxed lemon

freshly ground black pepper
1 spring onion (scallion), finely
    sliced, to serve
(*See page 8)

Drain the tuna and add it to a bowl along with the soft cheese, grated Cheddar, milk
and a little black pepper. Zest a little of the lemon and add 1 teaspoon of it to the bowl,
along with the juice of half the lemon. Mix well and serve on your jacket potato with a
few spring onion slices sprinkled on top.

Love your leftovers This topping will keep, covered, for 2 days in the fridge.

Cheesy chilli

GF*

EF

DF*

A flavourful chilli, packed full of protein and veggies, for a well-balanced family meal.

🍴 Fills 4 large jacket potatoes   **⏱ Prep and cook 30 minutes**   **❄ Freezable**

500g (1lb 2oz) lean beef mince
1 tsp sunflower or garlic-
    infused oil
1 small brown onion
2 large garlic cloves
2 tbsp tomato purée (paste)
1 x 400g (14oz) can of beans,

like haricot or kidney,
    drained and roughly mashed
a small can of sweetcorn in
    water
1 low-salt beef stock cube*
500g (1lb 2oz) tomato passata
    (strained tomatoes)

2 tbsp smoked paprika
1 tsp dried mixed herbs
½ tsp ground cumin
80g (2¾oz) smoked Cheddar
    cheese*, finely grated, plus
    extra to serve
(*See pages 8–9)

Put the mince and oil in a large saucepan over a medium–high heat. Dice the onion
quickly and add to the pan too, then, using a wooden spoon, break up the mince into
small pieces. Cook until the onions are soft and the mince has turned brown – this will
take around 5 minutes.

Meanwhile, mince the garlic then add to the pan, along with the tomato purée. Cook
for a further 2 minutes before draining the beans and sweetcorn and adding those to
the pan too. Crumble in the stock cube, then add the passata, smoked paprika, dried
herbs and cumin. Quarter fill the passata packet with water, swill around to catch all the
remaining tomato juice and add to the pan. Stir everything together well, then put the
lid on and cook for at least 20 minutes, but even up to an hour on a low heat is perfect.

Before serving the chilli, take it off the heat and stir in the cheese, allowing it to melt
into the sauce. Spoon over the cut jacket potato and serve with a little sour cream,
avocado and extra cheese on top.

Love your leftovers The chilli will keep in the fridge for 3 days, or freeze for 3 months.
Once defrosted, reheat in a saucepan until piping hot.

Wings and hasselbacks

Sweet, sticky chicken wings with crispy skin and succulent meat inside, are served alongside sweet red peppers and hedgehog hassleback potatoes.

GF*

EF

DF

⏲ 2 adults and 2 littles ⏱ Prep and cook 45 minutes ❄ Freezable

6–8 large new potatoes, washed
3 tbsp sunflower oil, garlic-infused oil, or butter*, for the potatoes
juice of 1 small orange or a satsuma

2 tbsp low-salt soy sauce*
2 tbsp sesame seeds
1 tbsp of honey (for over 1s) or maple syrup
2 tsp garlic granules
2 heaped tsp smoked paprika
2 tbsp cornflour (cornstarch)

1 low-salt chicken stock cube*
1.5kg (3lb 5oz) chicken wings
2 red peppers, cut into wide strips
1 tbsp garlic-infused oil
freshly ground black pepper
(*See pages 8–9)

Preheat the oven to 200°C fan (220°C/425°F/Gas 7) and line two very large baking trays with non-stick foil.

Start with the hassleback potatoes. Using a large sharp knife with a thin blade, cut thin slices at 3mm (1/8in) intervals across the top of each potato, ensuring you do not cut all the way through. You can lay two chopsticks on either side of the potato to stop the knife going all the way through, if you wish.

Place the potatoes on one of the prepared baking trays and coat in your chosen fat, turning the potatoes well to ensure they are fully coated and the fat is seeping between the slits. Put the tray in the oven and set a timer for 40 minutes. Turn the potatoes once or twice during cooking to coat in more fat and allow them to crisp up on all sides.

Meanwhile, make the wings. In a large mixing bowl or sealable food bag, combine the orange juice, soy sauce, sesame seeds, honey or maple syrup, garlic granules, smoked paprika, cornflour and a little black pepper, and crumble in the stock cube. Give it a really good mix, then add the chicken wings. Mix really well so that the meat is covered on all sides, then transfer the chicken to the other baking tray, separated so they are not touching. Now, add the sliced peppers to the remaining marinade, toss to coat and add the peppers to the tray too, nestling them between the wings.

Drizzle the garlic oil over the top of everything, then place the tray in the oven to bake for 30–35 minutes until the wings are starting to char slightly and the peppers have softened. You may need to swap shelves with the potatoes once or twice during cooking to ensure both trays are cooking evenly.

Serve up with a little extra green veg or salad, and the chicken and pepper cooking juices drizzled over everything, especially the potatoes. For little ones, remove the meat from the bone or cut the wings up through the joint so that it's easier for them to navigate eating the meat from the bone.

Love your leftovers Any leftovers will keep for 2 days in the fridge; reheat in the oven at 180°C fan (200°C/400°F/Gas 6) for 10–15 minutes until piping hot throughout. You can also put the wings in a bag with the marinade and place this in the freezer to marinate raw for up to 2 months. Defrost fully before cooking as per instructions above.

Potato curry with spiced flatbreads

The humble potato is the star of the show in this delicious curry. Serve as a main or side.

GF*
EF
V
Vg*
DF*

🍴 **2 adults and 2 littles** ⏲ **Prep and cook 45 minutes** ❄ **Freezable**

For the curry
1 large onion
2 tbsp garlic-infused olive oil
2 large garlic cloves
1kg (2lb 4oz) all-rounder
   potatoes, like Maris piper
400-g (14-oz) can coconut milk
2 tbsp tomato purée (paste)
2 tsp garam masala

1 heaped tbsp mild curry
   powder
4 lumps of shop-bought
   chopped frozen spinach

For the flatbreads
240g (8½oz) self-raising flour*,
   plus extra for dusting
1 tsp baking powder*

1 heaped tbsp garam masala
1 heaped tsp garlic granules
1 tsp mixed dried herbs
170g (6oz) Greek yogurt*, plus
   extra (or milk*), if needed
2 tbsp garlic-infused olive oil
1 tbsp nigella or (white or
   black) sesame seeds
(*See pages 8–9)

To make the curry, peel and grate the onion on a box grater, or finely dice. Add to a large saucepan over a medium–high heat with the garlic oil and sauté for around 5 minutes until translucent and starting to turn a little brown. Meanwhile, finely grate the garlic, then peel the potatoes and dice into bite-sized chunks, setting both aside.

Add the garlic, tomato purée, garam masala and curry powder, stir and cook for 2 minutes, without burning the spices. Quickly add the coconut milk and once melted, stir in the potatoes and spinach. Fill up the coconut milk can with water and add that to the pan, stir and put the lid on. Once gently boiling, tilt the lid to allow a little steam to escape and cook for 25–30 minutes until the potatoes are tender and the sauce has thickened. Stir occasionally, and add a splash of water at the end for a looser consistency.

To make your flatbreads, put the flour, baking powder, garam masala, garlic granules and herbs in a large mixing bowl and stir well. Add the yogurt and oil, then stir until it clumps together. If the mixture is too dry then add a touch more yogurt or a splash of milk. Tip the mixture out onto a floured work surface and form into a ball. Put a large griddle or frying pan on a high heat to warm up while you roll your first flatbread.

Cut the dough ball into 6 portions and make some room to roll out your flatbreads. Add a large handful of flour to your work surface, away from your direct rolling space, and use this to keep the surface and dough well floured to avoid it sticking to the rolling pin. Take the first piece of dough, dab the cut sticky side in flour, place on the work surface and press down to flatten it slightly. Dust your rolling pin and roll the dough out just once, then flip it over. Sprinkle a pinch of seeds on the dough, then roll them into it, patching any slightly sticky areas with flour. Roll it as thin as you can to around 2mm (¹/₁₆in) thick.

Lift the flatbread up carefully to avoid it tearing and lightly shake off any excess flour. Place in the pan, non-seeded-side down. Cook for about 2 minutes until it starts to bubble in patches and puff up, then flip with tongs and cook for a further minute on the other side. Transfer to a plate or wooden board and repeat with the remaining portions.

To serve, pile the curry into bowls and tuck a folded flatbread into the side of each dish. Adults, feel free to add a little salt to your curry, and for babies, mash any pieces of potato which are too small for baby to hold.

Love your leftovers The curry will keep for 2 days in the fridge, or freeze for 3 months. Reheat with an extra splash of water in a saucepan or microwave. The flatbreads can be stored for 3 days in an airtight container, or freeze for 3 months. Reheat in the microwave for 90–120 seconds, or on a baking tray in the oven with a little splash of water for 5–10 minutes.

Mushroom risotto

Silky mushroom risotto packed full of rich, earthy flavours, this is a family favourite in my house!

GF*

EF

V

Vg*

DF*

🍴 **2 adults and 2 littles** ⏱ **Prep and cook 35 minutes** ❄ **Freezable**

15g (½oz) dried porcini mushrooms

1 low-salt chicken or vegetable stock cube*

1 medium brown onion

35g (1¼oz) unsalted butter*

200g (7oz) chestnut mushrooms

2 fat garlic cloves, grated or crushed

150g (5½oz) arborio risotto rice

a large handful (about 40g/1½oz) hard cheese, such as Cheddar*, grated

freshly ground black pepper

(*See pages 8–9)

Boil the kettle. Put the dried mushrooms in a jug and crumble in the stock cube. Fill with 650ml (22fl oz) of boiling water from the kettle, stir and set aside to let the mushrooms soften.

Peel and finely dice the onion as small as you can. Add 25g (1oz) of the butter to a medium-sized saucepan and allow it to melt while adding the onions. Sauté for 3 minutes while you chop the chestnut mushrooms. Slice each mushroom into 3 or 4 slices, then dice roughly into smaller pieces. Add the mushrooms to the onions, along with a little black pepper and cook for 5 minutes.

Meanwhile, remove the soaked mushrooms from the broth and put on a chopping board. Run a knife over the mushrooms to cut them into small pieces, as fine as you can but no need to be precise. Add these to the pan, along with the garlic and risotto rice. Cook for a minute, before adding all of the mushroom stock.

Give the pan a good stir using a wooden spoon. Rest the spoon over the pan and place a lid on top so that the spoon leaves a gap allowing a little steam to escape. Simmer the risotto for around 20–25 minutes, or until the rice is fully cooked, stirring every so often but no need to continuously stir. Add a splash more water from the kettle if it looks to be drying up too quickly.

Take the pan off the heat and add the remaining butter, along with the grated cheese, and stir to melt them into the rice. The risotto will suddenly become silky and creamy.

For little ones, you can serve as is or blend a little to smooth out any larger lumps for young babies, if you would like. Ensure there are no large lumps of mushroom in any portions for under 2s.

Adults, you can add a touch more cheese and a little salt to your portion, if you wish.

Love your leftovers Rice must be cooled down within the hour for it to be safely stored and reheated. Therefore, spread the risotto on a cold plate to cool very quickly, then spoon into a bowl, cover tightly and refrigerate for up to 2 days. To reheat, put it in a saucepan with an extra splash of water or stock and allow to simmer until piping hot throughout. You can also freeze the risotto for up to 3 months – defrost thoroughly in the fridge overnight before reheating, as above, within 24 hours.

Rebecca's garlic bread salmon

Succulent, soft, flaky fish topped with a crispy garlic crumb.

GF*

EF

DF*

🍴 1 adult and 2 littles ⏱ **Prep 10 minutes, Bake 30 minutes** ❄ **Freezable**

a large handful of new
   potatoes
1 tbsp garlic-infused olive oil,
   plus extra for drizzling
3 tbsp panko breadcrumbs*
1 large garlic clove, crushed

finely grated zest and juice
   of ½ a large lemon
½ tsp dried mixed herbs
30g (1oz) Cheddar cheese*,
   grated

2 x 120g salmon fillets or any
   flaky firm fish fillet
freshly ground black pepper
(*See pages 8–9)

Preheat the oven to 200°C fan (220°C/425°F/Gas 7) and line a large baking tray with non-stick foil.

Slice the potatoes into 5mm (¼in) thick slices and lay flat on the prepared tray, avoiding too much overlapping. Drizzle with a little garlic oil and grind a little black pepper over the potatoes, then pop in the oven to start cooking; set your timer for 10 minutes.

Meanwhile, put the breadcrumbs in a bowl with the garlic, lemon juice and zest, herbs, Cheddar, a little more black pepper and the 1 tablespoon of garlic-infused oil.

Once the potatoes have been in for 10 minutes, take the tray out of the oven, flip each potato slice over and make a space in the centre of the tray for the fish. Add the salmon fillets to the tray, skin-side down, then spoon over the crumb mixture generously. Pop it all back in the oven for a further 15–20 minutes until the salmon is cooked through.

Serve the salmon and potatoes with fresh vegetables or salad and a bowl of yogurt, if wished, gently flaking the fish into chunks for little ones.

Love your leftovers The salmon can be stored in the fridge for up to 24 hours, or freeze for up to 1 month. If frozen, defrost first in the fridge, then reheat in a hot oven until piping hot throughout.

Note If you don't have any breadcrumbs, you can simply whizz up a slice of bread in a food processor to make your own instant fresh breadcrumbs. This works well if you're struggling to find gluten-free breadcrumbs.

Easy oven-baked chicken and mushroom shawarma

GF*

EF

DF*

A real family sharing meal, perfect to let the kids help themselves and decide how they want to construct their plate. Leave out the mushrooms if they don't float your boat.

🍴 2 adults and 2 littles   ⏱ Prep 10 minutes, Bake 30 minutes   ❄ Freezable

6 skinless, boneless chicken
    thighs
1 tbsp smoked paprika
1 heaped tsp ground cumin
½ tsp ground cinnamon
1 tsp ground turmeric
1 heaped tbsp cornflour
    (cornstarch)
3 fat garlic cloves, finely
    grated
finely grated zest and juice

of 1 unwaxed lemon
3 tbsp garlic-infused olive oil
4 large flat mushrooms
freshly ground black pepper

For the garlic dip
4 heaped tbsp plain Greek
    yogurt*
1 small garlic clove, finely
    minced
juice of 1 lemon

To serve
your favourite chopped salad
    bits, such as cucumber,
    peppers, shredded lettuce,
    tomatoes, onions
pickled cabbage
pickled gherkins
pitta breads or tortilla wraps*,
    warmed in the oven, if wished
hot sauce (optional)
(*See pages 8–9)

Put the chicken in a large sealable food bag along with the spices, cornflour, garlic, lemon zest and juice, 2 tablespoons of the garlic oil and a little pepper. Seal the bag and give it a very good mix – it may help to release some of the air from inside the bag. Squeeze the chicken around the bag with your hands – this not only helps to coat the chicken in all the flavourful spices, but also helps tenderise the meat a little. You can now bake this straightaway, or marinate in the fridge for up to 24 hours.

When you are ready to cook, preheat the oven to 200°C fan (220°C/425°F/Gas 7) and line a large baking tray with foil.

Tip the chicken out onto the baking tray and unravel the meat so the thighs lie flat in an even layer and are not overlapping. Add the mushrooms to the empty marinade bag, reseal and give it a gentle shake to allow the remaining marinade to stick to the mushrooms. Add the mushrooms to the same baking tray, gill-side down. Drizzle the remaining 1 tablespoon of oil over the mushrooms, then, if your little ones are over 4, add a very tiny sprinkling of salt, if you wish. Bake in the preheated oven for 25–30 minutes until the chicken is cooked through and turning crispy at the edges.

Meanwhile, make the dip – mix everything together in a small bowl and season with a little black pepper. Prepare the salad bits and arrange them, with the pickles, on a sharing platter or in bowls for everyone to help themselves.

Once the chicken is cooked, remove from the oven and allow to rest for 5 minutes before slicing everything into 1.5cm (⅝in) wide strips, including the mushrooms. Place a couple of pitta breads at the bottom of a large serving bowl and tip the chicken and mushrooms on top including any resting juices. All these yummy juices will soak into the bread – my absolute favourite part! Serve with hot sauce for the adults, if you like.

Love your leftovers Any leftovers can be kept in the fridge for 2 days and are truly delicious cold in a tortilla wrap – lunchbox goals!

One-pot chicken and orzo

The perfect one pot family dish; easy to throw together and has a little hidden veg.
Win, win, win!

GF*

EF

DF

⊘⊘ 2 adults and 3 littles ⏱ **Prep 5 minutes, Bake 40 minutes**

1 low-salt chicken stock cube*
1 large courgette (zucchini)
2 garlic cloves, crushed
finely grated zest and juice
    of 1 unwaxed lemon
2 tbsp finely chopped chives

200g (7oz) dried orzo pasta*
6 chicken thigh fillets (skin on
    and bone still in)
garlic-infused oil spray
freshly ground black pepper
(*See page 9)

Preheat the oven to 190°C fan (210°C/415°F/Gas 6–7) and find a large, high-sided
ceramic baking dish large enough to fit all of the chicken pieces in with a little room
to breathe.

Crumble the stock cube into the baking dish, then add 400ml (14fl oz) of boiling water
from the kettle and stir to dissolve the stock cube.

Grate the courgette and add it to the baking dish, along with any juice from the board.
Add the crushed garlic, zest and juice of the lemon, chives, orzo pasta and a little black
pepper. Stir it all to combine well.

Cut the excess overhanging fatty skin from the chicken thighs, leaving the main piece
still attached and covering the chicken meat, then nestle these thighs on top of the
pasta mixture, skin-side up. Spray a touch of garlic oil on just the skin of the chicken,
and season with black pepper and a little salt if your little ones are older.

Place the baking dish in the centre of the preheated oven and bake for 35–40 minutes
until the pasta and chicken are cooked through and the chicken skin is crispy and
browned. Serve with extra veg or salad if you wish.

For little ones under 2, remove the meat from the chicken bone and cut into finger strips
so they can pick it up and feed themselves.

Love your leftovers This will keep for 2 days in the fridge. Cover the dish with foil so it
doesn't dry out, and reheat in the oven until the chicken is piping hot throughout,

Inside-out chicken Kievs

GF*

EF*

DF*

How many times have you taken a chicken Kiev out the oven to find that all the garlic butter has escaped out of the centre? So let's just skip that faffy step and coat the outside of the chicken in garlic butter instead – much easier and arguably tastier!

🍽 2 adults and 2 littles ⏱ **Prep 15 minutes, Bake 30 minutes** ❄ **Freezable**

45g (1¾oz) unsalted butter*, softened
2 large garlic cloves, grated
1 tbsp chopped fresh parsley
finely grated zest and juice of 1 small unwaxed lemon
80ml (2½fl oz) milk*

80g (2¾oz) plain (all-purpose) flour*
1 medium egg* (or use an extra 50ml/1¾fl oz milk*)
1 tsp garlic granules
100g (3½oz) panko breadcrumbs*

4 skinless chicken breasts
500g (1lb 2oz) new potatoes
garlic-infused oil spray
freshly ground black pepper
(*See pages 8–9)

Preheat the oven to 190°C (210°C/415°F/Gas 6–7).

Make up the garlic butter by mixing the soft butter with the grated garlic, parsley, lemon zest and a little black pepper in a small bowl.

In a flat-bottomed bowl, mix the milk, flour, egg, lemon juice and garlic granules to make a smooth batter. Tip the panko breadcrumbs onto a plate. Now to assemble: pat the top of the chicken breasts with a piece of kitchen paper to dry them off. Divide the garlic butter into four and spread a portion over the top of each breast. No need to be neat here – just use the back of a teaspoon to spread it as evenly as you can.

One at a time, pick up a chicken breast by the pointy end and place in the batter, buttered-side up. Use a spoon to apply batter over the top of the butter, then lift up again by the pointy end and place in the panko breadcrumbs, again using a spoon to dust breadcrumbs over the top. Press the crumbs down a little to ensure the chicken is well coated. It's easier if you handle the chicken with one hand and keep the other clean to use a spoon – you won't get too messy this way. Transfer the coated chicken to a large baking tray and repeat to coat the other 3 fillets.

Cut the potatoes into 5mm (¼in) thick slices and arrange them on the baking tray around the chicken, trying not to overlap them too much. You may need to put a few potatoes on a second tray so they are not overcrowded, as this will prevent them turning crispy. Spray the potatoes and chicken with a little garlic oil.

Transfer the trays to your preheated oven and bake for 25–30 minutes until the chicken is cooked through and the potatoes are crispy. If you feel the potatoes could do with a little extra time, scoop the chicken out onto a board and let the potatoes have an extra 5 minutes while the chicken rests.

Serve up with green veg or a side salad. For little ones, slice the chicken into 2cm (¾in) strips so it's easier for them to hold and feed themselves.

Love your leftovers These will keep for 2 days in the fridge, and are delicious cold. You can also freeze the breadcrumbed raw chicken on a tray, then bag up once fully frozen. Bake from frozen for 40–45 minutes, or until the chicken is piping hot throughout.

Throw-it-all-in tomato and lentil gnocchi bake

GF*
EF
V
Vg*
DF*

The perfect family meal as you simply need to bung it all in an oven dish, stir and let the oven do its thing – no fuss and delicious! When shopping for the passata and chopped tomatoes, try to find the best quality your money can buy as this will really affect the flavour of the final dish.

🍴 3 adults and 2 littles ⏲ Prep 5 minutes, Bake 40 minutes ❄ Freezable

400g (14oz) passata (strained tomatoes

1 x 400g (14oz) can chopped tomatoes

1 heaped tbsp smoked paprika

1 tsp golden caster sugar (optional)

2 tsp dried mixed herbs

2 garlic cloves, crushed

1 x 400g (14oz) can cooked green lentils in water, drained

1 low-salt chicken or vegetable stock cube*

2 medium carrots, peeled if you wish

500g (1lb 2oz) fresh gnocchi*

60g (2oz) Cheddar cheese*, grated

60g (2oz) smoked Cheddar cheese*, grated

freshly ground black pepper

(*See pages 8–9)

Preheat the oven to 180°C fan (200°C/400°F/Gas 6) and find a large ceramic oven dish, about 1.8–2 litres (60–70fl oz) in volume.

Add the tomato passata and chopped tomatoes to the dish. Now, add the paprika, sugar, if using, herbs, garlic and drained lentils, then crumble in the stock cube and give it a really good stir. Finely grate the carrots and add these too, along with the gnocchi and half of each cheese. Give it a final good stir and top with the remaining cheese and a little black pepper to taste.

Place the dish on a large baking tray to catch any splatters, then pop in the middle of the preheated oven to bake for 30–40 minutes until the tomato sauce has thickened and is bubbling and the cheese is golden and crisp on top. Allow to stand for 5 minutes before serving with green veg or a salad on the side, if you wish.

For little ones under 2, cut the gnocchi in half lengthways, or into quarters if they are particularly big.

Love your leftovers The bake will keep for 3 days in the fridge; transfer to another baking dish big enough to fit the amount you have left snuggly, top with a little more cheese and bake until bubbling. You can also freeze leftovers. Once defrosted at room temperature or in the fridge, reheat in the microwave for 3 minutes, or place in the oven as above.

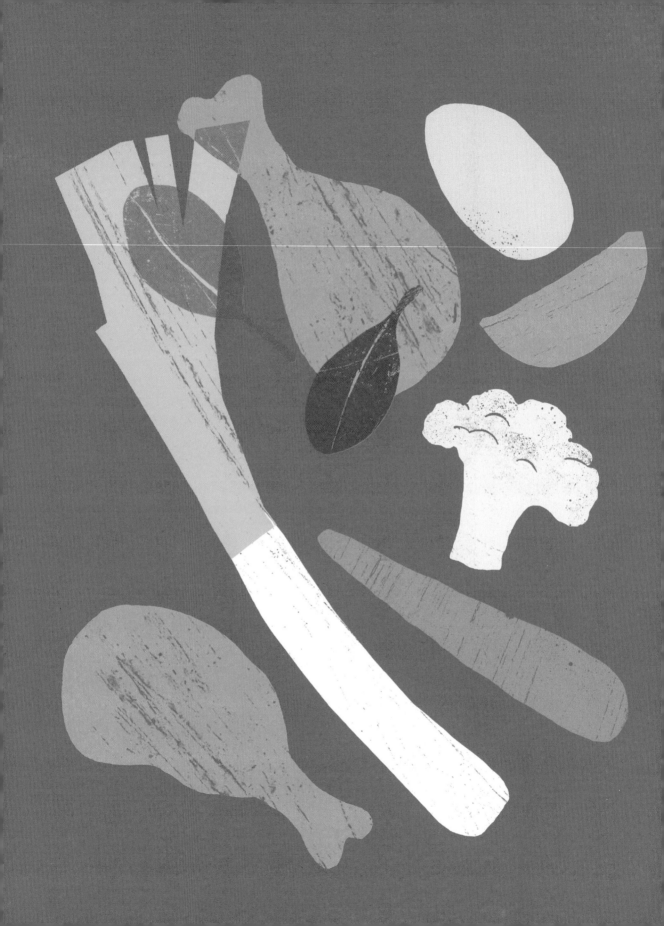

Weekend winners

The weekend is all about celebrating family moments, to gather together with your loved ones, enjoying meals that you can take a few extra moments to prepare. That tiny little bit of effort will be rewarded with happy full tummies, I promise you.

Proper family fish pie

Fish, prawns, peas, eggs, broccoli mash and a cheesy crust – the ultimate family comfort!

GF*

DF*

🍴 **2 adults and 3 littles** ⏲ **Prep 30 minutes, Bake 25–40 minutes** ❄ **Freezable**

For the mash topping
800g (1lb 12oz) all-rounder
   potatoes
1 small head of broccoli (about
   250g/9oz)
50ml (1¾fl oz) milk*
25g (1oz) unsalted butter*
70g (2½oz) Cheddar cheese*,
   grated

For the filling
4 medium eggs, shells washed
500ml (17fl oz) milk*
1 low-salt vegetable stock
   cube*
35g (1¼oz) unsalted butter*
3 tbsp cornflour (cornstarch)
50g (1¾oz) Cheddar cheese*,
   grated

½ tsp Dijon mustard*
250g (9oz) frozen peas
400g (14oz) frozen or fresh fish
   pie mix
200g (7oz) frozen or fresh raw
   prawns (shrimp)
freshly ground black pepper
(*See pages 8–9)

Preheat the oven to 180°C fan (200°C/400°F/Gas 6) and find a large, deep ceramic oven dish, about 1.8 litre (60fl oz) in volume.

Set a large pan of water (hot from the kettle) on to boil. Meanwhile, peel the potatoes and chop into 5cm (2in) chunks. Add to the boiling water and cook for 12 minutes.

Cut the broccoli into florets, removing most of the stalk but keeping enough that the broccoli pieces hold together. Add to a colander and wash under the tap. Prick the eggs for the filling with a needle to avoid them bursting. Once the potatoes have had 12 minutes, add the broccoli and eggs to the pan and boil together for a further 8 minutes.

Meanwhile, start the sauce by putting the 500ml (17fl oz) of milk in a jug, crumble in the stock cube and microwave for 2½ minutes to warm it up. Melt the 35g (1¼oz) of butter in a non-stick saucepan, then add the cornflour, stir and cook for 2 minutes. With a whisk in one hand and the milk jug in the other, slowly add the milk, stopping often to give the pan a really good whisk and remove any lumps. Once all the milk has been added, allow the sauce to bubble away for 5 minutes or until super thick. Remove from the heat, stir in the 50g (1¾oz) of cheese, the mustard, peas and a little black pepper. Set aside.

Back to the mash. Once the broccoli and potatoes are soft, scoop out the eggs and put them in a bowl filled with cold water. Drain the broccoli and potatoes and put them back in the saucepan. Mash with a potato masher or ricer, then add the milk and butter for the topping, along with 30g (1oz) of the grated Cheddar. Stir well, then set aside.

To assemble the pie, put the fish and prawns in the oven dish. Pour over the sauce and mix well. Peel and quarter the eggs and arrange over the sauce, then spoon over the mash. Sprinkle the remaining cheese over the top of the pie. Place the dish on a baking tray to catch any sauce that bubbles over, and bake for 20–25 minutes if the fish was fresh, or 30–40 minutes if the fish was frozen. Allow to stand for 5 minutes before serving.

For little ones, you can serve as is or mash with the back of a fork so the sauce and fish mixes into the mash. Finely chop the prawns, if you wish, or serve as finger food.

Love your leftovers Leftovers will keep for 2 days in the fridge if refrigerated promptly after cooling, or store in the freezer for 1 month and defrost in the fridge before reheating. Reheat until piping hot, ensuring the fish is piping hot.

Mince and onion pie

This dish is bit of a hybrid one from my childhood. Mince and onions was a staple dish on our family menu and, growing up in Northumberland, I love the traditional dish of leek pudding, which is a steamed suet pudding with leeks inside. So, I've combined the two, adding a few extra tweaks of my own and, oh my, the result is truly delicious!

GF*

EF

DF*

🍴 3 adults and 3 littles ⏱ Prep 25 minutes, Bake 45 minutes ❄ Freezable

For the filling
1 tbsp garlic-infused oil
2 brown onions, finely diced
  or grated
500g (1lb 2oz) beef mince
  (5% fat)
2 garlic cloves, minced
2 tsp dried mixed herbs
1 tbsp Worcestershire sauce*

2 low-salt beef stock cubes*
1 tbsp cornflour (cornstarch)

For the topping
1 large leek, sliced (about
  200g/7oz prepared weight)
280g (10oz) self-raising flour*,
  plus extra if needed
140g (5oz) shredded suet*

70g (2½oz) Cheddar cheese*,
  grated
1 tsp mustard* or ½ tsp
  mustard powder
freshly ground black pepper
(*See pages 8–9)

Preheat the oven to 180°C fan (200°C/400°F/Gas 6) and find a large ceramic oven dish, about 1.8 litre (60fl oz) in volume.

Put a large saucepan over a medium–high heat and add the oil and onions. Cook for 3 minutes before adding the mince. Break up the meat with a wooden spoon and cook together with the onions, stirring often, until you see no red meat left. Add the garlic, mixed herbs and Worcestershire sauce and cook for another minute.

Meanwhile, boil the kettle, measure 800ml (28fl oz) of boiling water into a jug and crumble in the stock cubes. Add this to the mince and onions and stir, allowing it to come up to a boil. Put the cornflour in a small cup and stir in a little dash of cold water from the tap to turn it into a paste. Once the mince is bubbling, stir in the cornflour slurry – it should thicken slightly. Now turn the heat down to medium–low and allow the mince to simmer away while you make the topping.

Slice the leek down the centre, keeping the root still attached. Wash it well under cold running water, with the open side down so any dirty water runs away. Shake briefly to remove excess water, then slice the leaves as thinly as you can using a large sharp knife.

Add the sliced leeks to a mixing bowl, along with the rest of the topping ingredients. Give it a really good mix to coat the leeks in the flour mixture. Pour in about 200ml (7fl oz) of cold water, or enough to bind the dough, stirring with a wooden spoon until the mixture starts to clump together. If it feels too sticky, add a touch more flour.

Tip the dough out onto a clean work surface and bring it together, patting it down to a large flat sheet of dough (any shape is fine), about 2cm (¾in) thick. Using a large knife, cut the dough into 12 pieces.

Continued on page 134

Continued from page 132

Now to assemble: pour the mince and gravy into your baking dish, then top with the pieces of leek dough, piecing them together like a puzzle. The finished pie will look like it's got a cobbled top. Don't worry if there are some gaps, as gravy will bubble up between them making lots of yummy textures.

Bake the pie in your preheated oven for 40–45 minutes until the top is crispy and the dough is light and fluffy inside. The gravy should have really thickened now too.

Serve in bowls with extra steamed veg, if you wish. Cut the topping into finger strips for little ones to feed themselves, and help them with spooning the mince and gravy.

Love your leftovers Leftovers will keep for 2 days in the fridge. Reheat in the oven until piping hot throughout – you may need to give it an extra splash of water if a lot of the gravy has soaked up into the topping.

You can also freeze this dish before or after baking. If frozen before baking, place in the oven at 180°C fan (200°C/400°F/Gas 6) from frozen and cook for around an hour, or until piping hot and bubbling throughout. If frozen already baked, place in the oven from frozen and bake for around 20–30 minutes or until piping hot throughout.

Veggie swap You can make this dish vegetarian by swapping the mince for veg like butternut squash or plant-based mince and using vegetable stock cubes and a vegetarian suet.

Showstopper mac and cheese

Hidden veg, gloriously savoury and flavourful cheese sauce, soft pasta and a textured topping – a real family crowd pleaser.

GF*

EF

V*

Vg*

DF*

🍴 Serves 2 adults and 3 littles ⏱ **Prep 30 minutes, Bake 20 minutes** ❄ **Freezable**

30g (1oz) unsalted butter*, cubed, plus extra for greasing
400g (14oz) dried macaroni pasta*
100g (3½oz) cured chorizo* (about half a ring) (optional)
150g (5½oz) white button mushrooms

1 large courgette (zucchini)
800ml (28fl oz) milk*
1 low-salt chicken stock cube*
2 large garlic cloves
2 heaped tbsp cornflour (cornstarch)
100g (3½oz) smoked Cheddar cheese*
150g (5½oz) Cheddar cheese*

4 tbsp panko breadcrumbs*
garlic-infused oil spray
freshly ground black pepper
(*See pages 8–9)

Preheat the oven to 200°C fan (220°C/425°F/Gas 7) and grease a roughly 20 x 30cm (8 x 12in) ovenproof dish with butter.

Set a large pan of boiling water over a high heat and cook the macaroni for around 8 minutes, or until tender. Once done, drain, return the pasta to the saucepan and set aside, reserving a mugful of the cooking water.

Meanwhile, get on with the veg-packed sauce. Set a large heavy-based, non-stick frying pan over a medium–high heat. Peel the chorizo and cut in half lengthways. Cut each half into two lengthways, then slice into 1cm (½in) cubes. Add to the dry frying pan and sauté for 2–3 minutes to release the flavourful oils in the chorizo – keep stirring to avoid the chorizo becoming crispy. Remove the chorizo with a slotted spoon to keep the paprika-spiced oil in the pan, transfer to a small bowl and set aside.

While the chorizo cooks, coarsely grate the mushrooms by cupping each mushroom in your fingers, placing the wide fleshy part on the grater and allowing the mushroom to break down. Don't worry if there are some larger bits that have crumbled away – a few large lumps is okay. Discard the stalks. Now grate the courgette, discarding the woody stem at the top.

Add the grated veg to the chorizo oil in the frying pan, along with a really good grinding of black pepper. Stir, then flatten the mixture with a spatula. Cook the veg for 5–10 minutes, stirring often but always pushing the veg into a flat, even layer so that it cooks as quickly as possible.

While the veg cooks, measure the milk into a jug and microwave for 2½ minutes. Once warmed through, crumble in the stock cube and set aside.

Finely mince or grate the garlic cloves and add to the veg pan. Once the garlic has been in the pan for a few minutes, and the veg is super soft with just a little moisture left, add the butter and the cornflour. Stir really well and cook for a further 3 minutes,

Turn over to continue the recipe and see how it looks

Continued from page 135

moving continuously until the mixture becomes very sticky and is starting to form a crust at the base of the pan. Use a rubber spatula to stir it all and ensure it doesn't burn.

Now, add a quarter of the heated milk and quickly stir very well to incorporate any large lumps into the liquid. Use your rubber spatula to help lift the caramelised veg from the base of the pan – this is where all the flavour is. This mixture should thicken very quickly, so before it becomes a gloopy mess, add another quarter of the milk and stir again. Once you have a loose sauce, add the remaining milk. Using small gentle circular motions, stir the thick floury veg into the runny milk, then let it simmer for around 5 minutes until thickened well enough to coat the back of a spoon. Stir often to ensure the sauce doesn't stick to the base of the pan.

This is when you can grate your cheeses quickly and mix them together. Once the sauce has thickened, remove from the heat and add most of the cheese, reserving a handful (about 50g/1¾oz) for the top, and stir until melted. Add the sauce to the large pasta pan and stir it into the macaroni. Add a little splash of the pasta cooking water if the sauce feels too thick, but be careful not to add too much – nobody wants a watery mac and cheese. Transfer the saucy pasta to your prepared oven dish.

Quickly whip up a topping by adding the panko breadcrumbs to the chorizo, along with the reserved cheese. Stir together, then sprinkle the chorizo crumbs over the pasta in the dish. Spray the topping with a little garlic oil to help it crisp up and avoid burning. Transfer the dish to the preheated oven and bake for 20 minutes, or until golden brown on top.

Allow the mac and cheese to stand for 5 minutes before serving with a little salad or steamed veg.

If serving to little ones, remove the crispy chorizo from their portion and spread the pasta over a cold plate to cool quickly. Macaroni-shaped pasta is fine for all ages, but children under 1 may find it easier to eat pasta spirals or rigatoni, so they can hold the shape easier.

Love your leftovers The mac and cheese keeps well in the fridge for up to 2 days – reheat in the oven or microwave. The sauce keeps very well in the freezer for up to 3 months; freeze in portions and defrost in a hot oven or microwave with an extra splash of milk until piping hot throughout.

Easy white chicken lasagne

A comforting family classic given a new twist.

GF*

EF*

DF*

🍴 2 adults and 2 littles, plus leftovers ⏱ Prep 20 minutes, Bake 30 minutes ❄ Freezable

1 tbsp garlic-infused oil, plus extra for the dish
400–500g (14oz–1lb 2oz) skinless, boneless chicken thighs, cut into thin strips
800ml (28fl oz) milk*
2 low-salt chicken stock cubes*

50g (1¾oz) unsalted butter*
2 heaped tbsp cornflour (cornstarch)
2 large garlic cloves, minced
80g (2¾oz) Cheddar cheese*, grated (optional)
300g (10½oz) frozen peas

1 tsp Dijon mustard* (optional)
150–200g fresh lasagne sheets* (or dried sheets, cooked)
50g (1¾oz) smoked Cheddar cheese*
freshly ground black pepper
(*See pages 8–9)

Preheat the oven to 200°C fan (220°C/425°F/Gas 7).

Heat the garlic oil in a large non-stick frying pan over a medium–high heat. Add the chicken strips and sprinkle over some black pepper. Cook the chicken, turning regularly, until browned all over and almost fully cooked through, about 7–10 minutes.

Measure the milk into a large glass jug, crumble in the stock cubes and microwave for 2½ minutes on high to take the cold edge off. Set aside until needed.

Once the chicken is done, turn the heat down to low, spoon the chicken into a separate bowl and set aside. Add the butter to the now empty frying pan and allow it to melt and brown for a moment to bring out the nutty flavour. Add the cornflour and garlic and whisk in, cooking for a minute. Remove the pan from the heat and add a splash of the warm milk, quickly whisking until the milk is incorporated. Quickly add a little more milk and keep whisking, until you have a thick, smooth paste. Now, you can add a good slosh more of the milk, whisking the thick paste into the liquid. Once you see no lumps, add the remaining milk. Place the pan back on the heat and cook for around 5 minutes, whisking often, until the sauce has thickened and coats the back of a spoon.

Take the sauce off the heat. Add the chicken, Cheddar cheese, if using, frozen peas and Dijon mustard and give it all a good stir.

Grease the base of a 2–3 litre (70–105fl oz) ovenproof dish and add a quarter of the chicken sauce mixture. Cover with a few sheets of lasagne ensuring all the chicken sauce is covered. Add another quarter of the sauce and layer with more pasta, then repeat again and finish with the final quarter of the sauce as the top layer. Sprinkle over the smoked Cheddar and a little extra black pepper. Bake in the preheated oven for 25–30 minutes until bubbling and the cheese on top has turned dark brown and crispy. Allow to stand for 5 minutes before serving.

For little taste testers, serve the lasagne cut into small pieces to offer on a spoon, blend it for early taste testers, or serve in finger-sized chunks to allow little ones to get stuck in with their hands. Adults, feel free to season your plate with a little extra salt.

Love your leftovers Leftovers will keep for 2 days in the fridge, or freeze for up to 3 months. Defrost thoroughly, add a splash of milk down the edges and bake for 20 minutes at 200°C fan (220°C/425°F/Gas 7) or until piping hot throughout.

Top tip If you have plenty of leftover cooked meat from your Sunday roast, add this to the thickened sauce instead of browning the uncooked meat first.

Ricotta and tuna stuffed giant pasta shells

GF*

EF

DF*

Soft and creamy tuna filling, stuffed into comically giant pasta shells, on a bed of rich tomato and pea sauce. The shells are perfectly shaped for little fingers to handle.

🍴 **3 adults and 3 littles**   ⏱ **Prep 20 minutes, Bake 25 minutes**

200g (7oz) dried conchiglioni*
  (giant pasta shells – can
  substitute cannelloni tubes)
250g (9oz) frozen peas
1 tbsp cornflour (cornstarch)
500g (1lb 2oz) passata
  (strained tomatoes)
1 tsp dried mixed herbs

1 tbsp Worcestershire sauce*
  (optional)
2 headed tsp smoked paprika
1 tsp sugar (optional)
2 tsp garlic granules
1 low-salt chicken or vegetable
  stock cube*
2 x 110g (3¾oz) cans tuna in

spring water, drained
250g (9oz) ricotta cheese*
  (or thick dairy-free cream
  cheese)
70g (2½oz) Cheddar cheese*,
  grated
freshly ground black pepper
(*See pages 8–9)

Preheat the oven to 200°C fan (220°C/425°F/Gas 7).

Set a large pan of boiling water from the kettle over a high heat and cook the pasta shells according to the packet instructions.

Meanwhile, put the frozen peas and cornflour in a large baking dish and stir so that every pea is coated and the cornflour starts to dissolve. Add the tomato passata, herbs, Worcestershire sauce, if using, smoked paprika, sugar, if using, and 1 teaspoon of the garlic granules. Crumble the stock cube into the passata packaging and fill with hot water to a third of the way up. Stir well to help the stock cube dissolve and then pour into the oven dish. Give the sauce a really good stir and set aside.

In a small bowl, mix together the tuna, ricotta, 30g (1oz) of the Cheddar, a little black pepper and the remaining 1 teaspoon of garlic granules.

Now, drain the pasta into a colander and hold it under the cold running tap to cool the pasta enough to handle. Now you're ready to assemble.

Hold a pasta shell in the cup of your hand, holding it open slightly. Take a tablespoon of the tuna mixture, point the spoon inside the pasta shell and use your thumb to scrape the filling inside the pasta. Place the shell in the pasta sauce, open-side up, and repeat until you have used up all of the filling. Once the shells are arranged neatly and snuggly in the dish, top with lots of grated cheese and a little black pepper. Place the tray in the preheated oven for 20–25 minutes to melt the cheese and crisp up the topping.

Serve in bowls with extra boiled veg, if you like. You can serve the stuffed shells whole to little ones, or slice in half lengthways.

Love your leftovers Leftovers will keep for 2 days in the fridge. Reheat in the oven for around 15 minutes until piping hot.

Top tip If your kiddos prefer their veg mixed in with their meal, rather than on the side, add a small grated and squeezed courgette (zucchini) to the tuna mixture. Alternatively, wilt some spinach and squeeze out the excess moisture, then chop and add that to the tuna mixture.

Bolognese polenta bake

GF*

EF

DF*

A cosy warming dish to huddle around on a cold autumnal day. Rich Bolognese ragu is topped with a firm, cheesy polenta topping.

⫴ 2 adults and 3 littles   ⏱ Prep 25 minutes, Bake 25 minutes   ❄ Freezable

1 tsp garlic-infused oil

500g (1lb 2oz) lean beef or lamb mince

1 brown onion, grated or finely diced

2 large garlic cloves, finely grated

500g (1lb 2oz) tomato passata (strained tomatoes)

1 low-salt beef stock cube*

2 tsp dried mixed herbs

2 tbsp Worcestershire sauce* (optional)

2 tsp smoked paprika

1 tsp sugar (optional)

freshly ground black pepper

For the polenta topping

1 low-salt chicken stock cube*

1 litre (35fl oz) milk*

180g (6¼oz) fine polenta (cornmeal)

30g (1oz) unsalted butter*

100g (3½oz) smoked Cheddar cheese*, grated

2 tbsp breadcrumbs*

(*See pages 8–9)

Preheat the oven to 200°C fan (220°C/425°F/Gas 7).

Heat the oil in a large frying pan, add the mince and fry for 3 minutes, breaking it into small pieces with a spatula as you go. Add the onion and continue to cook for another 3 minutes. Once the meat has browned all over, add the garlic and tomato passata. Fill the empty passata tin or carton a quarter full and swill the water around to catch as much tomato as you can, then add that to the pan too. Crumble in the beef stock cube and add the mixed herbs, Worcestershire sauce, if using, smoked paprika, sugar, if using, and a little black pepper. Stir and allow the sauce to bubble away while you make the polenta.

Crumble the chicken stock cube into a large saucepan, add the milk and allow it to come up to a simmer. Meanwhile, measure the polenta into a mug. Once the milk is just starting to show little bubbles, with a whisk in one hand and the polenta in another, sprinkle in the polenta while whisking continuously to avoid lumps forming. Allow it to cook for around 5 minutes, stirring often, until it thickens to a very thick creamy porridge.

Remove the polenta from the heat, add the butter and two thirds of the cheese and stir to melt them into the polenta. You can now serve this alongside your mince Bolognese, but it's even tastier if you combine the two and bake it in the oven.

Pour the Bolognese into a large baking dish large enough to fit it all in with a little space left above for the polenta. Dollop spoonfuls of the polenta on top, leaving some little gaps between each spoonful to let the sauce come up and bubble around it.

Place the dish on a large baking tray to catch any tomato splatters, sprinkle over the remaining cheese and the breadcrumbs, and finish with another good grinding of black pepper. Bake in the oven for 20–25 minutes until the polenta has set and there is a delicious golden crust.

Serve with steamed or boiled green veg.

Love your leftovers Leftovers will keep for 2 days in the fridge, or 3 months in the freezer. Reheat in the oven until piping hot.

Hidden cheesy veg-stuffed pizza

Packing veggies and cheese into the pizza base is an utter game changer. They add a delicious softness, which makes this pizza super moreish and comforting. Don't be alarmed by yeasted dough – it really does just take 5 minutes prep at a time when you have a breather in the morning. Or even make it the night before, then time just does its thing.

EF

V*

Vg*

DF*

🍴 **Makes 3 pizzas** ⏱ **Prep 15 minutes, plus proving, Bake 15 minutes** ❄ **Freezable**

Dough
500g (1lb 2oz) white bread flour
7g (¼oz) fast action dried yeast (or 2 tsp)
1 tbsp garlic-infused olive oil, plus extra for the bowl
1 tsp caster sugar
1 small courgette (zucchini)
a big handful (approx 60g/2oz) of grated Cheddar cheese*
semolina or flour, for dusting

Sauce Option 1 – extra veg
1 small courgette (zucchini), grated
200g (7oz) passata (strained tomatoes)
2 garlic cloves, crushed
1 tsp dried mixed herbs
1 tsp smoked paprika
freshly ground black pepper

Sauce Option 2 – super speedy
2 heaped tbsp tomato purée (paste)
1 tsp smoked paprika
1 tsp dried mixed herbs

Toppings
your favourite pizza toppings such as: thinly sliced ham*, thinly sliced mushrooms, sweetcorn, pineapple chunks, chopped peppers
1 mozzarella ball*, thinly sliced, or a large handful of grated Cheddar cheese*
(*See page 8)

First, start to make your pizza dough. To a jug, add 330ml (11¼fl oz) of lukewarm water from the tap – ensure it isn't too hot, as this will kill the yeast, but a little warmth helps activate it.

Measure the bread flour into a large bowl, add the yeast, oil and sugar and stir well. Make a well in the centre and pour in the warm water. Using a wooden spoon, mix until the dough starts to clump together, then tip it out onto a clean work surface and knead the dough by moving it around continuously for around 3–4 minutes. Play a nice song and by the time it's up, the dough should have come together into a ball, be smooth to the touch and spring back when you press your finger gently into the side. Try to avoid adding too much flour; if it feels sticky to begin with, just keep working it and it will come together. Or if you really need to, add a tiny amount of flour to help it along. Sometimes stopping, scraping your hands down and washing them will help. Cover your hands in flour before you begin kneading again. Alternatively, you can do this in a stand mixer with a dough hook, kneading for around 2 minutes until smooth.

Place the dough ball back into the mixing bowl, add a touch more oil and roll the dough in it to stop it sticking to the bowl. Cover the bowl tightly with the back of a plate, then a tea towel to keep it warm. Place the bowl in a warm location for a minimum of 1½ hours until risen and doubled in size. If you wish to prove the dough for longer, place the bowl in a cooler spot, or even in the fridge if you wish to leave it overnight, and let it come to room temperature before baking.

Preheat the oven to 220°C fan (240°C/475°F/Gas 8) and dust a large baking tray with flour or semolina.

Now, prepare the sauce. For option one, add all the ingredients to a saucepan and allow to simmer for 15 minutes. For option 2, simply put everything together in a bowl with 2 tablespoons water and stir together. Set aside until needed.

To finish the dough, grate the courgette and squeeze out some of the moisture, then add it to the dough along with the grated cheese. Get your hand into the bowl and start to work the veg and cheese into the dough. If it becomes a little tricky in the bowl, tip out onto a work surface and knead together so all of the courgette and cheese is incorporated. This won't take long, and try to avoid kneading the dough too much at this stage.

Cut the dough into 3 equal portions. On a flour or semolina-dusted surface, roll out a dough portion to a circle or rectangular shape, around 2mm (1/16in) thick. Transfer to the prepared baking tray and top with a few spoonfuls of the sauce, spreading it out almost to the edge. Scatter over your favourite toppings (not too much or the pizza will become soggy), then finish with either mozzarella slices or grated Cheddar, or both! Either roll out another, or just get this pizza baking while you roll and top the other pizzas. Bake in the preheated oven for 12–15 minutes until the base is crisp and the cheese is golden and bubbling.

Love your leftovers If you have some pizza left over, this will keep in the fridge for 2 days; bake in a hot oven for 5–10 minutes until crispy again. Or freeze raw or cooked, adding an extra 5–10 minutes onto the baking time until crispy and piping hot.

Turn over to see how it looks

Cheat's buttermilk 'fried' chicken burgers

GF*

EF*

DF*

A healthier take on this proper comfort food classic – but I promise you, you won't miss out! Cutting the chicken into smaller pieces means it crisps up better in the oven, so you get lots of crunchy bits in your burger. It also slices well, so those with little fingers can enjoy their chicken too!

🍴 Makes 6 burgers   ⏱ Prep 15 minutes, plus marinating, Bake 25 minutes   ❄ Freezable

300ml (10½fl oz) milk*
    (see note below)
juice of 1 small lemon
500g (1lb 2oz) skinless,
    boneless chicken thighs
1 tsp dried mixed herbs
1 tsp garlic granules
1 heaped tsp smoked paprika

For the coating
2 tbsp sunflower oil
160g (5¾oz) self-raising flour*
3 tbsp panko breadcrumbs*

1 tsp onion powder
1 heaped tsp garlic powder
2 tsp smoked paprika
1 egg*, whisked (skip if egg
    free)
20g (¾oz) unsalted butter*
freshly ground black pepper

For the lemon sauce
mayonnaise* (or yogurt* for
    little ones)
1 tbsp lemon juice
hot sauce (optional)

To serve (optional)
6 brioche buns, sliced open
Your chosen burger fillings,
    such as: gherkins, pickled
    red cabbage, shredded
    lettuce, tomato slices, etc
(*See pages 8–9)

Put the milk and lemon juice in a large bowl. Allow it to sit for 5 minutes – this will soon start to slightly curdle and turn into buttermilk. (Alternatively, you can use 300ml (10½fl oz) of buttermilk if you can find it, and skip the lemon.)

Open out each chicken thigh and cut in half widthways. Add the chicken to the buttermilk along with the herbs, garlic granules and paprika. Stir, then cover and place in the fridge for a minimum of 2 hours, or preferably overnight. The acid in the buttermilk will work its magic on the chicken to tenderise the meat, resulting in super moist and juicy chicken.

When you're ready to cook, preheat the oven to 200°C (220°C/425°F/Gas 7) and cover a large baking tray with 1 tablespoon of the oil.

In a large flat-bottomed bowl, combine the flour, breadcrumbs, onion and garlic powders, paprika and a generous grinding of black pepper, stirring well. Add the whisked egg to the marinated chicken and stir well to incorporate the egg into the buttermilk.

Continued on page 150

Continued on page 150

| **Note** If you are using a dairy-free milk with lemon juice to make the buttermilk substitute, opt for soy milk, which thickens better than other plant-based milks.

WEEKEND WINNERS

Continued from page 148

One at a time, dip the pieces of chicken into the flour mixture to evenly coat and place on a clean plate. Once all of the chicken has been coated, dip each piece of chicken back into the buttermilk mixture and then into the spiced flour again, patting down well to ensure it is coated on all sides. Place the coated chicken on the oiled baking tray, ensuring the pieces are sitting at least 2.5cm (1in) apart from each other. Drizzle the top of each piece with a little of the remaining oil; you may find it easier to distribute it evenly by using a spray bottle of oil. Place a tiny knob of butter on the top of each piece of chicken. Bake in the preheated oven for 20–25 minutes, flipping each piece of chicken after 13 minutes, until crisp and golden.

While the chicken is cooking, make a quick sauce by adding the mayo or yogurt to a bowl, with a little squeeze of lemon juice plus some black pepper. Adults, feel free to add a dash of hot sauce to your sauce, too.

Now to assemble your burgers. Place two pieces of chicken on the bottom half of the brioche bun, top with your chosen toppings, add the sauce to the other half of the bun and sandwich it all together. Serve with oven chips from page 164 and/or a side salad.

If serving to little ones who haven't quite mastered the art of eating a burger (their time will come!), cut each chicken piece in half lengthways to form two finger strips and serve with brioche bread fingers and the fillings separately on the side.

Love your leftovers Leftovers are delicious cold in a sandwich. Keep in the fridge for 2 days, or freeze for 3 months. Unbaked nuggets can also be frozen, then cooked from frozen for approximately 25 minutes, or until the inside is piping hot.

Curried spatchcock chicken

Spatchcocking essentially means to flatten the chicken. This helps to cut the roasting time, making it a perfect family meal to whip up when you don't quite have enough time to roast a whole chicken in the traditional way. This version, coats the chicken in warming flavoursome spices, giving you the most wonderful crispy skin and tasty cooking juices to coat those potatoes. Turn over to see how it looks.

GF

EF

DF

⚙ 2 adults and 2 littles   ⏱ Prep 10 minutes, Roast 1 hour   ❄ Freezable

1 whole small–medium
   chicken (preferably
   free-range)
1 tsp ground turmeric
1 tsp smoked paprika
1 tsp mild curry powder

1 tsp garam masala
1 tsp dried mixed herbs
2 tbsp garlic-infused olive oil
finely grated zest and juice of
   1 lemon
2 large garlic cloves

a thumb-sized piece of ginger
12–16 medium–large new
   potatoes, unpeeled and
   halved lengthways
freshly ground black pepper
salt (optional)

Preheat the oven to 170°C fan (190°C/375°F/Gas 5).

Spatchcock the chicken as shown overleaf.

Put the chicken in a large bowl, along with the turmeric, paprika, curry powder, garam masala, herbs, 1 tablespoon of the garlic oil, the zest and juice of the lemon and a good grinding of black pepper. Peel the garlic and finely grate the flesh into the chicken bowl. Then remove the skin from the ginger and finely grate this in too.

Now, get your hands stuck in and give it a really good mix. If you wish, you can also do this in a large sealable plastic bag, which will save you staining your fingers yellow.

Put the chicken in the centre of a large baking tray, skin-side up, with the legs pointing outwards. Tip the new potatoes into the empty bowl or bag and give it a good mix so the potatoes are coated in the remaining marinade. Arrange some of the potatoes around the chicken and, if needed, add the rest to a second baking tray. Try not to bunch the potatoes up too closely or they won't crisp up and cook evenly.

Drizzle the chicken and potatoes with the remaining oil and, if you're cooking for over 3s, sprinkle the chicken skin with a little salt. Salty chicken skin is one of the best things in life in my opinion, so if you adults really don't want to miss out, just ensure that baby's chicken portion doesn't include any skin.

Roast for 50–60 minutes until the chicken has browned and cooked through fully. To check this, make a small cut into the deepest part of the breast – if the meat is stringy and white thrroughout, it is done. Allow to rest for 5 minutes, then toss the potatoes in the resting juices before serving.

Love your leftovers Leftovers will keep for 3 days covered in the fridge, or freeze for 3 months. Defrost fully, then reheat in the oven for 10–15 minutes until piping hot throughout. If the chicken hasn't previously been frozen, you can also freeze the chicken raw, already marinated, then defrost fully in the fridge and roast as above – the flavour will be even more delicious this way.

1 Place the chicken on a board and cut away any strings.

2 Untuck the legs, if necessary.

3 Stand your bird up and cut down one side of the backbone.

4 Now cut down the other side of the backbone and remove it.

5 Turn the bird over, so it is breast-side up, and press down to flatten out the bird.

6 There you have it - easy spatchcocked chicken!

Classic roast chicken and gravy

GF*

EF

DF

Roast chicken has always been my favourite roast; it makes the best gravy and everyone always fights over that crispy skin!

🍴 **Serves 4–8** ⏱ **Prep 30 minutes, Roast 1½–2 hours**

2–3 large carrots
1 yellow onion
1 bulb of garlic
1 small lemon
1.2–2kg whole chicken
(preferably free-range)
1 tbsp garlic-infused oil

1 tsp dried mixed herbs
1 tsp salt (optional)
1 low-salt chicken stock cube
freshly ground black pepper

For the gravy
250–300ml (9–10½fl oz)

low-salt chicken stock*
1 tbsp Worcestershire sauce*
(optional)
1 tbsp low-salt soy sauce*
1 heaped tbsp cornflour
(cornstarch)
(*See page 9)

Preheat the oven to 180°C fan (200°C/400°F/Gas 6) and find a roasting tin big enough to fit your chicken with lots of wiggle room, and with sides at least 5cm (2in) deep.

Wash the carrots and place them in the roasting tin. Halve the onion (no need to peel) and nestle it between the carrots. Halve the garlic through it's equator, slicing through all of the cloves, and squeeze one half between the veg in the centre of the tray. Do the same with the lemon, placing one half in the centre of the tray too.

Make a note of the weight of your chicken, then remove the strings from the chicken and place the remaining lemon and garlic halves inside its cavity. Place the whole bird on top of all the veg, breast-side up — the veg 'trivet' will help the air circulate, cooking the meat evenly, and will also help make some delicious gravy.

Drizzle the garlic oil over the chicken skin and then sprinkle over the herbs, a little black pepper and the salt, if using. The salt is definitely not needed, but there is nothing better than crispy, salty chicken skin in my book. If you're serving this to little ones, you can remove the skin from their portion before plating up.

Crumble the stock cube into a jug and add 200ml (7fl oz) of boiling water. Stir to dissolve the stock cube, then pour it into the tray, ensuring you don't make the chicken skin wet. Add more boiling water from the kettle until liquid covers all of the veg.

Place the tray in the centre of the preheated oven. Make sure nothing is cooking on the shelf above the chicken, although having items cooking underneath is okay. Calculate the cooking time, allowing 40 minutes per kg, plus another 20 minutes. Use a large spoon to baste the chicken once or twice while cooking, and if all the juices dry up, add more hot water from the kettle down the side of the tin. Once cooked, the skin should be very golden and crispy. To check it is cooked through, make a small cut into the deepest part of the breast – if the meat is stringy and white thrroughout, it is done. Remove the tin from the oven and carefully transfer the chicken to a warm dish to rest for 20–30 minutes. If you're worried it will get cold, you can cover the dish with foil and then a tea towel too, however, do note the skin won't be as crispy if you do this.

Now you can make the gravy. Set a large sieve over a medium-sized saucepan and pour the entire contents of the roasting tin into the pan, allowing the sieve to catch all of the veg.

If the pan has lots of crispy bits stuck to the base, this is all flavour and we don't want to get rid of it. Pour the chicken stock into the roasting tin and place it on the hob over a medium heat. Use a wooden spoon to scrape the crispy bits from the tin into the stock, then pass the stock through the sieve into the gravy saucepan. Alternatively, add the stock directly to the cooking juices in the saucepan. Finally, add the Worcestershire sauce, if using, and soy sauce.

Set the pan over a medium heat and allow it to come up to a boil. Meanwhile, put the cornflour and 2 tablespoons of cold water into a small bowl and stir until the flour has dissolved. Once the gravy is boiling, with a spoon in one hand stirring well, quickly pour the cornflour paste into the centre of the pan and keep stirring for a minute. It should start to thicken instantly. Turn the heat down and allow the gravy to simmer away for 10 minutes to reduce a little and let the flavour intensify. If you're serving to older children and adults, add a pinch of salt here, too. And if you prefer a very thick gravy, make up a little more cornflour paste and add this to the pan, cooking for a few more minutes to take away the flour taste.

Serve your chicken and gravy with simple boiled potatoes, or go the full hog and serve with all the trimmings from pages 158–61.

Love your leftovers Leftover chicken and gravy will keep for 2 days in the fridge. Reheat the chicken in the oven – with a splash of gravy over the top and covered with foil to stop it drying out – at 180°C fan (200°C/400°F/Gas 6) for 10–15 minutes until piping hot throughout. The gravy can be reheated in a saucepan for 5 minutes until bubbling.

Waste not If you have plenty of leftover roast chicken, head to page 138 to use it up in a delicious chicken lasagne. Or stuff in a quesadilla, use it to top a pizza, or cook into pasta dishes. And adding cold chicken gravy to a leftover-chicken sandwich is cracking!

Rebecca's roasties

Crunchy on the outside, soft on the inside, and arguably the best part of a roast dinner!

♈ 2 adults and 2 littles ⏱ **Prep 20 minutes, Roast 1 hour**

1kg (2lb 4oz) all-rounder potatoes like King Edward, Maris Piper or, my personal favourite, Rooster potatoes

4–5 tablespoons of fat (goose fat*, sunflower oil or olive oil)

6 large garlic cloves (don't use small ones)

Preheat the oven to 190°C fan (210°C/415°F/Gas 6–7).

Put a very large pan of water on the hob to start heating up. This will take a while, so peel and cut the potatoes into large (about 5cm/2in) chunks. Add them to the water to start cooking as the temperature rises. Once boiling, cook the potatoes until they are just cooked and an inserted knife slides in easily – this will take approximately 10–15 minutes. Cooking fully results in extra soft insides to your finished roasties.

While the potatoes are boiling, add your chosen fat to a very large, heavy-based roasting tin, and place in the oven to heat up for at least 10 minutes.

Once the potatoes are cooked, place a large colander in your sink and carefully pour in the potatoes to drain away the water. Allow the potatoes to steam and cool for 5 minutes in the colander – this helps dry the potatoes, resulting in crispier outsides.

Once your oil is hot, very carefully remove the tin from the oven. With oven gloves on, pick up the potato-filled colander and give it one or two firm but careful shakes to slightly ruffle up the edges. As the potatoes are fully cooked, you want to try and avoid completely mashing them – the aim is to get lots of small fluffy bits on the outside of each potato.

Very carefully, tip the potatoes out into the hot oil, plus any smaller pieces left at the bottom. Using two wooden spoons, very carefully turn each potato over so that it is covered in oil on all sides. Place the tray back in the oven and bake for 25 minutes. Remove the tray from the oven and turn over each roastie. Nestle in the garlic cloves and place the tray back in the oven to bake for a further 25–35 minutes or until golden and crisp to your liking.

Serve the roasties alongside your roast dinner with lashings of gravy. For little ones, chop them in half or mash with the back of a fork.

Love your leftovers Potatoes will keep for 2–3 days in the fridge, or 3 months in the freezer. Reheat in a hot oven with a little extra drizzle of oil for around 10 minutes from chilled or 15–20 minutes from frozen, or until piping hot throughout.

The perfect Yorkshire puddings

GF*

V

Vg*

DF*

If cooking a delicious Yorkie which is crispy on the outside and soft on the inside is your nemesis, follow my foolproof method to make the perfect accompaniment to your Sunday roast... or any midweek meal in my book!

🍴 **Makes 12** ⏱ **Prep 5 minutes plus resting, Bake 30 minutes** ❄ **Freezable**

4 medium eggs
about 200g (7oz) plain
 (all-purpose) flour*

about 200ml (7fl oz) milk*
sunflower oil, for cooking
(*See pages 8–9)

Place a large jug or bowl with a spout over some weighing scales, setting the weight to zero. Crack the 4 eggs into the jug and check how much they weigh – it should be around 200g (7oz). Now add that same weight in flour, and the same in milk. For example, if the eggs weigh 206g, add 206g of flour and 206ml of milk.

Use a whisk to combine really well until you see hardly any lumps. One or two is okay, these will break up as the batter rests. Once combined, place the batter in the fridge. This relaxes the gluten in the flour after all the vigorous mixing, resulting in crispier Yorkshire puddings. It also lowers the temperature of the batter so that when it hits the hot fat, it will rise quicker and soak up less fat. Allow the batter to rest for at least 20 minutes, but you can do this up to 6 hours in advance.

When you're ready to bake, preheat the oven to 220°C fan (240°C/475°F/Gas 8) – or if you're cooking a roast dinner, once the meat is out of the oven and resting, crank the heat up to make the Yorkshire puddings.

Fill a 12-hole muffin tin with 1 teaspoon of oil in each hole, then place it on the top shelf of the oven. Ensure that this shelf isn't too high, or when the Yorkshires rise they may hit the top of your oven – you may need to move the shelf down one notch. It is also important that there are no other baking trays in the oven above the Yorkshire pudding tray, as this prevents a high rise, but having something on a shelf underneath is completely fine.

Once the tray has been in the oven for around 15 minutes and the oil is piping hot, get the batter out of the fridge and give it one last gentle stir if it looks like it has separated a little. Then very, very carefully remove the tray from the oven, closing the oven door behind you to avoid letting any heat escape. Pour in enough batter to fill each hole three-quarters full, and very quickly get the tray back in the oven and close the door. Allow the yorkies to bake for 20–30 minutes, or until they have turned a deep golden brown colour and are visibly crispy on top. Do not open that door for the first 20 minutes of cooking or they run the risk of sinking.

Serve whole, alongside a roast dinner, with a pool of gravy inside! For little eaters, tear into strips lengthways and soften in gravy if needed.

Love your leftovers You can reheat cold Yorkshire puddings in a hot oven for around 5 minutes until crispy again, or freeze them for up to 3 months. Bake at 220°C fan (240°C/475°F/Gas 8) from frozen for around 10–12 minutes until crispy and piping hot.

Cauli and broccoli cheese

This veg-packed side dish is the perfect accompaniment to your family Sunday roast! Pictured on page 156.

Pictured on page 156.

4 adults and 2 littles   **Prep 20 minutes, Bake 35 minutes**   **Freezable**

GF*
EF
V
Vg*
DF*

50g (1¾oz) butter*
a splash of sunflower or garlic-infused oil
1 large leek
1 low-salt vegetable stock cube *

600ml (21fl oz) milk*
½ large head of cauliflower
1 small head of broccoli
2 tbsp cornflour (cornstarch)
1 tsp Dijon mustard*

150g (5½oz) Cheddar cheese*, grated
2 tbsp breadcrumbs*
freshly ground black pepper
(*See pages 8–9)

Preheat the oven to 190°C fan (210°C/415°F/Gas 6–7).

Set a large frying pan over a medium–high heat. Add 10g (⅓oz) of the butter, plus a splash of sunflower or garlic oil to stop the butter from burning, and allow to melt.

Meanwhile, slice the leek down the centre, keeping the root still attached and wash it well under cold running water. Shake briefly to remove excess water, then slice as thinly as you can using a large sharp knife. Add the chopped leeks to the warmed frying pan and sauté for 5 minutes until soft, then decant into a small bowl and set aside.

While the leeks are cooking, crumble the stock cube into the milk and heat for 2 minutes in the microwave or in a separate saucepan.

Prep the cauliflower and broccoli by cutting them into small florets. Put them in a saucepan and cover the veg with boiling water out of the kettle. Let the water come to the boil again and cook for 1 minute, then turn off the heat and drain. Set aside.

Once the leeks are done, add the remaining butter to the pan, allow it to melt then stir in the cornflour and allow the flour to soak up the butter. Don't worry if it seems a little dry right now. Cook for a couple of minutes to cook out the flour taste, then take the pan off the heat. With your whisk in one hand and the milk jug in another, slowly add half of the milk, a little at a time, whisking continuously to ensure that the mixture doesn't go lumpy. Once you have a very thick but smooth sauce, add the remaining milk, mustard and a little black pepper and stir to incorporate. Allow the sauce to bubble for a few moments until it is thick and smooth. Once thickened, take the pan off the heat and add half of the cheese – it may split if you add the cheese when it's too hot. Stir to melt the cheese and it will suddenly turn super silky. Add the leek, broccoli and cauliflower to the cheese sauce and stir well. Pour into a large ovenproof dish big enough to fit it all in – the larger the dish, the more crispy bits you'll have. Sprinkle over the remaining cheese, the breadcrumbs and an extra little grinding of black pepper.

Bake in the preheated oven for 25–35 minutes until bubbling and the cheese on top has turned deliciously golden. Serve as a main or on the side of your favourite roast.

Love your leftovers This can be kept for 2 days in the fridge. Reheat in the oven for 25–35 minutes until piping hot. You can also freeze the dish (without the cheese sprinkled on top) and cook from frozen. Simply pop in the oven for 35–45 minutes, sprinkling over the cheese halfway through cooking.

Leek and mushroom stuffing balls

I have been making this dish as a side to my roasts all my adult life, perfecting the recipe over time, so I'm really excited to share it with you, pictured on page 157. These delicious veg-packed stuffing balls are the perfect accompaniment to your Sunday lunch. You can also use this mixture to stuff inside a joint of meat for a showstopper meal.

GF*
EF*
V
Vg*
DF*

🍴 **Makes 10 balls** ⏱ **Prep 15 minutes, Bake 25 minutes**

1 large leek (or large brown onion), roughly chopped
250g (9oz) button chestnut mushrooms
25g (1oz) butter*
4–5 thick slices of bread*
1 garlic clove, crushed

1 tsp dried sage
2 eggs*
garlic-infused spray oil
freshly ground black pepper
(*See pages 8–9)

Preheat the oven to 190°C fan (210°C/415°F/Gas 6–7) and set a large frying pan over a medium heat.

Put the leek and mushrooms in a food processor and whizz until they have broken up into small pieces. Tip them into your frying pan with the butter and a little black pepper, and sauté until nearly all of the moisture has cooked out of the veg and you have a thick purée. Keep stirring with a rubber spatula to ensure it cooks evenly and doesn't stick to the bottom of the pan. This will take around 5–7 minutes.

Meanwhile, toast 4 slices of bread and cut into cubes, as small as you can. This stuffing has a slightly chunkier texture, but if you prefer a smoother stuffing, whizz the toast in a food processor to form fine breadcrumbs. Put the bread in a bowl along with the garlic and sage.

Once the mushrooms and onions have softened, add them to the bowl. Give the mixture a stir for a few moments to help cool it slightly, then add the eggs and mix really well. If the mixture feels too wet, toast the final slice of bread, chop and add to the mixture.

Divide the mixture into 10 portions and roll into balls (be careful if it is still hot). Place on a baking tray big enough for the balls to sit without touching each other. Spray each stuffing ball with a few squirts of garlic-infused oil and bake in the preheated oven for 20–25 minutes until golden and crisp on the outside.

Serve with lashings of gravy to soak into the bready texture.

For little ones, cut the balls half so they can enjoy their stuffing as a finger food, or chop finely and stir through their meal.

Love your leftovers The stuffing will keep for 2 days in the fridge, or 3 months in the freezer. You can freeze the balls baked but, for best results, freeze once the stuffing balls have been rolled but not yet baked. Pop them in the oven and cook from frozen as above, adding an extra 5–10 minutes to the cooking time, until piping hot throughout.

Loaded Mexican sweet potatoes

A feast for the eyes but, most importantly, a feast for the belly. Packed full of flavour, and lots and lots of goodness!

GF

EF

V

Vg*

DF*

⏲ 2 adults and 2 littles ⏱ Prep and cook 50 minutes ❄ Freezable

3 large sweet potatoes
1 tsp garlic-infused oil
1 large ripe avocado, peeled, stone removed and roughly diced
juice of 1 lime
2 salad tomatoes, finely diced

1 x 400g (14oz) can of black beans in water, drained
1 x 260g (9¼oz) can of sweetcorn in water, drained
1 small garlic clove, crushed
60g (2oz) smoked Cheddar cheese*

freshly ground black pepper
4 tbsp soured cream* or yogurt* to serve (optional)
a little fresh coriander (cilantro), to serve (optional)
(*See page 8)

Preheat the oven to 170°C fan (190°C/375°F/Gas 5). Wash the sweet potatoes well, then pat dry with a piece of kitchen towel. Prick the potatoes all over with a fork or knife, then place on a lined baking tray. Rub the oil into the skin and cook for 40–45 minutes until an inserted knife slides in easily.

Once the potatoes have been in the oven for 35 minutes, start to prep the toppings. Make the guacamole by adding the avocado to a small bowl, plus the juice of the lime. Mash with the back of a fork, then stir in the diced tomato and a little black pepper.

Take the sweet potatoes out of the oven and put them on a chopping board, then set aside to let them cool for a moment.

Put the black beans in a microwaveable bowl and use the back of a ladle or a potato masher to crush them, popping each bean and mashing a little. Add the sweetcorn, along with the garlic and a grinding of black pepper. Cover the bowl and microwave for 3 minutes. While this heats up, grate the cheese, then add it to the bowl once it's out of the microwave, stirring immediately to help the cheese melt into the beans and corn.

Slice each sweet potato in half lengthways and, using a tablespoon, scoop out the flesh of the potato, keeping a 1cm (½in) border of sweet potato still attached to the skin. You'll be left with 6 sweet potato boats. Place the scooped potato onto a board or into a small bowl and mash with a fork before stirring into the warmed beans and sweetcorn.

To serve, place two halves onto each adult plate, and one half on the kids' plates. Spoon the bean mixture into the centre of the sweet potato, and top with guacamole and a little soured cream and coriander, if you wish.

For little ones under 2, you can serve the sweet potato in finger strips, and the accompanying elements separately on a spoon.

Love your leftovers Everything will keep for 2 days in the fridge, and you can reheat the beans and sweet potato in a microwave until piping hot. Any sweet potatoes which you haven't cut open yet can be wrapped in foil and frozen for up to 12 months. Place in a hot oven from frozen and bake for 20—25 minutes or until piping hot throughout. The bean mixture can be frozen separately for 3 months and, once fully defrosted, reheated in the microwave for 2–3 minutes or until piping hot.

Breaded squash rings and easy oven chips

Crisp on the outside and deliciously soft on the inside – the most delicious way to use up that butternut squash that's been sitting in your kitchen for ages!

GF*

EF*

V

Vg*

DF*

🍴 **2 adults and 2 littles** ⏱ **Prep 10 minutes, Bake 25 minutes** ❄ **Freezable**

1 medium butternut squash (or the equivalent in fresh pumpkin)
about 50g (1¾oz) plain (all-purpose) flour*
2 medium eggs*, beaten (or 100ml/3½fl oz milk*)
1 tsp smoked paprika

about 90g (3¼oz) panko breadcrumbs*
garlic-infused oil spray

For the chips
500–600g all-rounder potatoes, such as Maris Piper

1 tbsp sunflower oil

For the lemon dip
3 tbsp Greek yogurt*
juice of ½ lemon
1 garlic clove, crushed
freshly ground black pepper
(*See pages 8–9)

Preheat the oven to 180°C fan (200°C/400°F/Gas 6) and line large baking tray with non-stick foil or paper.

Peel and slice your potatoes into chunky chips. Either add to a large bowl with a touch of water at the bottom and cook in the microwave on high, or place in a saucepan of boiling water, and cook for 3 minutes for both methods.

Meanwhile, peel the squash using a knife or veg peeler, then cut widthways into 1cm (½in) thick discs. Where there is seedy pulp inside, run your knife around the inside to remove the seeds, being careful not to cut into the flesh. If using pumpkin, cut the veg into finger strips.

Drain the potatoes and place on a baking tray large enough for the chips to sit in an even layer. Set aside while you finish the squash.

Set up a dredging station with three wide flat-bottomed bowls. Put the flour in one, the beaten eggs in another, and finally combine the smoked paprika and the breadcrumbs in the last bowl. Dip a piece of squash firstly into the flour, dusting off the excess. Then place in the beaten egg and use a fork to help turn it over to coat both sides – if you can see dry flour, the breadcrumbs won't stick. Finally lift place the piece of squash into the breadcrumbs, coating all over and pressing it down gently to ensure the crumbs are stuck well. I like to keep one hand dry to handle ingredients like the flour and breadcrumbs, and the other hand for when handling the veg when wet, that way you don't become a big sticky mess. Pop the coated squash onto your baking tray and repeat with the rest.

Give each piece of breaded squash a squirt of oil and drizzle a little sunflower oil over the potatoes and bake for 20–25 minutes, flipping both the squash and chips halfway through.

While the veg bakes, make the dip by stirring all the ingredients together.

Serve the squash rings whole or cut in half, with the chips and a little yogurt for dipping.

Love your leftovers Leftovers will keep in the fridge for 3 days, or freeze for 3 months. To reheat, bake in the oven until piping hot throughout – approximately 10 minutes from fresh or 20–25 minutes from frozen.

Turkish lamb and spinach scrolls

GF*

EF

DF*

This is my take on a soft, spiced, stuffed flatbread without the fuss. Serve as an indulgent weekend lunch on its own or as part of a picky tea.

🍴 Makes 12   ⏱ Prep 20 minutes, Bake 12 minutes   ❄ Freezable

1 red onion, grated

2 tsp garlic-infused oil

400g (14oz) lamb mince

3 cubes of frozen chopped spinach

1 tbsp smoked paprika

1 garlic clove, grated

2 tsp dried mixed herbs

2 tsp ground cumin

1 low-salt chicken stock cube*

250g (oz) self-raising flour*, plus extra for dusting

1 tsp baking powder*

125g (4½oz) Greek yogurt*

a splash of milk*, if needed

50g (1¾oz) Cheddar cheese*, grated

freshly ground black pepper

For the cucumber dip

½ large cucumber

5 heaped tbsp Greek yogurt*

1 small garlic clove, crushed

(*See pages 8–9)

Preheat the oven to 220°C fan (240°C/475°F/Gas 8).

Put the onion and 1 teaspoon of the garlic oil in large frying pan and sauté for around 3 minutes until soft. Add the mince and cook for a further 3 minutes until starting to brown. Add the spinach, paprika, garlic, 1 teaspoon of the herbs, the cumin and a touch of freshly ground black pepper, and crumble in the stock cube. Mix the spices into the meat and let the mince brown further. Stir often and use a wooden spoon to break up the spinach as it starts to defrost. Cook until any excess liquid has evaporated and the spinach has defrosted, then remove the pan from the heat and set aside.

Add the flour, baking powder, yogurt, and the remaining 1 teaspoon of herbs and 1 teaspoon of garlic oil to a mixing bowl. Stir to combine, adding a few splashes of milk until the dough just starts to come together. Tip it out onto a clean work surface and briefly knead to form a ball. Dust the surface and the top of the dough with flour, then using a rolling pin, roll the dough out to a rough rectangle, just under 1cm (½in) thick.

Gently but evenly, scatter the spiced lamb over the dough, taking it right up to the edges, then sprinkle over the cheese. From a short end, roll the dough up to form a long sausage. Cut into 12 discs and place them on a non-stick baking tray on their side, with the spiral side up. Arranging them fairly close together will give a softer result, or if you prefer a crispy edge, ensure the scrolls are well separated.

Bake in the preheated oven for 10–12 minutes until the dough has puffed up and is golden and the scrolls are springy when gently squeezed.

While they bake, make the sauce. Coarsely grate the cucumber and, in batches, squeeze out most of the liquid over the sink using your hands or a clean tea towel. A lot of liquid will come out. Add the cucumber pulp to a small bowl along with the yogurt, garlic and a little black pepper. Stir and serve alongside the scrolls.

Love your leftovers Leftovers will keep for 3 days in the fridge, or freeze for 3 months. Defrost before reheating. To reheat, splash the tops with a touch of water and place in the oven until piping hot throughout.

Fishball ramen

Enjoy a big bowl of warming broth, delicately flavoured with Asian aromatics. Filled with noodles, peas and delicious balls of prawns and fish, it's a great finger food for little ones.

GF*
EF*
DF

🍴 2 adults and 2 littles, plus leftovers   ⏱ Prep and cook 30 minutes

For the broth
200g (7oz) noodles* (the type is up to you)
10g (1/3oz) dried mushrooms
a thumb-sized piece of ginger, roughly chopped
3 garlic cloves, halved
1 large spring onion (scallion), roughly chopped
1 low-salt chicken stock cube*
1 low-salt vegetable stock cube*
1 tsp sesame oil (optional)

1½ tbsp low-salt soy sauce*
100g (3½oz) sugar snap peas or mangetout (snow peas)

For the fishballs
150–200g (5½–7oz) prawns (shrimp)
400g (14oz) skinless, boneless firm white fish, such as cod or haddock, cut into chunks
1 small garlic clove, sliced
½ tsp finely grated fresh ginger

1 spring onion (scallion), chopped
1 tsp cornflour (cornstarch)
2 tsp garlic-infused oil

To serve (optional)
4 hard-boiled eggs* (optional)
chilli oil
fresh chillies
(*See page 9)

Set a medium-sized saucepan of boiling water on a high heat and cook the noodles according to the packet instructions. Drain and pour back into the saucepan, then fill with cold water so they don't dry out. Set aside until needed.

Meanwhile, make the broth. To a large saucepan on a medium heat, add about 1.5 litres (52fl oz) of boiling water from the kettle. Add the dried mushrooms, ginger, garlic and spring onion and allow to simmer for 5–10 minutes.

While the broth takes on flavour, make the fishballs by adding all of the ingredients to a food processor and whizzing until smooth. Divide the mixture into 8 equal portions and roll into balls. Set aside until you need them.

Back to the broth, the mushrooms should have softened up by now and the liquid turned a brown colour. Use a small strainer to scoop out all of the mushrooms, garlic, ginger and spring onion and discard. Crumble the stock cubes into the broth and add the sesame oil and soy sauce. Stir and cook for a moment, then drop in the fishballs. Allow to simmer and after 5 minutes, add the sugar snap peas. After another 5 minutes of cooking, drain the noodles and add them to the pan to heat through. Once the noodles are hot and the fishballs have taken on a slightly pink shade and are very firm to the touch, everything is ready.

Serve in bowls with a halved boiled egg on top, if you wish. Adults give yourself a little extra soy sauce and chilli on top, too, if you like an extra kick. If you can get hold of crispy chilli oil, it works deliciously on here. If your little ones haven't quite mastered using a spoon, you can serve the ramen elements on a plate and the broth in a cup.

Love your leftovers Leftovers will keep for 24 hours in the fridge. Reheat in a saucepan until bubbling and the fishballs are piping hot throughout.

Slow cooker superheroes

The ultimate family mealtime hack – quick prep, with a long
and slow simmer while you get on with your day, returning
to a family feast which practically cooked itself.

Winter apple porridge

Wake up and come downstairs to your kitchen smelling delicious and breakfast cooked for you! Thick and really creamy porridge, flavoured with winter warming spices, is the perfect way to start a cold and frosty morning.

⦀ 2 adults and 2 littles ⏱ **Prep 5 minutes, Slow cook 7 hours** ❄ **Freezable**

2 sweet red eating apples
200g (7oz) rolled porridge oats*
400ml (14fl oz) milk*
a handful of seedless raisins

2 tsp ground cinnamon
2 tsp vanilla extract
1 tsp mixed spice
(*See pages 8–9)

Best to get this porridge cooking right before you head to sleep. Firstly, find a large heatproof glass or ceramic bowl that fits inside your slow cooker pot, preferably with high sides.

Peel the apples, then coarsely grate them around the central cores. Add the apple pulp, plus any juice which has leaked onto the chopping board into the bowl, along with the rest of the ingredients and 550ml (19fl oz) water. Stir really well to ensure the cinnamon and mixed spice have been incorporated into the liquid and are not just floating on the top.

Cover the top tightly with kitchen foil. Place the bowl in your slow cooker, put the lid on and cook on LOW for 6–7 hours. If you fancy a lie in, the porridge should stay warm in the slow cooker for a few more hours if the lid hasn't been removed.

When ready to eat, give the porridge a really good stir, as it may be a little thicker at the bottom, mix it so the consistency is equal throughout.

Serve with a little drizzle of maple syrup or honey for over 1s, if you wish, and fresh fruit on top.

Love your leftovers The porridge will keep for 2 days in the fridge, or freeze for 3 months. To reheat, put it in a saucepan with a splash of water and reheat gently over a low heat. Or put in a microwaveable bowl, stir in a little extra water, and heat in 30 seconds bursts, stirring between each, until piping hot throughout.

No slow cooker? This porridge cooks perfectly in a saucepan too. Use 200g (7oz) of oats and about 1 litre (35fl oz) of milk with no extra water. Simmer for 4–5 minutes, stirring continuously until thickened.

Slow cooker broccoli slice

This slice is like a crustless cheesy broccoli quiche, delicious and simple with a salad and some bread. Prep in the morning and that's lunch sorted for later.

GF

V

DF*

🍴 3 adults and 2 littles   **⏱ Prep 5 minutes, Slow cook 1½–3 hours**   **❄ Freezable**

1 head of broccoli	85g (3oz) Cheddar cheese*,	1 tsp onion powder
125g (4½oz) cream cheese*	grated	(*See page 8)
8 medium eggs	1 tsp garlic powder	

Cut a piece of non-stick baking paper to slightly larger than the circumference of your slow cooker pot. Crumple it up into a small ball, then unravel it so it's flat again, which will make it more pliable. Press the paper into the base of your slow cooker pot.

Wash the broccoli and cut into very small florets. If you wish, you can remove as much of the stalk as possible and finely chop that too. Add the broccoli to the slow cooker on top of the baking paper.

Add the cream cheese and 4 of the eggs to a mixing bowl. Using a balloon whisk, mix the cream cheese into the egg until you can see no lumps, then add the remaining eggs, grated cheese and garlic and onion powders. Whisk well to combine. Pour the egg mixture on top of the broccoli and give it a little poke to ensure the broccoli is sitting mostly under the liquid and distributed evenly.

Take four squares of kitchen paper, still attached in a long line, and fold it over in half. Place over the lip of the slow cooker pot, and if it doesn't reach all the way round, repeat with another double layer of kitchen roll. Place the lid of the slow cooker on, and gently tease the paper so it is tight and doesn't droop down into the food. This will soak up any excess moisture, so that the slice doesn't become too soggy.

Cook for about 1½ hours on HIGH, or 2–3 hours on LOW, until the egg mixture feels firm and the broccoli has softened. Remove from the slow cooker, using the baking paper to lift it up, and cut into 8 sections, or into finger strips if serving to little ones under 2 years.

Love your leftovers The slice will keep in the fridge for 2 days, or freeze for 2 months. Reheat in the oven or microwave until piping hot throughout.

Top tips You can swap the broccoli for other veg you have in your fridge, like grated courgette (zucchini) or carrot.

If you would like to bulk the dish out, add some chopped ham, cooked potatoes, or chunks of bread, which will soak up some of the egg.

No slow cooker? Chop the broccoli into very small pieces, then pour the egg mixture into a baking tray lined with baking paper. Bake at 180°C fan (200°C/400°F/Gas 6 for 15–22 minutes until the egg mixture has set and the broccoli is cooked through.

Chickpea and butternut squash dahl

A hearty vegan meal, creamy in texture and full of protein and goodness from the lentils and chickpeas, making it well balanced and nutritious for all the family.

GF*

EF

V

Vg

DF

⅋ Serves 2 adults and 3 littles ⏱ Prep 5 minutes, Slow cook 3–8 hours ❄ Freezable

1 butternut squash, peeled and cut into 2cm (¾in) dice

1 x 400g (14oz) can chickpeas in water

300g (10½oz) dried red lentils, rinsed

2 low-salt vegetable stock cubes* (gluten-free, if necessary)

1 tbsp garam masala

1 tbsp mild curry powder

a good grinding of black pepper

2 heaped tsp dried mixed herbs

2 tsp smoked paprika

1 x 400g (14oz) can coconut milk

1 x 400g (14oz) can chopped tomatoes

1 brown onion, finely diced

2 garlic cloves, grated

Put all of the ingredients, including the water from the can of chickpeas, into the slow cooker, along with 350ml (12fl oz) of boiling water. Give it a really good stir and put the lid on. Cook on HIGH for 3–4 hours or LOW for 6–8 hours. Once done, use a wooden spoon or rubber spatula to give the dahl a really good stir and mash the soft butternut squash into the sauce a little.

Serve the dahl with rice or naan breads, or even as a pasta sauce. Adults, you may want to season your portion with a little salt or even a dash of chilli sauce, if you like.

Love your leftovers The dahl will keep for 3 days in the fridge, or freeze for 3 months. Reheat in a saucepan or in the microwave until bubbling and piping hot throughout.

No slow cooker? Put all the ingredients in a large casserole dish, place the lid on tightly and bake in an oven set to 140°C fan (160°C/315°F/Gas 2–3) for 2-3 hours, or until the lentils have softened. You can also cook this dish in a saucepan on the hob over a low heat, simmering for 30–40 minutes.

Nina's favourite tender lemon garlic chicken

GF*

EF

DF*

When I made this throw-it-all-in-one-pot dish for my three year old Nina, the "yummy" noises she was making filled me with happiness. "This is so good mummy, you have to put it in your new book." Well, Nina, it's going in!

🍴 2 adults and 2 littles ⏱ Prep 10 minutes, Slow cook 5 hours ❄ Freezable

500g (1lb 2oz) skinless, boneless chicken thighs
finely grated zest and juice of 1 large unwaxed lemon
2 large garlic cloves, finely grated
2 tsp dried mixed herbs

1 low-salt chicken stock cube*
35g (1¼oz) unsalted butter*, cubed
500g (1lb 2oz) mini new potatoes
freshly ground black pepper
(*See page 0 for substitutions)

To the slow cooker pot, add the chicken thighs, zest and juice of the lemon, garlic, herbs and a little black pepper.

Crumble the stock cube into a jug and add the butter. Pour over 175ml (5½fl oz) of boiling water from the kettle and allow to dissolve. Pour over the chicken and cook on LOW for 3–4 hours or until the chicken is just starting to fall apart. Add the potatoes and cook for a further 1 hour until they are super tender.

Serve with steamed veg and a little crusty bread to soak up the juices. For little taste testers, slice the potatoes in half lengthways or mash them into the chicken juices, which is delicious for us adults too, by the way!

Love your leftovers The dish will keep for 2 days in the fridge, or freeze for 3 months. Defrost thoroughly before reheating until piping hot in the oven or microwave.

No slow cooker? Put all the ingredients in a high-sided baking dish that is large enough to fit the chicken and potatoes in one layer. Bake at 200°C fan (220°C/425°F/Gas 7) for 30-40 minutes until the chicken is cooked through and the potatoes are tender.

Chinese-style spare ribs

GF*

EF

DF

Super soft pork ribs coated in a sticky sauce delicately flavoured with Chinese spices; for such minimal effort, you'll be surprised at how delicious these are! As the meat is incredibly soft, they are perfect for serving to little taste testers.

⅔ Serves 2 adults and 3 littles ⏱ Prep 30 minutes, Slow cook 4–7 hours ❄ Freezable

150ml (5fl oz) low-sugar and -salt ketchup

1 tsp Chinese five-spice powder

1 tbsp soft brown sugar (optional)

1 x 90g (3¼oz) pouch of apple purée (see page 10)

4 garlic cloves, minced

1 tsp ground ginger

1 tbsp cornflour (cornstarch)

2 tbsp sesame seeds

1 low-salt chicken stock cube* (gluten-free, if necessary)

1kg (2lb 4oz) pork spare ribs, cut between each bone

freshly ground black pepper

To your slow cooker pot, add the ketchup, five-spice powder, sugar, if using, apple purée, garlic, ginger, cornflour, sesame seeds and a little black pepper. Crumble in the stock cube and give it all a really good mix.

Add the ribs, stirring again to coat the meat well in the sauce. Arrange the ribs so they sit in an even layer in the sauce, which will help them to cook evenly. Place the lid on your slow cooker and cook on HIGH for 4 hours or LOW for 6–7 hours.

Once done, they are ready and delicious to eat straight away. However, to take the ribs to the next level, I urge you to take one more step. Preheat your oven to 200°C fan (220°C/425°F/Gas 7) and line a very large baking tray with non-stick foil.

Using tongs, or two forks, carefully transfer the ribs to the baking tray, spacing them out. Be careful at this stage as the meat is really tender and falls apart easily.

Use a rubber spatula to give the remaining sauce in your slow cooker a really good stir, then spoon a generous amount onto each rib, coating the top side completely.

Place the tray in the preheated oven and bake for 15–20 minutes until the edges have charred slightly and the heat has caramelised the sugars in the sauce, bringing out the flavour.

Serve the ribs with oven chips and a side salad for the ultimate home takeaway!

For little ones under 2, let the ribs cool slightly, then pull the meat away from the bone. Ensure you have removed any cartilage too – a slight squeeze with your fingers on any meat serving to baby will determine if there are any lumps inside.

Love your leftovers The ribs will keep in the fridge for 2 days, or freeze for 3 months. Defrost, then reheat in the oven for 10–15 minutes until piping hot throughout.

> **No slow cooker?** Put all the ingredients in a roasting tin large enough that they sit snuggly. Mix up the sauce ingredients and pour over the meat, mixing well. Cover the top tightly with foil and bake at 140°C fan (160°C/315°F/Gas 2–3) for around 2 hours, or until the meat is falling off the bone. Then bake on a separate tray, as above.

Slow cooker pulled pork

Don't be alarmed by this list of ingredients; use what you already have in your spice rack – it's going to be delicious, trust me! This is great served in a burger bun, or in a toasted sandwich or wrap. Serve alongside a small bowl of the meat juices to dip your sarnie into. You can also use the meat to make lasagne or bulk out pasta dishes. But my favourite way is to get messy and make pulled pork tacos, served with my rainbow slaw, overleaf.

GF*

EF

DF

🍴 Serves 6   ⏱ Prep 10 minutes, Slow cook 4–8 hours   ❄ Freezable

1 tbsp smoked paprika

2 tsp garlic granules

1 tsp ground cumin

2 tsp dried mixed herbs

2 heaped tsp plain (all-purpose) flour*

1.5–2kg (3lb 5oz–4lb 8oz) pork shoulder, string removed

1 tbsp sunflower oil

1 low-salt chicken stock cube*

2 tsp mustard sauce or powder*

2 tbsp Worcestershire sauce* (optional)

2 tbsp apple cider vinegar

1 heaped tbsp soft brown sugar (optional)

4 tbsp low-sugar and -salt ketchup

1 tbsp low-salt soy sauce*

1 large brown onion, peeled and halved

1 small garlic bulb, cut in half crossways

(*See page 9)

Put the smoked paprika, garlic granules, ground cumin and dried herbs in a small bowl. Stir well, then spoon half of this spice mix onto a plate along with the plain flour and mix the spices into the flour. Roll the pork in the spiced flour so that it is coated on all sides.

Set a large frying pan on a high heat and add the oil. Lay the pork in the centre and cook hard and fast on all sides to generate some dark colour and crispiness on the outside of the pork. This will add lots of flavour and help the pork to stay super juicy.

Meanwhile, add the remaining spice mix to a large jug with 300ml (10½fl oz) boiling water from the kettle. Crumble the stock cube and add it to the jug along with the mustard, Worcestershire sauce, vinegar, sugar, if using, ketchup and soy sauce. Give it all a good mix and add it to the slow cooker along with the onion, garlic bulb and pork. Put the lid on and cook on HIGH for 4–5 hours or on LOW for 8 hours.

Once the meat is really tender and breaks away easily, it is done. Transfer the meat to a large bowl and use two forks to shred it up. Take the onion out of the sauce and discard. Squeeze the garlic cloves out, discarding the skin, and mash the soft garlic into the sauce. Then add the shredded meat back to the cooking juices and give it a good mix.

You're now ready to enjoy this meat however you like; I love it in tacos. For this, toast a couple of mini wraps in a frying pan or over an open flame on a gas burner, then mound up a little pile of the pulled pork and some slaw on the taco, fold over and enjoy!

For little ones, it'll be easier for them to enjoy this meal deconstructed.

Love your leftovers Pulled pork leftovers will keep really well for 2–3 days in the fridge, or 3 months in the freezer. When reheating in a saucepan or microwave, ensure it is piping hot throughout before serving.

No slow cooker? Bake in a large lidded casserole dish in an oven set to 130°C fan (150°C/300°F/Gas 2) for 5–7 hours, or until falling apart.

why not try it with ...

Baby-friendly rainbow slaw

Coleslaw tends to consist of chopped raw crunchy veg, which can be tricky for baby to eat. Even though this recipe does use raw veg, we're going to grate it so that it is much easier for little ones to enjoy.

GF*

EF

V

Vg*

DF*

⑪ 2 adults and 2 littles   ⏱ Prep 10 minutes

2 medium carrots
½ small red cabbage
½ small white cabbage
2 red eating apples
6 tbsp Greek yogurt*
1 tbsp apple cider vinegar

½ tsp Dijon mustard*
  (optional)
freshly ground black pepper
finely chopped chives, to
  garnish
(*See pages 8–9)

Wash the carrots (but no need to peel) and coarsely grate them on a box grater. Then remove and discard the outer leaves of the cabbages and grate those too. Slice the flesh from the apple, cutting around and discarding the central core. Cut the apple into 2–3mm (⅛in) thick matchsticks.

Put the yogurt, vinegar and mustard in a large bowl. Mix this all together, then add the grated veg and apple, season with a little black pepper and stir well.

Garnish with chopped chives and serve alongside your favourite picky-style meals.

Top tip If your little ones are older, you can replace a few tablespoons of the yogurt with mayonnaise.

Slow cooker meatballs

With the surprising addition of pasta in these meatballs, you're left with really tender meat which isn't overly bready. Pictured on page 188–189.

GF*

EF*

DF*

🍴 2 adults and 2 littles, plus leftovers   ⏱ Prep 10 mins, Slow cook 2–6 hours   ❄ Freezable

2 brown onions, peeled
4 large garlic cloves
1 medium courgette (zucchini)
1kg (2lb 4oz) tomato passata (strained tomatoes)
1 tbsp tomato purée (paste)
50g (1¾oz) Parmigiano-Reggiano cheese*, finely grated

4 tsp smoked paprika
1 tbsp Worcestershire sauce*
1 bay leaf
1 tsp dried oregano
1 tsp caster sugar (optional)
2 low-salt beef stock cubes*
500g (1lb 2oz) beef mince (12% fat), or 250g (9oz) each of beef mince and pork

mince (5% fat)
4 tbsp orzo pasta* (or breadcrumbs*)
1 tsp dried mixed herbs
1 medium egg*
50g (1¾oz) Cheddar cheese*, finely grated
freshly ground black pepper
(*See pages 8–9)

Gather a large mixing bowl for the meatballs and set up the slow cooker on your work surface with the lid off.

Using a box grater, coarsely grate the onions. Take half of the grated onions in your hands and gently squeeze some of the juice into the remaining onions. Put the dryer onion pulp into the bowl and tip the wet onion pulp into the slow cooker.

Now, using the fine side of the grater, mince the garlic cloves, adding half to the meatball bowl and half to the slow cooker.

Back to the coarse side of the grater, grate the courgette. Gather a little of the pulp in your hands at a time, hover over the slow cooker and squeeze so that the juices fall into the slow cooker pot, then put the dry courgette pulp into the meatball bowl.

To the slow cooker, add the passata, tomato purée, 20g (¾oz) of the Parmigiano, 3 teaspoons of the smoked paprika, the Worcestershire sauce, bay leaf, dried oregano, sugar, if using, and a grinding of black pepper. Crumble in the stock cubes, ensuring there are no large lumps. Give it all a very good stir and get on with the meatballs.

Add the mince, orzo pasta, mixed herbs, remaining 1 teaspoon of smoked paprika, egg, a little black pepper, the remaining Parmesan and all the grated Cheddar. Now it's time to get your hands in there – it really helps mix it all up more quickly and evenly.

Once the mixture is well combined, roll it into golf ball-sized meatballs and place each one in the slow cooker tomato sauce. You should get around 16 meatballs. Put the lid on, and cook on LOW for 5–6 hours, or HIGH for 2–3 hours.

Serve the meatballs and sauce with pasta, cutting the meatballs in half for little ones.

Love your leftovers This will keep for 2 days in the fridge, or will freeze for 3 months. Reheat in a saucepan or in the microwave until each meatball is piping hot throughout.

> **No slow cooker?** You can also cook this recipe in a large, lidded casserole dish on the hob over a medium-low heat, or in the oven set to 170°C fan (190°C/375°F/Gas 5), for 2–3 hours.

why not try it with ...

Easy cheesy garlic bread

🍴 **2 adults and 2 littles, plus leftovers** ⏱ **Prep 5 minutes, Bake 12 minutes** ❄ **Freezable**

GF*
EF
V
Vg*
DF*

2 part-baked baguettes*
40g (1½oz) unsalted butter*, softened
40g (1½oz) cream cheese*

1 tbsp fresh flat or curly leaf parsley, finely chopped
4 garlic cloves, finely grated or minced

1 mozzarella ball*
freshly ground black pepper
(*See pages 8–9)

Preheat the oven to 200°C fan (220°C/425°F/Gas 7) and line a baking tray with non-stick foil.

Make diagonal cuts down the length of both uncooked baguettes, around 2.5cm (1in) apart. Ensure you don't cut all the way through, but far enough that the bread opens and you can get the filling inside. You may need to prize the slits open a little to ensure you can get the filling into each slice in the bread.

Mix the butter, cream cheese, parsley, garlic and a generous grind of black pepper together in a bowl. Using a dinner knife, spread inside each slice of the loaves. If you find it easier, you can fill a small sandwich bag with the filling, then squeeze the mixture into one corner, snip off the tip and pipe the mixture between the slices of bread.

Now make a final cut down the centre of the top of each baguette, ensuring you keep both ends intact, which will help the baguette to hold its shape when baked in the oven.

Cut the ball of mozzarella in half and slice into 5mm (¼in) thick slices, then stuff it down the centre slit in each baguette. Place the baguettes on the prepared baking tray and bake for 10–12 minutes until the bread has browned nicely and the cheese has melted.

Serve with salad as a simple lunch, or on the side of your slow-cooked meatballs or favourite pasta dish.

Love your leftovers Garlic bread will keep for 2 days in the fridge, or will freeze for 1 month. This is best eaten warm, so reheat any leftovers in the oven until piping hot throughout.

If you wish, you can freeze one baguette before baking and pop it in the oven from frozen; bake at 200°C fan (220°C/425°F/Gas 7) for around 15 minutes, or alternatively bake for 5–10 minutes if the garlic bread was cooked before freezing.

Make it quick! You can make this on a much smaller scale using a slice of toast as the base and topping with a little garlic butter and cheese.

Pork and apple orzotto

A throw-it-all-in kinda dish that makes your home smell delicious while you wait for dinnertime!

GF*

EF

DF

🍴 3 adults and 2 littles ⏱ Prep 10 minutes, Slow cook 3–6 hours ❄ Freezable

650g (1lb 7oz) pork shoulder
    steaks, fat trimmed, cut into
    2cm (¾in) wide strips
a drizzle of oil
1 brown onion, finely diced
1 low-salt chicken stock cube*
1 bay leaf
2 tsp Dijon mustard*

2 large garlic cloves, minced
1 heaped tsp dried mixed
    herbs
200g (7oz) orzo pasta*
2 large red eating apples,
    cored and cut into wedges
freshly ground black pepper
(*See page 9)

Put half of the pork and a drizzle of oil in a large frying pan over a high heat and cook until browned all over. This is what will give the final dish its colour and extra depth of flavour, so take a moment to allow it to get some lovely dark charred edges before transferring to your slow cooker pot. Repeat to brown the other half of the meat.

If your frying pan is dry, add a touch more oil, then turn the heat down and sauté the onion for 3–5 minutes until translucent. Allow the onion to soak up the flavours from the pork cooking juices in the bottom of the pan. Dissolve the stock cube in 400ml (14fl oz) water, add to the onions and stir, then transfer it to the slow cooker pot with the pork. Add a little black pepper, the bay leaf, Dijon mustard, garlic and the mixed dried herbs to the slow cooker and stir. Put the lid on and cook for 2½ hours on HIGH or 4–5 hours on LOW.

After this time, the pork should be soft and break down with a little pressure. If there is lots of fat sitting at the top of the slow cooker pot, you can skim away a little if you wish using a large spoon. Now add the orzo pasta, apple wedges and 275ml (9½fl oz) boiling water. Stir and cook on low for 30–40 minutes, or until the pasta is cooked through. Add a touch more water if you feel the dish is too dry.

Serve as is, with a little green veg on the side – or a fresh salad works very well too. If feeding little ones under 9 months, mash the pork into the orzo using the back of a fork. The apples can be enjoyed as finger food, or also mashed into the dish too.

Love your leftovers The orzotto will keep in an airtight container in the fridge for 2–3 days or frozen for 3 months. Reheat with an extra splash of water until piping hot throughout.

No slow cooker? Follow the instructions above, but cook in a wide, high-sided, lidded frying pan. Brown the pork and cook it for 1 hour on low with the lid on, or until the meat is really tender. Then add the pasta and cook with the lid off for 10–15 minutes until cooked through.

Slow cooker spag bol

GF*

EF

DF

There's something about a Bolognese sauce that has had time to cook for hours – the flavours have developed, the veg is soft and the whole meal is as comforting as you remember from your childhood.

🍴 **Serves 6** ⏱ **Prep 20 minutes, Slow cook 3–8 hours** ❄ **Freezable**

750g–1kg (1lb 10oz–2lb 4oz) mince (10–15% fat) – either all beef or 50/50 beef and pork

3 rashers of smoked bacon, thinly sliced (optional)

3 medium carrots, peeled (if you like) and diced

3 celery sticks, finely diced

1 large brown onion, finely diced

a drizzle of garlic-infused olive oil, optional

3 fat garlic cloves, minced

2 tbsp tomato purée (paste)

1 heaped tsp dried mixed herbs

1 tbsp Worcestershire sauce*

1 heaped tsp sugar

1 tbsp smoked paprika

2 low-salt beef stock cubes*

500g (1lb 2oz) tomato passata (strained tomatoes)

1 x 400g (14oz) can chopped tomatoes

freshly ground black pepper

(*See page 9)

Put the mince and bacon, if using, in a large dry frying pan and cook until the mince has browned and is taking on a darker colour – this will take around 5–7 minutes. Transfer the meat to your slow cooker pot. At this stage you can scrunch up a few pieces of kitchen paper and dab into the meat to remove some of the excess fat, if you wish.

Meanwhile, in the same frying pan in which you cooked the meat, fry the carrots, celery and onion in the remaining meat juices. Add a touch of garlic-infused oil if you feel like your pan is very dry. Sauté the veggies for around 5 minutes until soft, then transfer to the slow cooker.

While everything is frying, add the garlic, tomato purée, mixed herbs, Worcestershire sauce, sugar and paprika to the slow cooker, along with a good grind of black pepper, then crumble in the beef stock cubes. Now, add the tomato passata, and half fill the carton with water from the tap, swilling it around to loosen any of the excess tomato hiding in the packet, and add to the slow cooker. Add the can of chopped tomatoes and do the same, quarter filling the can and swilling around before adding the liquid to the slow cooker.

Once everything has been added to the slow cooker, give it a very good stir, then put the lid on and cook on LOW for 6–8 hours or on HIGH for 3–4 hours.

Once ready, serve the sauce with a pasta shape of your choice and with a little grated cheese on top. Adults, you can season your portion on your plate if you feel it needs it.

Love your leftovers The sauce will keep for up to 4 days in an airtight container in the fridge, or freeze for up to 3 months. Defrost and reheat on the hob or in the microwave until piping hot throughout.

> **No slow cooker?** Cook everything in a large saucepan with the lid on for as long as you can – 20 minutes on a medium heat will do, but if you can leave it ticking away on low for 2-3 hours then the sauce will have a real depth of flavour.

Hearty goulash soup

Having a Hungarian background, goulash to me has always been a family favourite soup. A hearty, comforting broth packed full of goodness with deliciously succulent meat, tender potatoes and soft peppers that just melt into the sauce.

GF* **EF** **DF**

🍴 **2 adults and 2 littles, plus leftovers**   ⏱ **Prep 10 minutes, Slow cook 4 hours**   ❄ **Freezable**

1 tbsp sunflower oil
1 large brown onion, finely diced
1 tsp caraway seeds (optional)
600–700g (1lb 5oz–1lb 9oz) diced stewing beef or lamb shoulder
1 red pepper
1 yellow pepper

2 large carrots
6 fresh tomatoes, quartered, or 1 x 400g (14oz) can good-quality chopped tomatoes
3 garlic cloves, finely diced
2 tsp dried mixed herbs
3 tbsp sweet, mild paprika
2 fresh or dried bay leaves
2 low-salt beef stock cubes*

1 tbsp cornflour (cornstarch)
350g (12oz) potatoes (I prefer new potatoes as they hold together well, but any all-rounder like Maris Piper or King Edward will do)
(*See page 9)

Heat a teaspoon of the oil in a large heavy-based frying pan over a gentle heat. Add the onion and soften for 2 minutes, then add the caraway seeds, if using, and cook for 2 more minutes. Once translucent, add the onion and seeds to the slow cooker pot.

Return the pan to the heat and crank up the temperature to high. Add the remaining oil, then, in two or three batches, fry the diced meat until browned and caramelised on the edges. Add to the slow cooker pot.

Meanwhile, deseed the peppers and cut into 1cm (½in) wide strips, or finely dice if your little ones prefer (not "bits", as my Nina calls them). Peel and cut the carrots into 2.5cm (1in) chunks. Add both to the slow cooker pot, along with the tomatoes, garlic, herbs, 2 tablespoons of the paprika and the bay leaves, then crumble in the stock cubes.

Once all the beef is added to the slow cooker pot, deglaze the pan to extract as much flavour as possible – add 300ml (10½fl oz) of boiling water to the pan and use a wooden spoon to scrape any crispy bits from the bottom, then add this liquid to the slow cooker. Stir really well, cover and cook on the HIGH setting for 2 hours.

Once the two hours is up, add the remaining 1 tablespoon of paprika, the cornflour and a little cold water to a small bowl or mug and mix to make a runny paste. Peel the potatoes and dice them into 2.5cm (1in) chunks.

Now, the meat should be starting to get soft, but it won't be fully falling apart yet. Give the goulash a gentle stir, and add 400–500ml (14–17fl oz) of boiling water (depending on how soupy you would like it). Add the cornflour paprika paste and the potatoes and give it all a really good stir. Place the lid back on and cook for a further 2 hours on HIGH.

Serve the soup in deep bowls with a dollop of sour cream and some crusty bread for dunking. Adults, this dish is delicious as is, but if you wish to add a sprinkling of salt to your bowl, it really helps the flavours to pop.

Love your leftovers The soup can be kept for 2 days, or frozen for up to 3 months. Reheat in a saucepan on the hob until piping hot throughout.

No slow cooker? This dish can also be made in a large lidded saucepan on the hob, simmering on a medium-low heat for 2–3 hours, and adding the potatoes halfway through cooking.

Slow cooker lamb curry

This rich curry is one to look forward to all day while it cooks away in your kitchen. Perfect with flat breads for dipping into the creamy sauce.

GF*

EF

DF*

🍴 2 adults and 2 littles   ⏱ **Prep 15 minutes, Slow cook 6 hours**   ❄ **Freezable**

600g (1lb 5oz) lamb shoulder
1 tbsp sunflower oil
2 large garlic cloves
a thumb-sized piece of fresh ginger
1 medium brown onion

1 tsp ground turmeric
2 tsp mild garam masala
1 tbsp smoked paprika
1 x 400g (14oz) can finely chopped tomatoes or passata (strained tomatoes)

150g (5½oz) Greek yogurt*
1 low-salt chicken stock cube*
3 tbsp very thick cream*
(*See pages 8–9)

Cut the meat into bite-sized chunks and trim off most of the fat – if there is a little left, that is totally fine.

Add the sunflower oil to a large non-stick frying pan and fry the lamb in batches until charred nicely on the edges. If you cook it all together then it will stew and you won't get the browned edges that give your curry extra flavour. Transfer each batch of meat to the slow cooker as you go, and repeat until it's all done.

While the meat fries, prep the aromatics. Peel the garlic and ginger, then finely grate to a purée. Coarsely grate the onion.

Once all the meat has been transferred to the slow cooker, add the grated onion to the frying pan to soak up the last of the lamb juices in the bottom of the pan. Fry for 2–3 minutes to soften the onion – you can add a tiny splash of water if the pan feels too dry and the onion is catching. Add the garlic and ginger purée, along with the spices and cook for 1–2 minutes, adding a touch more water if needed. It's important to not burn the spices, but toasting them here will release their flavours and give your curry a stronger flavour.

Add the tomatoes and yogurt to the onion paste and stir it all together, then pour it into the slow cooker pot, using a spatula to ensure you transfer every last bit of the sauce. Crumble in the stock cube, stir and put the lid on. Cook on LOW for around 6 hours.

Forty minutes before the end of the cooking time, add the thick cream; this softens the flavour and gives the curry a lovely rich texture.

Serve the curry with rice, naan breads and veg. For little ones, serve large pieces of meat as finger food, or mash it into the sauce.

Love your leftovers The curry will keep for 3 days in the fridge, or freeze for 2 months. Reheat in a saucepan until piping hot and bubbling.

Top tip Swap the lamb for chicken or root veg, like butternut squash, for an alternative flavour. These will take less cooking, so reduce the time by 2 hours, or cook until tender.

No slow cooker? Simmer the curry in a saucepan over a low heat for 40–60 minutes until the meat is tender.

Slow cooker gammon

GF*

EF

DF

Soft and tender meat that just falls apart with a fork, coated in a delicious mustard glaze, and crisped up in the oven for maximum flavour, this is a real show stopper for your Sunday family roast and is my Christmas Eve tradition! This recipe has a few different spices that help give the gammon its flavour, but will be still amazing without, so if you would like to leave them out don't let it stop you from making this one.

🍴 **4 adults and 2–4 littles** ⏱ **Prep 40 minutes, Slow cook 3–6 hours** ❄ **Freezable**

Approx 2kg (4lb 8oz) joint of smoked gammon (preferably with a nice layer of fat on the outside)

1 brown onion

1 garlic bulb

½ tsp coriander seeds (optional)

2–3 allspice berries (optional)

2 juniper berries (optional)

4 cloves (optional)

1 tsp black peppercorns

For the glaze

2 tbsp wholegrain mustard*

1 tbsp Dijon mustard*

2 tbsp honey (if planning on serving to under 1s, use maple syrup instead)

a good grinding of black pepper

(*See page 9)

Put the gammon joint in your slow cooker with the strings or casing (not the plastic packaging) still attached as this will hold it together as it cooks. Cut the onion in half and top and tail the garlic bulb to expose the ends of the cloves and add these too. Add all of the spices and pour in enough water to come a quarter of the way up the side of the joint. Put the lid on and cook on LOW for 6 hours or HIGH for 3–4 hours.

Once the gammon is almost cooked, line a baking tray with non-stick foil and preheat the oven 220°C (240°C/475°F/Gas 8) – the hotter the better as you want to really caramelise the crust. Carefully lift the joint out of the slow cooker using two large forks and place on the prepared baking tray. Allow to cool a little while you prepare the glaze.

Mix all the glaze ingredients together in a bowl and season with a good grind of black pepper. Remove any strings or outer casing from the meat and gently rotate the joint so that the fatty section is facing up. If your joint has the skin on it too, carefully remove this leaving a layer of fat still attached to the joint. Using a knife, score a criss-cross pattern into the fat, ensuring not to cut through into the meat. Pour the glaze over the joint, using the back of a spoon to spread it evenly across the entire top side of the joint. Quickly put the gammon in the oven before all of the glaze drips down the sides. Bake for 15–25 minutes or until the top has turned deliciously dark and crispy, using a spoon once or twice during cooking to baste the joint with the glaze at the bottom of the pan. Remove from the oven and allow to rest for at least 15 minutes before serving.

Love your leftovers Gammon is one of my favourite things to have in the fridge: great in sandwiches; dice and toss through pasta; use it to top pizza; or cook into an omelette – the possibilities are endless. It will keep for 5–7 days in the fridge, or freeze for 1–2 months. Defrost fully before reheating until piping hot in the oven or a frying pan.

> **No slow cooker?** Instead, put the meat in a pan of water and bring to the boil, then lower the heat to low and simmer for 20 minutes per 450g (1lb) plus an extra 20 minutes, before glazing and placing in the oven as per the recipe above.

Top tip Gammon is a salty piece of meat, therefore it is advised to only offer a very small amount to taste for little ones under 1 – exposure and variety is a great thing.

Proper beef stew and dumplings

A hug in a bowl on a cold, rainy day. The best thing about beef stew is the smell that fills your house throughout the day. The anticipation brings me so much joy!

GF*
EF
DF*

🍴 1 adult and 1 little ⏱ **Prep 20 minutes, Slow cook 4–8 hours** ❄ **Freezable**

5 celery sticks

1 medium brown onion

3 small carrots

2 tbsp sunflower oil

2 tbsp plain (all-purpose) flour*

750g (1lb 10oz) lean diced stewing beef

2 large Maris Piper potatoes, peeled and quartered

1 tbsp Worcestershire sauce* (optional)

2 fresh or dried bay leaves

3 garlic cloves, minced

1 heaped tsp dried mixed herbs

2 low-salt beef stock cubes*

freshly ground black pepper

For the dumplings

200g (7oz) self-raising flour*, plus extra for dusting

70g (2½oz) beef or vegetarian suet*

50g (1¾oz) Cheddar cheese*, finely grated

(*See pages 8–9)

Finely dice the celery, onion and carrots. Add all this veg to a large heavy-based frying pan with a little drizzle of the sunflower oil, and cook for around 5 minutes until the vegetables have started to soften. Stir occasionally to ensure they cook evenly.

Meanwhile, on a plate, coat the beef in flour and shake off any excess.

Transfer the softened veg to your slow cooker pot and put the empty frying pan back on the hob over a high heat with a little more sunflower oil. Brown the meat in the pan in batches, making sure it has plenty of room, until the outside is dark brown with crispy edges, but the inside is still raw. Transfer to the slow cooker.

While the meat browns, add the remaining ingredients and a generous grind of black pepper to the slow cooker pot. In a large jug, mix the stock cubes with 800ml (28fl oz) of boiling water until fully dissolved, and add this liquid to the slow cooker too.

Give everything a good stir then put the lid on. Cook, preferably, on LOW for 6–8 hours, or on HIGH for 4–5 hours, until the meat is tender and falls apart with gentle pressure.

This is delicious as it is, with the potatoes adding a little thickness to the stew. However, if you're like me and love a really thick and hearty stew, 1 hour before it's ready, add dumplings. To make these, measure all the ingredients into a mixing bowl, season with black pepper and give it a stir. Trickle in enough cold water to make a slightly sticky, mouldable dough – about 160ml (5¼fl oz). I find wetter dough makes lighter dumplings.

Now, stir the stew well and keep the lid off. Flour your hands, then take a small amount of the dough and roll it in your hands gently to form a rough golf-ball-sized dumpling. Plop it into the stew and repeat with the rest – the dough should make around 10 dumplings. If your dough is too sticky to shape, use a spoon to dollop the mixture into the stew, or add a touch more flour until it's dry enough to handle.

Try to add the dumplings neatly without overlapping each other, then put the lid on and on cook on HIGH this time until they have doubled in size at least. Don't be tempted to take the lid off your slow cooker as this will affect their rise. The anticipation for the final reveal is worth the wait!

SLOW COOKER SUPERHEROES

No slow cooker? Cook the stew in a lidded casserole dish in an oven set to 160ºC fan (180ºC/350ºF/Gas 4) for 2–3 hours until the meat is tender, then add the dumplings and cook for another 30 minutes.

Tropical rice pudding

GF · EF · V · Vg* · DF*

This comforting dessert brings a little sunshine to your day with flavours of coconut, pineapple and peach. Whack it all in the slow cooker in the afternoon and enjoy a delicious no-added-sugar treat after dinner.

⅝ Serves 6   ⏱ Prep 5 minutes, Slow cook 2½–6 hours   ❄ Freezable

30g (1oz) unsalted soft butter*, for greasing
160g (5¾oz) pudding rice
1 x 400ml (14oz) can coconut milk
550ml (19fl oz) milk*

2 tsp vanilla extract
1 x 425g (15oz) can pineapple chunks in juice
1 x 415g (14¾oz) can peach slices in juice
fresh fruit, to serve (optional)

demerara sugar, to serve (optional)
(*See page 8)

Generously grease the bottom and sides of your slow cooker pot with butter to avoid the rice pudding sticking.

Put all of the ingredients, including the juice from the tins of fruit, into the slow cooker and give it a little stir to combine. Put the lid on and cook for 2½–3½ hours on HIGH or 4–6 hours on LOW. It will be ready when the rice feels soft.

When you initially take the lid off, it may seem like the rice pudding has split, but don't worry – use a rubber spatula to give it a really good mix and it will all come together.

Serve in bowls as is, or with a little extra fruit on top or a sprinkling of demerara sugar.

For babies under 12 months, mash the pineapple in their portion gently with a fork to break it up.

Love your leftovers The rice pudding will keep for 2 days in the fridge, or freeze for 3 months. Defrost and reheat with an extra splash of milk, as it will really thicken as it cools.

No slow cooker? Add everything to a wide, low-sided baking dish, including the juice from just one of the cans of fruit. Bake at 140°C fan (160°C/315°F/Gas 2–3) for 2 hours, checking after 1½ hours to see if the rice is tender and the liquid has been absorbed.

Something sweet

Family treats that are very low in sugar, but still have maximum yumminess. I've worked really hard to create recipes that you can enjoy together every so often. You might choose to serve just a small portion to baby as part of a balanced diet or even reduce the sugar content further when you know your baby has eaten something higher in sugar recently. It's really great to offer a wide variety of tastes and textures to little ones, and remember it's important to consider their sugar and salt intake across a whole week, and not just individual meals.

Hot or cold chocolate milk

Cuddle up cosy on a cold autumn day with a blanket and a mug of warm hot chocolate, or use the same recipe for a refreshing glass of chocolate milk during the summer months. Refined-sugar free, it's a much healthier alternative to shop-bought varieties.

GF

EF

V

Vg*

DF*

⏲ Makes 2 large mugs   **⏲ Prep 5 minutes, Cook 5 minutes (optional)**

450ml (16fl oz) milk*
  (see page 8)
6 small soft dates, pitted
1½ tbsp unsweetened cocoa
  powder
1 tbsp maple syrup (optional)

Add all the ingredients to a blender and whizz until smooth. At this stage you can strain the milk through a fine sieve if you wish, but it's not necessary.

The chocolate milk is now ready to drink cold, or you can pour it into a small saucepan and heat gently on a medium heat for 3–5 minutes until just simmering. Stir frequently to prevent the milk sticking to the base of the pan, as well as creating a lovely foamy top to the hot chocolate.

Love your leftovers Unheated chocolate milk will keep in the fridge for 2 days. Give it a mix before serving.

Note Babies under 12 months old should have their usual breast or formula milk as their main drink, with additional water to help to learn cup usage skills. Therefore, this hot chocolate is best served to little ones over the age of 12 months, and children under 3 years old should be served smaller portions than older children.

You can freeze the milk into ice lolly moulds to make chocolate ice pops too.

Peach melba tarts

Crispy flaky pastry topped with a gloriously sweet peach jam filling and a soft raspberry for a hit of fresh zinginess. Sprinkle over a little icing sugar for the big kids and I promise you these little tarts will not stick around long!

⦚ Makes 12 tarts ⏱ Prep 15 minutes, Bake 14 minutes

a little melted butter* or oil,
  for greasing,
1 tbsp plain (all-purpose) flour*
225g (8oz) Peach Chia Jam
  (see page 23)

2 tbsp cornflour (cornstarch)
½ x 375g (13oz) sheet of
  ready-rolled puff pastry*
12 large fresh raspberries
1 egg* (or 20ml/¾fl oz milk*)

icing sugar, to dust (optional)
(*See pages 8–9)

Preheat the oven to 180°C fan (200°C/400°F/Gas 6) and grease a 12-hole tart tin or shallow muffin tray with a little melted butter or oil. Sprinkle over a spoonful of plain flour and tap the sides of the tray to ensure the flour sticks to all the melted butter. Tap out the excess flour into the sink.

Put the peach chia jam in a small saucepan and bring to a gentle simmer.

Meanwhile, in a small bowl, mix the cornflour with 3 tablespoons of cold water from the tap to make a paste.

Once the jam is starting to bubble, add the cornflour paste and stir continuously. It will start to thicken immediately. Cook for a further 3–5 minutes until you have a very thick paste. If the jam is too runny, it'll give the tarts soggy bottoms. Transfer to a large cold bowl and set aside to cool while you prep the pastry.

Unroll the pastry sheet halfway and cut down the side of the roll. Place the remaining pastry in an airtight bag and save in the fridge for another recipe (or more tarts when these get gobbled up quickly!). Roll your piece of pastry into a tight sausage, then cut into 12 equal slices. One at time, place the pastry disc on its side in the centre of your palm and press it flat with your other hand until you have a large, flat pastry circle, approx 5mm (¼in) thick. Press the pastry discs into your prepared tin, ensuring the pastry is moulded into the base of the holes.

Beat the egg (or use a little milk) and brush over the sides and top of the pastry, avoiding the central base as this is where the filling will be.

Add a heaped tablespoon of the jammy filling to each tart to fill them almost to the top. Place a raspberry on top, pressing it a little into the jam. Pop the tarts in the oven to bake for 12–14 minutes until the sides of the pastry have puffed up and turned golden and the base of the pastry has browned a little and is visibly cooked.

Allow to stand in the tin for 2–3 minutes before popping each tart out of the tray using a dinner knife. Place on a cooling rack to cool before digging in. You can dust the tops of the tarts with a little sifted icing sugar to add a touch more sweetness, if you wish.

Love your leftovers The tarts can be stored in an airtight container at room temperature for up to 3 days, or freeze for 3 months. Defrost at room temperature and enjoy cold, or reheat in a hot oven for about 5 minutes until piping hot.

Speedy apple pie turnovers

GF*

EF*

V

Vg*

DF*

With a few shortcuts, you can whip up these turnovers in no time at all. Using grated apple not only means that you don't need to precook it and let it cool before filling the pastry, but that the apple is a safe size to be enjoyed by all the family, from 6 months of age. They're also great for packing up and taking on the go!

Makes 6 turnovers   Prep 15 minutes, Bake 25 minutes

1 tbsp cornflour

1 tbsp fresh lemon juice

1 heaped tsp ground
cinnamon

1 heaped tsp golden caster

sugar (optional)

1 x 90g (3¼oz) pouch of apple
purée (see page 10)

3 red eating apples

1 x 375g (13oz) sheet of

ready-rolled puff pastry*

1 egg* (or a splash of milk*)

1 tbsp demerara sugar
(optional)

(*See pages 8–9)

Preheat the oven to 190°C fan (210°C/415°F/Gas 6–7) and line a large baking tray with non-stick baking paper.

Put the cornflour and lemon juice in a small mixing bowl and stir until smooth. Add the cinnamon, caster sugar, if using, and apple purée and stir to combine.

Peel the apples and, using the coarse side of a box grater, grate each apple around the central core, discarding the core. Working in batches, squeeze a little of the grated apple over another bowl to remove as much juice as you can. Transfer the pulp to the apple purée bowl and mix well. (The squeezed apple juice is delicious to drink – add a touch of sparkling water for a refreshing combo!)

Take the pastry out of the fridge and gently unroll. If you feel it is starting to tear, wait a few moments so that it warms and softens a little. Once unrolled, cut it into 6 squares; cut one solid line down the centre so you have two long strips, then cut each of these into 3 squares.

Divide the apple mixture evenly between the pastry, spooning it into the centre of each pastry square. Whisk the egg in a small bowl, or decant a little milk, and brush a little onto the exposed pastry – this is to help the pastry parcels stay sealed when baking. Fold over one corner of each pastry to form 6 filled triangles. Transfer to the prepared baking tray and, using a fork, crimp the edges together to ensure they are well sealed. If your fork is sticking to the pastry, dip it into the egg or milk to stop the stickiness.

Brush the top of each pastry with the remaining egg (or milk) and cut two short slits through the pastry to allow the steam to escape during cooking, ensuring your pastry will be crisp and the filling won't leak out. If you wish, you can sprinkle a small amount of demerara sugar over the top of each turnover, which will give a lovely crunch, but this step is completely optional. Pop the pastries in the preheated oven to bake for around 20–25 minutes, until the pastry has puffed up and is golden brown on top. Transfer to a cooling rack to cool a little before digging in.

To serve to little ones, cut into finger length strips so it's easy for them to hold.

Love your leftovers The turnovers can be stored in an airtight container at room temperature for up to 2 days, or freeze for 3 months. Defrost at room temperature and enjoy cold, or reheat in a hot oven for 5–10 minutes until piping hot.

Apricot almond Danish pastries

These are super simple to make and are naturally sweet, using fruit as the main sweetener. Whip up a batch of these delicious pastries and your house will smell like a French patisserie all afternoon!

GF*

EF*

V

Vg*

DF*

Makes 8 Prep 10 minutes, Bake 20 minutes ❄ Freezable

2 x 400g (14oz) cans apricot halves in juice, drained

2 heaped tbsp ground almonds

1 tsp almond extract

1 x 375g (13oz) sheet of ready-rolled puff pastry*

1 egg* (or milk*)

1 tbsp icing sugar, to serve (optional)

(*See pages 8–9)

Preheat the oven to 190°C fan (210°C/415°F/Gas 6–7) and line a large baking tray with non-stick baking paper.

Set aside 8 apricot halves for the tops, then put the rest in a blender or food processor and whizz until super smooth. Add the ground almonds and almond extract and whizz again until combined.

Unroll the puff pastry sheet and cut it into 8 equal rectangles. Transfer them to your baking tray, spacing at least 2.5cm (1in) apart. Place a slightly heaped tablespoon of the filling mixture onto the centre of a pastry, then add an apricot half, pressing down slightly so it's secured in place. Repeat to make 8 pastries.

Beat the egg in a small bowl, then, using a pastry brush, brush a touch of egg onto the exposed pastry of each Danish, focusing mainly on the corners. Fold over each corner, approximately 2.5cm (1in) into the pastry, so that each one is now a rough circular shape. Egg wash the other side of the pastry edges, and any other exposed dry pastry you can see.

Bake in the preheated oven for 15–20 minutes, or until the pastry has risen, and turned golden and flaky. Allow to stand for a minute, before transferring to a cooling rack using a thin fish slice or offset spatula, and dusting with a touch of icing sugar, if you desire.

For under 1s, avoid adding the sugar dusting and cut into finger strips to serve.

Love your leftovers Store in an airtight container for 2 days. They are best served slightly warmed, so reheat in a preheated oven for 5–10 minutes. They can also be frozen for 1 month; thaw thoroughly before reheating in the oven.

Crumbly cinnamon biscuits

EF*

V

Vg*

DF*

Cold and miserable Saturday afternoons are made for biscuits with tea, or milk for the little ones. These glorious little mouthfuls are low in sugar – and it's a good job as I bet you can't just have one!

🍴 **Makes 20 biscuits** ⏱ **Prep 15 minutes, Bake 14 minutes** ❄ **Freezable**

200g (7oz) plain (all-purpose) flour, plus extra for dusting

130g (4½oz) cold unsalted butter, cubed*

30g (1oz) golden caster sugar

1 tsp vanilla extract

2 heaped tsp ground cinnamon

1 egg yolk* (or a small dash of milk*)

(*See pages 8–9)

Preheat the oven to 180°C fan (200°C/400°F/Gas 6).

Measure the flour, cubed butter, sugar, vanilla and cinnamon into a mixing bowl. Using the tips of your fingers, gently rub the butter into the flour until it resembles breadcrumbs.

Add the egg yolk, and using a metal dinner knife, mix the yolk into the crumbs until it starts to clump together. Tip it all out onto a clean work surface and briefly knead to bring the dough together. (You can also make the dough in a food processor, but it's very important that you pulse only very briefly, because if you overwork the dough, your biscuits will be chewy rather than crumbly.)

Cut the dough in half, placing one half in the fridge, covered, while you work on the other. Using a rolling pin, roll the dough out to around 7mm (³⁄₈in) thick – no need to get a ruler out, you just want it to be a little thinner than a centimetre. Dust the work surface, rolling pin and the top of the dough as you go, and keep moving it around to avoid the dough sticking to the work surface. If it does, use a spatula or thin dinner knife to gently slide under the dough to separate it. If it is very warm in your kitchen, you may find it easier to chill the dough for half an hour before rolling out, to prevent a sticky mess.

Using a cookie cutter roughly 8cm (3¼in) in diameter, or an upside-down drinking glass, stamp out as many biscuits as you can, rerolling the offcuts of dough to use it all up. Repeat with the other half of the dough.

Transfer the biscuits to a large non-stick baking tray and bake in the preheated oven for 11–14 minutes, until the biscuits are just starting to turn a little darker and the very edges are slightly browned.

Remove from the oven and allow to cool on the tray for a couple of minutes before using a spatula to transfer to a cooling rack. The biscuits will feel quite soft when first out of the oven, but will firm up as they cool down.

Love your leftovers Store in an airtight container for up to 1 week. Unbaked dough can be frozen for up to 3 months. Allow to defrost, then roll out and bake following the recipe above.

Jam sandwich biscuits

These shortbread vanilla biscuits with a jammy filling are a childhood classic. Trouble is, most recipes are rather high in sugar. These are a much healthier version.

EF*

V

Vg*

DF*

⏱ Makes 12 biscuits   ⏲ Prep 20 minutes, Cook 10 minutes

135g (4¾oz) unsalted butter*, softened

45g (1½oz) fruit sugar or golden caster sugar

2 tsp vanilla extract

1 medium egg* (or 60ml/2fl oz milk*)

240g (8½oz) plain (all-purpose) flour, plus extra for dusting

1 tbsp cornflour (cornstarch)

For the jam

60g (2oz) frozen blueberries

1 tsp vanilla extract

1 tbsp golden caster sugar

1 tbsp cornflour (cornstarch)

(*See pages 8–9)

Preheat the oven to 180°C fan (200°C/400°F/Gas 6) and ensure you have two shelves evenly spaced in the oven.

Measure the butter, sugar and vanilla into a mixing bowl, then beat well using a wooden spoon or in a stand mixer. Once the butter is light and fluffy, add the egg and beat again. It may look like it has split, but it's okay, just mix it well and it'll come together. Sift in the flour and cornflour and stir. It will feel like the mixture is too dry, but keep mixing, it will come together in around 30 seconds. Once the dough is starting to clump together, tip it out onto a clean work surface and bring it together into a ball of dough.

Cut the dough in half and, one half at a time, roll out to about 5mm (¼in) thick. Dust the work surface, rolling pin and the biscuit dough with a little flour. Cut out 6cm (2½in) circles using a cookie cutter, rerolling the excess dough to make more biscuits. Lift the biscuits onto a non-stick baking tray – using a thin offset spatula will help.

Find something you can use to make a small hole in the tops of half of the biscuits, preferably around 1.5cm (⅝in) in diameter – a little heart cookie cutter or an apple corer or even the handle end of a wooden spoon which you can shimmy into the centre.

Bake the biscuits in the preheated oven for about 10 minutes, or until the edges are just starting to turn slightly golden. Remove them and transfer the biscuits to a cooling rack.

Meanwhile, make the jam by adding the frozen blueberries to a small saucepan along with 2 tablespoons of boiling water, the vanilla extract and the sugar. Bring the mixture to a boil, and use a potato masher to break down the fruit. Separately, put the cornflour in a small bowl along with 2 tablespoons of cold water and stir to form a paste. Pour the cornflour mixture into the fruit, mixing continuously with a spatula. The mixture will thicken pretty instantly. Allow to cook for another minute, stir very well, then transfer the jam to the cornflour bowl to cool.

Once everything is at room temperature, spread a teaspoon of the jam filling onto each of the whole biscuits. Place one of the biscuits with a hole on top to sandwich together.

Love your leftovers Unfilled biscuits will keep in an airtight container for 1 week at room temperature, while the jam will keep for 5 days, covered, in the fridge. Biscuits that have been sandwiched with jam will keep for 1 day, but will soften over time, so it's best to sandwich them the day of eating to keep them crisp.

Dairy-free chocolate and banana brownies

V
DF

Soft and decadent, the classic treat redesigned to make it low in sugar and friendly for all. For big kids, you could add in choc chips or chopped nuts, or both!

🍴 Makes 16 brownies ⏱ Prep 10 minutes, Bake 22 minutes ❄ Freezable

4 medium eggs
80g (2¾oz) golden caster
   or fruit sugar
2 medium ripe bananas,
   peeled
2 tsp vanilla extract

100ml (3½fl oz) olive oil, plus
   extra for greasing
100g (3½oz) plain (all-purpose)
   flour
50g (1¾oz) unsweetened
   cocoa powder

Preheat the oven to 180°C fan (200°C/400°F/Gas 6). Grease the base and sides of a 20cm (8in) square brownie tin with a little olive oil. Cut a strip of non-stick baking paper large enough to line the base and two opposite sides of the baking tin. Trim the two overhanging sides to 2cm (¾in) above the edge of the tin – this stops the paper moving in the fan oven and sticking to the batter before it's baked.

Using an electric hand whisk or stand mixer, whisk eggs and sugar together for around 5 minutes until the mixture is pale and fluffy and has more than doubled in size. Meanwhile, prep the other ingredients. (If you don't have a stand mixer and need to hold the whisk while it does its thing, prep the other ingredients first and then move onto the eggs.)

Put the bananas in a separate large mixing bowl and mash with the back of a fork to get them as smooth as you can. Add the vanilla extract and oil and mix well. Measure the flour and cocoa powder into another separate bowl ready for when you need it.

Once the eggs and sugar are ready, add to the mashed banana mixture. Use a rubber spatula to very gently mix it together, being very careful to not overwork the eggs and lose all of the air you've just spent time adding. Once you see no large lumps of banana, stop mixing. Set a sieve over the bowl and sift in the cocoa powder and flour. Again, use the spatula to very carefully combine the flour into the wet batter, stopping as soon as the mixture looks combined, with no large lumps of flour.

Pour the batter into the prepared brownie tin – do this slowly and from a low height, and if you spot any lumps of flour, quickly stir them into the batter. Level out the top of the batter gently, spreading the mixture into the corners, then place the tin on the middle shelf of the preheated oven and bake for 17–22 minutes. Check after 15 minutes; if it still has a little wobble in the centre of the batter with a gentle shake, then place it back in the oven for a further few minutes until it has just set.

Allow the brownie to stand in the tin for 10 minutes before lifting it out onto a board using the baking paper flaps as handles. Leave to cool for a further 5 minutes before cutting into 16 squares.

Love your leftovers The brownies will keep for 3–4 days at room temperature. For extra yumminess, blast a brownie square in the microwave for 15–30 seconds to heat up before serving – they will be pretty hot, so let it cool a moment before serving to little ones.

Blueberry cheese scones

Fluffy cheese scones with bursts of juicy blueberries that take just 10 minutes to throw together. If you love jam on a cheese scone, you'll adore these for afternoon tea or lunch!

EF*

V

Vg*

DF*

🍴 Makes 8 large scones ⏱ Prep 10 minutes, Bake 15 minutes ❄ Freezable

300g (10½oz) self-raising flour

50g (1¾oz) cold unsalted butter*, cubed

150g (5½oz) fresh blueberries

150g (5½oz) Cheddar cheese*, grated (optional)

70ml (2¼fl oz) milk*

2 medium eggs* (see tip below)

(*See pages 8–9)

Preheat the oven to 220°C fan (240°C/475°F/Gas 8) and line a large baking tray with non-stick baking paper.

Sift the flour into a mixing bowl and rub the butter into the flour with your fingertips until it resembles fine breadcrumbs. This will take a minute or so. Shake the bowl a few times to help any larger lumps of butter that are hiding lift to the surface. You can also whizz this briefly in a food processor, if you wish.

Add the blueberries and grated cheese, if using, to the flour mixture, reserving a little cheese for sprinkling on top of the scones before baking.

In a separate bowl, whisk together the milk and eggs. Now, pour this into the dry ingredients, reserving a little for glazing. Using a round-bladed knife, mix the wet and dry ingredients together until the mixture starts to clump. You want to work the mixture as little as possible, as overworking may result in flat scones.

Tip the mixture out onto a clean work surface and bring it together with your hands. Flatten the dough with your palm to form a flat circle around 2–3cm (¾–1¼in) thick. Avoid using a rolling pin as you may overwork the dough or roll it too thin, which would result in flatter scones. Use a sharp knife to cut the circle into 8 triangles, like a pizza, and transfer to the prepared baking tray. Brush the tops with the reserved egg and milk mixture, making sure not to let any liquid drip down the sides, then sprinkle over the rest of the cheese.

Place the tray in the preheated oven and bake for 10–15 minutes until well risen and golden on top. Serve in finger strips to little ones, with a little unsalted butter. Delicious with the peach chia jam from page 23.

Love your leftovers The scones will keep in an airtight container for 3 days. To serve warm, reheat in the oven until piping hot. If you can't eat them all, freeze for up to 3 months, and thaw in the oven for 5–10 minutes, or until defrosted and piping hot.

Egg free? You can sub the eggs for an additional 115ml (3¾fl oz) of milk if your family can't eat them, but the scones won't be quite as fluffy.

Rebecca's banana muffins

Light and fluffy little cakes, flavoured with naturally sweet bananas, these are a childhood classic that you'll never get too old for.

EF*

V

Vg*

DF*

⏛ Makes 12 muffins   ⏱ Prep 10 minutes, Bake 25 minutes   ❄ Freezable

3 medium ripe bananas (plus 1 for decoration, optional)

120g (4¼oz) unsalted butter*, melted

60g (2oz) golden caster sugar or maple syrup (optional)

100ml (3½fl oz) milk*

1 tsp vanilla extract

1 tsp ground cinnamon

3 medium eggs*

300g (10½oz) self-raising flour

1 tsp baking powder

1 tbsp demerara sugar (optional)

(*See page 8)

Preheat the oven to 180°C fan (200°C/400°F/Gas 6) and line a 12-hole muffin tray with non-stick paper cases.

Mash the bananas in a mixing bowl using the back of a fork, then add the butter, sugar, milk, vanilla extract, cinnamon and eggs. Beat until well combined.

Sift in the flour and baking powder and gently but quickly stir into the batter. Stop mixing once just combined to avoid overworking the batter as this will result in dense little muffins.

Divide the mixture between the 12 muffin cases. If wished, slice another banana and decorate the top of each muffin. You can sprinkle a little demerara sugar on to the tops, too, which will give the muffins a lovely golden sheen, but this step is totally optional.

Bake in the preheated oven for 20–25 minutes until golden, risen and an inserted skewer comes out clean.

Love your leftovers Store the muffins in an airtight container for up to 3 days, or freeze for 3 months.

Pear and ginger cake

Delicately spiced with ginger, it will surprise you how low in sugar this moreish cake really is. Whip this up for a family gathering and see smiles all round.

V

DF*

🍴 **Serves 8–10** ⏱ **Prep 20 minutes, Bake 1 hour** ❄ **Freezable**

150g (5½oz) unsalted butter* (see page 8) softened, plus extra for greasing

80g (2¾oz) soft dark brown sugar, or slightly less if preferred

1 x 290g (10¼oz) can pitted prunes in fruit juice (175g/6oz drained weight)

300g (10½oz) self-raising flour

1 tsp bicarbonate of soda (baking soda)

2 tsp vanilla extract

2 heaped tsp ground ginger

2 tsp ground cinnamon

2 medium eggs

400g (14oz) can of pear halves in juice (230g/8oz drained weight)

demerara sugar, to decorate (optional)

Preheat the oven to 170°C fan (190°C/375°F/Gas 5) and grease and line a 20cm (8in) springform cake tin with non-stick baking paper.

Put the butter and sugar in a mixing bowl and beat until pale and fluffy. Drain the prunes, catching the juice in a bowl, and add the prunes to the mixing bowl. Beat again for a few moments to break up the fruit – don't worry if it looks like it's starting to curdle.

Add the flour, bicarbonate of soda, vanilla extract, ginger, cinnamon and eggs to the bowl, along with 80ml (2½fl oz) of the prune juice. Whisk well until a smooth batter is formed, but stop beating as soon as the mixture comes together to ensure you don't overmix.

Pour the batter into your prepared tin and level the top. Arrange the pear halves on top, then sprinkle over the demerara sugar, if using. Bake on the middle shelf of the preheated oven for 50–60 minutes until an inserted skewer comes out clean. Check after 30 minutes and if the top is starting to brown too quickly, make a foil hat and place it over the cake tin to prevent the top of the cake from burning.

Allow to cool for 5 minutes in the tin before running a knife around the inside of the tin and removing the sides. Place the cake, with the base still attached, onto a cooling rack and set aside until it is cool enough to handle, then remove the base and serve.

This cake is delicious slightly warm with a little drizzle of single (light) cream or custard.

Love your leftovers Store the cake in an airtight container for 3–4 days, or freeze for 3 months, defrosting at room temperature.

School dinner sprinkle cake

V

DF*

A British classic with no introduction needed. This version has a low-sugar sponge, with the option to go healthy or not so healthy on the toppings.

🍴 **Serves 12** ⏱ **Prep 20 minutes, Bake 25 minutes**

1 x 90g (3¼oz) pouch of fruit purée (see page 10)
80g (2¾oz) fruit sugar or golden caster sugar
80ml (2¾fl oz) milk*
250g (9oz) unsalted butter*, softened, plus extra for greasing
350g (12oz) self-raising flour
1 tsp baking powder

2 tsp vanilla extract
6 medium eggs

For everyday icing (great for babies from 6 months and if you're trying to watch your sugar intake)
150g (5½oz) cream cheese
50g (1¾oz) plain extra thick yogurt*

1 tbsp icing sugar (optional)
20g (¾oz) multicoloured sprinkles, or fresh berries

For treat icing (for days when you just fancy a little treat)
200g (7oz) icing sugar
50g (1¾oz) multicoloured sprinkles
(*See page 8)

Preheat the oven to 180°C fan (200°C/400°F/Gas 6). Grease and line a 20 x 30cm (8 x 12in) tray bake tin with non-stick baking paper.

To a large mixing bowl or stand mixer bowl, add the ingredients in the following order: first the fruit purée, followed by the sugar, milk and butter. Sift in the flour and baking powder, then add the vanilla extract and finally the eggs. Using an electric hand whisk or the stand mixer fitted with a paddle attachment, briefly combine until the ingredients bind to a smooth batter with no lumps, then stop mixing immediately. Be sure not to overwork the batter as this will result in a dense sponge.

Pour the batter into the prepared cake tin and level out with a spatula, creating a slight dip in the centre so that the cake rises evenly. Bake on the middle shelf of the preheated oven for 20–25 minutes until risen, golden brown on top and an inserted sharp knife comes out clean. Allow to stand in the tin for 5 minutes before tipping out onto a wire cooling rack and allowing to cool completely. Leave on the wire rack with the bottom of the cake facing up – this will be the flattest side and perfect for icing.

While the cake cools, make the icing. For the low-sugar option, mix together all the ingredients, except for the sprinkles or fruit, then spread over the cold cake, topping with your chosen decoration. It's best to decorate with sprinkles just before serving, as the water in the icing will result in the colours of the sprinkles bleeding over time.

For the sugary option, sift the icing sugar into a medium size bowl, then with a small jug of cold water in hand, gently and very slowly trickle in a small amount of water, stirring continuously until you have a very thick but pourable consistency. Spread this over the top of the cake, followed by a generous dusting of sprinkles.

To serve, cut into squares and serve as is or with a good dollop of custard.

Love your leftovers If you have iced the cake with the treat icing, it can be stored in an airtight container at room temperature for 2–3 days. If you have iced with the everyday icing (with cream cheese), store in the fridge for 1–2 days.

Pineapple and cherry upside-down cake

V

DF*

Impress your loved ones with this beautiful fruit-topped cake – soft vanilla sponge with naturally sweet pineapple and glorious ruby red cherries giving a wonderful ombre colour effect.

🍴 Serves 8–10   ⏱ Prep 15 minutes, Bake 45 minutes   ❄ Freezable

1 x 400g (14oz) can of pineapple slices in fruit juice (approx. 6 rings)

130g (4½oz) frozen dark sweet cherries (unsweetened)

200g (7oz) unsalted butter* (see page 8), softened

80g (2¾oz) fruit sugar or golden caster sugar

4 medium eggs

1 x 90g (3¼oz) pouch of fruit purée (see page 10)

2 tsp vanilla extract

260g (9¼oz) self-raising flour

1 tsp baking powder

Preheat the oven to 170°C fan (190°C/375°F/Gas 5). Grease and line a 20cm (8in) springform cake tin with non-stick baking paper.

Carefully transfer the pineapple slices to the base of the cake tin, trying not to break up the rings. Reserve the pineapple juice in the tin for later. Arrange the rings so that they fit snuggly and neatly together, then squish a frozen cherry in the middle of each circle. Press the remaining cherries into any space between the pineapple slices so that you can't see any of the base of the cake tin, focusing on the edges, which will give the cake a wonderful ombre effect. Set aside while you make the cake batter.

Using an electric hand whisk or stand mixer, cream the butter and sugar together until light and fluffy. Add the eggs, fruit purée, vanilla extract, flour and baking powder and mix very briefly until all the ingredients have combined into a smooth batter. Be sure not to overmix as this will result in a dense sponge.

Dollop the batter over the fruit, then spread out gently, trying not to move the carefully-arranged fruit underneath. Level the top, leaving an ever so slight dip in the middle – this will help the cake rise evenly.

Bake on the middle shelf of the preheated oven for 35–45 minutes until golden brown and an inserted skewer comes out clean. Do not open the door before 25–30 minutes or the cake may sink. If the top is starting to colour too quickly, loosely place a piece of kitchen foil over the tin to prevent the top of the cake from burning.

Once done, remove from the oven, and gently spoon over 5–6 tablespoons of the pineapple juice left in the can to help keep the sponge super moist.

Allow to cool for 5 minutes in the tin before running a knife around the inside of the tin and removing the sides. Turn out onto a wire rack, remove the cake tin base and peel away the baking paper. Allow the cake to cool a little, then serve on its own or with a healthy portion of vanilla custard.

Love your leftovers Store the cake in an airtight container at room temperature for 2–3 days, or in the freezer for 2–3 months. Defrost at room temperature, then reheat in the microwave or oven until soft and piping hot throughout.

Coconut and jam lamingtons

Fluffy, low-sugar vanilla sponge coated in a simple berry jam and coconut –
a showstopper everyone will love.

V

DF*

⑪ Makes 12 squares ⏲ Prep 30 minutes, Bake 25 minutes ❄ Freezable

1 x 90g (3¼oz) pouch of fruit
purée (see page 10)
80g (2¾oz) fruit sugar or
golden caster sugar
80ml (2¾fl oz) milk*
250g (9oz) unsalted butter*,
softened, plus extra for
greasing
350g (12oz) self-raising flour

1 tsp baking powder
2 tsp vanilla extract
6 medium eggs

For the coating
300g (10½oz) frozen berries of
your choice – choose sweet
varieties for a sweeter finish
2 tsp vanilla extract

20–50g (¾–1¾oz) golden
caster sugar, to taste
(optional)
3 tbsp chia seeds
about 250g (9oz) unsweetened
desiccated (dried shredded)
coconut
(*See page 8)

Preheat the oven to 180°C fan (200°C/400°F/Gas 6). Grease and line a 20 x 30cm (8 x
12in) tray bake tin with non-stick baking paper.

To a large mixing bowl or stand mixer bowl, add the ingredients in the following order:
first the fruit purée, followed by the sugar, milk and butter. Sift in the flour and baking
powder, then add the vanilla extract and finally the eggs. Using an electric hand whisk
or the stand mixer fitted with a paddle attachment, briefly combine until the ingredients
bind to a smooth batter with no lumps, then stop mixing immediately. Be sure not to
overwork the batter as this will result in a dense sponge.

Pour the batter into the prepared cake tin and level out with a spatula, creating a slight
dip in the centre so that the cake rises evenly. Bake on the middle shelf of the preheated
oven for 20–25 minutes until risen, golden brown on top and an inserted sharp knife
comes out clean. Allow to stand in the tin for 5 minutes before tipping out onto a wire
cooling rack and allowing to cool completely. Leave on the wire rack with the bottom
of the cake facing up – this will be the flattest side and perfect for icing.

To make the jam. Put the frozen berries, vanilla extract, sugar, if using, and 100ml (3½fl
oz) of boiling water in a medium-sized saucepan. Set over a medium–high heat and
cook for around 5 minutes until the berries have softened. Carefully blend the mixture
until it is super smooth, either with a stick blender or by transferring the mixture very
carefully to a food processor or blender. Once smooth, transfer the berry liquid back
onto the heat and add the chia seeds. Stir and allow to bubble for a further 5 minutes
until thickened. Pour the jam into a cold, wide-bottomed bowl and set aside to cool.

Once the cake is cool, cut it into 12 squares. Put the coconut into another bowl. The
next part is a little messy, so try to keep one hand for each task. Take each cake square
and dip the sides and top into the jam, keeping the base clean, then dip the cake into
the desiccated coconut. If your jam feels too thick to coat the cakes, add a dash of
water and stir it through to loosen the consistency.

If you prefer, you can simply generously spread lots of jam on top of the cake before it
has been cut, then cover in coconut before portioning into squares.

Love your leftovers Leftover jam that hasn't been used can be kept in an airtight container for 2 weeks in the fridge. The cake will last in an airtight container at room temperature for 2–3 days. Blast it in the microwave for 15 seconds if the sponge is starting to feel a little stale. The cakes will also freeze for 3 months – defrost at room temperature before enjoying.

Rebecca's plum and apple crumble

Crumble is an absolute classic dish that recalls happy childhood family memories. Make your own memories with this comforting pud, suitable for the whole family.

GF*

EF

V

Vg*

DF*

🍴 3 adults and 3 littles   ⏱ Prep 10 minutes, Bake 40 minutes

6 large ripe plums
2 Bramley apples
1 heaped tsp cornflour (cornstarch)
1 x 90g (3¼oz) pouch of apple purée (see page 10)
40g (1½oz) golden caster sugar

2 heaped tsp ground cinnamon
200g (7oz) plain (all-purpose) flour*
120g (4¼oz) cold butter*, cubed
75g (2½oz) porridge oats*

45g (1¾oz) demerara sugar (optional)
(*See pages 8–9)

Preheat the oven to 180°C fan (200°C/400°F/Gas 6).

Cut the plums in half, remove the stones and slice each half into 4. Peel, core and cut the apples into similar-sized chunks to the plums.

Put the fruit in a baking dish, about 1.5l (52fl oz) in volume. Add 80ml (2½fl oz) of water, then add the cornflour, apple purée, caster sugar and cinnamon. Stir well to allow the cornflour to dissolve and distribute evenly. Set aside while you make the topping.

Measure the flour and butter into a mixing bowl, then rub together with the tips of your fingers until the mixture resembles breadcrumbs and you can see no large lumps of butter. Shake the bowl every now and then and any large pieces of butter will shimmy to the surface, making it easier to spot them. Stir in the oats and demerara sugar, if using, then scatter over the fruit mixture. Avoid pressing the topping down, as this will result in a firm, not crumbly, topping.

Transfer the dish to the middle shelf of the preheated oven and bake for 30–40 minutes until the top is golden brown and you can see the fruit bubbling away underneath.

Allow to stand for at least 5 minutes before spooning into bowls and serving with custard or cream.

Love your leftovers Leftovers will keep for 3 days in the fridge. Reheat in the oven or microwave until piping hot throughout.

Chocolate cheesecake

I like to smuggle healthy ingredients into my desserts where I can, and the avocado in the topping also helps this no-bake cheesecake become super creamy too. This serves 8–10 adults, but a few more if your diners are little!

GF*

EF

V

Vg*

DF*

⧗ Serves 8–10 ⏱ Prep 30 minutes, plus at least 1 hour chilling

For the base
180g (6¼oz) porridge oats*
100g (3½oz) unsalted butter*, melted
90g (3¼oz) soft dried pitted prunes
2 tbsp almond butter (replace with an extra 30g/1oz of prunes to make it nut free*)

For the topping
1 large ripe avocado (or 2 small)
300g (10½oz) cream cheese*
70g (2½oz) golden caster sugar
4–5 tbsp unsweetened cocoa powder

180ml (6fl oz) double (heavy) cream* (see tip below)
fresh berries, to decorate
(*See pages 8–9)

Line the base of a 20cm (8in) springform cake tin with non-stick baking paper.

Put the oats in a food processor and briefly whizz for 5 seconds to break them up slightly. Add the melted butter, prunes and almond butter to the processor and blend until well combined and starting to clump together. Spoon the mixture into the prepared cake tin and, using the back of the spoon, press it down into the base of the tin, levelling the top. Put the tin in the fridge while you make the topping.

Wipe out the food processor bowl and add the avocado. Give it a brief whizz to start breaking it up, add the cream cheese and sugar, then sift in the cocoa powder. Whizz until it looks fairly smooth – a few lumps right now are okay.

In a separate bowl, add the cream and whisk until it thickens but still falls off the spoon very easily – don't make it too thick here. Using a spatula, add the cream to the food processor, and scrape down the sides so that all the cream cheese and avocado is in the centre and will mix with the rest of the ingredients. Whizz one final time until it looks super smooth, but ensure you don't overmix at this stage as you don't want the cream to separate.

Take the tin with the base out of the fridge, scrape the cheesecake mixture into it and level it out. Place the cheesecake back in the fridge to completely cool and harden – 1–2 hours will be fine, but preferably overnight.

To serve, run a knife around the edge of the cheesecake and remove the springform sides to the tin. If you can, use a palette knife to lift the cheesecake from under the baking paper, but if you're worried it will break, leave the tin base attached. Decorate with sliced strawberries and blueberries, or raspberries and slice into wedges.

Love your leftovers The cheesecake will keep in the fridge for 3 days.

Make it dairy free Replace the double cream with another avocado and use plant-based cream cheese and butter.

Conversions

If required, we recommend you follow the conversions as listed on the individual recipes, however, here is a handy list of standard conversions should you need them for anything else.

Dry measures

15g	½oz
30g	1oz
60g	2oz
90g	3oz
125g	4oz (¼lb)
155g	5oz
185g	6oz
220g	7oz
250g	8oz (½lb)
280g	9oz
315g	10oz
345g	11oz
375g	12oz (¾lb)
410g	13oz
440g	14oz
470g	15oz
500g	16oz (1lb)
750g	24oz (1½lb)
1kg	32oz (2lb)

Length measures

3mm	⅛in
6mm	¼in
1cm	½in
2cm	¾in
2.5cm	1in
5cm	2in
6cm	2½in
8cm	3in
10cm	4in
13cm	5in
15cm	6in
18cm	7in
20cm	8in
22cm	9in
25cm	10in
28cm	11in
30cm	12in (1ft)

Australian tablespoon conversions to UK spoon measures

½ tbsp	2 tsp
1 tbsp	1 heaped tbsp
2 tbsp (8 tsp)	2½ tbsp
3 tbsp (12 tsp)	4 tbsp
4 tbsp (16 tsp)	5 tbsp
5 tbsp (20 tsp)	6½ tbsp
6 tbsp (24 tsp)	8 tbsp

Volume measures

75ml	2½fl oz
90ml	3fl oz
100ml	3½fl oz
120ml	4fl oz
150ml	5fl oz
200ml	7fl oz
240ml	8fl oz
250ml	9fl oz
300ml	10fl oz
350ml	12fl oz
400ml	14fl oz
450ml	15fl oz
500ml	16fl oz
600ml	1 pint
750ml	1¼ pints
900ml	1½ pints
1 litre	1¾ pints
1.2 litres	2 pints
1.4 litres	2½ pints
1.5 litres	2¾ pints
1.7 litres	3 pints
2 litres	3½ pints
3 litres	5¼ pints

Oven temperatures

130°C	110°C fan/250°F/ Gas ½
140°C	120°C fan/275°F/ Gas 1
150°C	130°C fan/300°F/ Gas 2
160°C	140°C fan/325°F/ Gas 3
180°C	160°C fan/350°F/ Gas 4
190°C	170°C fan/375°F/ Gas 5
200°C	180°C fan/400°F/ Gas 6
220°C	200°C fan/425°F/ Gas 7
230°C	210°C fan/455°F/ Gas 8
240°C	220°C fan/475°F/ Gas 9

Index

Penguin Random House

Publishing Director Katie Cowan
Art Director Maxine Pedliham
Senior Acquisitions Editor Stephanie Milner
Managing Art Editor Bess Daly
Copy Editor and Food Stylist Rebecca Woods
Editor Kiron Gill
Nutritionist Lucy Upton
Designer Amy Cox
Proofreader Nicola Graimes
Indexer Vanessa Bird
Jackets Coordinator Lucy Philpott
DTP and Design Coordinator Heather Blagden
Production Editor David Almond
Production Controller Stephanie McConnell
Prop Stylist Robert Merrett
Photography by Andrew Burton
Illustrations by Ana Zaja Petrak

First published in Great Britain in 2021 by
Dorling Kindersley Limited
DK, One Embassy Gardens, 8 Viaduct Gardens,
London, SW11 7BW

The authorised representative in the EEA is
Dorling Kindersley Verlag GmbH.
Arnulfstr. 124, 80636 Munich, Germany

Text copyright © 2021 Rebecca Wilson
Rebecca Wilson has asserted her right to be identified as
the author of this work.

A CIP catalogue record for this book
is available from the British Library.
ISBN: 978-0-2415-3469-4

Printed and bound in China

For the curious
www.dk.com

This book was made with Forest Stewardship
Council ™ certified paper - one small step in DK's
commitment to a sustainable future.
For more information go to www.dk.com/our-green-pledge

Thank you

This book would never have happened
without my darling Nini – you are my
inspiration and motivation, thank you
to no end. I am so proud of you, to
have helped create all of this. Thank
you to Stu, and all my friends and
family for your support, patience and
encouragement too – you're all
amazing.

My agent Darryl, thank you for always
being there – your trusted advice never
fails to help me see clearly on this crazy
journey. Steph, the fantastic editor
whose vision helps bring my recipes
to life, thank you for everything.

To all at DK: Katie, Bess, Amy, Kiron,
Max and Heather who have made this
book as beautiful as it is. Becci – food
stylist and word wizard – thank you for
keeping me on track, and Andrew,
on the photos, you've made this book
look incredible. This book wouldn't be
as amazing as it is without you all.

PLEASE NOTE

• All eggs are medium (UK) or large
(US) unless otherwise specified.
• Those following strict allergen diets
should always check the packet for
guidance about suitability.
• Soy sauce is normally very high in
salt and so is not recommended for use
in baby or toddler foods. Instead,
choosing a low-salt soy sauce can be a
good swap for the whole family – but be
careful as each brand is different, with
some still containing too much salt. Try to
choose a low-salt variety that has less than
6g/100mls of salt on the label.